CORRUPTIONS

CORRUPTIONS

A Novel of Washington

James T. Shea

ISBN: 1452862206
ISBN-13: 9781452862200

Library of Congress Control Number: 2010907009

This novel is a work of fiction. Names, characters, places and incidents are either prod-
ucts of the author's imagination or are used fictitiously. Any resemblance to actual
events, locales or persons, living or dead, is entirely coincidental.

Printed in the United States of America
First edition
1 3 5 7 9 8 6 4 2

To Elaine,
    My love,
My anchor,
    My muse.

Chapter 1

Corruptions start small in Washington.

I jerked as Bobby Darin's "Mack the Knife" blared from my shirt pocket. I'd been lost in a difficult client memo, floundering for the right way to pass on some particularly bad news. The ringer was set to mute, but not for calls from any number associated with Uncle Harry.

Fumbling the phone from my pocket, I dropped it, only to kick it under my desk. We'd gotten all the way to MacHeath's jackknife by the time I could get it open. I took a breath.

"Ed Matthews," I intoned in my best take-me-seriously voice.

"Eddie." It was Belinda from Harry's office, one of just two people in the world who called me Eddie and got away with it. "You have to get up here, now. Within fifteen minutes."

"I'm, ah, I'm kinda in the middle of some..."

"Eddie, now." Dead air. She meant it.

"I'm at the office. Fifteen will be tight, but I'm out the door."

* * *

Our offices were on Connecticut Avenue, just north of Farragut Square. Fifteen minutes would definitely be tight, but Harry's office was in the Dirksen Senate Office Building, on the north, or Senate, side of the Capitol Building, so it was possible—depending on the cabbie. Coming out the front door of our building, I walked quickly south to L Street, a one-way aimed in the right direction. The crosstown light was red, and I scanned the few cabs visible in the wait for a green. As they started toward me, I let one go by—he'd been at the stop line when the light changed and started up too slowly—stepping out to flag down the next cab through, the one veering left to right, right to left, looking for advantage. He screeched up next to me, just missing my shoe.

Climbing in and slamming the door behind me, I saw I'd lucked out—a West African driver, by the look of him and his accent as he chattered into his cell phone. Barring an accident between here and Dirksen, I should make it.

D.C. cabs have mostly two kinds of drivers—the African and South Asian immigrants who drive like bats out of hell while yammering nonstop on their phones, and the old-time D.C. residents, almost all black gentlemen, urbane, pleasant, a guaranteed interesting conversation if you want one, but the slowest drivers God ever placed on this earth. There's no middle ground, no somewhat fast but still interesting drivers, just mad jabbering foreigners and D.C. gentlemen.

"Dirksen Senate Office Building."

Seemingly ignoring me, the driver took off at a breakneck pace, never pausing in his call. He shot down L Street, catching up to the flow of traffic that had passed him as I entered the cab and moving quickly into a game of dodgems. I watched from the backseat, admiring his work, especially the way he sped up when the light at 15th Street went yellow, sliding left to pass the slowing limo in front of him, and then right to squeeze by another cab, entering the intersection just after the light went red as the opposing traffic started up.

I had to give it to him—this was one hell of a driver. Knowing I'd make it to Harry's on time, I leaned back to focus on the meeting and began wondering what Uncle Harry could need that was so time sensitive this early in the year.

It was a crisp, clear Thursday in January, about twenty-five degrees but feeling colder with the damp winter wind, and there wasn't much going on. Washington had slipped quietly into 2007, the beginning of the end for George W. Bush's eight years in office, the early stages of another crazy-mad race for the White House already underway. For me, it was the beginning of yet another year lobbying in support of America's foreign policy by representing friendly countries before Congress. At least, that was the simple way to put it. The full story was a lot more complicated, but then again what story wasn't?

I'd stumbled into lobbying, but over time became very good at it. Growing up, I'd always been interested in people's interactions and how they influenced one another. In college I pursued a Sociology degree, learning what made groups of people tick; law school just reinforced those skills. As a third child, I was a natural mediator and, arriving in Washington, found that my skills translated well in a town where success often lay in finding the middle ground between opponents. The fact that I enjoyed understanding people made me a good listener, and the more I retained from what they told me and then shared with colleagues, the more successful I was.

I'd leveraged that into a Vice President title at Michael McPherson & Associates, a boutique firm that specialized in small countries with big problems. Starting out, I'd been pretty naïve about our clients, but we only worked for the good guys, or at least clients that seemed to be good guys. Sometimes I got too caught up in the show, and I had a serious weakness for good food, great wines, and Johnny Walker Black. But my specialization—figuring out exactly how much of a client's agenda we could achieve and then helping convince the client why that was all we could get—gave me an edge and meant I made a difference. Maybe I had too much fun at it, but I'd always felt like I was doing something with a purpose.

This was looking to be a slow year, for us and for Washington. With Democrats in control of Congress and the war in Iraq still heading south, the Bush Administration would get precious little through Congress and into law, but then again, with a razor-thin margin in the Senate, the Democrats couldn't get much done either. Add to that the number of Senators running for President, especially on the Democratic side, and none of us in the lobbying business expected much out of the year. Except, of course, for the little tidbits here and there that we could slip into those few bills that would slink through the process. After all, that was what the clients were paying us for. And while I might wonder what Harry needed from me, it didn't really matter: he got whatever he wanted whenever he wanted it.

That was just the way life was when your uncle was a United States Senator.

The Honorable Harrison J. Fuller, elder statesman of Pennsylvania Democratic politics and the state's senior Senator, was a man to be reckoned with. Twice Chairman of the Energy and Water Appropriations

Subcommittee, once before the Republicans took Senate control in 2002 and now again since they'd given it up in 2006, he'd been a mainstay in the Senate for a couple of decades. A liberal Democrat who got along with colleagues on both sides of the aisle, Harry was a colorful speaker in Senate debates, a brilliant wheeler-dealer, and an Appropriations Committee member who could slip more crap into a funding bill than anyone other than Senate legends Ted Stevens of Alaska and Bobby Byrd of West Virginia, the two biggest earmark hounds in the history of the sport. While not in their league—let's face it, they stuffed more money per capita into their godforsaken states than anyone with a conscience ever could—Harry was nonetheless a serious player and, thanks to my delightful Aunt Helen on my mother's side, was also my uncle.

Like most members of Congress, Harry is a people person with crowds but a shy, withdrawn, and even gruff sonofabitch in person. He wasn't someone you'd ever get close to, and having known him as long as I had, I could tell when he was "on" and when he wasn't. Over the years, he'd gotten to the point where he was "on" pretty much all of the time, even at home, and it was only his good fortune in marrying Helen that gave his dinners with guests or his evenings out with supporters any inkling of a human touch. It's a common curse in Washington, that loss of humanity that comes after years and years of being in public office, people wanting something from you virtually every minute of your life, never knowing if there was anyone left who was putting your interests in front of his own. Somehow they can't give up though—the Members, staff, and hangers-on who make up the Washington machinery—can't give up the addicting inside knowledge and sense of power that hold them in a vise grip. Well into his fifth Senate term, Harry was as trapped as any of them, watching out for Pennsylvania and especially for the political future of one Harrison J. Fuller.

I hadn't seen him since election night, when we stood together in his Georgetown mansion watching a crushing Democratic defeat of the President and his party, turning a twenty-eight-seat Republican House majority into a thirty-two-seat Democratic edge and flipping the Senate from Republican to Democrat with the slightest margin, fifty-one to forty-nine if you counted the two "independents," Bernie Sanders of the People's Republic of Vermont and Joe Lieberman of, well, his own little world. Harry and I stayed late into the night, drinking his exceptionally fine cognac, watching results that were giving Harry his first full committee chairmanship, the relatively useless Committee on Rules and Administration but a chairmanship nonetheless. We'd both gotten good and drunk, something Harry's hollow leg seldom let him do, and I awakened the following morning on that same sofa, a blanket over me and Aunt Helen standing guard with a hot cup of black coffee, three slices of dry toast, and four or five Excedrin.

Glancing out the window toward Union Station, I considered calling Belinda back to get a sense of what I was heading into. Then again, I told myself, I'll just get whatever I need out of her when I got to Harry's and wing it from there. Answering Harry's periodic calls was pretty standard, and I'd always been able to skate through. Harry had a good staff, but like so many Senate offices, they were better at keeping constituents happy than at accomplishing anything in legislation. They could get just the right tone in response to a crackpot letter writer, or find the best photo op to put Harry in the *Philadelphia Inquirer* or the *Pittsburgh Post-Gazette*, or draft resolutions that spoke in somber tones of some great issue of the day but in point of fact said nothing at all. When Harry needed something real accomplished on the Senate Floor or just the right piece of report language to get action out of the Administration, he called me.

My cabbie pulled to the right by the security booth at First and D Streets NE, still about a block from Dirksen's back door, but the closest you could get in this post-9/11 world. He'd done it without any red lights—at least, none that we stopped for. I tipped him $3 on top of the $5 one-zone fare.

Sliding out the door, I jogged over to the building, where I lucked out again: no school kids heading through security or, worse, veterans groups lighting up the metal detectors—you can kill a good twenty minutes while the detectors boop and beep at every cane, leg brace, orthopedic shoe, and other metal debris trapped inside their insides. Heading left inside the door, I made for the stairs—Dirksen's elevators, while faster than Russell, were still slow this time of day, shortly after 1:00 p.m., as staffers en masse returned from lunch. Better a mad dash up the three flights of stairs, arriving breathless, than late for whatever Harry needed.

I half ran down the hall, slowing as I neared the office to catch my breath. Entering, I said a quick hello to Joanna, the pretty young receptionist, and kept right on going. Harry's office was a home away from home for me or, better yet, an office away from the office. I could drop by any time I wanted, borrow a phone to make calls, or a desk and some poor intern's computer if I needed to draft up an amendment or some talking points. I had to be a little more polite to people than at the company, but other than that, I could pretty much act like I owned the place.

Uncle Harry's personal office was two rooms over, the first full of cramped staff cubicles, his senior people stuffed into tiny little areas made palatable by the Senator's presence just a few feet away. The second smaller office housed Belinda, keeper of Harry's schedule and the one who had the most influence on the old man. She'd been with him forever, from back when he was a member of the Pennsylvania State Legislature, and he just never let her leave.

Trim, a touch dowdy, Belinda Morgan reminded me of a 1970s-era librarian, precise in her movements, vaguely aware of the concept of style, but never seeming to primp for anyone. She was always there for Harry, in that odd symbiotic relationship of two old pros who know each other's every move, unwilling to walk away from this seat so close to power. For all I knew, she'd been in love with him over all the years in that Tracy-Hepburn kind of way, locked out of marriage by my Aunt Helen and uninterested in joining the parade of paramours. Belinda knew Harry inside and out, kept all his little secrets, saw through his weaknesses better than Helen did, and knew where the bodies were buried.

So I wasn't ready for Belinda's first words, pointing me back out the door I'd just come through after a quick, meaningful glance at her watch. "Stand over there, just outside the office. When the Senator's door opens, walk in as if you're just arriving."

Given her tone, I backed up without thinking and moved a few feet into the next room. A couple of the staffers looked up and smiled, and then looked confused as I smiled back blankly, but stayed where I was while trying to look like I knew what was going on.

I watched through the door as Belinda buzzed Harry's office. "Senator, your call from the White House will be coming through any time now." I laughed in spite of myself; the White House never called Harry, and no real White House call would ever be announced like that.

Even from where I was standing, I could hear the dull bass of Harry's voice approaching the door, the voice of a man used to talking to crowds, his apologetic tone recognizable through the solid oak. Sure enough, as it opened, Harry was rapidly explaining his problem. "So very sorry, but, well, they scheduled this call only this morning. All I can say is it's a, ah, a very important call, and I really will be on for a while." Then he emerged through the doorway, the Honorable Sen. Fuller, his white hair flowing, in his dark green suit, the one best tailored to his newfound weight. I could hear murmurs of concern from the office, from whoever was in there with him.

"Eddie!" It was a hiss—low, but urgent. I'd forgotten my cue.

I stepped into the room. "Good afternoon, Uncle Harry." Instinct told me to go with the familiar rather than give His Excellency the full Senator treatment the way I usually did when strangers were present.

They were all in the room now, four of them, a very odd mix: an old man, Nepalese maybe, no, Chinese in origin, in a limp suit that fit more like a sack; a young guy, same racial mix but much more comfortable in his similarly dark suit, holding the old man up; and two corporate types, Washington regulars, white guys in expensive suits looking very much at home. One of them, slightly older, maybe midfifties, slid up to Uncle Harry, continuing their conversation in a conspiratorial tone. I couldn't hear what they were saying—the other white guy drowned him out, explaining to the old man in loud, slow English about the White House being where the President, America's leader, lives—but even over his jabber, I could see that the older guy and Harry knew each other well.

"Nephew!" Harry never called me nephew. Turning to his guests, he proclaimed, "What a stroke of luck! This is my nephew, Ed Matthews, who I told you about, the lobbyist. One of the best, very effective on the kinds of issues you are faced with. I never go to my Committees or to the Floor without consulting Ed."

Whoa, he's laying it on thick, I thought. Even though this was a first for me, it was pretty obvious what was happening, so I responded first by looking sheepish and all aw-gosh-Uncle-that's-too-much before stepping up to respond.

"Really, Senator, I just try to help when I can—working the bills all day every day, I just have an advantage from knowing every step of the process." I paused for effect. "I'm just glad you give me the opportunity to help. It's an honor for me."

Harry beamed as he turned back to his visitors, one hand raised to point over at me. "You'd want to consider other candidates, of course, if you decide you even need a lobbyist, but Ed here really is among the best." Inside, I smiled: plausible deniability, combined with a direct handoff that meant he thought they'd sign me.

Looking at me, Harry winked. He knew I could take it from here, just as he knew that I knew I'd owe him big time for whatever he was handing over. After his own pause for effect—something we in Washington did all the time—he turned to the old Asiatic man to begin his goodbyes.

From the corner of my eye, I could see Belinda had picked up the phone and was discreetly dialing. That seemed odd for a moment, since Harry, an inveterate gabber, was just starting the ritual of handshakes and thank-yous and wasn't anywhere near ready to place a call. She glanced at me and smiled as the phone on Uncle Harry's desk began ringing. Looking down again and then at Harry, she said, "That must be the call, Senator." She paused theatrically before punching a button on her phone with a flourish, picking up what I assumed could only have been her own call. "Senator Fuller's office."

After listening to dead air for a moment, she put her hand over the mouthpiece. "It's … the one you've been waiting for."

Harry was still trying to get away from the first guy, but raised his arms in defeat as he retreated toward his office.

I took my cue and began to shepherd my new friends out of the office. Harry nodded with his best "duty calls" look, backed into his office, and shut his door. Belinda pushed another button on her phone and then rose to help out, coming from behind her desk with arms outspread, mumbling something about it being "so good of you to come," moving slowly enough to appear polite but basically shoving us all out of her office. What a pro, I thought.

I led the way out and into the hall, pondering the fact that I was left with what looked like our firm's newest client. I had no idea who they were, where they were from, or what they needed—for the life of me, I couldn't figure out Grampy or the kid, but the cut of the suits on the two white guys meant somebody with money needed some kind of help. In the foreign aid game, if I played this right, that could work out to a retainer somewhere in the neighborhood of $300 to $360K a year. This was turning into a very good day.

* * *

The client pitch. A meeting I'd done many times, but never on my own, certainly never in the lead or, worst of all, without knowing at

least a little something about the potential client. This time, I didn't
know *anything* about the potential client. Still, if I couldn't dance my
way around that problem, they'd probably drum me out of the Lobbyists
League. After all, we were mostly just song-and-dance men, primed for
precisely this kind of meeting.

"So you can assist with our cause?"

On leaving Harry's office, they'd limoed me up Pennsylvania Avenue
to the Willard and invited me in for a discussion over drinks in the
bar. One of Washington's grandest and oldest hotels, the Willard was
completely redone in the Reagan era after crashing into utter disrepair
in the 1960s. Horribly overdone and gaudy, it was a dark, plush mon-
strosity of a hotel that showed well to impressionable out-of-towners
but always grated on me.

In the car, I'd been able to figure out who was who. Bao Yan-hu, the
elder man in the ill-fitting suit, seemed at first blush to be the nominal
client, while the one who hung back with Harry, Edward Kincaid, acted
like he was the one who would be signing off on any checks. Each had a
hanger-on—Bao had his grandson Charlie, and Kincaid had a fellow lawyer
by the name of John Hendrickson. They were with something called the
Dungan-American Friendship Society, a name that meant nothing to me.
In point of fact, I didn't know what a Dungan was, although it seemed safe
to assume the old man was one of them.

In the chitchat during the ride, Hendrickson had played the role of in-
termediary with Bao and Charlie, paying close attention to their comments
and questions while Kincaid ignored us all, working on his Blackberry the
whole way. Here, in the Willard Bar, the scene in the car replayed itself as
Hendrickson placed himself between Bao and Kincaid, who in turn mo-
tioned me to the seat next to him—definitely the decision maker.

"Well, I believe that you need help," I responded to Charlie's question,
"and I know that our firm is positioned as well as anyone else in the city to
do it." I took a long pause, staring unblinking at my guest. I was still flying
entirely blind here, and the conversation up to now had given me no clues
as to what they were looking for. The way Harry handed them off to me, I
wasn't sure if they thought I knew all about them—meaning I couldn't just
come right out and ask what I wanted to, "so who the hell are you?" But it
had to be something foreign aid related, or foreign aid bill related at least.
I'd just have to figure it out. "I can't promise I'll succeed, but I know the

Senator cares about your issue, and I don't think he would have introduced us if he didn't feel we could help."

Charlie smiled. "I am most pleased, as is my grandfather." He had a wonderfully lyrical way of speaking, an Etonian accent born either of an English school out in his little speck of the world, or of his being sent to England for high school or university. "Senator Fuller told Mr. Kincaid that something good would come if we visited Washington, and I believe it is so."

So this had been planned, but nobody told me in advance. It struck me as odd that Harry hadn't said anything, but then again, he had his little secrets, lots of them, and I guessed that this was just another. I turned my attention to Kincaid to get a sense of what the guy in charge was looking for. "Tell me more about what you need."

But it was Hendrickson, the other suit, who answered. Goddammit, I thought, I haven't gotten two words out of Kincaid.

"The Dungan-American Friendship Society is concerned about the plight of the Dungan people of Kazakhstan. As you know, President Nazarbayev grows increasingly erratic, even despotic, and the people fear that their window of freedom following the collapse of the Soviet Union is again closing. We seek only Congressional support and commitment to protect the Dungan people."

Wow, I thought, that was slick. Short, to the point, the twenty-second pitch you make to a Congressman as he's walking down the hall on his way to a vote or at a fundraiser when he's trying to determine what you want for your money. This guy clearly knew the game—so, I wondered, what the hell do they need me for?

Problem was, despite what he thought, I didn't know anything about President Nazawhatchamacallit. I let that slide, though. If I was recalling right from occasional glances at *Washington Post* articles on the region, this was pretty much the standard story of the Stans: dictators getting ever more despotic. And asking a question like "President who?" would just make me look like an idiot. Still, I had to say something.

"So tell me, why do the Dungan feel especially threatened?"

Charlie leaned forward, excited. "We are a different people, outsiders in our own country. We have been in Kazakhstan for 150 years, and we are Muslims, but still we are outsiders. We are a Sinitic people, and we do not intermarry with our fellow countrymen, so we remain ... outside."

10

I raised my eyebrows and nodded slowly. It was a delaying tactic—Sinitic? Sinitic? They weren't from the Sinai, with features that were clearly Asiatic. "Chinese?" I said, realizing only from their faces that I'd said it aloud. Another pause, clutching for something to say that would sound like I knew what I was doing. "You're from western China, if I recall right." Sort of a statement, sort of a question, and in any case a safe bet with the Stans all lying due west of China.

"Yes," Charlie smiled, "we were from the west of China. It was in the Hui Rebellion that we were forced to depart China, and our forefathers fled to what is now Kazakhstan. There were few of us then, and we are only fifty thousand now. And like all non-Kazakhs in our country, we are afraid."

I nodded sagely again. After a few years in Washington, everybody in town can pretty much nod sagely all night long if they have to, it's like a sport. Get enough lobbyists drunk in some Capitol Hill bar, you can set off a couple of hours of raucous laughter imitating various Congressmen trying to look sage in televised Committee hearings. Here, though, while I could nod as much as I wanted, I was starting to worry about how long I could maintain the charade. Central Asia was a bitch to keep up with in the best of times, trying to tell one Stan from another, and even among us foreign-aid lifers, all most of us knew about Kazakhstan was that Borat came from there. What with all hell breaking out in that whole region thanks to the Taliban, Osama, and the wars, it was impossible to track: What country do we have secret bases in? Which dictator do we like? How many troops from which Stan were in the Coalition of the Willing? So for all I was ducking and dodging, trying to find out what they wanted without giving away too much of my own ignorance, I knew I had to give them something.

"We must secure an official Congressional statement of support for your people," I said. That was easy—a couple of paragraphs in a Committee report would do. "We must be sure that the government of Kazakhstan is put on notice."

Charlie translated this for his grandfather, who nodded and smiled.

I waited until he was finished. "And of course, we will provide you with weekly updates of our activities, reports on what Committee actions, our plans, and any efforts by our opponents." Again, nothing that difficult—this was standard practice for every client.

Again Charlie translated, and once again Bao looked over at me and smiled. I had to admit it—this guy was great, late eighties or so, hunched, quiet, but with eyes that saw everything. He didn't seem to need to understand every word, since Charlie only translated snippets of the discussion, just the key parts I assumed, whatever they were. But Bao watched us like a hawk, like he was reading us from the way we moved, or gestured, or from the tone of our voices. He said something in reply, a thin reedy voice with a sing-songy tonal quality, surely a Chinese dialect and not the Russian I assumed to be spoken in much of the Stans. Wizened, I thought with a smile, wizened was the word that came to mind; I finally knew what that meant.

"My grandfather is most grateful for your willingness to help our people," he said, "and we will be thankful for whatever you can do to assist."

Gratitude is nice, but I needed to know whether there was any money here. "I will have to research the issues a little further and talk to my employer, of course, but I feel that we should be able to agree to a representation for this calendar year at a rate of $375,000. That's less than our standard $425,000 fee, but I believe that I can talk my partners into that concession."

Charlie's eyes widened; he wasn't prepared for this. "That is a very great deal of money."

Hendrickson leaned in, turning away from Charlie to speak directly to me. "Our organization is well funded," he said, "but we need to discuss this matter with the Board of Directors when we meet next in February. That amount seems rather high for this level of work."

It was, well over the norm, but I expected them to try to talk me down. I decided to leave his comment alone and see what happened next.

Charlie started again to object, but Hendrickson held up his hand to stop him. "This really is not something to concern yourself with, Charlie," he said, glancing back slightly. Looking around to me, he paused before continuing. "But as I said, we will discuss this. The Board members take their concerns very seriously, and we are prepared to fund this operation."

Charlie looked troubled, but Bao continued to smile over at me. He almost seemed to understand what we were discussing, although Charlie hadn't thought to translate this part of the conversation.

Okay, I thought, you do have money—and I was right that the suits control it. But I still didn't know what their decision process was, as in what this Board would need to know about us. I leaned in to ask but was cut off.

"This is not a FARA client." This from Kincaid, his first words since we arrived at the bar, coming out of nowhere. FARA—the Foreign Agents Registration Act, a pain-in-the-ass piece of law requiring anyone working for foreign nations or groups to register with the Justice Department—is one of those inside-the-Beltway things that nobody ever talks about. Obviously, a U.S. trade association wasn't a foreign entity, even if foreign policy was involved, so they wouldn't be a FARA client. But why did he care?

"The Friendship Society," he continued, "is a 501(c)(6), an educational organization under the tax code. Generally, we focus on trade—the Dungan produce almost all the vegetables grown in Kazakhstan, and we worry most about their country's access to European markets." That sounded somewhat plausible, I guessed, although not sensible. If it's access to the European markets, what was I supposed to do? I made a mental note to check on Kazakh trade statistics—assuming I could find any. "But we are incorporated in the U.S. through Mr. Hendrickson's law firm in Chicago. So FARA does not apply."

"Yes, I thought so," I replied with a smile. "That is much easier on us, though, so I'm glad to hear you confirm it." I waited, but it seemed that he had what he wanted, for after staring back for a few moments he turned to his drink and withdrew from the conversation again. I couldn't figure him out at all.

Hendrickson cut in again, pulling my attention away from Kincaid. "So we understand one another?"

"I think we do."

"When the Board makes its decision following the upcoming meeting, what will we need to finalize our arrangement?"

Looks like I landed me a client, I thought, suddenly losing interest in Kincaid. Maybe now Michael will take me a little more seriously.

* * *

On the street outside the Willard, I watched them drive away, headed to National for the 7:40 p.m. nonstop to O'Hare. Could it be that easy? I wondered. They'd asked for nothing in writing other than a couple of firm brochures—no proposal, nothing to outline our plans. When I'd offered to fly out to make a presentation to the Board, they even avoided a commitment on that, promising to get back to me. The most specific requirement

I got out of them was that the association needed "representation," whatever that meant. Three hundred and seventy-five thousand dollars for representation? Well, if they were willing to bite, that was up to them, and the $375,000 would be a bundle for the firm and a huge breakthrough for me. A huge breakthrough.

Pulling out my cell, I put in a call to Uncle Harry. Per our standing agreement, I called Belinda first despite the time and was surprised when she was at her desk to take the call. She put me right through.

"Ed, how did it go?"

"Great, Uncle Harry, once I got over the shock and figured it out, for Chrissakes."

"I knew you'd catch on quick enough." A low rumble of a laugh slid down the line at me.

"Just wanted to say thanks—it looks like they want to do a deal with us, and do it soon."

"With you, Edward," he corrected me. "This is your deal."

"I can talk to Michael…"

"No." A pause. "No, this is your deal. It's what you want, your own client—you've said that for years now."

"It's still not my company, though, and Michael is …"

"You can make it work. You need to make it work. I'm not in the business of delivering up clients for Michael McPherson."

"Okay, okay. I'll make it work. I have no fucking idea how, pardon my French, but I'll make it work."

That quiet, low rumble again, his real laugh rather than the loud, toothy one reserved for constituents. After a pause, he continued, "Ed?"

"Yes, sir?"

"You realize this puts you in the Big Leagues, right? Are you ready for that?"

"I've been waiting for this for a long time, Harry. A very long time."

There was another pause on the line, longer this time. Perhaps Harry noticed something I missed: I hadn't answered his question. Waiting for something and being ready for it, those were two entirely different things.

"Good night, Ed, and good luck," he said. And the line went dead.

14

Chapter 2

"Need I remind you that they're not even a country?"

Charlotte looked up from her chopping, glaring at me, carving knife raised. I laughed.

It was only a few days after my first meeting with the Dungan, and while I'd had several days to revel in my euphoria, my wife, Charlotte, and I were still trying to come to grips with what this client-to-be entailed. It was part of a much larger discussion, and occasional argument, about what I wanted to do with my life after spending a decade or so of it helping our foreign friends. As long as I was just working for Michael, I had some freedom of action; now that I was bringing in my own client, though, that made it all seem more permanent.

I turned to the other counter to grab some plates and headed for the dining room. Make yourself useful, I thought, just do it in another room. Placing the plates around the table, more slowly perhaps than was necessary, I tried to think of a response that might rescue the conversation. This was an increasingly important issue between us, and I hadn't yet found an easy answer to her worries.

Her basic argument was simple: I was working for everyone *but* America. As a lobbyist, you have to believe that you're working for the good guys, people who deserved what they were asking for—or at least people who were just as deserving as anybody else. In foreign policy lobbying, it's tougher: that $30 million I wanted for Morocco could just as easily go to a jobs program in Detroit. (Actually, it couldn't, but only for all sorts of crazy budget rules that could all be circumvented anyway.) Over about three or four years, Charlotte and I had been talking more and more about this "why not America?" question, as I successfully lobbied for small African nations, countries emerging out of Yugoslavia, tiny trade associations, and now a friendship society whose purpose I still wasn't entirely sure of.

"Can't you ever do anything for Americans?" she'd ask.

"Foreign aid and foreign policy work *is* for America," I'd answer.

"Americans," she'd glower.

The issue was bigger than that; it was about the whole question of lobbying. Lobbying is one of those fields where there isn't really a "you," only a "them," the client. I'd spent my career finding government money that other people could spend (or more likely, misspend), getting meaningless snippets of language signed into law, pushing resolutions that honored the Right Honorable Anybody from Anywhere for doing something the average person might do any day of the week. Just for them, the client, the people paying me to do it. She wanted to know what I wanted out of life.

Like I had any frigging idea.

So there I was, setting the table, trying to stay out of her way while thinking that we still had time for a quickie before Mourad, Halima, and the others showed up—if I could somehow get Charlotte to chill about my future, move a little faster with the cooking, and give me a few minutes in the sack, or on the sofa, or wherever. Glancing forlornly over at the couch, I knew that would never work: ever since I'd told her about the Dungan, she'd been more upset about my "furriners" than ever. Until we settled that, I knew there wouldn't be a whole lot of sneaking off for quickies.

* * *

I hadn't seen it coming, that evening following my meeting with the Dungan when I first told her about my potential client. I waited until we were both home—she after a staff meeting that ran late, me after a long walk home in the cold replaying the client pitch meeting in my mind to be sure I'd read it right. I was still warming up in the living room when she arrived, my back against the couch, a glass of Cabernet half-drunk next to me, reading some articles in that day's *Post* I'd skipped over earlier. Charlotte came through the door weighed down by her long winter coat, an overlong scarf she'd nabbed from me, and two briefcases—one for the laptop and some papers, the other just for papers. As she shed them, layer after layer, she asked me how my day had gone.

I started right in on the story, focusing less on the gymnastics of getting to Harry's office—a tale she'd heard many time before—and more on the clients, their attitudes, their interactions, the old man and his link to the boy, Kincaid's silence vs. his partner's openness. I spoke fast in my excitement, missing some of the details, so I had to go back to what I'd glossed over. She headed from the closet to the kitchen as I rambled on, grabbing a plate, cheese, some crackers, and sliced ham that she rolled up as we talked, while I leaned in through the hot-dog window opening into the kitchen from the dining/living room space. She listened, taking it all in, considering it, as we walked back over to the couch, her with the food, me with the wine and a second glass. As usual, she heard more than I said as she mulled through their behaviors, laughing at the right places but apparently unsure where the story was headed. She especially wanted to know about the exchange with Kincaid about FARA and his partner's agreement on the money. She wasn't as sure as I was yet, but I knew in my heart I'd win her over. After all, it wasn't until all her questions were done that I told her the best part—it would be my very own client.

"They're not hiring Michael. They're hiring me."

"What?" She looked up from where she'd been picking at another cracker; I noticed that her body went perfectly still. "What do you mean, you? You work for Michael."

"Well, Harry told me, I ... I ... they said they wanted me," I stumbled, caught somehow, feeling like when my mother used to catch me stealing candy; suddenly the mood shifted. "I spoke to Harry after ... he said it was my client, not Michael's. Michael can't stop that."

"How deep into this business do you want to get? I thought you wanted to get out." She leaned back, her face suddenly flushed, and turned away to look out into the alley behind our apartment, on the light snow that had begun to fall, at the trees and the fire escapes as it gathered, anywhere but at me.

I turned to look out with her, my heart sinking as I did. I'd been so excited about the idea of a client, of finally breaking through and landing something that was mine, I hadn't foreseen this at all. "Jesus."

"You've talked about being unhappy in this business for years now, being miserable with the constant chatter, the lack of satisfaction, your need to do more." Her voice was rising with every word, and her knuckles were white around her fork. She turned to look at me. "I thought you were serious."

"Honey, I … I dunno. I said it's time to think about doing something else. I said it's time we look to the future. I said, shit, I don't know. I…" This was going downhill fast. I ran through my memory, trying to remember what I'd said about my career. Hell, everyone complains about his career, I thought, looking down at my wineglass. Sure, these last couple of years I'd been complaining some too, but it wasn't like I had even the slightest idea of what else I might do. I certainly wasn't ready to leave yet. Glancing over at her, I gave her a skeptical look and, not sure what to say, just shook my head a little.

"Jesus Christ. Is that the best you've got?" She stood then, dropping a cracker on her plate and turning quickly away. "I'm going to bed."

"Honey," I called.

The infuriating thing in all this was that Charlotte was really hot when she was angry, a little pistol, a thin, smallish figure with an intensity that would blow you away. She had a fire in her eyes, especially when she was impassioned, and her cheeks colored with a warm glow. She always got her whole body into it somehow, and watching her rise and begin to leave, I felt my desire rising and hated being so confused. "We should talk," I said quietly, not quite like I meant it.

Charlotte stopped by the living room door for a moment and turned. "I'm not the one with nothing to say. All you've got for me is 'um, uh, uh, um.' That doesn't cut it." She shook her head and, turning back, walked on toward the bedroom, her stockinged feet sliding just a little on the wooden floor.

* * *

"It's like I've been telling you for years—the Arab states have to recognize that the war in Iraq changed everything." Peter laughed, his short, hard-to-read laugh, the one that always left me unsure whether he was serious or not, that seemed to give him an out if he offended any of us. "They've got no choice."

Peter Chase was in his element, playing to the crowd, spouting bullshit to see what kind of reaction he could get. He was one of the most arrogant people I knew, matched only by Philip Galsworthy, who unfortunately for the rest of us was sitting directly across from him. If we're not careful, I thought, these two idiots will drag us into a three-hour debate on Iraq— hardly the way to spend an evening among friends.

Eight of us were settled in at dinner, scattered around the table, Charlotte at one end near the kitchen and me at the opposite, with the couples split up around the table. Charlotte had insisted on sitting with Mourad on one side and her good friend Kevin Carlson on the other, if only because she couldn't stand listening to Peter and especially hated the sight of Philip, Kevin's partner. I had Halima, Mourad's wife, to my right, and Alexis, a beautiful young thing unfortunately married to Peter, on my left. Peter and Philip faced each other across the center of the table.

"Jesus, Peter, you are so full of shit," I responded to his laughter.

Charlotte started and, with a quick glance at Halima, said, "Ed, our guests."

Halima smiled. "No, Charlotte, reeeeally," dragging it out the way native Arabic speakers do, "I agree: he eees full of shit."

That brought a laugh from just about everyone. Halima—petite, generally quiet but always impish when she piped up—smiled at Charlotte and then me. Even an Embassy wife can have a sense of humor, she seemed to be saying.

Her husband Mourad reached out to Charlotte. "In Morocco, we do not encourage our wives to be so bold," he said. He paused as he glanced over at his wife. "Except when they are speaking with people like *Monsieur* Chase, *ces hommes complètement de la merde*, so to speak." Halima tittered, while Peter looked a little confused.

"Full of shit," I translated. Peter laughed, this time for real.

I liked Mourad, liked him a lot. Morocco was a former client of ours, and Mourad my former client manager, then Second Secretary at the Embassy, but now the Deputy Chief of Mission. We had a lot of fun; the Government had hired us to earmark some money, and thanks to Mourad's contacts and mine, we'd worked out the deals we needed to secure a $12 million earmark about two months into the year. That allowed us to spend the year hanging out without a lot of worries whether we'd get anything done. So we'd take staffers to Orioles games or to the Kennedy Center, and out to a nice dinner somewhere—with Mourad paying the bills, we avoided the restrictions at the time on lobbyists paying for food. It was a good deal. It didn't hurt that Charlotte and Halima got along like gangbusters, either.

This was our first dinner of the year, the first with guests, that is. We entertained at home a lot, mostly because bringing friends in to eat had never been considered buying them a meal. Besides, Charlotte and I had always loved cooking, if only because it gave us such a sense of achievement: when we cooked a meal, we got to sit right down and eat it. Instant gratification. In a city like Washington, where most things took months if not years to finish, everybody needed a little of that or they'd go crazy. Some people played golf, day in, day out, raining or not; some people shopped. Us, we cooked.

As we always did with the first dinner of the year, this was something of a "round the horn" dinner, bringing together people from throughout the process who seldom saw one another. Peter and his lovely wife Alexis were a bicameral couple—he on the Senate side, she on the House. She was wasting her time as a secretary on the House Foreign Affairs Committee, a starter job she'd never been able to get out of, while Peter was one of my Senate-side go-to guys, this term working as defense and foreign policy staffer for the Senate Majority Leader, a killer job in this status-conscious town. On looks alone, Alexis was totally out of Peter's league, except for the whole "older and wiser" thing he had going; in truth, they were intellectual equals, but he never seemed to give her any credit for that and used his long years in the Senate to play the senior statesman in the family. I had no idea what she saw in him, but then again was smart enough to realize that maybe I was just biased—blue eyes, blonde hair, I'd always been a sucker for all that.

The last couple was another two-fer, two authorizing committee staffers, and a different Washington tradition at that: another gay Washington power couple, Kevin Carlson and Philip Galsworthy. Kevin worked on the Democratic side of the House Foreign Affairs Committee, Philip the Republican side of Senate Foreign Relations. I'd actually introduced them several years back, shortly after Kevin's then partner moved to Seattle to run for City Council. They were an absolute odd couple—both half-in, half-out of the closet depending on whom they were with. Philip's fellow Republican staffers politely ignored the fact that he was gay, as did the whole Heritage Foundation crowd. Kevin was very "out," at least in Democratic circles, where being gay was prized in a staffer as evidence of an employer's openness to diversity. In this way, Kevin and Philip's opposing political philosophies were a plus: since they never socialized together at political functions, Kevin didn't have to try to pretend to be in the closet, and Philip didn't have to worry about being dragged out of his.

Kevin and Charlotte had known each other from their first D.C. jobs together working for Rep. Charles Peterson, a liberal Democrat from Washington State. It was pure coincidence and sheer luck that Kevin's job put him in a position to help me out, the kind of luck that happens all the time in Washington. I liked Kevin, if only because he held Charlotte's hand through a couple crappy bosses after she left Peterson's office, a shoulder to cry on, giving her advice and then job leads that rescued her from bad situations. He even provided the lead on a job in the office of her latest asshole boss, Rep. Heaney of Tennessee, but she didn't blame him for that one. I'd always thought that Heaney was someone she was able to live with, that either because by then she could take anything a boss could throw at her, or because there was something less obnoxious about him that let her put up with his shenanigans. Now, I thought as I watched them chatting, heads close together, maybe it's just that after three assholes in a row she'd given up on finding anything better and decided to stick it out—at least until I knew what I wanted out of life.

At a dinner party similar to this one, I'd introduced Philip and Kevin. I'd asked Philip to join at the last minute, after Kevin's relationship had gone bust and we had an empty seat to fill. I wasn't planning to set them up; I didn't even know until Kevin's gaydar went off that Philip was gay. I was just trying to fill out the dinner table, with Philip the right choice because I needed to a favor from him. So Kevin latched onto Philip—who, despite being an asshole, was a handsome guy; I got my favor from Philip; and I earned Charlotte's undying annoyance for bringing the two of them together. Charlotte had this thing about knowing who was right for whom. Philip definitely wasn't right for Kevin, and it was all my fault.

Tonight's was the kind of dinner party I liked most. For a process lobbyist—as opposed to an access lobbyist—this was the perfect collection of people. My job was to work the system, not any one individual in it. An access lobbyist knows one or two Members of Congress and leverages that to the limit, like Mitchell Wade and Brent Wilkes did when they bought Duke Cunningham for the thirty thousand or so pieces of silver he demanded. As a process lobbyist, I worked everyone, trying to get our clients to be item #3 on a whole bunch of request lists rather than item #1 on any of them. Subcommittee Chairmen loved granting wishes like those, wish #3 on five Members' wish lists. Think about it: they'd get five happy Subcommittee members because they were able to give them something and, by doing it, add to the number of votes for the bill.

Problem was, that meant a lot of balancing acts, especially when you needed to entertain lots of different people and put them in lots of different mixes, putting together dinners like this one where two-thirds of the agenda was fun and one-third work—just the intrusion of Washington into our social life that Charlotte hated. I glanced down the table to find her staring at me as the conversation rolled on around us. The grim smile on her face told me she was reading my thoughts again, listening about our social life being indistinguishable from my business life, and the fact that as long as I stayed in Washington as a lobbyist, we'd never get away from dinners like these, convening and entertaining our friends, not sure whether they were friends or just freeloaders. God, she knows me so well, I thought.

* * *

We'd met at Michael's house, at some party or other. Charlotte was relatively new to Washington then, working for a junior Foreign Affairs Committee member. There was something about her, some spark, some intensity that made me notice her immediately from across the room. She wasn't a traditional beauty, and she was tiny, but she was perfectly proportioned, had lovely carved features, and eyes—eyes that, well, they flecked and shimmered from green to brown and back again, and they drew me like some pitiful moth whizzing round and round the neighbor's bug zapper until the inevitable ZITZ!

The Foreign Affairs Committee Chairman, a short Italian immigrant from California who'd been in the Korean War and, from the look of his balding skull, generally forgot to wear his helmet, was chasing her around. She had a laugh—still has it—that could liven up a space, and she was laughing at the silliness of being courted by the Chairman while her date, a feckless young lawyer from one of the international trade firms, stood by and fumed.

We were in a group, carefully discussing American policy toward the Middle East, when Charlotte walked up. Talking about the Middle East was a tricky thing: if you had political ambitions, including good staff positions on foreign policy committees, you had to be careful not to be too pro-Arab for the prevailing tastes—tastes that were something of an ever-

22

shifting sand depending on whether Likud or Labor was running the Israeli government. When Labor was in charge, as it was this night, you could be a little less concerned. But still, you had to be careful.

"Why do we let them get away with it when they bulldoze Palestinian homes?" Charlotte said, jumping into the middle of our conversation.

We stopped for a moment, stood still, looking into our drinks or glancing warily at each other. There were four of us, together in a small cluster, chatting more than talking seriously about policy. Someone had mentioned the housing guaranties as she was walking by, but no one wanted to touch her comment.

"We were supposed to reduce the loan guaranties when they did that, right? Isn't that what the law said?" She wasn't going to stop.

I looked her in the eye, and she was laughing, mostly on the inside, but challenging us nonetheless. She was wearing a light summer dress, one that swung as she moved, and it was still rustling slightly as it settled. She was sexy, and I wasn't surprised she was being chased around the room. Looking past her, though, I saw the Chairman receding, slowly, sidling off toward the food table, trying to look nonchalant. By joining a conversation on the Palestinians, she had dropped him like a stone. I liked her immediately.

"Oh, but they included the standard national security waiver," I told her. "So it's up to the President to decide what's in the national security of the U.S. It's not our decision."

"That's convenient."

"There are those who say everything Congress does is convenient."

She snorted. "Not bad, but you haven't answered the question."

"I didn't plan to." I laughed, and she laughed too. So did the others, I think, although I wasn't paying attention. Besides, they were already realizing there was a spark here and the broader conversation was over.

That was the start, and that was the end; I was hooked from that moment on. I never did find out what happened to her date that night, but any woman who could ditch a Committee Chairman and a dweeb date, all while picking up a guy who at least seemed interesting—well, I just couldn't help myself. We were in our own little world the rest of the night, and for months, even years after.

The spark wasn't quite as powerful as it had been, but we never lost that deep connection. We seemed headed for a crossroads, but the connection was still there.

She was right in one way, of course. Washington takes over your life, invading every moment, involving itself in everything you do. Like entertaining. Charlotte loved entertaining, but she was right about this dinner. A dinner party for six "friends" included a former (and possibly future) client and his wife along with four Congressional staffers who, let's face it, were all potential lobbying targets. Every sign pointed to it being an event among friends, but with me as the lobbyist in the group, we were the hosts and paying for it all. We'd be reimbursed by the company, but that only made it worse—getting paid to have dinner with friends. Were they true friends? Were they friends because I paid for everything? Could I keep it social, or would I slip in a little business every half hour or so?

As Uncle Harry would have put it, "There is no line—live in Washington, and Washington's your life. Get used to it." It was getting harder and harder for Charlotte to live with that part of our lives. Still, I had to admit we had once again put on a great spread. Like I said, Charlotte loved entertaining; it was the guests she had trouble with.

* * *

I stood with Mourad on the fire escape while he smoked, looking in through the large French doors at the others. They were gathered around the sofa, Charlotte and Halima on opposite ends, Kevin and Philip gathered to Charlotte's left, and Alexis sitting cross-legged on the floor facing the couch. Peter stood to the side alone, watching. Looking at him, I wondered again at the ways of couples and why people pair up. As little attention as Peter paid to Alexis at the dinner table—other than to correct her occasional misstatements—he always ignored her for the rest of the evening. Kevin and Philip, the gay odd couple, hung together most nights, comfortably within reach but never touching. Alexis, though, might as well have come alone.

I looked to Charlotte, and wondered how my actions seemed, wondered how our relationship appeared to my friends. At these parties, I loved to mingle, walk the room, and work my way back to Charlotte, pass on a story, snatch a kiss, and then move on again perhaps or stick with her for a while, connecting and separating and connecting again. She was more likely to find a spot and sit in it, letting the party come to her, the flies attracted to the bright light of her laughter and spirit. But how do they see us? I asked myself.

"So where are they again, exactly?" Mourad caught me by surprise with the question, and turning as he took a slug from his scotch, I paused to remember the conversation at hand. He was looking at me with real curiosity in his eyes. The Dungan, I remembered, I'd asked about the Dungan. Mourad had served in Ankara, Turkey, and knew the Stans well, but he'd never heard of my new client.

"I can't say I'm entirely clear on that myself. As far as I can tell they're on the southwestern-most edge of Kazakhstan, but I'll still have to find a better map." The maps I'd reviewed so far had given me nothing. "Maybe the Georgetown library, or GW. There isn't a lot on them on the Web, and Google and Wikipedia have only been of marginal help so far. The best information I'm getting so far is off Christian Web sites focused on peoples that need 'saving' from their non-Christian beliefs." I smiled thinly. "I'm not entirely sure I can trust those."

He snorted and looked down into his scotch. "I wouldn't," he replied, raising it in mock toast before taking another hit.

A shiver ran through me in the cold, damp air. We'd been somewhat lucky, since the temperature was back into the high forties during the day and the snow mostly gone from the ground. It was typical of Washington, a heavy, wet late January snow followed by a quick warming, the disruptions limited to the day of the storm and a day or two after. I'd worn a sweater for the party, knowing the ritual—this was my third trip out here with Mourad and his *Gauloises* so far this evening—but sweaters don't keep out the damp.

"So what do they need?"

"Well," I responded, "we're in the cagey phase where they're trying to get me to tell them what I can produce, and I'm trying to figure out the minimum they need to keep them happy. They're definitely not looking for an earmark, but I'm not sure how much or how little language they want."

Mourad turned to face the street and flicked his cigarette out over the yard of Eleanor Walters, our downstairs neighbor, and into the alley. I made a mental note to go pick it up once they left, for he'd placed it expertly in her parking space, and I just didn't need another scene with her. I'd given up smoking many years before, but knew from experience Eleanor's intense dislike for cigarettes and smoking.

"It's very strange," he said. "A people without a country hiring a lobbyist for something they can't or won't define." He turned back to look at me. "Tell me again about the lead guy, the one on his Blackberry?"

"I don't know. He hardly said a word." It still struck me as odd—a high-priced, high-end lawyer as much from his style as his attitude, representing a couple of guys whose outfits screamed, "communist tailors made this suit!" He'd also been the last one out the door from the meeting with Harry, the one who cozied right up to him as the group entered his lobby. So he was the one Harry knew, but Harry hadn't passed anything on about him, and I didn't know him from Adam. "So what's out there anyway?"

"Well, if it's where you say it is," he replied, "there's nothing but sand and maybe some oil." He looked over at me and shrugged. *"Il n'y a rien là."* Nothing there.

Discussions with Mourad were one of those rare places where my college French came in handy. I'd minored in French, mostly so I could take Junior Year Abroad somewhere in France. I'd ended up in Provence, far enough from the mobs of American students in Paris that I was actually able to learn the language. Unexpectedly, it turned out to be surprisingly useful in the lobbying business, for developing relationships with clients like Morocco and people like Mourad.

I winced as he took out another cigarette and lit it; I took a long, slow drink from my own scotch, holding it in my mouth in the vain hope of it warming me a little. "But there's no significant reserves there, and no way to get it out, no pipeline." He furrowed his brow as he looked at me. "I don't get it."

I smiled thinly. I didn't have a clue either, but didn't want to tell him that. It wouldn't be good for the mystique I've so carefully worked on over the years, even if Mourad was one of the few who could see right through me. So I changed the subject. "Tell me about the area."

"Well, we've been working the Stans for a lot of years now." Kyrgyzstan, Uzbekistan, Kazakhstan, Turkmenistan—all those sandpit former Soviet republics scattered along the southern edges of the old Russian empire. "We've had people in there ever since the Berlin Wall came down, figuring that independence was inevitable at that point." Mourad grimaced. He left unsaid why they'd been there, working to keep the mainly Turkic populations on the moderate side of the Islamic equation, hoping to counter the influence of neighboring Iran's Shi'ite radicals and Saudi Arabia's wealthy Wahhabi fundamentalists. "You know the drill: Sunni Turkic populations that have never embraced Islam with the fervor of their southern relatives. They've been under Russian or Soviet rule since forever and don't know how to be free—so they've all evolved into autocracies, where we maintain our silent struggle to keep them moderate."

"Sounds like your kind of client, Sweetie." I turned to find Charlotte sticking her head out the door. She smiled at Mourad and then looked back over at me. "You look a little chilly."

Bless you, sweetheart; even annoyed with me, you still care. In point of fact, I was freezing my ass off and starting to shiver. Mourad laughed, "You should have said something," and taking one long last drag on his cigarette and then tapping it out, he expertly flicked it out to join its fellow butt in Eleanor's parking space. I really need to get out there as soon as they leave, I thought, or she will freak.

* * *

Kevin and I stood by the table, choosing among brandies. These were harder to charge back to the company, but I had a weakness for a good brandy, and Hill staffers seldom had access to the ten- or fifteen-year-old stuff. So Michael looked the other way when I every once in a while charged off an entire bottle with one of these meals. "So what's the Committee up to this year?"

Kevin pursed his lips, unsure which bottle would give him the most bang for my buck. "Not much, it should be quiet. We won't know much until the President sends up the budget, but we're hearing it's just more foreign aid cuts, except for Iraq—and we'll spend the year fighting like hell over that."

It was always a bad year for foreign aid, but since Bush's Iraq War, it had gotten a lot worse. That wasn't my concern, though, at least not for this conversation. "When's your first hearing on the bill? The SecState hearing?" As I spoke, I reached for the Armagnac and held it up for Kevin—he looked relieved at not having to choose. I was relieved that he didn't know to take the $240 Remy XO cognac I had hidden in the back. I poured us both a glass of the Armagnac.

As I poured, Kevin leaned in a little too eagerly. A nice enough guy, good at keeping his boss happy and a good friend to Charlotte, but a pompous ass sometimes, like in fine restaurants or when drinking what he thought was fine brandy. At least he heard my question, I thought as he replied, "Rice? Her? Early February, I think. Why?"

"Oh, I've got a really good question, on religious freedom in the Stans," I said. "After the inevitable Iraq questions in the first round, most Members will probably just do another one on Iraq. This one will stand out, and it's a natural for the cameras. I figured I'd give it to someone who can use it for some credit back home."

We were discussing the once-a-year hearing where the foreign affairs committees drag the Secretary of State up before the cameras at the beginning of the annual foreign aid process, trying to get a little airtime on the TV news back home. And Kevin's boss, Rep. Edgar Kleinmayer, yet another Massachusetts Democrat, came from a part of the state that was full of émigrés from the former Soviet Union. It was a natural for him.

Kevin coughed into his snifter, caught just on the verge of a sip. "I'll take a look at it." He peered at me over his glasses. "I might be able to use it."

"Well..." I dragged it out. I had him, but I needed to reel him in. "Thing is, I need this one asked while the cameras are still rolling. I mean, it's *the* question on the Stans, and freedom of religion is a very big deal in those communities."

More to the point, it was a big deal for me. I needed to know what kind of opposition we might be up against if and when we landed the Dungan as a client, and the easiest way to do that was through a softball question thrown on the table to see if anyone reacted. The Secretary of State hearing, one that everyone would be watching, was the best place to do it, but only if the question was asked live on TV during the hearing, instead of submitted in writing after the fact. I needed this and could probably only pull it off with someone like Kevin. So I had a lot more riding on this conversation than he probably thought I did.

"Shit." Kevin stared down into his Armagnac, pondering perhaps the price I'd just attached to it. He looked back up at me. "Is that what you want?"

"It's what I need."

Charlotte paused briefly on her way back from the kitchen, balancing three refilled wine glasses in her hands. "Catching up on a little business, sweetness?"

Gotcha.

Chapter 3

"So you've all been sitting on your asses while I was gone? Or have you just been out charging off high-priced meals to the company accounts?"

Michael was back from his latest vacation, three weeks in Jackson Hole over Christmas and well into the New Year. He and Alice had headed out of town on their annual Christmas ski trip, kids in tow, other family members flown in to give a distant hotel that homey Christmas feel. Michael wasn't among the city's super rich, but rich enough to be bored by a life and lifestyle responsive always to the Congressional calendar: the budget prep throughout the late fall and early winter, budget submission in January or early February, foreign aid policy debates considerations in March and April, the lengthy Easter Recess with its vacations and CODELs, foreign aid funding in June and July, the August Recess for visits to the beach and perhaps more CODELs, and then the sprint to the finish—sometime early in October in election years and just before Christmas in the off years. It's a schedule with many breaks, but always at the same time—so spur-of-the-moment trips, romantic getaways, and pretty much anything spontaneous in life was out of the question. The richer they got, the more Washingtonians compensated by chasing the ever more lavish; the rest of us just lived with it.

Michael had rescheduled our weekly Monday morning staff meeting to Wednesday to accommodate his return, all of us squeezed into our "conference room"—a larger-than-usual office held for the firm's hoped-for expansion and meanwhile reconfigured for such meetings. Everyone was there, a strange little group so typical of the smaller Washington lobbying outfits: Michael, the company president, at the head of table; our two Senior Vice Presidents, D. Wellington Richards, the old CIA hand, and Tom Lebont, our right-winger contact into the odder fringes of the Republican party, on either side of him; our new intern, Michelle Edgerton, just out of grad school and cursed with the worst title in all of Washington; and me, the company's Vice President for Legislation. In Washington, titles are everything, so you almost have to have at least a vice president title on your card to get in the door, even with staffers. As a result, the city is plagued with inflationary titles masking very thin companies, legions of vice presidents yet virtually no one serving under them. McPherson & Associates was typical, four senior officials and one lowly intern, gathered in our weekly staff meeting.

"Come on, Michael, it's January," I said. I didn't want the meeting to go this way, Michael all high and mighty on us. He's a great guy down deep, but the longer and longer he owned the company, the deeper and deeper that "down deep" kept getting.

I needed to find a way to tell him about the Dungan, about my bringing in a client that Uncle Harry insisted be mine, not his. Knowing there was no way he would do anything other than flip out over it, I had to bring it up at just the right moment, but things weren't getting off to a good start. "January's a time for wining and dining, figuring out what people are planning, and starting to set out strategies for the year. It's not like there's anything else going on."

"That's the time you have to be telling them what to do, to be selling our clients' needs." Michael barely even glanced up from the legal pad he was scribbling on, franticly copying notes of that morning's cell phone calls into an intelligible form. Few things were scarier than being a passenger in Michael's car when he was taking notes, and even fewer things more illegible than the notes he took. "That's the time to make things happen."

On the one hand, he had a point. The only achievement I could point to since the November elections—not counting the ten pounds of seasonal weight gain I'd be spending the next six months trying to get rid of—was getting Kevin, a relatively junior staffer, to have his boss ask some meaningless question about religious tolerance on behalf of a client we hadn't even signed yet. On the other, it was bullshit, and Michael knew it: nobody paid attention to much of anything until they knew what was in that year's budget, especially in the middle of a war like Iraq, sucking up so much money per week that every other account in the budget was bound to suffer.

But it looked like Michael, coming back from vacation, had decided to play at being the boss. Just what I didn't need.

Michael was our Big Cheese, an Assistant Secretary of State many years ago, a political appointee who slipped from one State Department bureau to the next, somehow serving as Assistant Secretary of State for three utterly different regions of the world under two Presidents and three Secretaries of State. He was lucky—named Assistant Secretary the first time at the tail end of an Administration when his sponsor was Vice President, and then sliding into the others as the sponsor moved up. He had been a lobbyist before heading into State, so it was only natural when he headed out that he would rejoin the ranks, this time representing foreign governments and their interests before Congress. He had some connections and some name recognition, he had the balls to promise anyone just about anything, and he had just enough chutzpah to put his name on the door—Michael McPherson & Associates. He liked the control that came with running a small company, but it had its downsides: the serious targets—big-money clients like Turkey, Egypt, Pakistan—could tell we were razor thin, making it impossible for Michael to reel them in. But he had clients, and some of them he did pretty well by. Others, well, at least we always gave it our best shot.

"Ed and I have a meeting with the Ambassador of the United Arab Emirates scheduled for two weeks from today," Wellington said, pointing down the table at me and nodding. "It's our annual review meeting. It's the soonest he's available. I've asked Ed," pointing again, "to join me to explain our Congressional strategy."

Wellington, or Weller as I'd nicknamed him several years back, was the senior statesman at the table—at least in terms of age and that certain air New England Yankees bring to government service. I liked Weller, despite his incorrigible stuffiness and a bad tendency to panic when Michael was in one of his moods. A delightful old guy trapped by tradition in terribly ill-fitting Brooks Brothers suits, his real name was Douglas, a normal first name, but back when he started out in the State Department, you needed a name like W. Averell Harriman or P. Fotherington Weatherington, or some equally East-Coast-Harvard-Yale-Princeton-my-forebears-arrived-on-the-Mayflower kind of name to be taken seriously. So, as he finally admitted one drunken evening in the Hawk and Dove, he'd started going with Wellington, his paternal grandmother's maiden name. He'd forgotten, though, that he was named Douglas after his mother's father. Pissed her off, he told me that night, pissed her off for years.

Today, as usual, Wellington had set himself down immediately to Michael's right, his preferred seat, where he could lean in conspiratorially as he spoke, an old agency habit he apparently saw no reason to break: it reminded us all where he came from. He glanced down the table to where I sat, the far end opposite Michael, and raised an eyebrow with a look that said, "I'm sending you a message." Swell, I thought, he's telling me something, probably about how helpful he's being and how he's tossed me a softball or some such. I had no idea what he was doing, but that was normal: you should meet a former CIA agent some time and see if you have the slightest clue half the time what the hell he's talking about.

"We have a strategy?" Michael looked up, glaring at me.

I smiled. "Yeah, we do. And this time, Wellington, could you let me explain it from the start so you don't confuse the Ambassador?" Wellington glanced down, seemingly smiling at the memory.

To Weller's right, his prepped-out protégé Michelle, daughter of "an old family friend" undoubtedly also descended from Yankee Brahmins, looked slightly shocked that I would mock her protector. Nice kid, but too pampered growing up to work very hard. Daughter of a Democratic powerhouse lobbyist, she had only joined us six months before, just back from her post-graduation jaunt across Europe, and was still learning the ropes. It took a full legislative year, from January through December, to truly understand the lobbying process and how to work the Hill. For her that year was just starting, and I didn't feel good about her ability—or desire—to understand how it all worked. Her adoration for "Welly," her nickname for him, didn't help.

"So you want to tell me this plan?" It was Michael, still grimacing.

"We're going to try—and I do mean try—to do something in the House bill, working with Will Richardson. He's likely to say no, but at a minimum I'll get a promise to support us in Conference out of him. Then we'll get the amendment into the Senate Appropriations bill, Will backs us in Conference, and we're done."

"What Senator?"

I paused. "I'm still working on that."

Michael snorted. "Helluva plan. So far you've found someone to refuse to help."

He had a point. This was definitely our most difficult assignment this year, getting the UAE, the United Arab Emirates, to be added to the list of Major Non-NATO Allies—what we called the MNNA list. It was something that would be hard to do in the best of times, but appeared damned near impossible in the middle of the War on Terror, when every Arab government, including our allies, was deemed suspect by Washington. It wasn't so much that Congress was afraid of the governments going rogue on us, but instead that the political risk of supporting Arabs at this time was infinitely higher than the risks associated with ignoring them.

The trick was, this wasn't about status at all, but rather about getting them an expensive air defense system, the ARCHON, one of the Air Force's most advanced systems, for one of their military facilities or other. It was too new a system to sell them, but for some exceedingly "black" reason that Wellington wouldn't talk about, the Administration considered its transfer to the UAE essential. As long as no one knew about it. Hence the MNNA status, where it could more easily be snuck through.

"Besides," Michael continued, "it's Wellington's client. What do you think we should do, Wellington?"

I cringed inside. While a terrific guy, Wellington didn't have a strategic-planning bone in his body, at least not for the peculiar strategies needed for success with Congress.

"Oh, well, Michael," Wellington intoned in his best State Department bass, "Ed and I have strategized extensively on this meeting, and we're in total agreement." Turning to face me, he smiled benignly.

Michael just grinned his Cheshire-Cat grin. "Oh, I see. That explains why Ed can't name a Senate sponsor and has to warn you about not getting ahead of him in the meeting with the Ambassador."

Wellington looked stricken. Nice try, Weller, I thought, but it looks like nothing is going to work right today.

"How about Koliba?" I asked, since only a change in subject would get Michael off my back. "That's where we have serious problems to worry about."

Going into this year, we had four clients, with the Dungan a possible fifth. Two of the clients weren't my problem, a Caribbean apparel association that was a pure trade client; and the Greece-America Association, a ridiculous little group out of Michigan looking for report language. At least until we signed the Dungan, the other two clients were where I'd be earning my keep: the United Arab Emirates with their Major Non-NATO Ally amendment, and Ernest Koliba, President of Golongo.

Koliba was our most contentious client, the one who paid the most and listened the least. Golongo was another of those thin slivers of a country you find in West Africa; on a map, you'd want to take a left at Nigeria and you'd find it squeezed in there somewhere around Ghana. Like so many countries in the region, it had a long history of military dictatorships, broken only by the occasional failed spurt of democracy. Koliba had been elected president in the latest of those, about eighteen months earlier, and seemed very much the people's president at first. We'd been hired right after the elections. He took our advice once or twice, shifting a crazed internal security chief to a position where he could do less harm, watering down a bill or two in Parliament that would have gutted free speech. The past six months or so, though, while his presidency was getting more secure, the people around him were getting more and more corrupt and less willing to suffer the risks inherent in a democracy—so things like listening to Parliament or the courts started losing its appeal.

An outbreak of antidemocratic tricks started in the late fall, as the foreign aid cycle was nearing its end. Koliba's people engineered a mayoral election in the capital for a Koliba clone, who received 96 percent of the vote. We'd only gotten away with that because the opposition candidate was an equally corrupt thug, not someone U.S. democracy advocates wanted to see in office. But just after Christmas, while Michael was skiing, Koliba sacked four of the seven Supreme Court justices—surprisingly enough, the four who had just voted to uphold the bribery conviction of one of his subcabinet ministers. To the extent that there are "moderates" on human rights—people like Human Rights First as opposed to the more rabid Human Rights Watch—they worry most about freedom of the courts. When you lose them, you pretty much lose the battle. So I'd been e-mailing Michael during his vacation all the stories off Google News and telling him that unless we could come up with a serious plan, we were screwed in terms of keeping Koliba's aid pipeline open.

Michael, as usual, didn't agree. "Koliba'll be fine," he replied, barely looking up from some memo he'd started editing. "You got all hot and bothered last year, and we came out fine."

"Jesus, Michael, you know it can't be any worse," I responded. Dammit, I thought, I hate it when he dismisses me, especially when I'm right. "The way Koliba's screwing around with the courts, even our friends think he's off the deep end. Our enemies hate him even more than before, and they're out for blood."

Michael kept writing, a skeptical grimace sliding across his face.

"I been talking to the House Republican leadership on Koliba," Tom said, raising his left hand and pointing theatrically at some distant point across the street. Tom couldn't talk without waving his hands at something—must have been all that time he spent praying to Jesus. He'd started out on the Hill right out of two tours of Army duty in Vietnam and always claimed to have worked for some clandestine group or other running a "secret war" killing Cambodians and Laotians instead of North Vietnamese and Viet Cong. Or maybe they were Viet Cong, just in Laos and Cambodia. I could never tell—Tom was another one from the "I can't tell you that" school of life history. For all I knew, he spent the war in a bar in Da Nang serving Mai Tais while pretending to be an intelligence officer. Anyway, he ended up working for Republicans in the House, moving from office to office, and as the Members he worked for got more and more conservative, so did he. Hell, if you read his resume, the first two Republicans he worked for were pro-abortion New England Republicans, but as the Party slid westward and southward, so did Tom. He ended up "born ag'in" and a fixture on the Washington religious circuit. Eventually, it became his ticket into the private sector: within a month after sitting next to a very devout Caribbean Prime Minister at Washington's annual Prayer Breakfast, he left his Hill job and hung up a shingle, the PM as his first client.

"They tell me they understand his critical importance to U.S. policy in the region," he continued. "They say they'll keep an eye out for us."

"And I can get to Hollinger," Wellington said. "I'm sure I can make him see the importance of Koliba as an island of stability in that part of the world."

"Oh, Jesus, Hollinger," I said, almost without meaning to. Tom always invoked the House Republicans, and I always ignored him. But Wellington, well, he should have known better. Hollinger, the Intelligence

Committee Chairman on the Senate side—that Committee didn't consider the foreign aid bill, didn't oversee any foreign aid funding, didn't have anything to do with it. Sure, they were responsible for the "top secret" secure listening post that was the only reason Koliba got any money at all, but I had a foreign aid bill to worry about. "That's the wrong committee."

Wellington's nostrils flared ever so softly. Oops, I guess this time he really had been trying to help.

"We all know what committee has jurisdiction, Edward." It was Michael, and he was smiling that pencil-thin smile that meant he was getting angry, with his face just beginning to redden. Dammit, I thought, I've set him off again; that was pretty stupid since I only brought up Koliba to get his mind off the UAE and set up a conversation about the Dungan.

"Okay, okay, look," I said, "how's about we at least find some way to let some air out of the tires? Give the Members a chance to blow off some steam, to yell at somebody?" I looked around the table, trying to find someone who'd back me up. "There's a lot that's happened since the last bill, all of it bad, and we have to give people an opportunity to vent. Otherwise, we'll be at the end of the year, and they'll still be pissed off."

"You're just worried because the House staffers jump whenever the human rights weenies tell them to. Well, fuck 'em, they're just staff." He was glaring now, the redness deepening. That vacation doesn't seem to have done him much good, I thought, if he's stressing out this fast. "The rest of us will work the Senators, and they'll come around."

"Well, I just don't think it'll work this time." I was on the defensive. "We used that 'island of stability' bullshit all last year, reminding them up to the actual vote that the country had just been through free and fair elections and that at least they had an independent judiciary. Now that he screwed those up, it's hard to go back and tell them the opposite."

"It'll work fine." Michael was almost smiling now, something scary to see, especially since he was also beet red with anger. "You just keep working those staffers of yours. This'll be the first time Hollinger even hears about the place. He and the other Senators will realize how badly we need Koliba." He smiled encouragingly at Wellington and went back to his memo.

* * *

This was pretty much the way it had always been at Michael McPherson & Associates, and I'd made a nice career out of it so far. Michael made the decisions, Wellington and Tom got to play *eminences grises* in their own little realms, and I got all the, not to put too fine a point on it, shit assignments. At least, that's how it seemed. Charlotte's voice echoed in my head: "It will always be that way. It's his company, and he's got all the clients." The thing was, I was on the verge of bringing in a client, so what would happen next?

That was a tough question to answer, partially because of the structure of the place, partially just the history between Michael and me. Wellington and Tom weren't technically even part of the firm; they incorporated individually and had their own consulting clients. Their work with Michael was a peculiarly Washington kind of back-scratching: they helped out on Michael's clients if he helped out on theirs. Some money probably changed hands every once in a while depending on who called in more chits or whose calls and visits went higher up the Congressional food chain, but I had never been privy to Michael's books so I actually had no idea how that worked.

Michael worked the foreign aid lifers, the ones who joined the foreign affairs committees right after arriving in Congress and actually wanted to be on them. Wellington, who had only left the CIA a few years earlier, worked senior House and Senate leadership, mostly on the Democratic side, as well as the defense and intelligence crowd, the people he used to brief when he was in the Agency. Tom worked the Republicans we politely referred to as "issue oriented," the ones who saw foreign affairs as a place to do what they couldn't get done at home: they couldn't mandate sexual abstinence in the U.S., but they could prevent the Administration from funding family-planning programs in desperate Third World countries; they couldn't do anything about the moral decline in America, but they could make the world safe for Jesus by mandating that foreign aid recipients enact "freedom of religion"—in effect, freedom for evangelicals—in countries quite happy to be 99 percent Moslem or 99 percent Buddhist. I always found it the basest form of cynicism, imposing on our friends and allies things we wouldn't impose at home, but Tom never failed to assure me that it filled the campaign coffers come election season. And it made the members who followed that track tremendously responsive to fellow true believers, something Tom was making a career out of.

As for Michael and me, I'd been hired right out of a brief stint on the Hill. After college I got a master's degree in international affairs at the

Johns Hopkins program in D.C. The year I graduated, I'd taken a State Department internship in Africa, ending up in Mauritania, one of those Texas-sized countries that has more sheep than people and more camels than sheep. From Africa, I'd switched over to law school—six months in Mauritania told me the last thing I wanted was to be a Foreign Service officer—and from there into a one-year clerkship. I'd started out on the Hill in a House Judiciary Committee job, not realizing what a dead-end committee that was in years they weren't trying to impeach a President. I started looking around for something else after about six months and found Michael through a friend of a friend of an ex-girlfriend.

We hit it off right from the start. I was a rookie to lobbying, unaware of how different it was from being on the Hill, but was someone who knew a little about foreign policy, could write well, and could summarize the insane driveling on of a three-hour Congressional hearing on U.S. policy in the Horn of Africa into the two-page memo a foreign client might even read. I'd been with him eight years now, for a long time just him and me—well, and a long parade of secretaries who could only put up with him for six to nine months before moving on in disgust. Over time we'd picked up the Wellster and Tom, first to share some space when we moved into new offices and later in this odd partnership. More recently, Michael started hiring the interns, young kids mostly just out of their own master's programs in government, Georgetown's Foreign Service School or American University or wherever, all brainy and eager, just beginning their careers.

He was quite a guy, Michael, hell-on-wheels to work for, but he taught me the game and made me good at it—something I will never forget. And since the people Michael lobbied, the senior members of the House and Senate, ran the place—at least in name—he always held it over me that he was the one who made a difference for our clients. For several years running, I had been the one who wrote all of the company's bill and report language, passing it directly to the staffs and making sure that they inserted it in legislation precisely where and when we needed it. But that didn't make me the big dog: never mind that the members just went along with what their staffs told them; or that 90 percent of the time the members didn't even know what the bills contained; or that most of them scarcely knew Michael and didn't give a rat's ass about our country clients. Michael worked the members and I didn't, so he was the big dog.

Thing was, even though I was always the junior guy, the staff guy, no matter how long I stayed or how good I got, up to now I hadn't cared. As Charlotte never failed to point out to me, I had no idea what I wanted to do when I grew up, so sticking around as Michael's number two seemed to be a job made in heaven.

Up to now.

* * *

I shifted fruitlessly in my seat, buried in the springless black Naugahyde directly behind the driver, and drew my heavy coat around me to ward off the damp, miserable cold. I'd headed for the Hill right after the staff meeting, just to get out of the office, and took the first cab I saw. Another Nigerian, I thought, but this one must be new; it looked like he was heading for the tempting but always slow "shortcut" through Washington's pitiful excuse for a Chinatown. I didn't care—I was just looking to get out of the office. Even if I didn't accomplish anything, at least I'd be able to clear my head a little.

I stayed on the Hill much of the day, not learning anything and losing a nice chunk of time at some defense industry exhibit for staffers and Members in a Rayburn caucus room. I headed back to the office in the late afternoon, arriving around 4:00 p.m., in the hopes of getting to Michael before the day ended.

Checking in with his latest secretary, Laura, I learned that Michael was free until a five-thirty meeting at a bar nearby. In between times, he was just catching up on paperwork and e-mail. I decided to wait until the last minute before going to see him: the farther away from that disastrous staff meeting he was, the better.

I kept focusing on how I'd screwed up the meeting that morning and what it might mean for this next conversation. We'd gone through every single client—the UAE, Koliba, the Greece-America Alliance, the Caribbean trade association—and somehow I managed to put myself in the hot seat on every single one, even the ones I didn't work on. Either I had a strategy that Michael hated, or I had no strategy at all, something he hated even more. And every time he asked a question, I shot back some flip-ass answer that just made it worse. Eventually, I just sat there and let Sherman run through Georgia. He was back, he was cranky, and he was loaded for bear. So of course I didn't bring up the Dungan, but I knew that if I didn't get to him before the end of the day, the inevitable discussion would go much worse.

At five fifteen, I tapped lightly on his open door and walked in. Michael was behind his desk, fluorescents turned off, reading by the light of the tall brass desk lamp. There was a certain formal, dark atmosphere to his office, an air of semi-elegance that was only undercut when you actually sat in the furniture or leaned against his desk. It was all show, like the deep mahogany veneer of the desk. Like lobbying itself, I thought.

Without looking up, he started back into our earlier discussion. "There doesn't seem to be anything worth a shit going on around here."

"Michael, give me a break. That was all pretty unnecessary this morning."

"Yeah. Maybe." He paused momentarily in his scribbling as he said it, which I took for something of an apology. Not much of one, except that Michael never apologized. So maybe waiting had been a good thing.

"We have a line on a new client." It was a snap decision, going with the direct approach, and it seemed to work. Michael looked up at me. "Uncle Harry introduced me to a trade association a couple of weeks ago. The Dungan-American Friendship Society. They're interested in hiring us."

"The what?"

"Dungan-American Friendship Society—Asiatic ethnic group out of Kazakhstan. Just looking for some advice and report language, and willing to pay."

"Pay what? And why?"

"I told them our standard fee for such representation is $375,000, and they didn't balk," I responded. "I know it's the rate for a country client, but I threw it out there figuring they'd talk me down. Their lawyers didn't seem to balk at the price."

Michael looked out the window for a moment and then back at me. "That's a whole shitload of friendship." His eyes narrowed, and he waited. "Again, why?"

"Well, Harry's never steered us wrong."

"No, not Harry, for Chrissakes. Them. Why would some bullshit group from the middle of nowhere spend that kind of money for report language?"

He had a point: report language—quite literally, language, anywhere from a sentence to a paragraph or two, in the reports that were always issued when a Committee approved a bill—didn't have the force of law. But if you wrote it right, using the right tone, had the right Committee members sneak it into the report, and then had them follow up as needed with nasty phone calls to the appropriate Administration official, in that case report language was not something easily ignored. We always used the right Committee members and always had them make those follow-up phone calls.

"Why do any of our clients spend that kind of money?" I responded to him. "For the prestige, the knowing they're on the inside. The knowing that Senator Harrison Fuller personally recommended their advisor."

"It's not Harrison Fuller's company. It's mine."

"Well, he does want it to be my client."

"Fuck him. Not up for discussion." Reddening, he started up from behind his desk, sliding his papers together.

"Michael, look..."

"I said, it's not up for discussion." He closed his briefcase and moved quickly out from behind the desk. "We're done here. I have a meeting. Tell Charlotte I said hello."

"Yeah. I will." I watched his back as he headed out the door.

That went about as I expected. At least it wasn't public, not for the entire office to see, as it would have been this morning. Maybe that meant I could talk him back from this first offer.

Sure, I thought, shaking my head, and maybe pigs can fly.

Chapter 4

"SHERMAN!" Her pet name for me. She didn't have to shout it out, but she usually did anyway.

Eleanor was at her desk. Across the room from me, sure, but across a front office, not some cavernous Committee room, and the place was empty except for her two younger assistants, our friend Alexis and another staffer, Terri I think her name was, at their noticeably smaller desks. They sat facing each other and alternated between looking at me and looking at each other, smirking at Eleanor's greeting, knowing there was a really, really good Washington story there and that it probably involved cheap, tawdry sex. Of course, that was the effect Eleanor was looking for. And they were right; the sex *was* cheap, and tawdry too. But still.

People never die in Washington; they just move from one job to the next, showing up when you least expect it, usually somewhere where your very survival depends on whether they remember what happened when your paths crossed five years back. It was always the hardest lesson to teach young lobbyists: just because the new foreign policy staffer to a junior Subcommittee member was an uninformed idiot didn't mean that you could treat her that way, because years later, when she was a Special Assistant to an Assistant Secretary of State, she'd remember how you treated her and she'd screw you for it. First lesson to new hires: be careful, be very careful.

The other people who never disappeared were old girlfriends or, well, whatever it was you'd call what Eleanor and I had that summer so long ago. Eleanor hadn't just not disappeared. Oh no, she was my ex-lover from a *very* long time ago, my former landlady, my current downstairs neighbor, *and* the executive assistant to the Chief of Staff of the House Foreign Affairs Committee, all rolled into one. It was beyond incestuous and often felt that way given the twenty-year age difference between us, but it was so much one of those "small world" Washington stories that most people never even blinked when I told them. *If* I told them, of course—it was never great for the reputation telling people you used to sleep with somebody almost twenty years your senior. At least not for guys.

Anyway, here I was, on the visitors' side of the room, behind the half-wall and doorway that led to the Foreign Affairs Committee staff offices. And here was Eleanor, in a very cushy job with two assistants of her own, a job where she could talk on the phone to Congressmen and other supplicants, read all the interesting memos, but still pass the actual work on Alexis, Terri, and the many other assistants running around the halls of the Committee. She had landed well.

"Hello, Eleanor. How's the Committee treating you this morning?"

"Well, fabulously as ever." She smiled at me, that wide, happy smile that brought back so many memories. Eleanor and I truly did go way back, back to my intern days in Mauritania.

* * *

I first got to know Eleanor in the back seat of a dilapidated 1960s Chevy wagon—a mammoth car, beaten to shit by sun, sand, and heat —on a crazy drive across the Sahara to some godforsaken nowhere in the middle of the desert. As that summer's Embassy intern, I met her briefly when I first came to the office, introduced around the building by our admin officer. I'd seen her at the constant Embassy dinners and parties, weaving among the crowds, her laugh a raucous, wild sound, bringing life and pleasure to more than just the small group she might be talking to. A roving secretary serving a three-month TDY, temporary duty, in the Nouakchott Embassy, Eleanor was a State Department lifer who spent her career flitting from mission to mission, filling in for those on vacation or sick leave, knowing she could get away with murder since she was the Embassy's last resort. Twice divorced, with a twenty-something daughter in grad school in the States, she was always in search of the new, the different, the adventurous. How she'd decided she'd find it in this hellhole I'll never know, but she had balls—I'll give her that. Mauritania was a miserable place to serve out time, but Eleanor seemed to enjoy every minute.

I was just out of Johns Hopkins. Looking back, I was awfully young for my age and lucky to run into Eleanor: she stripped me of any innocence I had left.

It was a miserably hot day, but in the Mauritanian summer, they always are. Perched on the westernmost edge of Africa, Mauritania is all Sahara desert but for a thin strip of land along its southern border, the Senegal River. The days are hot and dry, except when the wind is up, when they are hotter and drier and the air is full of sand. With fewer people than camels or sheep, it's a country where you make your own fun—or, more precisely, you make up things to fill your time and call them fun. We were on one such outing, a two-night romp deep in the desert to visit the home of our *marabout* driver, our holy man, a virtual stranger who for, no apparent reason, invited us to his "home" and whose invitation we, also for no apparent reason, accepted.

"Goddamn, he's a terrible driver," I moaned. "What am I doing in this crazy-ass country?"

Eleanor chuckled from the rear, where she was crammed between another Embassy secretary and our *marabout*'s wife. It was she who somehow found our host, brought him to the Embassy, and then accepted his invitation on behalf of all of us—"well, shit," she explained later, "I can't go *alone*." So here we were.

We'd left town around 11:00 a.m., idiotically heading out into the Sahara just as the day was beginning to get unbearably hot, and it was almost one thirty now, the heat blasting up from the desert floor and off the hood of our ageless Chevy. Staring through the windshield at the unending sameness of the desert around us, I was struggling to keep myself awake. It was always like this, the heat draining you and beckoning you to sleep. I could feel myself sinking deeper into the seat, feeling the sweat pouring down along my spine. The more I slid away, the more I could feel the sand, the sweat, the heat on my clothes, and then they too slipped away, images taking their place, images of Eleanor laughing, images of the hot sun beating on me, images of taking her in hand and pulling her toward me...

The jolt threw me forward, the sense of our car careening out of control snapping me awake, the adrenaline rush intense as I grabbed at the dashboard to steady myself. We were bouncing across the hard-packed sand,

and as I looked up, I could see our *marabout* rousing himself slowly from sleep. From the rear, I could hear Eleanor's ever-present cackle, yet another adventure for a woman I was certain was just waiting for that one ultimate moment that would send her plunging to her death. Leaning forward to peer through the windshield, though, I could see this wouldn't be it.

We were some fifty yards off the road, racing along at an oblique angle, our driver muttering something in Arabic, his wife surely from her tone cursing him wildly under her breath, and the rest of us in various states of disarray. The desert here seemed hard and somewhat rocky, and the surface only slightly worse than the road we'd been driving on. He edged the Chevy slowly to the left, bringing us back to the macadam surface, and smiling over at me, he mumbled, *"vous etiez aussi endormis"* in that crushingly terrible accent. Yes, we were also asleep, I thought, but we were not driving, *mon ami.*

Two sleepless hours later, we arrived at a group of tents, eight or nine of them, with a good-sized herd of camels nearby. "Honey, we're home," I called out the car's window, to no one in particular, and with no response other than Eleanor's wild laughter. We weaved slowly across the hard sand to our tents, women to one tent, me to another, where I fell into a dead sleep, the kind brought on by a long drive in an ancient Chevy set on "broil."

That afternoon and evening brought us wonder after wonder, waking from our slumbers to aged goat roasting on a spit, to our *marabout*'s African slaves hard at work tending the herds and cooking our meal, to a feast of goat and couscous carefully eaten one-handed with our right hands the way they'd taught us in Embassy culture classes, to our fortunes told by the *marabout*, quietly, in private, like the great life secrets that they were, and especially to the deep, endless power of the Sahara desert glimmering by the light of the stars. Massive, high dunes hid each meaningless spot in the desert from the next in an endless cycle. For the first time, I understood what it was to be truly alone in an undiscovered place, hidden from anyone or anything that knew of me or that I knew of, alone in this strange, desolate land with these strange, wonderful people whose lives were encompassed by this massive emptiness. In the firelight, I watched them, the *marabout* and his family, circled close to the fire, murmuring in the strange *Hassaniyeh* dialect, telling stories, I imagined, of the origins of the world, or of the first hajj, Mohamed's hajj, and the rides across the sands in discovery of this distant life.

Hours later, rising from a deep, deep sleep, I stumbled from our tent, slowly waking to the fact that I'd never asked our host if there was an appropriate place to pee—or my colleagues how far from the tent would be diplomatic. The Milky Way, loud in the depths of the night, brought me to wakefulness, its bright light shimmering across the windswept sands, the chill air held back by the blanket I'd thrown around my shoulders. I tripped forward, watching the stars not the sand, past the camels shifting and lowing in the dark, toward the first dune I saw, a low face that I struggled up, feet slipping back as I climbed, falling forward to crawl up and over into the emptiness.

Once over the ridge, I took only a few steps, glancing back at the tents as they disappeared behind the crest, recognizing the foolishness of my modesty even as I continued that discreet extra few steps that ensured no one could see me. Dropping the blanket, I stared up at the line of stars, watching intently as I relieved myself, the strong hard stream hitting the sand an anomaly in the silence that surrounded me.

Climbing back a few steps up the slope, I squatted down, drawing the blanket around me as I took out my Marlboros. I was entranced, watching the next ridge in the light, knowing I could walk there quickly, cross it, turn left, cross another, turn right, turn myself around, and disappear into the emptiness. The sand was a living thing to me, the world alive in a way I'd never known. Dragging deep on the cigarette, I pulled the smoke in, feeling it reach into every small nook, every crack and crevice of my lungs, feeling it inside me like this enormous, living snake of sand crawling across the world before me, unending, unbending to time or space or the touch of humanity. I was at home like I'd never been before.

"That's a foul and disgusting habit."

It was Eleanor, on the ridge above me, looking down. Much later I learned that she'd been awake for two hours, waiting to see if I went out, waiting for me. Now, though, in this place she seemed an apparition, her native Mauritanian dress blowing lightly at her ankles, her thin, strong legs showing in flashes through the fabric, her smirking face masked in the deep folds around her head.

She took what remained of my virginity that night, there on the blanket, naked in the cold air, our warmth pulled from one another. Had I dreamt of the moment, it would have been some younger woman, a Peace Corps worker perhaps, not Eleanor at all. But I wasn't dreaming, and this place was my place, and it needed so desperately to be shared, given, held onto. At twenty-three, afraid of my own shadow in so many ways, clumsy with women, I learned at last to let go of my fears and feed into the people and planet around me. And Eleanor was my guide.

* * *

Eleanor had come to the Hill after tiring of the State Department's many postings, the constant travel, and the unpredictable bosses. Like many State employees, between her housing allowances, her hazardous duty pay, and her salary, she had saved up a pile of cash to invest in D.C. real estate. She parlayed small investments into the purchase of five condos when her California St. apartment building was converted in the 1980s, back when D.C. real estate was affordable. One of those condos I'd later bought for twice what she paid for it, which was how I ended up living upstairs from her.

Now in her late fifties, Eleanor had been with the Committee for about eight years, an irreplaceable asset who knew someone in just about every office in the State Department and, even better, how to ferret out every single secret in the building. She was the State Department's greatest nightmare come to life. And she was loving every minute of it.

"Well, you're looking lovely as ever," I said, as I opened the door in the half-wall on my way to Eleanor's desk. That drew a giggle and a smile from Alexis, and saying "hi" to her, I once again marveled at the brown in her eyes. I couldn't help noticing she was decked out that day in her dark blue dress, the one with the neckline, such that somehow every male visiting the Committee that day would slide to her side of the office to ask whatever question he might have.

I stopped for a second; Alexis never wore that dress to work, only to Committee receptions and Embassy parties. I looked again at Eleanor, glanced back with a smile at Alexis, and continued toward Eleanor once more. She had that small smirk I'd seen often, the one that said she could tell my mind was working.

The Committee was holding its annual hearing with the Secretary of State that day, the best-attended hearing of the year. That meant that several Committee members would make their way to the hearing room through the same door I'd come in and would see Alexis just as I had. They would notice. So that was it—Alexis was in the hunt for a job, something better than this receptionist gig, hoping some Congressman might notice her—or more precisely, when he noticed her, he might think of a job in his office where she could have something more interesting, and better paying, to do. She hadn't said anything at our recent dinner, but she was definitely in the hunt. Some bell was ringing in the back of my head about that, but I couldn't seem to nail it down.

"Sherman, you're just saying that."

"Hmmm?"

"I think," Eleanor responded, "you said something about me looking lovely a moment ago."

"Yes, sorry," I said, shaking my head, "I was remembering a question I had about today, but I can ask it later." Turning fully toward Eleanor now, I smiled, arms out in supplication. "I came to see if you can help me out. I have to check in with Kevin, but he'll never agree to a meeting this close to the hearing. So I'm hoping I can slip back there," pointing to the staff offices behind her, "and chat with him for a second."

I paused, just long enough. "And yes, of course I'm just saying that, but that doesn't make it any less true." Cocking my head a little, I gave my best sheepish grin.

"Get back there, silly, but keep it fast and don't let the Chairman see you." She narrowed her eyes as if she was reconsidering. "You know he hates lobbyists running around back there."

I kept moving, bearing right into the back offices before Eleanor had even finished. As I passed, I winked, only for her, and mouthed a silent thanks. What a sweetheart.

* * *

Kevin was on the phone, his back to the door, comfortable in the knowledge that only fellow staffers were there with him. It was 8:15 a.m., after all, and Committee hearings don't start until nine thirty at the earliest. So he had reason to believe he was safe.

"Hey, Kevin," I said, quietly, just enough to let him know I was there, giving a "don't worry about me—take your time" wave when he turned, shock on his face. I pretended not to notice.

He said, "Hold on one sec," as he turned to hit the hold button. "Jesus, how do you do that? Did the girls leave the front room empty again?"

Every single assistant on that Committee knew there was a history between Eleanor and me, although none, to my knowledge, knew what it was. But none of the "girls," as they're still affectionately and condescendingly called, ever ratted us out to the professional staffers. Maybe because the professionals always insisted on calling them "girls," I thought, and had trouble remembering their names.

It's the corollary to rule number one for lobbyists, the one about always treating people well—the staffers go on to more senior jobs, but the assistants are there forever, so never, ever overlook the support staff.

"Oh, I had a quick meeting back here. I just figured that while I was here I'd stop to check on that question we agreed on, the question about religious freedoms in the Stans. Just double-checking that he'll be asking it live from the dais." Dozens of questions get written up for every hearing, and they'll all eventually get asked and answered—but 96 percent in writing. Kevin promised me over the Armagnac that ours would be asked, but for all I knew he'd made ten such promises.

"Shit, well, you know you're not supposed to be wandering back here." He looked down at his desk, and then back at me, and grimaced. He was caught and was having trouble finding a way out. He looked at the receiver in his hand. "Listen, ah, look, I gotta finish this call, but we'll get to it when the third round of questions comes around."

You sonofabitch, I thought, as Kevin hit the flashing button on his phone and returned to his call. Getting some boob Congressman to ask a question at a Committee hearing might not sound like a big thing, but for me it mattered: in the early stages with a new client, you need to turn over a lot of rocks, and even though we hadn't signed the Dungan yet, this was one of the few hearings where I could get a question on the table that people would notice. Like I said, if there were people out there keeping an eye out for anything Kazakhstan, they'd notice this question, and I'd hear about it. But only if the question was asked live, with the cameras rolling, while Secretary Rice was still sitting there.

My problem was that Kevin's boss, the Honorable Edgar Kleinmayer, wouldn't be caught dead hanging in for the third round of questioning. Not for this hearing: even the staffs referred to this as their annual "clusterfuck" hearing, cameras all over the place, the room mobbed, every member in attendance down to the last fresh-scrubbed, blow-dried freshman from east

Oklahoma or wherever, there for their one shot to get the Secretary of State on record on an issue they cared about, to posture for the lobbyists scattered through the room and the constituents watching at home, maybe even to hit the rare home run by asking that one question that puts the Secretary on the spot more than the others, makes her squirm just enough that CNN Headline News would cover it. Or, even better, the nightly news on local TV. But the networks would head out after the first round of questioning, and the higher-paid lobbyists, when they even showed up, would head out somewhere in the middle of the second, followed quickly by most committee members. So by the third round of questions, it would be down to the Chairman, stuck there out of politeness to the witness, and the most junior committee members, fresh enough to the game that they'd still think the Secretary was listening to what they were saying rather than just spouting off the same circuitous blather that she'd been using to answer questions all morning.

Kleinmayer was senior enough that his second round of questions would come by about eleven thirty, so by staying he wouldn't have pissed away anything more than the morning. But there was no way he'd be staying beyond that.

I was ready for this, though, and ready for the outburst that was sure to follow, so I held my ground with my best poker face on, waiting for Kevin to finish. Friend of Charlotte or not, I needed this guy, and he'd made a commitment to me; he wasn't getting off that easy.

Clearly annoyed by my presence, he raced through the end of his call and turned to stare. I paused for a moment, grimacing, and then said, "Listen, you know, I'm sure you have other important issues, but I'm kind of stuck here. This is a really important question for us, and I have to get it in while people are still watching the hearing—and that means second round. I thought you made a commitment."

"Oh fuck." He turned back to his desk and looked at his phone as if hoping for a call, something, anything to give him time to think. No call. "Look," he said, turning back to me, "we've got a problem: we promised AIPAC," the American Israel Public Affairs Committee, the heart and soul of the Israel lobby, "we'd ask a peace process question."

"Peace process? What peace process?"

"Screw you. You know we've got to go with that question." He was right: if you made a promise to AIPAC, you didn't break it. Me, well, people broke promises to me all the time. But AIPAC? Wasn't going to happen. "And after that, he has to ask something on Iraq, or he'll look like he doesn't care about the troops."

I waited for a second to let that pass and then reached into my briefcase. Handing over a thick folder, I said, "Freedom House, Human Rights Watch, Forum 18, the State Department, the UN High Commission, report after report after report on human rights issues in Kazakhstan. This is *the* question for human rights in this hearing. I wasn't kidding."

Kevin glanced up at me as he opened the folder, and began flipping through the documents. It was an impressive pile, even for someone as hardened as Kevin. And as staffer to a Democrat out of Massachusetts, it played to just the right politics.

The irony, of course, was that I could scarcely stand the human rights crowd and seldom gave them the time of day. Weenies one and all—that was my motto for them. But here, in this meeting, leaning on those dweebs just might work for me.

"We are talking about the *Boston Globe* here, Kevin," I continued, pushing my luck a little. "If there's anything that's going to get Kleinmayer into the *Globe* report on the hearing, it's not going to be support for the troops. It's going to be something like this. And the reports are the kind of visual he can wave for the cameras."

He continued to flip through them, stopping occasionally to read segments I'd highlighted in yellow. I waited, silent, giving him a little room to breathe.

"All right," he said after a long pause. "We'll do it."

* * *

Leaving the Committee offices by the side door, I turned right to head for the long line waiting outside the Committee room. There I found the kid who was linestanding for me, making a little extra cash so I could have a seat for the hearing. Capitalism at its best—when I first started on the Hill, lobbyists all used to line up themselves or send their junior associates to wait for a few hours until the Committee doors opened. Even then, depending on staff, media, and important constituents (read, "donors") brought into the room by their member of Congress, there might only be five or six seats for the public. So some enterprising soul outsourced the whole business, hiring students and the unemployed to stand in line and read the paper for $10 or $12 an hour—not a bad gig if you could get it.

The kid recognized me and began gathering his schoolbooks in preparation to leave. "Wait a second, kid. I'm not ready yet."

"It's Larry, Mr. Matthews." He shook his head as he settled back down, rolling his eyes to his fellow linestanders.

"Right, Larry. I know." Actually, I had no idea, but I guessed that he'd stood in line for me before. Jesus, I thought, you gotta love a town where even the linestanders have attitude. "Look, Larry, sorry," I said, glancing toward the Committee offices, "I just need to catch somebody on her way into the hearing. And call me Ed, for Chrissakes."

I remembered what that bell going off in my head earlier was. I'd heard through the rumor mill that Rep. Toby Kelton, Democrat of Oregon, needed a new Foreign Operations Subcommittee staffer. I knew Toby and his chief of staff and could easily place a call to the latter recommending Alexis. If I could place her in that job, I'd earn points with all of them. But while I knew she was smart, what I most needed was to know whether or not she paid attention to what was going on around her. With Peter always dominating the conversation when the four of us were together, I had absolutely no idea.

Pulling out my Blackberry while I waited, I looked down the line at the now suspicious faces. "I'm staying here for now, but only one of us is going into the room." The grumbling slowed to a dull roar, but I wasn't sure that I'd convinced them; years ago you could get away with cutting in line for hearings, but once the whole process had been privatized, it was a lot more vicious.

It was a good forty minutes later when as Alexis walked toward the hearing room. I stepped out of line to cut her off. "Can I ask you a quick question?"

"Sure," she smiled, and I led her across the hall. Washington's version of a private conversation, crossing the hall to put fifteen feet between you and everyone else. Usually it was the best I could do, especially on this kind of drop-by.

"Any surprises expected in there today?"

She was taken aback; she hadn't expected a serious question. "Nothing much, it's all just post-State-of-the-Union stuff, one side attacking, the other side mimicking the President's line."

Nicely put. "Nothing interesting in the questions?"

She paused and thought. "Well, of course, the Committee intends to closely question the Secretary on…"

"No, c'mon, really, it's me—not the Committee line, please. I'm just curious, nothing out of the ordinary, unexpected?" I waited. This would tell me something.

"Well, maybe." She looked around and, finding no one overly close, leaned in toward me. "Fairchild's bringing in some constituents. He's going to sandbag the Secretary. Some country in the Middle East, something about their kid being imprisoned unfairly." She smiled up at me. "No one knows but you, me, and the television camera crews."

Shit, I thought, that didn't sound good. It was what I was looking for— she had been listening—but it might actually be one of our clients. I stared at the wall for a second and then noticed she was still waiting. "Mind if I ask one more question?" She pursed her lips, but nodded—a "yes, but..." move. "I take it you're looking for a more interesting job?" I asked.

Her cheeks reddened sharply, and she looked around a little wildly. Stepping a little closer, whispering, "Is it that obvious?"

"Not really, but I keep an eye out." I tried to look innocent, like it wasn't her plunging neckline that gave it away. I doubt that I succeeded, although I recall clearly that I was able to keep myself from checking out her boobs as she leaned in. "But you're not just looking to change jobs— you're looking for something better?"

"God, please, I'm going nuts doing nothing but smile all day." She laughed. "I'm looking for a policy job—you know, my degree's in International Relations."

"Send me a resume. I think I might know someone on Foreign Ops who's looking." I paused for a second, wondering whether or not to blow my innocence on the whole neckline thing, but decided I had to since I had my own reputation to protect. "And do us both a favor." This time I leaned in. "Don't wear that dress to the interview. He votes like your typical liberal Democrat, but he's pretty conservative personally and surprisingly shy. You'll scare him to death."

She blushed again, deeper this time, and thanked me for the help. "That's okay, really." I wanted to ask if Peter was helping her find something interesting, but from what I'd seen of their relationship, I decided not to. Glancing over her shoulder at the increasingly long line outside the hearing room, I quickly changed the topic. "Now, though, I should find my placeholder—looks like the natives are getting restless, and you're the only one who can set them free."

* * *

Four hours later, I was over on the Senate side, in the Dirksen Senate Office Building, meeting with my grade-A, number one, absolute go-to guy, the first guy I went to when I was having problems, the one guy who could almost always help me sort them out. I'd met Roger Bauman in my very first year in Washington, one of two critical friendships that dated from that year. Roger was a lifelong staffer who moved from office to office within the Senate over the years, never heading off to the Administration or into campaigning. Such staying power required tact and patience, and Roger was expert at both. Quiet and cautious, with a wide range of tics and twitches that kept anyone who didn't know him off balance, he was hard to get close to. But he was well worth the time and effort, being incredibly well read, encyclopedic in his knowledge of what was happening in Washington at any given moment, and a generous friend to the few of us who got past his strange exterior.

I could never explain my friendship with Roger since most everyone else I knew was scared of him. It wasn't so much a social friendship—no beers and dogs while watching a football game—but rather one built entirely around our shared interest in how Washington worked. I always tried to explain it to Charlotte by the fact that we shared an interest in listening, in understanding what made people tick and why they did the things they did. He was the one person who got that side of me.

I wasn't scheduled to see Roger, but Fairchild's move over at House Foreign Affairs turned out just as I'd feared: it *was* about our client, and I needed some ideas. "It was damned well staged, Roger. Fairchild handled it very well."

Just as Alexis had predicted, Sam Fairchild, Republican from Illinois, surprised Secretary Rice during the hearing, going after her about a young woman by the name of Karen Jameson, imprisoned somewhere in the UAE on suspicion of being a terrorist. A liberal Republican, one of the five or so left in the House, Fairchild could normally be trusted to handle Administration witnesses with care: not only was George W. still in the White House, but his own constituency was increasingly moving to the right, leaving Fairchild to walk a fine line between supporting the leader of his party and voting his conscience. This time, though, it was a local issue, and he'd castigated the Secretary for the Administration's lackadaisical response to the student's imprisonment. Me, I knew nothing about it.

"After his questions, Fairchild made a point to walk around to the back of the hearing room to speak to a well-dressed couple seated near the back. The woman had been crying, so I figure it was the kid's parents, and the State Department folks were watching the whole thing very closely."

"What did he have to do that for?" Roger stared at me through his heavy black glasses, his left eye twitching. He had a wonderful habit of expecting me to answer the unanswerable and an impressive ability to unnerve me despite his unimpressive physical presence.

Roger was small, thin, and slope shouldered, his white dress shirt and thin black tie hanging off him. He blinked rapidly, his nose wrinkling up like a rabbit, when he was nervous, and nervous was his normal state of mind. His desk was bare but for a stacked in- and outbox, both almost empty, a small pile of whatever papers he needed at that moment, a phone, and his computer monitor. Roger hardly seemed to use the computer, preferring to have notes written for him and work the old-fashioned way, face-to-face with nothing to record the conversation. I often felt he'd missed his calling when he decided not to become a monk, but everyone else I worked with always underestimated him, so I'd long before decided that his look was carefully considered. He was the smartest guy in the place and the best horse trader in a Committee full of them.

Today, though, he wasn't happy and decided to take it out on me. When I first walked in, he gave me one of his trademarked "what-are-you-doing-here?" looks, and now he was still staring, waiting for me to answer his question. He was the critical player in our UAE amendment since Coherence Electronics, the prime contractor manufacturing the ARCHON, was based in his boss's home state of Michigan. Rep. Fairchild's actions could threaten to make the Senator's amendment a whole lot more difficult than he'd planned for.

Our UAE amendment was pretty straightforward, a single line in the appropriations bill declaring the United Arab Emirates a "Major Non-NATO Ally" of the United States. Established in the 1980s for the Israelis and piggybacked on by Egypt first and then many others over the years, MNNA was mostly just an opportunity to get in line for discarded military equipment the Army, Navy, Air Force, et al, no longer wanted. The Coast Guard and the Reserves got first crack at the stuff, followed by the Indian tribes, and then the MNNAs in order of priority. Among those, the Izzies went first, and I could never understand what would be left after they got through with the list: they're exceptionally attentive when it comes to getting free stuff from the U.S., and I had to figure there would be so little of any use left once they'd picked everything over that other countries would be left with spare parts from broken-down trucks, jeeps, and penny-ante ships the military wanted to dump. But MNNA had turned into a big deal among Arab countries, part of the ongoing I'm-a-better-friend-to-the-evil-Satan-America-than-you-are competition they always seem to be embroiled in.

Whatever, it was our job to get it, and Roger was ready to help. Sort of. Mostly, he expected us to get it done. "So what next?"

"Hey, don't look at me. I have no idea."

"No, you idiot, what happened next?" He shifted in his chair, straightening his body and settling himself firmly in the exact center of desk. His standard, old-style wooden desk was far too big for him and made him seem smaller than he actually was. Reaching to his left, he shifted his pile of papers almost imperceptibly, straightening them I guessed, and resumed his staring at me, a disconcerting look despite the furious blinking.

I chuckled. "Nothing else happened." At least, nothing else Roger needed to know right then. I'd gotten my Dungan question asked just like I'd wanted, with the cameras rolling and had Michelle back in the office recording the hearing off CSPAN so we could digitize the video and ship it off once they signed on as a client. But that wasn't anything Roger cared about. "You know, the hearing went on, and for all I know, they're still over there babbling away. I just thought I'd get the hell out of there and see if you might have some ideas."

"Nothing." He turned to his left, glancing randomly at his computer screen. By now, it would be showing his screensaver, random photos from a walking tour through Greece he'd gone on the year before. Dry, ascetic, barren landscapes. Just where I'd have expected Roger to go. "How do you plan to fix it?"

"I told you," I laughed, "I've got no idea. I'll think about it, though, if it makes you feel any better."

"You better fix it, if you want that amendment in our bill."

So it was my job. In theory, his Senator needed the amendment as much as we did, but Senators have lots of things they need and build their record on winning more often than they lose. For a lobbyist, though, losing an issue can mean losing a client.

This was a serious problem: the whole plan for our MNNA amendment was to sneak it through the process without anyone knowing about it. Parents who were smart enough to show up at the SecState hearing and get their Congressman to rip the Secretary a new one, people like that were likely to notice. And to put up a stink.

At the same time, some kid jailed on terrorism charges wouldn't be easy to spring out of prison, which I already knew was the only way to get the 'rents to shut up. In the post-Abu Ghraib environment, with the U.S. still holding a few hundred Arabs, Africans, and South Asians in a rat-infested prison in Nowhere, Cuba, it would be next to impossible to convince any Arab governments to spring an American citizen, no matter how slim the accusations. And for all I knew, she really was a terrorist.

This was definitely not good.

But hell, if it wasn't difficult, they wouldn't have needed us, would they?

Chapter 5

"Tell me again why you insisted we come to this hearing?"

"You mean us, Michelle, or just you?" I was whispering a little more fiercely perhaps than was necessary and, from the corner of an eye, saw heads turning on the other side of the Committee room aisle. I ignored them.

Michelle shifted heavily, her look of disgust aimed at me as much as at the Senators spread across the dais. I'd come in late, about forty-five minutes into the hearing, but nothing appeared to have happened other than Administration witnesses droning on and on as they read through their prepared statements. I was pretty happy not to have missed anything, but less than thrilled with my colleague's attitude.

Admittedly, Senate Budget Committee hearings—like those of their House counterpart—are hardly the most enjoyable assignments, listening to dyspeptic old men, and the occasional dyspeptic old woman, mumble and rant and moan about the excesses of the Federal budget. The Budget Committees have only limited authority, but make up for it through unlimited debate. As the Congressional year commences, they meet, they meet some more, and then meet some more, getting testimony from every agency and department there is, and finally, after more discussion than you'd think possible given the Committee's pathetic role in the overall process, issue out a slimmed-down, chopped-up version of the budget the President sent them that year. Foreign aid is invariably slashed, and a wide range of crazy budget maneuvers inserted in the bill to make room for ever-more defense spending and a hefty slather of Congressional pork. Slip in a few new programs here, and add a nice dollop of education spending programs there, all in the name of "good government." Then push a resolution to the Floor that's insanely partisan, and hang around for the next six to eight months wondering first if it has a prayer of passing the Senate and then if anyone is going to pay the slightest bit of attention to it.

"You know what I mean," she replied. "It's the Budget Committee, for heaven's sake. They never *do* anything."

"They meet, they talk, they sometimes talk about our clients, they pass a budget, they set foreign aid limits for the year, they ... they do a lot." I was struggling a little here, as I always did with the new kids, these interns we rolled through every year. The need to be there from the first day of the session until the last, the need to listen carefully to understand the context of it all, where you fit, how you fit, whether or not your clients mattered enough to show up as items for discussion within a Committee like the Budget Committee—usually a very bad sign—it was all hard to understand. Washington is all about the ebb and flow of the process, especially for people like us, working at the edges of the Congressional debate where small changes and vague hints of interest could be turned into an amendment, or report language, or a minor change to the law that we could influence to the benefit of our clients.

The kids, though, they always wanted answers, simple and direct, and they wanted to know why they had to do something, why they had to "waste" their time sitting through these meetings that they could never see the point of. Especially the ones like Michelle, the Mayflower descendants.

Glaring at me, she leaned in to add, "They don't accomplish anything."

"It's what the clients pay us for, and what we pay you for." I was tired of this argument, tired of the many times I'd been through it without ever convincing anyone I was right. I suppose it didn't help that I often skipped the Budget hearings, sending the kids in alone, or that when I did attend them, like today, I showed up late and always had one of them with me to take notes. Truth be told, Michelle was right in that Budget Committee hearings are almost always a waste of time, as well as a fright to sit through. She was only there because, once every three years or so, somebody would say something that mattered, something that would come back to haunt us, and for all any of us knew, this was one of those years. That was reason enough.

Besides, I thought, I've paid my dues and now it's your turn—not that I could ever say that aloud. I found myself rubbing my forehead, feeling a headache coming on. Sensing more than seeing Michelle's body English in the chair next to me, I was envisioning her inevitable run back to Weller, telling him how stupid it was to waste her time this way, given who she was and how well she knew the process. Not something I needed these days, since I had my own reasons to keep Weller happy at the moment.

Goddammit, I thought, why won't the kids just shut up and pay their dues?

* * *

Three days later, I was covering a Senate State/Foreign Operations Sub-committee hearing, this time alone. I didn't mind. I actually enjoyed this committee. That day, though, it was just my luck to arrive as Raymonda Clayton, Staff Director for the subcommittee Republicans, stepped off the elevator closest to the hearing.

Shit, I thought. I'd planned to get into the room and its back row of seats before she even showed up.

"Ray! It's been too long!" I smiled broadly, something that did not come easily when seeing my former lover. She glared at me. We both knew it was a lie, that it could *never* be too long between our meetings, for my disastrous relationship with her was semi-legend in the small Foreign Ops world.

We met right after she arrived in Washington, a neophyte in the city's internecine battles but, unbeknownst to all of us, a vicious and dreaded opponent back home in the halls of New York State's small and clubby leg-islature. She struck me as young, pretty, smart, ambitious, and a boatload of fun; the whole evil, psycho, I'll-make-you-miserable-if-you-cross-me side of her didn't come out in those early years. I'd been in Washington for about three years when we met and had enough experience with the place to help her learn. And I had lots of fun for a year or so, as she used me to learn the nature of the business, the best sources for information on the Hill, and the various and sundry roles played by Washington's many lobby-ists, the ones playing in the big pond rather than the kiddie pool that was

New York's legislature. She led me on, letting me see the small-minded, bitterly partisan weasel of a Senator whom she worked for, his insistence on helping out only those lobbyists with the deep personal pockets and many close, personal friends who could pay for his reelection campaign, and telling me how hard she had to work to get anything "real" done. There was so much her boss could do on his Committee assignment, the Appropriations Committee slot he'd somehow wrangled (*that* should have told me something, since true novices never got Appropriations seats), if only I could help her out and show her the ropes. Like they weren't joined at the hip. But I couldn't see it.

I had such a great time, experiencing all those Washington novelties that one finds in a first D.C. love. The free Smithsonian you can walk to during lunch, catching a Monet exhibit in the East Wing while talking about the bill that would be on the Floor that afternoon. The fundraisers you can go to, her for free as a staffer, me for $500 or so to show my support to some Member or other while scarfing down hors d'oeuvres, canapés, and especially a couple glasses of decent free wine. Spring lunches on the lawn in front of the Capitol, loud, boisterous dinners at Millie and Al's, company-paid box seats at the Kennedy Center, constituent-paid Orioles games down in the new Camden Yards in the years before the Nationals rolled into Washington. It was all new, it was all fun, and we lived it up as much as we could.

The sex was fabulous, of course, but then again don't all great books and movies tell us that sex with the devil is the best kind? And a devil she was, as she proved when our relationship moved into years two and three, and I slipped from her loving partner slowly into her backwash. Looking back, it still scared me, even after five years of marriage to Charlotte. I'd started out as the teacher, the good guy, the helper, but over time the power shifted. I wrote all her legislation, gave her all my secrets, pointed out the lobbyists whose only route to success was money, not talent or a sense of the system, pointed out the ones on the fringes, the ones who seemed most desperate to gain a foothold in the secret societies that were the committees and their staffs, told her all of it. She sucked it in, sucked me dry, and left me spent wondering just how I could have been so stupid.

Luckily I had all my friends to tell me just how stupid I was. They could see it coming, they told me later, and had tried to warn me. Warn me? I never remembered any of those conversations, but they may well have happened: I just wasn't listening. She was my first real, true love, and I was in too deep to hear what anyone had to say. So I always gave them the benefit of the doubt and accepted their assurances that they tried to help, but mostly just for effect since I was struggling to forget that whole ugly period of my life.

Like I said earlier, though, people never disappear in Washington. They just get more powerful.

Still smiling, I continued, "So what can we expect out of the hearing today?"

"Don't give me that shit," she snapped. "You're just here to suck some money out of the Federal Government on behalf of your clients."

Well, I thought, that was one way of putting it. I decided not to contest the point.

"Ray-ray," a pet name for her I'd long lost the right to use, "I'm hurt. What do you take me for?"

She came to a dead stop and stuck a finger in my face. "Don't *ever* call me that."

I made an innocent face and said, "Oops. C'mon, Raymonda, I was just kidding." Raymonda. God, who would ever curse a child with a name like that? No wonder she'd grown up to be a bitch. "Cut me some slack, okay? It has been a long time since I've seen you."

I smiled slightly, not sure which way she'd go, lighten up on me or smack me one across the face. The longer you knew her, the more explosive she could be, and one or two of those smacks had been a part of the long, slow decline of our relationship.

"Yeah, right." She turned and headed for the hearing.

Watching her back, I tried to think of something further to say. Usually with a staffer, especially one so involved with a Committee I worked, I'd want to give her something that I'd heard at another Committee, or offer to help do something in the bill, or suggest a problem that I thought might be headed down the pike. With Raymonda, though, any such comment would just get me into more trouble.

More trouble from Raymonda I didn't need, because it was her boss, Republican Joseph Belkin of New York, whom Uncle Harry had identified as the best candidate for our UAE MNNA amendment. So I was going to be depending on Ray a whole lot later on in the year, and the less I did to make that unpleasant—or any more unpleasant than it was already going to be—the better.

She disappeared into the hearing room without looking back.

I walked over to my linestander, who'd waited patiently through the exchange. "Larry," I said, half as a question, half a statement. He snorted lightly and nodded.

* * *

A little over a week went by before my next assignment, this time for what looked to be a particularly tedious hearing on North Africa and the Middle East. It was another of those hearings we needed to be at, in case a nugget or two might be revealed, but it was also one of those narrowly focused things—three hours on the Middle East and North Africa, rehashing the same questions over and over? that seldom provided anything new. Given the tendency of all Congressional hearings to open with witnesses reading from opening statements, copies of which could be picked up on the way out of the hearing, and thanks to the fact that—in the spirit of "training"—I'd been able to send Michelle up to take notes, I was able to arrive fashionably late.

I noticed her in the back row, looking sour, as I squeezed through the door into the room. Closing the door quietly behind me, I leaned back against it, taking the space among the standing-room only crowd that I'd created by opening the door. It was a cheap trick, but always worked.

A hand clasped my shoulder, and I glanced back around. It was Mourad, who I'd apparently squeezed out of the space I was standing in. "Thank you, my friend," he whispered to me. "Now I've got somebody's handbag against my ass."

Checking out the dais to see whether I needed to pay attention, I whispered back, "Is she cute?" That got me an elbow, but no response.

I was always amazed at how excruciating Congressional hearings could be to sit through, but—as a cog in the wheel producing inane questions to be asked—attending these hearings was part of my job and part of my penance for manipulating the system. I checked my watch; it was only three fifteen, meaning that I'd only missed about forty-five minutes of the hearing for a Subcommittee that tended to go two, two-and-a-half hours a shot. The day's topic—terrorism in North Africa—was always much worse than the average, in the efforts of the Administration to say as little as possible and in those of the Subcommittee members to make a big splash. There were those in the room who found it useful, I supposed, but there was absolutely nothing that was going to occur that we could even remotely claim credit for, and well, let's face it, the minutiae of U.S. policy toward every vitally important nation in North Africa, discussed in excruciating detail over a three-hour period, was enough to put even a died-in-the-wool foreign aid junkie like me to sleep. Adding insult to injury was the single most monotone witness in the history of Washington, Assistant Secretary of State for Near East and South Asia Richard Murcheson, who at the moment was providing an extended response in which he seemed to say, the more I listened, little more than "no."

What always put this hearing over the top, though, was Rep. Timothy Wiggins, a conservative Republican from Florida, making his now-infamous presence known. Ever since 9/11, every single Member of Congress has tried to stake out their own little antiterrorism turf to rail about; Wiggins had been pretty successful by targeting the out-of-the-way North Africans. Beginning in 2005 and especially in the time since, his choice proved prescient as bombings in North Africa, and especially Algeria, began to skyrocket.

I always tried hard to ignore his racist rants and almost never reported on them since they only served to piss off Arab clients some minimal amount more than they upset the State Department careerists they were aimed at. Mourad, though, couldn't ignore them. As Wiggins got ready for his second round of questioning, behind me I heard him say in a low voice, "Oh, Jesus, here he goes."

I leaned back and whispered, "How come you guys never say, 'Oh, Allah, here he goes'?"

He glanced around before answering me. "We never mock our religion." Leaning closer, he added in a whisper, "Asshole."

I laughed lightly. "Hey, sorry," I whispered back. "You don't actually report back to the Ministry what this dick has to say, do you?"

"If only I were so lucky," he responded. "The international media quote everything he says, to show what racists you all are."

In the hall after the hearing, while waiting for Michelle to make her way through the crowd, I asked Mourad if he'd heard anything more about Kazakhstan or the Dungan. He chuckled, saying that his contacts in the Ministry had been surprised that he knew of their existence since they're virtually invisible even inside the country. "This is either the easiest client you've ever had, or there's something strange going on," he said. "I'd still be careful."

"It couldn't be going any smoother or easier," I said as Michelle came through the hearing room door, looking glum. I turned to her and waved.

"Well, yes, that's what I mean," Mourad replied. I looked back at him. "Anyway, the guys from the Ministry want to meet with you sometime. They're planning a visit sometime later this year, so I'll put you on the list for the reception."

"Jesus Christ Almighty," Michelle interjected, "two of those in one day is unforgivable. Why do you make me sit through those things?"

Several young girls, school kids by the look of them, here to see how government worked, blanched and hurried away down the hall in a pack. Sorry, girls, I thought, but this *is* how government works—mostly, it just pisses people off.

Mourad laughed and said his goodbyes. I looked at Michelle, still glaring at me, and responded, "Let's go get a coffee."

As we stood by the elevator, I asked, "So I take it this morning's hearing was bad."

"Awful. The Subcommittee is in firm agreement: they hate Koliba."

That's peculiar, I thought. There hadn't been any Sub-Saharan Africa hearings scheduled that day. "Sorry, Michelle, which Subcommittee were you at?"

She scowled at me and, stepping into the elevator, smacked the "B" button. Following her, I tried to look noncommittal, thinking to myself, how do I piss her off like that?

The foreign aid authorizing committees—House Foreign Affairs and Senate Foreign Relations—each had a whole bunch of subcommittees, one for each region of the world. Each Subcommittee would hold its own sets of hearings, and its own mark-ups—the official title for a mass editing session—of any foreign aid bills moving that year, before sending the bills to the full Committee and then the Floor. Hearings set the stage for those bills and gave a platform for committee members looking to get noticed. But with all the Subcommittees meeting at the same time, in no discernible order, we were always spread out across the Hill. I just couldn't remember where she'd been.

"My God," she finally said, as she stalked off the elevator. "Western Hemisphere, you sent me to Western Hemisphere"—the subcommittee on the Americas.

"That's what I thought," I lied. "But what the hell is Western Hemisphere doing talking about Koliba?"

"Chavez," she replied.

Hugo Chavez, the Bozo-in-Chief of Venezuela? Mr. I-Think-I'll-Poke-A-Stick-In-The-Americans'-Eyes? "What in the hell does Chavez have to do with Koliba?"

"He gave a speech last week praising Koliba's willingness to stand up to American pressure on its internal affairs, especially from the 'villains,' he called them, in the Congress. They ended up yelling about both Koliba and Chavez. It was a disaster."

"Great," I said. "More people focused on Koliba."

"Ed," Michelle said, stopping to turn toward me, "you can't be surprised. The guy is a monster."

Dammit, I thought, just what we needed, Michelle joking around over what assholes our clients are. "Don't ever, *ever* call any of the clients 'monsters,' or any other names," I responded, leaning in so close that she pulled away. "I don't care what's going on or what they're doing. They're paying us to represent them in Washington, and the last thing we need is for people to hear that we think they're monsters, or criminals, or whatever. Just keep your feelings to yourself, all right?"

She was furious, but she nodded. Only after a long pause and a stare, but she nodded.

"Thanks. And I'm sorry, but look around, okay?" The halls were a constant haze of movement, staffers coming through on their way in for weak coffee, or maybe just to get their heads out of their offices. It wasn't mobbed, but it wasn't empty either.

I looked back at Michelle. "Look, maybe we're all thinking it sometimes, but we have to play this game straight. You say it once, it'll roll right out the second time." It was true; in this business it was easy to slip, easy to loosen up and forget, and once you did you couldn't take it back. "We have to make it through the year. I know it sucks, but we have to make it through. Okay?"

"Fine," she said, still glaring at me. After a long breath, she glanced around. "I'm going back to the office," she said, turning to enter an elevator that had just opened. I stood waiting as the door began to close, undecided what to do next, but wanting her gone before I decided. The elevator door closed on her.

Oh well, I thought, staring at the closed doors, another cup of coffee couldn't hurt. It might even tide me over until that night's fundraiser.

* * *

"Oh, the Congressman will be so delighted you could make it, Mr. Matthews," the pretty little bobblehead gushed.

Sure he will, I thought, especially when you tell him I just forked over six grand to get in the door for some free shrimp and mediocre wine. I smiled at her, though, and dutifully placed my nametag on my right lapel. "At least he's someone I like," I said, "which isn't true at most of these things."

She stopped dead at that and stared at me. God, I hate fundraisers, I thought, meaning the people, the people who raise funds as opposed to the events—although those mostly suck too. But the people, they're leeches, calling to harass you into attending their events, always asking for more money even when you've maxed out—"How about your wife? Is she supporting the Congressman this year?"—smiling through these events like we're all happy, friendly, and buddy-buddy when we hate them for sucking us dry. And they're also the dimmest bulbs in the city.

Fundraisers and fundraising, the bane of a lobbyist's life. Used to be they were an occasional annoyance, the periodic $250, $300, or even $500 check to a Member's campaign committee. Starting in the mid-1980s, though, when Dick Gephardt and Tony Coelho decided their Democrats needed to catch up to Republican corporate money, the stakes got much higher. Over the next decade, Democratic Party politics was transformed into a vast moneymaking machine, during the period when Ronald Reagan and his ilk were transforming Republicanism into a conservative, semi-Christian cult of believers and nonbelievers, the Scientology of the American political system. When the believers took control of both Houses of Congress while George W. Bush was in the White House, the culture of political money and the culture of belief for belief's sake merged into one, allowing the truly corrupt—like Jack Abramoff, Bob Ney, and Duke Cunningham—and their hangers-on—the Ralph Reeds, Grover Norquists, and the like—to run rampant through the halls of power. Since then, the American body politic has been racing downhill on roller skates, with most of us just along for the ride. In the post-Abramoff era, those who survived, and often thrived, were the ones who recognized that the problem in the system wasn't us, it was *them*—the goody-two-shoes House and Senate members who railed against the evils of lobbying while refusing to admit that *we* couldn't corrupt *them* unless they were willing to take the money. By the time of this fundraiser, another serious effort at lobbying reform, one that would lead to yet another reform act, was well underway. But serious political reform? Or fundraising reform? Off the table.

Very few people actually said what they meant at fundraisers, but I always found it a great icebreaker. One time some stranger asked me what I did for a living, and when I told him I was a lobbyist, he called two friends over so I could repeat myself: "I'm a lobbyist." They marveled at my actually admitting it, rather than using one of the code words: lawyer, consultant, strategic advisor, whatever—the weasel words most lobbyists use to hide their true identities. Admittedly, when you were ranked below taxmen, garbage pickers, and gravediggers among America's most respected professions, you had an image problem. But c'mon, a fundraiser was a bunch of us all gathered together to snag some food and face time with a Member of Congress in exchange for cash. What was the point of pretending?

The bobblehead had gotten her wind back and, with a smile, was leading me directly over to the Honorable Rep. Will Richardson. Six thousand nine hundred dollars—or more precisely, six $1,150 checks from six different people, all of whom could later be dunned for another $1,150 before the primary, let alone the additional $2,300 they'd be asked for before the general election—was a significant enough bundling of cash to get you brought over to the Congressman. While every U.S. citizen could give up to $2,300 per candidate per election, not many do, and with elections running $2 million for a Congressional seat and $10 million or more for the Senate, picking up $2,300 contributions one at a time was like spitting into Lake Erie. It was bundled checks, a group of checks from a whole batch of individuals, that were the only way to get noticed in Washington. So that was how we played it.

"Congressman, sorry to interrupt, but I'd like to introduce..."

Turning, Richardson flashed me his million-dollar smile, the one that got him elected. "Ed," he said, "how you doing, you crazy fool?"

"Great, Will. How are you?"

Glancing back to excuse himself from the suits he'd been talking to and with a quick conspiratorial wink to the bobblehead, Will put his arm around my shoulder and began walking me away from the crowd. I went with the flow and, from behind me, heard her voice saying, "Oh, you know each other." Well, duh.

"Thanks so much, Sweetie," Will said without looking back. To me, he said with a laugh, "I thought I'd get you away before you bit her head off."

"Yeah, right. What's her name?"

He laughed. "Suzie?"

"Jesus, you're banging her." Will never knew the names of the help unless he was banging them. And "banging" was the appropriate term here; "relationship" wasn't a word in Will's vocabulary.

William Elliott Richardson, after Roger the second critical contact I'd made my first year in Washington, had always been something of a horndog. Six foot one, lean, lanky, always tanned, with a constant air of being in charge, of knowing, Will had that special swagger that the handsome seem born with. In my early days in Washington, we'd hung out a lot, back before I'd gotten married, when we could pair up for nights on the town hunting for ladies. We'd dress up in our power suits, Will in his blue buttondown shirts with red ties, the combination that set off his olive skin the best, his monstrously ugly Yale class ring prominent on his right hand. Of course, I was more one of the Pips in these encounters than the Gladys Knight, more the guy who could be ditched if there was a woman on her own or could serve as a passable wingman on those nights when she was out with a friend. There was something minimally degrading about the whole thing, always playing second fiddle and ending up with a fellow second fiddler, each of us knowing it. I never got much in the form of dates out of the relationship, but over time, the more I got to know Will, the more I liked him for his smart, serious approach to the business of politics and governance. If he couldn't keep it in his pants—and from his knowing Suzie's name he hadn't changed in that sense—that wasn't my problem.

"So whadja bring me?" he asked with a smile.

I laughed. "Six checks, sixty-nine hundred."

"Nobody maxed out?"

"Hey, c'mon," I responded. "We max out this early in the cycle, and you've got no reason to let me into your next fundraiser." He laughed with a shrug that said, "true enough."

A waiter came by with glasses of wine and what appeared to be mineral water. I reached for the wine, but Will stopped me. "Bring my friend a glass of the Markham, would you?" The waiter turned back, and Will added to me, "The stuff on the trays is shit."

I smiled my thanks.

"How do you get them to give to me, anyway?" Will asked.

"Hey, if I have to drop $25,000 a year in political contributions," an informal (read: nowhere in writing) agreement we had at the company as the minimum we'd put into the pot, "I'm at least going to demand they shell out to at least one or two people who I feel like financing."

He laughed, not quite as sincerely this time. "But what do you get?"

"Well, actually, now that you mention it, more than usual," I responded lightly. "I've got a one-minute I could use dropped, and then I need to chat with you about a one-line amendment on Major Non-NATO Ally status for the UAE. It's not something I'm ready to surface publicly yet, but it's a major piece of our work this year."

He scrutinized my face carefully, as if to see whether I was anything holding back. After a pause, he said, "You're serious? About the amendment, I mean? I'm assuming your one-minute is just the standard bullshit."

"Yes, I am, and yes, it is," I responded, smiling, as I took an overly full glass of red wine from the returning waiter's tray. The guy's sharp as ever, I thought. It came from having been a staffer at one point; staffers know the details matter, while Members leave details to the staff. It's the primary reason that many of the most effective members of the House and Senate were once staffers. "The one-minute's just an innocuous statement about ethnic freedoms in the Stans, as a starting point for a new client we're working on."

Every day they're in session, the U.S. House of Representatives begins with one-minute speeches that give Members the opportunity to stand in front of C-SPAN—well, technically, in front of the House, but since none of their colleagues are listening they're only there because of the TV cameras—to spout some drivel about a local fire chief who retired, a basketball team that won the state championship, a one-legged dog that rescued an old lady from certain death in a fire. It's total crap, but for lobbyists, it's a gold mine: some Congressman talked about your client on the Floor of the House.

"Yeah, but the amendment? I'm guessing it's something we need to talk over." I nodded in response.

Will squeezed my arm, turning to his left in search of his next target. He had what he needed from me, and it was time to move on. "Set it up with Maureen," his personal secretary, he said. "Just you and me, lunch. Let's do Voce before they shut those free lunches down."

Free for him, he meant. That lobbying reform bill I mentioned was targeting lobbyist-purchased meals, so we needed to sneak it in before the bill passed.

"Thanks for the Markham," I responded as he began to walk away. As a last gesture, he pointed to the waiter and then to my glass, nodding, indicating I should continue to get the better wine. Ah, well, I thought, watching his back recede, at least I'd get some decent buzz on and could maybe make a meal out of the food trays scattered around the room. Charlotte was working late, so there wasn't any reason to head home soon.

Besides, fundraisers have always been Washington's best source for unfiltered gossip: a cross section of people in the business who seldom cross paths, all standing around solely for the purpose of being seen, all desperate to impress. When you hung around with your friends in Washington, they would talk about the things they thought you'd be interested in. At a fundraiser, no one knew what I'd be interested in, so they'd talk about job openings, rumors on subcommittee assignments, or the latest young staffer whose raucous YouTube videos from college were worth watching.

I looked around and saw Michelle from across the room—we made the interns pony up contributions too, although not usually as much as the rest of us, and hers had been one of the checks I'd dropped off. She stood in a small group of attractive professional women chatting together, all striking elegant poses and dressed to the nines, a couple of suits hovering around the outer edges of their circle trying to find a way in. The men in this town weren't the only ones on the prowl most nights.

Well, I thought, if I'm going to waste an hour on mindless chitchat with strangers, I might as well spend it talking to beautiful strangers. Michelle wouldn't be too happy to see me, but that was nothing new. Taking a fortifying gulp from my Markham, I headed on over.

Chapter 6

"Well, as you know, Mr. Ambassador, there are things I simply cannot discuss."

Weller looked deep into his client's eyes, tilting his head ever so slightly, as if to say, "Do you understand the secret I am telling you?" His Excellency Ahmad Al Youssri stared back over the tops of his reading glasses, equally solemn, his eyes flickering as his focus went from one spot to another on Weller's face, looking for the truth or lie that lay hidden somewhere. I felt like I was watching a great Broadway play, two brilliant actors putting their all into the performance, from a seat on the stage.

Weller waited. Al Youssri blinked first.

"You know, of course," he said, looking down now to shuffle the papers on his desk, "that I must report to my Minister the success or failure of your efforts. Our being declared this 'Major Non-NATO Ally' of the United States is extremely important to our government as well as to the entire relationship between our two countries." He looked up again, focusing on Weller but taking me in as well. "We are entirely depending on you to accomplish this important objective."

The Deputy Chief of Mission—his reason for being present now evident—shifted uncomfortably in his chair, the scraping feet of the chair echoing loudly in the Ambassador's oversized office. He coughed politely into his hand, in case we'd missed the screech of the chair, and grimaced, that peculiar midpoint between a smile and a frown that diplomats perfect for moments like this, when they aren't supposed to take a position either way but have to show something.

I remained still, not ever having gotten that move down to the point where I was willing to use it when it counted. This was that annual strategy session at the Embassy of the United Arab Emirates, the one that Weller had mentioned at staff meeting, up amidst the hideously new and glaringly ugly embassies scattered along International Court in upper Northwest DC. These palatial buildings, seemingly designed by blind architects, were the polar opposite of the stately mansions on Washington's original Embassy Row, Massachusetts Avenue just north of Dupont Circle. It was even a pain in the ass getting here, a long drive up Connecticut Avenue to Van Ness.

The Ambassador sighed theatrically. Al Youssri was a typical client ambassador, an Ambassador E. & P., Extraordinary and Plenipotentiary as protocol liked to call them, who found himself in a position not at all plenipotentiary because his Minister of Defense had decided to hire a lobbyist, an Ambassador who absolutely, unequivocally detested our very presence in his office, let alone the fact that *we* represented his government in its dealings with Congress. As a result, these meetings were always something of a chess-game-cum-death-match as both sides tried to pretend that we were working together. Wellington, who'd brought in this client thanks to some still-unknown (at least by me) feats of bravado during his CIA days, was under strict orders to treat His Excellency with all due respect and civility. The Ambassador, whose training and career choice required that same respect and civility, generally expressed his rage in the same way as most Middle East ambassadors, by smiling constantly while speaking in short, easy-to-understand words. Today he was grinning like the Cheshire Cat.

"If, of course, you were able to participate in these meetings," he continued, "you would certainly communicate the results of any decisions to our Government's official representatives." "To me," he was saying.

Weller paused briefly before replying. Choosing a next step? Resisting the urge to strangle the man? No, that would have been Michael; he could never tolerate ambassadors, finding them useful for garden parties and for signing the checks, but utterly useless otherwise. From his days at the agency, Weller knew better. At least, he acted like he did.

"Surely, Mr. Ambassador, had this decision been as easy as the President, the Speaker of the House, and the Senate Majority Leader meeting in January to decide on what they would give the UAE and our other allies this year, I would not have sold my services to your Government." Weller smiled, almost genuinely. "It would not have been right."

This was one of those classic moments in lobbying, trying to tell your client just how stupid they were without actually saying the words. The biggest problem in working with Arab clients was the difference between the real world—well, sort of, Washington not actually being all that real, but you know what I mean—and the client's, a world of shadows, conspiracies, rumors, and lies. Nothing in the Middle East is as it appears, and the best and most trusted news source is the rumor, passing through the streets like wildfire. In government circles, the rumors are more sophisticated, and this one—the idea that the President, the leaders of Congress, and a couple of aides get together at the beginning of every year to plan out who they'll give foreign aid to and how much they'll give, with subsequent Congressional debates on aid just a show so that countries on the losing end blamed Congress, not the White House—had always been the craziest, and about the most common, of the bunch. It was somewhat understandable coming from a region where even the democracies were simply dictatorships by another name: one could comprehend how, when everything that happened in your country only happened with approval from somewhere on high, it would be difficult to believe that the world's only hyperpower was run by a political system as crazy as ours. It was tough enough to believe that such a system could produce a functioning government, let alone world preeminence. So they would assume it wasn't a democracy at all. At least, the ones that hired us did. It was the only reason we got paid, but it made our job just that much more maddening.

Weller's problem was particularly complicated: Ambassador Al Youssri was a Harvard alum, both undergrad and Ph.D., and had served in London and Paris for over sixteen years, having by now lived longer in the West than in his native land. So did he actually believe this crazy idea, or was it simply safer—since he'd brought in the DCM to keep watch—to play the Arab game?

I looked over at Shaikh Mohamed, the longstanding, long-suffering second-in-command, an old-school, traditionalist Bedouin in his stark white *dishdasha*, flowing robes reaching the floor and covering all but the tips of his Italian leather shoes. His *keffiyeh* was red and white in the Arabian Gulf style, and he kept his prayer beads busy, counting slowly through ninety-nine names over and over again. He was intent on our conversation, but his only contributions were those subtle shifts and coughs at the tensest moments of the meeting, movements that might have gone unnoticed had he actually said anything at all.

I couldn't read him, especially since Wellington had told me he was the Ambassador's uncle once or twice removed. Of course, everyone in government in these sheikdoms is somehow related, and amidst the royal families they have their own forms of democracy, families jousting for power against their cousins, uncles, and nephews. It reminded me of Boston in the 1970s, how when I was growing up and my younger brother would get in trouble somewhere, my Aunt Mary would come to the rescue, finding some policeman or court clerk in that town who was distantly related—"oh, you know Patrick, dear, he's your third cousin twice removed." I could never get them all straight, but they were always there, the Irish Mafia scattered throughout the region making things safe for their distant relations. Of course, Aunt Mary was never sitting on eighty billion barrels of oil—but on the other hand, I thought now as I stared at Shaikh Mohamed, her housecoats almost reminded me of that *dishdasha* he insisted on wearing.

Weller coughed, a real cough, and as I looked over, he smiled ever so slightly. He was putting down the tea he'd taken up for cover, and seemingly almost choking on it; leaning forward now, he placed the cup carefully on its saucer and glanced briefly at me before turning once again to the Ambassador. He'd thought of something.

"Of course, Your Excellency," he began, "if there were such a meeting—which I could never admit or deny—the President, the Speaker, and the Majority Leader would have to agree on the limits of what they would accept, and then require each nation to achieve those objectives in the Congressional process. Otherwise, it would be too easily discovered that they had conspired together.

"I'm sure that's why your eminent uncle, Minister Farouk, chose to hire us."

* * *

"Nice save."

Weller laughed and leaned forward to the cabdriver. "Two stops. I'll be getting out at the Cosmos Club, and my friend is headed up to the Capitol." He glanced at his watch before looking back at me. "Sorry you can't join me at lunch with Col. Fawzi. He always finds you much more amusing than me."

Fawzi was the real client here, head of the UAE's military mission and direct line to Farouk al-Basri, the Minister of Defense who'd retained Wellington's services two years back. As the UAE's official representative, the Ambassador was nominally the lead contact, but Fawzi signed Weller's contract every year, issued the checks, and made the direct-line calls to the Minister. He'd gotten Wellington in trouble once or twice, by passing timely information on American foreign policy shifts to the Minister when the Ambassador was still in the process of digesting our analysis and deciding how much to report back to his own boss, the Minister of Foreign Affairs, another cousin or uncle subsequently shown up by Farouk knowing more than he did and knowing it sooner. But that was okay—such foolishness was Farouk's favorite part of having Wellington in place, so it helped ensure his contract renewal.

Weller always met Fawzi for lunch after his meetings with the Ambassador, both to debrief but especially to head off any trouble Al Youssri might try to make in response to something Weller had said. And they always met far from the Embassy grounds, somewhere they were sure not to be seen by others on the Embassy staff.

In the end, the meeting had gone reasonably well. We'd explained the process we were planning for getting them declared a Major Non-NATO Ally and the potential benefits in terms of donated military equipment. Weller reported that he'd convinced the Defense Department's Near East Bureau to support the move, by arguing that it would serve as a backup to the investment they'd made in Qatar, which in turn was little more than a hedge against the possible loss of their naval facilities in Bahrain. As he'd told me earlier, "after 'who lost Iran?' in the 1970s, they like three or four levels of back-up." Anyway, the Ambassador seemed marginally mollified by the report, and we made it out of the Embassy in a pretty good mood.

Staring out the window, watching northwest Washington roll slowly by, I wondered for a moment about our decision not to discuss Karen Jameson. I'd told Weller about our would-be terrorist, and he was convinced the Ambassador would never raise the issue with us or be able to help solve it if we raised it with him. It was something Weller would need to work through his Defense Ministry connections. Still, I hated leaving it out there without *doing* something.

I started, remembering another problem, the low point of the day's meeting.

"Oh, Jesus, and thanks for that whole thing about getting this in the House Appropriations Bill," I said. "That'll never happen."

He looked surprised. He'd completely forgotten the strategy I'd laid out in the staff meeting with Michael, as usual remembering only the result—we could get it done—and forgetting the details. My whole strategy depended on the Senate: while I was going to try with Will Richardson in the House, Emirates always go over much better in the Senate, something about status and the special kinship Senators feel with any kind of royalty.

"What do you mean it won't happen?"

"Senate, I've always said Senate. I said I'd try in the House and fail, setting us up for Joint Conference. I think I've even been able to identify a Senator who, with a little nudge from Harry, might be willing to give us a hand." If Harry was actually able to deliver Sen. Joseph Belkin, Raymonda's boss and the ranking Republican on the Senate subcommittee, it would go a long way toward locking in the amendment. "Senator Belkin, from New York, lives out on Long Island amid the horse-y set and loves the sheikdoms. He's even got a Foreign Ops staffer I've known for about fifteen years. Just the kind of person I've been targeting from the start." Weller looked blank. "Great, well anyway, it'll work, but not in the House, in the Senate, and we nail it in Conference. And you just promised this guy a victory in the House."

Weller smiled wanly. "I'll tell Fawzi. But you should probably expect the Ambassador to be upset, at least until the Senate acts."

As the cabbie approached the corner of Florida and Massachusetts Avenue, Weller directed him to pull to the right, a move that would save me about five minutes on my way to the Hill. Opening the door, he paused, with his feet on the street outside, and turned back briefly to me. "That's why I need you, son. Keeping me honest."

* * *

Checking my watch as I approached Rayburn, I saw I had some extra time, probably enough to catch Charlotte for coffee. I had a dinner tonight, so we'd hoped to meet up.

Entering Congressman Heaney's office, I said a quick, polite "hi, how are you?" to Anna, the receptionist, and moved on. For all the brilliant, hard-working, and accomplished eye candy that Washington has to offer, some of those women are —well, not. Heaney was notorious for staffing his front desk with some of the dumbest, least competent women in Washington, women you wouldn't even want taking phone messages for you. But damn, they were gorgeous, stunning young kids working as front-desk jockeys, just out of college, starting out at the front desk in the hopes of landing something better but not showing the slightest bit of promise they'd ever get it. Anna was most certainly one of those, twenty-two or twenty-three, slender, oval face surrounded by waves of dark, full brown hair, and lush brown eyes I could just go swimming in for hours. But another of those Washington rules that had to be followed was that, while a five-minute chat about the weather with a gorgeous woman was a great break in any man's day, you absolutely did not even *notice* the women who worked in the same office as your wife. It just caused trouble.

"Hey, babe." I'd caught Charlotte heading toward her desk as I came into the back office. "Still have time for coffee?"

Charlotte's face lit up as she turned, and she gave me a warm smile. "Just give me one second."

As she headed back toward her cubicle, I felt a glow watching her walk away. She was in a dark wool skirt and jacket, one of her more upscale out-fits—she must have some group coming in from off the Hill for a meeting, constituents probably. I eyed her again, as if for the first time: tiny, five foot four, and petite—small bones, all in proportion, a nice tight butt, and short, tight brown hair. She'd never liked her body—breasts too small, not tall enough, a fear of weight tending to gather in her butt—but she was perfectly balanced, every inch matching up to every other inch, the epitome of proportion.

This coffee was something of a ritual, scheduled whenever we could. With Charlotte out of the house so early, generally before I even dragged myself out of bed, we never got to chat about the morning paper, that day's *Washington Post* front-page update on the scandal *du jour*, or whatever. Meeting like this was the only way to spend time together during the workday, and it was always so much better than falling all over each other first thing in the morning: we'd avoid the whole thing about me getting in her way in the bathroom and moving too slowly to do the breakfast dishes, or her having to adjust her time and energy level down a notch to keep from bowling me over. This way, we'd both be up to speed and well into our day. It was usually only a few minutes when we could fit it in, but it was, most importantly, something to carry us through for the next ten hours or so while we ran at Washington's pace.

Elbows on the table, two hands holding the mug to glean all the warmth from it, Charlotte smiled at me over Rayburn's dishwater coffee. "Glad you could make it." Even on days I was all over the Hill in meetings, I couldn't always find time for coffee.

"I needed the break," I said, smiling. "Remember? Today's some of the annual visits to the folks who hate us. I'm on my way to Wallingford over in Ellen Thomason's office. That'll be a nightmare." I laughed a little at the thought of yet another staffer yelling at me. "How's your day shaping up? The boss in?"

As I said earlier, Charlotte worked for one of the biggest assholes in the House. This wasn't just my opinion, it was pretty much everybody's. Members of Congress get elected for a whole lot of reasons, but there's never been a single one who got elected because he or she was a good manager. Most of them are bad at it, some of them excruciatingly so: Mikulski, LaFalce, Heaney, legends even among their peers. In those offices, having the boss in the office or not generally affected the entire tenor of the day. It was a Tuesday, meaning that the first votes for the week in the House wouldn't happen until somewhere around four o'clock this afternoon, so there was a good chance he was still on his way in from Tennessee.

"No, not yet, but you can already sense the approach of doom and feel everybody's mood shifting." She shook her head. "It's sad. They're good people—it's just that he's such a toad and they're all so scared."

"Why do you stay with him anyway?"

"Oh, he doesn't scare me, and besides," she said, looking down into her coffee as she spoke, "I was hoping you might be ready to find another career for yourself."

"Honey, I'm about to sign my first client, the first one that's mine," I said, a little more plaintively than I'd meant to. "You can't want me to leave now. I can make something out of this one."

"Jesus, Ed, they're not even a country, for Chrissakes."

I picked up my coffee and took a long slug—God, it is such bad coffee, I thought, but I needed time. "Well, not for now, but there have been dozens of countries that have emerged from the Soviet Union." Maybe not dozens, I knew, and fifty thousand vegetable farmers were never actually gonna be a country, but it was the best I had. Then again, maybe—I'd have to check all those post-Soviet countries, I thought; I hadn't followed the splintering of the Russian empire too well, and representing this client, I should know it enough to come up with a better answer than that. I searched, and said, "Besides, Ukraine wasn't an independent country at first."

"Ukraine has a history five thousand years old and is enormous, so don't even try that one." She grinned at me—she was clearly annoyed, but not so angry that she wasn't determined to keep it light. "Your guys sound more like fifty former Communists gathered around a Citgo station somewhere in the Urals deciding to pick a fight."

I laughed. "Look, it's my first client, and I want to make this work." I glanced at my watch. I wasn't prepared to argue this; I wanted this client, wanted to play it through. "Listen, I have to go. I don't want to be late for Wallingford—it will just give him more reasons to complain."

"Sweetie, I'm just saying…"

"I know, babe, you're saying it's time for me to think about a serious career, something I can be proud of, not some bullshit lobbying gig stuck in this place with all these people." I waved in the direction of the accumulating crowds, the dozens of staffers filing through, some stopping to sit for impromptu meetings. "I just, I don't know, it's different seeing it with my own client." I paused and then smiled at her. "Even if they do run a Citgo station."

"To what end? Freedom for Uzbeks?"

Kazakhs, I thought to myself, Kazakhs, but it's probably safer to let that slide. Having no serious answer for her, I choked down the rest of my coffee, gave her a kiss, and left.

* * *

Fourteen, fifteen, sixteen, seventeen, eighteen, green binding, looking down, scribbling a note like I cared what he was saying, looking up again, finding the green binding, nineteen, twenty, twenty-one, leaning a little left to see past his head from where he's slid over a little, twenty-two, twenty-three, and, little more left, yes, twenty-four, and that was the end of the row. Look down at notes, twenty-four, that's added to twenty-six on the bottom, twenty-two on the second shelf, thirty-five on the third, so that 107 books in that bookcase. Yep, 107. Next?

Franklin Wallingford, national security staffer for California Senator Ellen Thomason, was in full attack mode. This kind of meeting usually only happened once or twice a year, but when it did, the key was to sit there, listen, and take notes. At least, pretend to listen and pretend to take notes.

Meetings with Congressional staff were the lifeblood of our business, and I spent enormous amounts of time every year talking, and especially listening, to staffers. For one thing, I needed to get in to make the pitch for our clients. More importantly, though, I needed to find out what people were up to, what their interests might be, how the people who weren't helping us out might react to our plans, whether we could trade a vote here or there for something we needed, etc., etc. Most of the meetings I usually enjoyed, because I actually was interested in the foreign aid bill, and the foreign aid business, and I was almost always learning something new. This kind of meeting, though, this was torture. After a morning meeting with a client who couldn't stand us, going straight into a meeting with a staffer who couldn't stand another of our clients was definitely a frying pan/fire kind of a deal.

"Now I am going to read to you from the Constitution, the Constitution that Koliba endorsed, the Constitution overwhelmingly approved by the Parliament and the people, the Constitution yutta yutta yutta blah blah blah…"

He didn't actually say that last part, but well, let's face it, some of these people just weren't worth listening to, and I'd developed some defense mechanisms to keep from going crazy. This particular skill I learned from conversations with my father, a gab artist from way back, using an approach reminiscent of the classic *Far Side* cartoon of a dog listening to her master and hearing only her own name: "blah blah blah Ginger, blah blah blah Ginger." With Dad, it was more along the lines of "blah blah blah Gilbert and Sullivan, blah blah blah Rodgers and Hammerstein," but it worked pretty much the same. It served me well over the years, becoming almost as important as my ability to read things upside down on people's desks.

Wallingford leaned forward in his seat, pointing his index finger at me. With a start, I dialed back in to what he was saying. "How do you sleep at night?" he said. "How do you face yourself in the mirror in the morning?"

Ah yes, the old I-so-disagree-with-you-your-life-must-be-unbearable thing. I sleep very well at night, I thought, probably better than you, all wound up tight as a drum the way you are. Looking closely at him, though, at the fire in his eyes, I could see that the question was rhetorical and no answer was expected or desired. Letting my mind wander again, I wondered how long I'd be stuck here.

I'd known I was in trouble when Wallingford came out to the front office and asked me if part of my job was to report back to the clients what people in Congress had to say. When I responded yes, he'd asked if I minded if Mindy, or Buffy, or Candy, or whatever the preppy little intern by his side went by, joined us to take notes. As if we were going to discuss something momentous that he'd need notes on later, a lobbyist and a staffer—what, we were supposed to be making history here? I paused before answering to let him feel like he'd gotten one up on me in the vain hope that might reduce the amount of horseshit I had to sit through. I should have been so lucky.

Wallingford had been going on for about twenty minutes by the time I started counting the books behind him. Counting like that while pretending to pay attention actually took more effort than you'd think, so I was heading for the end of my rope here. It had to be close to forty-five minutes by now, but I didn't dare look at my watch.

What a job.

Twenty excruciating minutes later, I was on my way across to the House side of the Capitol, having learned what I needed. Near the end of the meeting, Franklin had gotten off his whining about Koliba and told me what he intended to do about it: he was working with staff on the SFRC, the Senate Foreign Relations Committee, to prohibit all funding for Koliba's government this year and would push to do the same thing in both the State/Foreign Operations Appropriations Bill and the Defense Appropriations Bill. A complete cutoff of money from all sources, which would mean that not only would Koliba not get any foreign aid—the money he didn't give a rat's ass about—but he also wouldn't get the $20 million in cash that the Pentagon gave him every year to pay for our "secret" CIA listening post. The classified pot of money, unknown to most of Washington, including poor Muffy-Buffy-Candy-Mindy-Whoever, since she blanched when Wallingford brought it up.

Now I had something I could work with.

* * *

About a week later, I met up with Will Richardson at Voce, my favorite Italian restaurant in Washington, one of the power restaurants along Pennsylvania Avenue and a particular treat since I could actually get a decent meal without having to order steak.

This was the dinner Will and I had agreed to at his fundraiser, and another of those leaps into the Big Leagues that Uncle Harry and I had talked about. I'd known Will for years and bought him one dinner a year ever since I signed on with Michael. This was looking like our last such dinner, what with both Houses of Congress pushing reform legislation that would prohibit lobbyists from feeding Members of Congress. More importantly, though, it was a major new step in my relationship with Will—not the dinner itself, but the fact that I was asking Will for something big. That was a change.

While Will had always been one of my "go-to" people in Washington, up to now it had only been for news and advice, not for action. Like I said, our relationship began as two guys out on the town but evolved over time as I came to recognize his quick mind and his understanding of the process. So on those pre-Charlotte nights we were out catting around, we'd talk Washington and bat ideas and options off each other. I'd feed him information on countries that seemed to interest him, and he'd feed me information back on various Subcommittee mark-up plans, on people who were pushing amendments against our clients, on people who might be looking to trade their support if I could help find them other votes in Committee. It was always mutually beneficial, and neither of us ever gave up anything critical, but it was the perfect symbiotic, grease-the-wheels Washington relationship. Like other similar relationships I had, it gave me the kind of inside access that defined "special interests" for most Americans and spurred the periodic cries for reform, for limits on lobbyists. These pleas have never worked, because no one has ever found a way to stop the free exchange of ideas without shutting down the entire system. If I was any indicator, though, the sentiment is well placed: I had access *way* beyond Joe Public Citizen, and this dinner was just another example of that.

"So what's this one-minute?"

I looked up from my arugula salad and smiled. He was getting right down to business. "I wasn't sure you'd remember," I said, smiling.

He said nothing, waiting.

Reaching into my jacket pocket, I took out a single sheet of paper, unmarked, with a brief speech on it. It was titled, "Kazakhstan: Promoting Ethnic Freedoms." I slid the paper, still folded, across to Will. "Here it is. Nothing major. Nothing to get you in trouble back home. Just taking a flyer, trying to see if anyone's listening. For our newest client, the Dungan-American Friendship Society." That wasn't quite true, since we hadn't signed them yet, but close enough.

"The what?"

"Dungan-American Friendship Society, a group worrying about the Dungan, a nomadic Asiatic people living in Kazakhstan. A pillar of the economy, a small, industrious group of Chinese origin surrounded by about nine hundred thousand Kazakhs. The contract isn't finalized yet, but they're worried about President Nazarbayev, who's increasingly erratic, and they just want someone—the U.S.—to notice they're there." I'd gotten it out pretty much just as I'd practiced, three quick sentences, simple, understandable, easy to grasp. Now I sat back to see if it sold.

Will looked down at the paper for a moment and then back at me. He was thinking, not about the text, but about what I'd said.

For those of us who weren't swimming in huge pools of campaign cash, trust had always been the true currency of Washington. Being someone who people trusted was a critical survival skill and the core of my success as a lobbyist. You didn't have to agree with other people, and you didn't have to try to make them feel good; you just had to be straight with them about whether you were going to help them out or whether you were going to try to screw them. Whichever you chose, the key was always to tell other people the truth and never ever get caught in a lie. I'd successfully cultivated that reputation, taking great care throughout my career to always tell the truth. Waiting for Will's decision, I could sense that my long cultivation was on the verge of paying off.

"So what's the point?"

"Credit with the client. An early chit demonstrating our effectiveness."

"You know these are a joke?" he added, tapping the paper with one finger as he reached for his wine glass with the other hand.

"New client. You start at square one." I smiled.

"Okay. Next week all right?" As I nodded, Will went back to his Caesar, leaving the paper where it was on the table, halfway between. By the time he would pick it up later that night, no one would remember that I was the one who'd placed it on the table. Just another move in the lobbying two-step.

* * *

An hour or so later, as he finished up his Delmonico, Will asked, "So what's this new thing? The UAE? What's that all about?"

We'd been chitchatting about the Committee, avoiding this topic for the last. The one-minute was an easy "yes" for Will, so it wasn't a risk to start out the meal with it. This, though, he might say "no" to—in fact I was counting on him saying "no" at first and then agreeing to my second option. But Members hated saying "no," and it was uniformly a serious conversation killer. There was nowhere to go with a conversation after a "no": what did you say next? So it was always safest to hold the big topic until the end of the meeting, or dinner, so you could clear on out of there without anyone feeling uncomfortable.

"It's something Congress hasn't done for a few years, designating a country a Major Non-NATO Ally. Israel, Egypt, South Korea, Australia, Thailand, Morocco, Pakistan—there's a batch of them. Our client wants the designation, but DOD hasn't allowed one to be named for a while. So we need it in Foreign Ops." I cut a sliver of swordfish off of the small scrap on my plate, stretching out the explanation with a little bit of silence. "Nothing too serious."

"That's it? It's pretty lame."

I laughed lightly, coughing as I did on the swordfish. "Will, I'm not talking to a rookie here. I'm talking to you. You know the UAE, you know how we work with them, and I'm betting that since I mentioned MNNA status at the fundraiser, you had someone in your office brief you on the issue." I paused, looking at him. He held his poker face, so I reached for my wine and took a long sip. A Barolo, rich and fruity, a wonderful wine, I thought for a moment, realizing that I might just miss meals like this. "So if you want the whole spiel, I can give it to you, but let's be serious. You don't need it and you probably don't want it." I smiled.

In point of fact, I wasn't ready to lay the whole story out on the table. Wellington had been pushing me hard not to talk to anyone about the ARCHON, the air defense system for which our MNNA amendment was developed, because it was so secret. I'd convinced him that whoever sponsored the amendment would *have* to know what it was really about, and that meant that Uncle Harry would as well. But he'd insisted I tell no one else at this point, which made my strategy for this dinner even easier. If I couldn't tell Will the whole truth, I wasn't going to push him very hard just yet.

Will glanced around for a moment, reaching without looking for his own wine glass and grinning ever so slightly as he brought the glass to his lips. He emptied the glass, and as I reached for the bottle, leaned back against the banquette.

"Yes, I did. The amendment doesn't make a lot of sense to me." He looked around again. No one was close enough for him to be worried about being overheard, so I knew he must have been playing for time. Doesn't want to say no to me, I thought; that's just what I was hoping for. "I just don't see a real need for it, and your client wanting it isn't enough for me right now."

"Well," I said, exhaling slowly for effect, "we need to find somebody to carry this one, and you were our only bet in the House." Picking up my knife and fork, I carefully speared the last piece of swordfish. Pausing before putting it in my mouth, I asked, "Your guy didn't talk to the Subcommittee staff, did he?"

He shook his head. "You said you weren't ready to go public."

"Thanks." I chewed thoughtfully. "What about Conference?"

His turn to look up from his plate. "What?"

"Conference, you know, that thing at the end of the year?" He smirked and quickly flashed me the finger as he reached for his newly filled glass. "I think we can get it in the Senate, but I'll need someone to ask the Chairman to accept it in Conference."

He paused, looking up and off to the right, his "tell" that he was actually considering something. "That might work," still looking away. "But it's too easy, too quick an alternative."

I looked around for the waiter. Will had said he had a party to go to, so we agreed to skip dessert. "I knew you'd never agree to offer it in the House. Too much exposure." As our waiter surfaced from the table he was looming over, I signaled him for the check and looked back to Will. "*I* wouldn't have agreed to it on the basis of what I told you, and that's pretty much all we've got for an argument." At least, it was all I could tell you right now. "I've known you a long time, Will. You weren't going to do it."

* * *

On the street outside Voce, I stood with Will until he could flag down a cab. One pulled sharply to the curb, and stepping off, he opened the curbside door. He turned before getting in.

"Interested in a small party?"

I smiled inside; from my experiences with Will, a "small party" could mean almost anything, from three girls he met in a bar somewhere to forty people drinking margaritas all night until they ended up in the streets of Capitol Hill in a mammoth conga line. Well, that last one only happened once, and back when Will was a staffer, but still, it could be almost anything.

Charlotte was waiting for me at home, and I was tired. I'd had a good night, getting something for the Dungan and getting a commitment to support our UAE amendment in Conference. "Thanks, but I'm going to pass."

"You sure?" he asked. "Someone dropped out at the last minute, and I'm short one guy."

Hmm. While I didn't know what kind of party he was throwing, I could guess from the context that the "someone" who dropped out was probably a fellow Member, meaning the woman he'd been paired with would have been a serious looker. Not like the old wingman days, I thought.

Tempting.

Except for my being all married and shit.

"Yeah, thanks, but I promised Charlotte I'd be home right after dinner."

"Your loss," he said, and climbed into the back of the cab. Watching them drive slowly off, I shook my head, wondering what I'd be missing out on, wondering how long Will could keep this up.

Standing there, I ran the dinner through my head. I'd gotten pretty much all that I needed from him, but was struggling with the one new idea he'd given me: in between our discussions of the Kazakhstan one-minute and the UAE amendment, he told me I should look to the religious right for support for my Dungan. It was the one place that Kazakhstan's government was vulnerable.

For years, evangelicals in the Republican Party had been more and more aggressive on freedom of religion overseas—or more precisely, freedom for proselytizing Christianity overseas. They'd pressed for a special office in the State Department pushing religious freedom, inserted requirements into human rights reports about the issue, ranted and railed about it for a long time. Will thought I should hop on that bandwagon.

For me, and certainly for my client, such a tack would mean a dance with the devil, a partnership with people we didn't agree with to get at a mutual opponent. Not that I had anything against Jesus; I liked him as much as the next guy. I just thought the U.S. Government had no place helping spread *anyone's* religion around the world, just as I thought other countries had no right to shove their religion—or, let's say, their crazy-ass Wahhabist version of a religion—down the throats of the Moslem world just because they were swimming in petrodollars.

Will pointed me toward the Christian wackos' most effective champion, Henry Little, a rabid little Idaho Republican whose very existence I could barely tolerate—not just pro-gun, but pro-assault rifle; not just antiabortion, but supportive of snipers who shoot at abortion doctors; not just antigay, but all purple in the face, hissing and spitting whenever gays are mentioned.

Little symbolized everything I hated in American politics, not because he believed all that stuff, but because of the way he used it. People's beliefs never bothered me either way. It was the way they used their beliefs for political gain, pulling Jesus out of a hat at some opportune moment like he was just another piece on the chessboard of Washington political gamesmanship. Same thing liberal Democrats always did with "the children," you know, the nameless thousands or millions of children whose lives will be saved or something by just about every amendment liberals put forth. "Let's do it for the children."

For me, using Jesus that way was always worse.

And here Will thinks I should ally myself with Little, I thought as I walked slowly up Pennsylvania Avenue toward the White House. It was way too early in the year to think about pursuing such an option, but it gave me a new and urgent assignment: to find some other way, some other agenda to push for the Dungan. What a miserable business this can be, I thought, dodging a cabbie as I crossed against the light at 13th Street—what a miserable business.

Chapter 7

"Veeee-je-tah-bers." Bao smiled, handing his menu back to the perplexed waiter.

Vegetables? Oh Jesus, I thought, running my eyes through the list of menu items, there probably aren't any vegetarian entrées. The big ticket Chicago lawyers who arranged lunch brought us to a typical, big-ass Chicago steakhouse, and nobody thought to ask Bao Yan-hu or his grandson about the old man's diet. Looking over at Hendrickson and Kincaid, it was evident that the one was clueless and the other, Kincaid, didn't seem to care about anything happening around him. As usual.

I turned to Charlie. "He's a vegetarian? Why didn't you say anything?"

"Grandfather insisted I say nothing," he replied, looking chagrined. "Among our people, the role of host is taken very seriously, and we do not criticize our hosts."

Well, that doesn't work, I thought. Among our people, the role of host has pretty much gone down the toilet, and most people don't spend two minutes thinking about their guests. Bit of a mismatch.

I waved the waiter over. "I'll have the New York strip, medium, and I'll start with the chopped salad. Bring him," pointing to Bao, "an entrée portion of the vegetable sides, some of each. Not just a pile of side dishes, but make it an entrée. Uh, lemme see, have them throw the asparagus on the grill, and do the same with the baked potato, slices or wedges of it so they brown." I handed him back the menu and glanced to my left to Charlie. "You're okay, right?"

Charlie smiled. "Yes, unlike my grandfather, I am a meat eater." He too ordered the strip, but "very well done" in the style of people who don't like meat but eat it anyway.

I smiled back and, reaching into my pocket, said, "Thinking fast on your feet is part of the business." I drew out a pair of chopsticks, a small piece of the research I'd done on the Dungan: one of the Chinese customs they'd retained was the use of chopsticks, especially among the older generation. Vegetarians, that I hadn't picked up on; chopsticks, though, I was prepared for chopsticks. Even had a spare pair for Charlie if he needed them.

Laying the chopsticks next to Bao's forks, I pointed to them and then to him, and smiled at him.

"Thah-nk you," he said with a broad grin and, picking them up, began to toy with his bread.

* * *

Michael and I had arrived at lunch a few minutes early, finding the table and setting ourselves up opposite one another. We'd flown to Chicago on an early morning flight, hoping to finalize our relationship with the Dungan in this meeting over lunch right after their monthly association board meeting. We would be heading back that same night, contract in hand. At least, that was the plan.

It was rude, of course, to seat ourselves when we weren't even the ones who'd scheduled the lunch, but we'd given up on ceremony to stake out exactly the spacing we wanted. Michael, figuring that he needed to convince the lawyers of his skills and knowledge of the system, wanted Kincaid on one side of him and Hendrickson on the other. Me, I wanted the opposite, Bao on one side and Charlie on the other. It was typical of us: Michael always went for the power and the money, while I liked to cozy up to the people who could help me understand the country, the society, their mores, and their customs. That was information I could use on the Hill to give staffers and Members a feel for the client, a sense of them as people, making it harder to treat them like statistics or "furriners" the way Congress normally treats every non-American.

We rose as they entered, while the maitre d' expertly guided them to our table. With Kincaid nowhere to be seen, Hendrickson let Bao take the lead, leaning on Charlie as he walked smiling toward us. "I am so pleased," he told Michael, as I introduced them around, "to meet you. I look forward to working with Mr. Matthews." He bowed ever so slightly.

Michael froze for an instant, and a thin plastic smile came across his face. "I am so glad that you are pleased with Edward. He has come so far in the time since he first came to work for me." He glared his smile at me, behind eyes of ice.

Well, that only took about fifteen seconds.

I too nodded deferentially, hoping to think of something that might ease the tension. But glancing at the others, I noticed Hendrickson standing back just far enough to watch for our reactions. He planned this moment or, at least, had known it was coming. So he's smarter than he lets on, I thought. I began to wonder if this might be more evenly matched than I'd expected and to hope I'd be on whichever side won.

* * *

"I would like to make a toast." It was Michael, acting out of turn again.

"We are so very pleased that you invited us to join you today," he said, looking slowly around the table at each of us, stopping almost imperceptibly as his eyes locked on mine, nodding ever so slightly before moving on to the others. He had a presence about him sometimes, where you just didn't see anyone else in the room; this was one of those moments. "We at Michael McPherson & Associates are very pleased to be considered for this important representation. Before we start with our business, I would simply like to express my personal appreciation for your willingness to consider my firm to assist you in Washington."

Subtle again, Michael, I thought, counting the "I's," "we's," and "my's" silently in my head. Raising my glass with a smirk, I leaned forward a little to drink but stopped, sensing rather than seeing something wrong.

Five red wine glasses in the air, one—Bao's—still on the table. Bao himself had joined his hands as if in prayer and bowed toward the table.

Turning to Charlie, I asked, "He doesn't drink, does he?" Charlie shook his head a little. Jeez, this lunch is turning into the Sacred cozying up to the Profane, I thought.

Through the early stages of our lunch, once Kincaid had strolled in a good twenty minutes late with no effort to explain, Michael was virtually ignoring Bao and Charlie, focusing on Kincaid and Hendrickson, talking up his many hard-earned successes. From what I could tell, he was regaling them with stories of his work in tax and trade policy, issues so far off track from today's topic that I guessed he was angling already for his next client rather than worrying too much about this one. He was most definitely "on," pitching his skills as intently as I'd ever seen him. He's reaching the point, I thought, where he is selling himself so constantly he's forgetting how to turn himself off. So different from my small companion, I thought, glancing down at Bao.

While Michael was pitching away, I was learning more about the Dungan, their homes, their lifestyle, and how Charlie came to be in America: a math prodigy picked up on by the old Soviet school systems and sent to Moscow for further training, he'd escaped to the Math Department at the University of Chicago for a doctorate and never gone back. Now he was CTO in a security software start-up that sounded like it involved five guys, all working from algorithms Charlie had developed.

Kincaid broke the ice first, taking a drink from his glass and shaking his head as he put it back on the table. He was disturbing to me in so many ways: he paid no attention to the Dungan, even though as their association's president he was technically working for them; he paid scant attention to Michael's spiel, something Michael wasn't picking up on; and he seemed strikingly bored. His eyes roamed about the room as if tracking who was eating with whom, or maybe just trying to keep his attention focused on something vaguely interesting. He had almost nothing to say, leaving Hendrickson to respond to Michael's questions about who was representing them in Washington and on what. The one pleasure I was getting—the fact that Michael was getting nothing more out of Kincaid than I had—was simultaneously disturbing, since Michael was so much better than me at breaking through people's barriers. Who is this guy, I asked myself, and what the hell is he doing?

Looking over at Bao as I drank, I saw that he was smiling, so either we hadn't done anything overly offensive, or he was so used to Americans ignoring him and his traditions by now that it was amusing. He muttered something brief to Charlie, who looked at Michael and said, "My grandfather says that you are most kind in your welcoming. We are most pleased to be here in this lovely restaurant to share with you this kind opportunity, and we look forward to learning more about you. Your colleague, Mr. Matthews," here, Bao looked directly to me and nodded, "has been most helpful in explaining your system, and we look forward to today's discussions."

Well, that was one hell of a lot more than whatever Bao had actually said, but was nice nonetheless. Especially naming me—the whole "who signs the contract?" question was hanging over us still, and he was pulling the discussion back a little bit toward their team. Things seemed to be going well enough.

* * *

"It is most unusual, that is all," said Michael, holding his Cuban like a defensive shield, "most unusual for a client to sign with individuals in a firm when the firm, after all, is here as a whole to serve our clients' interests."

I had to admit, I was calm at this point, abnormally calm despite the intensity of everything going on around me. My boss, the guy who'd made me in this town, was fighting like hell to make sure that *my* first client was his client, not mine. Hendrickson, their lawyer, had come to lunch expecting a fight and was fighting away, quietly, politely, as if they were discussing the precise shade of écru to paint the walls. My client-to-be—at least the person I saw as the client, the tiny thin old man who sat with a quizzical look, as if uncomprehending—watched the debate like you would watch a tennis match. Like me, Charlie stayed out of the conversation, occasionally translating in a low voice to give Bao a sense of it, I assumed, but mostly letting it all roll by in silence.

Somehow, I knew I didn't matter. So I just watched.

"My clients are prepared to sign for one year, for $360,000, if Mr. Matthews will sign the contract on behalf of the company." They'd nudged us down $15,000, on principle I supposed; lawyers had always struck me as unfailingly driven to demonstrate some value. "We will pay in two installments, one-half immediately, one-half in six months."

"But in our company," Michael said, his cigar bouncing as he spoke, "I sign all the contracts." He took a deep drag on the cigar. He was a horrible smoker when he was nervous, sucking in cigar smoke like it was a cigarette. As owner of a small foreign aid lobbying company, he was nervous a lot. Not for the first time, I found myself wondering how his family history was for lung cancer.

"But in your company," Hendrickson purred, "you can surely delegate that authority to your Vice President for Legislation." He gave me a thin smile and peered at me over the top of his glasses. Michael's eyes followed his, glaring at me.

I didn't react. I just waited, hoping someone would say something so I might be off the hook.

"It's not the way we do things."

Michael was making this painful. For me? For them? I couldn't tell. It was rather maddening, if only because I'd gotten so used to Michael over the years I thought I knew his every mood. This one, though, was new: I'd never seen him negotiating like this. I wasn't used to seeing him lose control, and that alone was making me tremendously uncomfortable.

Looking back, I think he knew it was over, but he just felt like he had to fight it.

"There is one small complication," Hendrickson said. Shit, I thought, we're so close; this could screw the whole thing up.

Taking the cue, Michael said, "Another complication?" Nicely played: making the signing already a complication.

"We cannot sign the contract until tomorrow. Today is Tuesday."

Michael and I looked at each other, and despite the tension, I almost laughed. "Tuesday?" I asked.

Charlie coughed and looked at me in embarrassment. "Our board meets each month on the seventeenth, which is a lucky day for Grandfather. This month, the seventeenth, today, is a Tuesday. Tuesdays are very unlucky days. The Dungan never begin a relationship or sign a deal on a Tuesday." He looked down at the table and continued, "It is very bad luck."

"Bad," Bao added, looking up at me. "Bad luck."

"Looks like I'll have to stay overnight," I said, to no one in particular.

* * *

The following morning, Hendrickson met me in the lobby of the skyscraper where the Dungan-American Friendship Society had its small office, and accompanied me to the fourteenth floor. Entering the office, which was little more than a conference room off the main hall, I was surprised to find Bao and Charlie waiting.

"Am I late?" I asked Hendrickson.

Charlie replied for him. "No, first we had to have the Board vote, to finalize our decision to hire you. We could not do that on a Tuesday either."

"Bad luck day, Tuesday," Bao intoned. "Good luck day today."

It had taken me a while, Googling "dungan," "tuesday," and a bunch of variations, but I finally found a reference confirming that, indeed, Tuesday was an unlucky day for the Dungan people. I'd cut-and-pasted the document into an e-mail to send to Michael; he'd been in a killer mood when he headed out to O'Hare for his flight to D.C., and I decided it was worth the trouble to prove to him that the Dungan and Kincaid weren't scamming him somehow—at least not about Tuesday. I hadn't found any rationale for why Tuesday was a bad luck day, though, so I wasn't sure that Michael would be convinced. At least he hadn't called me on the phone screaming about it. Yet.

"All we need to do now is sign the agreement," Hendrickson said, pointing me to an empty seat next to Bao.

My heart began to race, even though this had all been decided the day before. Michael had conceded before the end of lunch that I would sign the contract and headed out of town furious with me. Walking him to the cabstand, I'd pushed my luck, being ballsy enough to raise the split of revenues, the traditional finder's fee for bringing in the client, but he waved me off in disgust and just started walking faster. "Just sign the fucking contract and bring it back to D.C.," he said, struggling with his coat and then throwing it and his briefcase into the rear of a waiting cab.

Holding the door open, he turned back to me. "You may think this is all about you, and all about your client. It's not. It's about Harry. I don't trust the motherfucker, and you shouldn't either."

I looked at him, surprised. He was serious. "I'm being careful, Michael."

"Are you?" He glanced down at the curb, reddening a little more. From years of experience, I could almost hear the gears grinding as he worked through what he wanted to say. Then he surprised me again, turning back to stare at me. "You're great at your game, the best. But if Harry's fucking with us somehow, if there's a play here we can't see"—in his eyes I saw, "you can't see"—"you're not ready to face Harry down. You're ready for a lot, but not for that."

He stood staring at me for several more moments, but I had no response: I'd been expecting just about anything other than what he said. Finally, he turned to get into the cab. As he slammed the door, I could hear him tell the driver, "Just get me the fuck out of this town," and watched the back of his head as the cab sped off. I stood by the corner for several minutes, the Chicago wind whipping at my coat, my mind spinning without catching on anything specific.

Today, though, everything was going perfectly. They'd sent a driver to pick me up at the hotel, and he'd called ahead to Hendrickson as we were approaching the building. I wasn't even entirely sure what part of town we were in, since I didn't know Chicago well and, other than crossing over the river at one point, couldn't tell one set of streets from the others. It's one of those cities where all the skyscrapers—other than the Wrigley Building and the Sears Tower—pretty much look the same after a while. It didn't matter since Hendrickson was there by the car door to take me through security and up the elevators.

Hendrickson took the seat next two me and opened the folder in front of him. He signed the one-page contract on the bottom of the page and then signed the extra copy behind it. He slid the open folder, which I could see included a check, upside down, presumably the first $180,000, over to me.

This was it? I thought. I was deflated somehow, very aware of Bao smiling at me, Charlie watching us, and Hendrickson waiting, while I looked down at the folder. After all the excitement and the arguments with Michael, this was it? Two signatures? Then what?

"It is good." It was Bao, in a low voice, but enough to shake me out of my reverie. I looked him in the eye and knew he was reading me, recognizing my hesitation, knowing that there was something I felt was missing. He waited.

It is good, isn't it? I thought. Laughing a little, I looked down again, and this time signed my name once, twice, with a little more panache and a lot more care than I normally did. It was done.

As we walked back to the elevators, Hendrickson was apologizing for Kincaid's absence when I heard the "ding" of an elevator arriving. As I turned, Kincaid walked out of the elevator, and I noticed a look of surprise on his face just as the red light over his head winked out. Down? I wondered. For a moment, I asked myself where he could have been to be coming off a down elevator and promised to check in the lobby who the building's other tenants were. In the rush of goodbyes, though, and in the afterglow of having a $180,000 check in my pocket, I forgot.

I was halfway to O'Hare, replaying the signing in my head, when I recalled the image, the one seemingly wrong moment, the red light over Kincaid's head. Damn, I thought, I need to check that out. That feeling faded, though, as I once again patted my breast pocket, to be sure the check was still there. I leaned back and sighed, my first big payday in hand; there was plenty of time to worry about Kincaid and his elevator. Besides, this is a good luck day, I recalled, laughing; so it has to be nothing.

* * *

"Oh, Ed, I don't know. They're just very upset over there. Even at the thought of it."

Eleanor stared down into her drink, some obscure California red, eyes crinkled in concern, her chin sunk down into the grey turtleneck she wore over a charcoal skirt and under a navy blazer. She'd been well trained by State and still had some of that striped-pants, cookie-pusher style about her, looking more like an Embassy functionary than most Hill staffers. The perfect outfit for tonight's event, a Golongolese Embassy-hosted function honoring the nation's Vice President, Joshua Gangaran.

Gangaran's visit was the bone I'd been thrown for pitching a fit in our staff meeting over the desperate straits in which Golongo's president, Mr. Koliba, found himself. Gangaran was the country's front man, the pleasant face of an increasingly unpalatable regime, the small *d* democrat elected to office freely and fairly while Koliba and his people were focused on stacking the Presidential vote and not worrying much about the rest of the ticket. Tall, 6'2" at least, his skin the blue-black found only in Africa, Gangaran was Harvard trained and had run as a reformer, promising to reform from within. There were no indications that he'd had the slightest success so far, and for all any of us knew he'd been bought off by now, but he retained a veneer of respectability, and that was about all we could expect from any Golongolese these days.

Gangaran was in town for two days only, having arrived earlier in the afternoon for a visit to the State Department before tonight's reception, and with meetings on Capitol Hill the following days with the House and Senate foreign affairs committees. Tonight's was to be the friendliest part of the visit—the semiofficial, semi-open reception for U.S. Government folks and defense contractors with an interest in Golongo, along with those few members of the House and Senate and their staffs willing to be seen in public with him. It was one hell of a feed, the kind that desperately poor countries always insist on throwing for visiting dignitaries, their limited resources wasted on trays and trays of shrimp, pastry puffs, mini-quiches, and cut vegetables, along with a bar that exceeded the choices at even your best fundraiser. Still, getting people—serious people, like members of Congress—into the room was always hard, because there was nothing in it for them. So we'd called in a lot of chits to get at least a few people in from the Hill, something no good reception can do without. I'd had to beg Uncle Harry to come since he was absolutely our only shot of pulling in a Senator; he'd given me a lot of crap for it, but he promised to drop by at some point. That put me here for the duration.

I smiled back at my date, Eleanor, who I'd invited once Charlotte made it clear that she wouldn't be caught dead in the same room with Gangaran, reformer or not. It was something of a two- or three-fer, since Eleanor counted as a senior Congressional staffer on our list of attendees, I actually enjoyed spending time with her, and I'd asked her to nose around the State Department for some inside skinny on how Kazakhstan was faring inside the building these days. It was this last assignment that was disturbing her so much. "Eleanor, I just don't see what they could possibly flip out over. We're representing a few thousand vegetable growers, for heaven's sake."

She took a long drink. Watching, I was reminded how lovely she still looked to me, not in any classic sense, but strong, symmetrical features on a face whose every movement, every nook and cranny, every look I knew so well. It had been a short summer for us, but very intense, and one I'd learned so much. They tell me familiarity breeds contempt, but somehow my ongoing familiarity with Eleanor—and the knowledge that of all the many "familiars" in her long State Department career, I was the only one who came back to find a true friend and, in her own way, mentor—made her very special to me. "I think you're in trouble."

"Oh, well, shit, if that's all, I'm always in trouble." I reached to squeeze her hand, small, thinner now, with the slightest mottling. She squeezed back, laughing despite the annoyance. I turned, looking for Gangaran. "Come on, let's go meet a Vice President."

She drew back. "I mean it."

"I know you do, sweetheart." I turned to the shrimp tray and, picking one up, offered it to her. "I promise, we'll talk about it later," I said, leaning in toward her. She smiled slightly and opened her mouth. I fed her the shrimp, delicately, holding the tail tightly to squeeze the last of it out of the shell. My fingers brushed against her lips, and I let myself remember how good it felt to have her body close to me. "After we introduce you to the Veep."

I smiled at her. Maybe this is why I never told Charlotte about my summer with Eleanor, I thought. She knows about all the others, but this one, this was too close to the bone and retained too much intimacy, too many scenes like this, to admit.

* * *

I waited for Eleanor on the stoop in the courtyard where she was house-sitting, a small enclave hidden away from the Sahara in the form of most Embassy homes in Mauritania: a square one-story building, rooms scattered around an open air courtyard that attracted the cool air of the night and, with walls blocking the worst of the wind and sand, allowed for some semblance of a garden. She was getting a bottle of wine, a Californian purchased from the Embassy commissary. On nights like this, when the city's generator had failed again, this was the only place in the building that was even vaguely cool, and chatting over wine and maybe a little cheese was the only activity that made sense. With the Milky Way bright above us, it was desperately romantic as well.

"Are you going to tell me what the hell I was doing at that dinner?" I asked her. We'd just gotten in from another of my only-in Mauritania evenings, a dinner for three in the courtyard of some Moor's home—he, Eleanor, and I gathered around a small dish holding nothing but the boiled head of a goat. No lettuce, no trimmings, nothing, just boiled goat head. I'd been asked to come at the last minute, and my presence seemed to surprise our host as well. Through his tortured French, I sensed an effort to figure out who I was, this twenty-something young lad trailing after the Ambassador's secretary. I didn't mind; my French was just as butchered, and I was trying just as hard to figure him out.

"Well," she said, as she poured me a glass of the Cabernet, "after I accepted the invitation to dinner, I found out he only had two wives. I thought you'd block any plans he might have."

Taking the glass from her, I laughed again. "Why not just cancel?"

"And miss that goat head?"

Eating boiled goat head was pretty much what it sounded like: picking bits of meat off the face and skull of the poor beast, picking here and there desperately trying to find something edible, all while giving your host reassuring smiles as if this wasn't the strangest meal in your entire life. There was the inevitable offer of the eyeballs, a delicacy in this part of the world but one that even Mauritanians know Americans just don't eat; so he offered them, one at a time, we politely declined, and then we listened to the disquieting crunch as he chewed, lost in thought, picking at the skull in search of another morsel. "If I'd known you were coming, I would have brought a second head," he said as we snapped the goat's jaw to get at his tongue, slicing it into small pieces. Oddly, at least for me, that turned out to be the best part of the meal.

"You know I never say 'no' to a new experience." Eleanor rolled the wine in her glass, sniffing it, and glanced up at me with a smile. She'd sat down next to me and scooched over, sliding her hip against mine. My arm instinctively went around her shoulder.

"Oh, well, you know me," I replied, "I'll go along with anything."

She looked down into her glass before taking another long sip. "Yes, you will. It's one of you most endearing qualities, and one of your most annoying."

I didn't know how to take that, but decided to let it go. "So am I one of your new experiences? Does that explain us?" I asked her, leaning toward her.

"No, honey," she replied, kissing me lightly on my lips, "the sex explains us." She kissed me again, firmer this time, serious about it.

Three hours later, we were still there, under the Milky Way, on the mattress we'd dragged out from the too-hot bedroom and planted in the courtyard. Hot, sweating, a thin film of sand, the Sahara's ubiquitous sand, coating us, we lay in a loose embrace, letting the air float around us in a futile effort to cool down. "You're a sweet kid, you know that?"

I paused, wondering for a moment if that was a compliment, or a comment, or a what? "Thanks, I think."

"I mean it," she responded, sliding back into me, planting her firm butt against my lap, spooning, wiggling her way in. "You're sweet. It's a good thing."

I laughed and nuzzled against her neck, pulling her in with my left hand, playing it along her belly and down to her thighs. "Yeah, it's a good thing. Besides, it takes a lot less energy than the alternative." Pressing my hips against her, I could feel myself growing again, feel my prick harden. My fingers trailed up again, now to her crotch, to the damp patch of hair that I touched lightly. "Hmm," I said, into her neck.

She twisted, part into me and part away. "Jesus, Sherman, my pussy already hurts from the last two times," she said. "Don't you ever let up?"

Removing my hand, I drew back away from her. "Sorry." I lay flat, chastened, and looked up to the stars.

"Goddammit, Sherman," Eleanor said, rising up on her elbow. "You've got to learn to be more assertive."

"You said no."

"No, I said my pussy hurts a little. You said you wanted it." She grabbed me and squeezed, arousing me even more. "Don't you?"

Panting, I breathed, "You know I do."

Sliding her right leg over me, she sat on me and began moving, agonizingly slowly at first, and then just the tiniest bit faster. "I don't want it. But if you plan to survive in Washington, Sherman, you need to be able to use people sometimes. Especially the willing ones."

My breathing was getting more ragged, my need for her pulsing inside me. I fought it, feebly I admit, but I fought it. "Dammit, you said no."

Her response was to reach down and guide me inside her, grimacing only a little, and then begin grinding against me again, mechanically still but just that much faster. "Using people," she continued in a flat voice, "using people is the currency of Washington, Sherman. You have to do it to survive. We all do. Tonight I used you—now you use me." She held my wrists loosely as she rode me, holding me in place. I didn't, couldn't fight her.

"Slow down, dammit, you're going too fast..."

"But I'm not doing this for me, Sherman. This is all about you." With that, she raised up on me just that much more and slid down, slamming her pelvis against my belly.

"God damn you, it's too good. It feels too good," I said, sliding my arms out from under and, taking her by the wrists, flipping her over on her back in one smooth motion. I couldn't slow myself anymore; I hadn't learned that kind of control yet. I was moving faster, faster, and my breath was getting ragged.

"Look at me, Sherman." My eyes opened, looking down at her, seeking out some sign of pleasure, but all I saw was the look of someone almost at work, at an unpleasant task. "Not for me," she said.

At that, I exploded with a cry of pain, combined with intense, burning pleasure, exploded in her like it had been days or weeks, not an hour, since we'd last made love. A hard shiver ran through my entire body, and my arms buckled, dropping me down on top of Eleanor. I could feel my breath rattling through me, feel the spasms running down my legs as I kept coming, coming, like it was somehow new. I felt Eleanor's arms enclose me, hold me to her, and heard the lightest whisper saying, "It's the nature of Washington, using people. It's how you survive. You have to learn to like it."

God damn you, I thought, eyes closed, breathing hard, as little ripples of pleasure wove through me. Collapsing on top of her, I felt the thick sweat on our bodies mingling, sliding off our skin. I let out a deep breath. This does feel good, I thought. It's not me, not my way, but my God it feels good.

* * *

"Mr. Vice President, may I introduce my colleague, Ed Matthews, and his guest, the Executive Assistant to the House Foreign Affairs Committee's Chief of Staff, Eleanor Walters. She's here on behalf of the Chief of Staff, who was unable to make it."

Dammit, Tom, I thought, where the *hell* did that come from? I was livid and felt myself take half a step forward. Eleanor was here as a favor to me, not on some official Committee business, and wasn't ready to play that game. Worse, I never, ever put her into that kind of game; it was part of our unspoken deal, and Tom had just broken it.

Tom smiled thinly at me, his face drawn, while Eleanor stiffened on my arm. Tom had been in lockstep with Gangaran all night, hanging on one side of him like a Secret Service agent protecting the President. Grim, his face taut, Tom looked increasingly scared as the night went on, that some-kid's-gonna-break-the-china scared that parents get when they've got a houseful of four-year-olds at little Tiffany's birthday party.

We all knew the trip wouldn't go well, but that was the plan: bring Gangaran out so that he can get yelled at and defuse a little of the steam building in Congress. The State Golongo desk officer had told me his State and Defense Department meetings would definitely go about as badly (from his point of view) as I'd hoped. But being in this room, it seemed pretty clear that Tom was having trouble accepting the plan.

I counted three right-wingers from the House—Jack Tindal, conservative Texas Democrat from just southeast of Austin, and two nutjob Republicans, Louis Hadle of Alabama and Timothy Wiggins of Florida, the same Timothy Wiggins I'd recently watched rant and rave about terrorists from North Africa. His presence was yet another demonstration of the simple fact that your friend on one client could easily be your enemy on the next, and vice versa. More importantly, I knew that each of them would only have showed if Tom had begged them, and having three members of the House of Representatives show up a reception like this might give Gangaran and his ambassador the idea that Golongo had support in Washington. With an even bigger draw on his way over, Tom's claim that Eleanor was representing the House Foreign Affairs Committee was entirely the wrong message—in addition to pissing me off royally.

As I squeezed Eleanor's forearm lightly in reassurance, Gangaran stepped forward to her with a smile, looking her up and down in that strikingly blatant way foreign government officials always did. "Miss Walters, it is my very great pleasure."

The man was a hulk, built like a linebacker, with an incredible air about him. I felt like I wasn't there, and of course, he treated me that way. I wasn't bothered; it was a client thing—they all treated us like cattle.

Eleanor paused, her mouth open, for just a moment. *That* surprised me, for I'd never seen anyone get the better of Eleanor. Recovering, she flashed Tom a look that said, "do not ever do that to me again, asshole," and responded, "Mr. Vice President, it is an honor. My boss so regrets his inability to attend, but it was a national security matter. I'm sure you understand."

The tension in Tom's face eased ever so little. Gangaran tilted his head slightly and said, "Oh, but of course, Miss Walters. Tell me, tomorrow I meet with your Committee members. How will that go?"

Eleanor stiffened again. Not bad, I thought, that's twice in one night.

Uncle Harry's booming voice over my right shoulder saved the day. "Edward! Nephew!" he called, approaching quickly from the sound of it.

Letting go of Eleanor, I stepped forward to the Vice President, cutting between them while simultaneously turning toward the sound of Harry's voice. Conspiratorially, I leaned in to Gangaran. "Senator Harrison Fuller, Pennsylvania, Defense Appropriations member," I said. "Very important." Gangaran threw a glance at Eleanor, as if to follow up on his question, but I held tight and began Harry's introduction while he was barely in earshot. "Senator," I said, "we're so very pleased you could be here. I'd like you to meet Vice President Gangaran."

Harry stepped up, every bit the Senator, a little more regal tonight than usual, but I supposed that was the company: Senators relish meeting foreign leaders, perhaps since their own Presidents so seldom give them the time of day. I stepped back, to give them some room, while Tom and the Ambassador crowded in to pay their respects. Tom looked relieved, in that we'd pulled one Senator into the party, but still grim, since he knew Harry was something of a loose cannon. I'd warned Tom that Harry's one requirement for attending the event was that he could tell Gangaran "whatever the fuck" he pleased, as he so daintily put it, so Tom had reason to worry. But I'd pointed out that it was a small price to pay in exchange for getting him into the room, and with no other Senator on his dance card, Tom had been forced to go along.

As I turned toward Eleanor, standing still stricken off to my left, I heard Harry's booming voice. "Could I have a moment alone with His Excellency?"

Glancing back, I could see Tom looking beseechingly at me. I ignored him and took Eleanor by the arm as I approached, leading her away. "Jesus, I'm sorry."

"I wasn't prepared for that," she said. "That sonofabitch..."

"He's *my* problem, not yours," I replied, looking into her eyes. "Entirely my problem." I paused, to let that sink in. "Let's you and I go get a stiff drink."

At the bar, I ordered us both a Johnny Walker Black, rocks for Eleanor, mine with a splash of water. We were both tense, Eleanor because she wasn't there representing the Committee but as a favor to me, me because Tom had just crossed a huge line—screwing me with one of my most useful contacts—and I wanted to fry his sorry ass. Looking over at him, hovering with the trio of idiot right-wingers he'd brought to the party, I wondered how best to confront him.

"It really is your problem, isn't it, Sherman?" Eleanor asked softly.

"Hmm?"

"I think I feel sorry for Tom, for once." She smiled and laid her hand on my arm. "I do think you've learned over the years."

"I had a great teacher." Looking over again, I saw Tom and then past him this time, to Harry, deep in conversation with Gangaran, the Ambassador beside them looking deeply unhappy. Harry didn't seem angry, though, and neither did Gangaran; from here it looked like a serious discussion but not a confrontational one. Tom was watching them too, nervously: he'd stopped listening to his friends and was staring openly at the Vice

President, too far away to hear but smart enough not to walk into their conversation.

I looked back to Eleanor and raised my glass to clink against hers in a toast. "Yes, Master, I indeed had a great teacher," I said in my horrible faux-Chinese accent, "Glasshopper has 'rearned' from your wisdom." Taking a long slug of the scotch and relishing the burn as it went down my throat, I added, "You were going to tell me about Kazakhstan."

* * *

Eleanor wove one hell of a tale. It seemed that State was absolutely, positively freaking out at the thought of anyone representing *any* of the minority peoples scattered through the Stans, let alone Kazakhstan, perhaps the most problematic among them. It wasn't so much just the idea of someone working for them, an outcome State always hated because it made it harder for them to control the bilateral relationship. It wasn't even the new standard complaint about the delicacy of diplomacy in that part of our post-9/11 world and how lobbyists can undermine the objectives of American foreign policy—as if some bozo like me walking the halls of Congress could actually have an impact on foreign policy (something we never told the clients, but even on our best days we just nibbled at the edges). No, State was going totally overboard at the idea of another Kazakh group being represented in Washington because of the Vice President's office. Not Gangaran. *Our* Vice President.

"They are simply scared to death of that office. It's like a black hole over there, and they love nothing more than hanging a few State Department 'weenies'"—she did that annoying quote marks move here, as if that made them less weenie—"out the window by their toes."

"But there's no way they'd worry about a group as small as the Dungan. What's the big deal with some tiny stateless group just angling for some notice?"

"Their ties to Shaddock Mills."

Shit, I thought, that's a very bad combination. Shaddock Mills was just one among the current crop of lobbying firms working for the Government of Kazakhstan, but if they were close to Cheney's people, they were seriously connected. Shaddock Mills alone I could handle; the Vice President's office, them I could slip under the radar of. But if Shaddock Mills had friends in the Vice President's office and they were working together, well, that was going to be a problem.

It made sense that Cheney would be keeping an eye on Kazakhstan policy: he'd been there in 2006, praising the dictator Nazarbayev and promoting the idea of an oil pipeline through Kazakhstan that could bypass Russia. But hell, I'd figured that was little more than a routine visit to a friendly ally in the fight against terrorism, especially since the Kazakhs had oil. I might have to rethink that a little, I thought.

In my small corner of the world, Dick Cheney was a very big deal: the War on Terror had moved most corners of U.S. foreign policy into the "classified" realm, and Cheney was nothing if not the King of Classified, even more than the Prince of Darkness title that Democrats liked to put on him. Always ready to toss his own grandmother, or his Chief of Staff, under the bus if it suited him, Cheney had his fingers everywhere, at least everywhere that he and his conservative friends cared about. That was the beauty of the Vice President's office: Veeps could either do nothing at all, like most of them over the years or, if they had influence with the President, could sneak around behind the scenes shaping policy, undermining approaches they didn't like, supporting the ones they did, and reporting to no one except the President—and then in meetings where there was no one in the room but the two of them, so no one else ever knew what was happening.

It's the greatest black-box experiment in the world, only with real people and real power.

The link between Cheney's office and Shaddock Mills—whatever it was—was something I'd been totally unaware of, but I decided to play it cool. "Is that it?"

"Well, it's enough, Sherman. So you just be careful. Those people play for keeps."

Chapter 8

"Hi. Ed Matthews to see Alexis Chase, please."

The receptionist smiled and picked up the phone. "Please have a seat while I see if she's back there."

"Thanks." I stood, preferring to stay on my feet given the many hours spent sitting at my desk, at hearings, or in meetings over the course of a week. Turning around in the cramped space, I glanced at the reading materials in the dark brown, institutional bookcases against the walls. It was the typical innocuous mix of law books and reference materials that litter every Congressional office—no *Portnoy's Complaint*, *Huckleberry Finn*, or other potentially controversial works on display, lest some constituent or other get offended. No one ever complained just because the books were boring, so boring they would be.

It still being only early April, the office was relatively quiet. Capitol Hill offices move more slowly in the early months of the year, with lobbyist visits not as common as they would be later on, and visitors from back home not showing up until late spring or summer. It was the right time for someone like me, though, to get my face in front of people and test out what they were planning for the year. I needed to know what they wanted and how to help them out, as well as lay out my own needs and see how much they'd be willing to do. It was one of my favorite times of year, leaving a trail of breadcrumbs in offices around town and seeing who'd follow them to the end. It was one of the things I was best at.

The office for Rep. Toby Kelton, House Foreign Operations Subcommittee member and Alexis's new boss, was on the fourth floor of the Longworth House Office Building. Alexis had followed up on my lead and landed the job. Toby was grateful to find someone smart, talented, and good-looking enough that lobbyists would never mind getting fobbed off on her when Toby just didn't feel like seeing them. Alexis, according to her grateful phone call and nice note, was delighted to be working for someone who took her seriously and had her working in an area she loved.

This was my first visit since she'd gotten the job, a day to figure out whether her gratitude was just that, or if she felt she owed me anything and just how much that might be.

As the heavy wooden back-office door opened, Alexis appeared smiling, happy to see me despite this being just a drop-by. She waved to me. "C'mon back," she said, leaning against the weight of the door. As I took the door, she turned to head to her desk, the pleats on her knee-length skirt swaying as she did, her long, lovely legs running down to conservative navy pumps that matched the skirt and offset the yellow in her sweater. Much more appropriate dress for Kelton's office, I thought, but still incredibly attractive.

"Gee, you look different somehow," I offered cautiously.

She glanced back at me. "When in Rome," she smiled. Great dimple on that right side. "Your advice worked. Most of the other girls who interviewed with Toby came in the way I looked that day outside HFAC."

We reached her desk, like the rest a tiny cubicle with a too-large desk crammed into it. She swung around to face me, her skirt whirling again as she did. I kept my eyes on her face. "On the other hand, I've gone deep into debt buying an entirely new wardrobe."

I laughed. "Well, it's working."

She blushed. "So what's up?" she said, sounding all business for the moment.

"I just wanted to check in on the deadline for Committee requests, and see if there's anything I can do to help."

"Oh, and you don't *need* anything in the letter?"

Okay, she passed the first test: never trust a lobbyist. "Well, as you know, before you came on board here, Toby told Michael he would put in some report language on Famagusta for the Greece-America Association—that's one of ours." Not one that I ever worked on, I failed to add, but that was okay, I was just using it as a conversation starter. As she nodded, I continued. "And then there's the stuff Toby hasn't shown any interest in support-ing: Koliba, the Dungan, military aid for Africa," here she winced, "and our efforts to get MNNA status for the UAE."

"MNNA?"

Good, another test passed. There was no way she'd have heard about that program in her past job or, since we were the only people going for it, this one either. Most staffers, though, preferred to fake their way through conversations like this and then ask someone more senior what the hell we were talking about. It could be the boss's staff director, or the Subcom-mittee staff, or even people like me: after you've built up enough trust with people, they call you all the time looking for explanations of all the arcane and absurd programs too small for most people to notice. It was a call I never wanted to duck, because it told me what my peers and often my opponents were up to, making it easier to balance my strategies against everything else in the bill.

"Major Non-NATO Ally, MNNA, a DOD program to provide excess defense articles to key countries around the world. It started with Israel and Egypt a decade or so back and has since expanded to a bunch of countries. It's mostly for show, though, since the foreign recipients come in last on the list after the Reserves, the Coast Guard, and state governments. By the time you get to the bottom of that list, there ain't much left."

That wasn't the full story, given the plans to excess the ARCHON to the UAE. But this was only a test, since I'd be using Will Richardson on that amendment in Conference; so I figured it was enough information for now.

She was scribbling as I spoke and frowned down at her notes. "So why?"

"The status thing matters to a lot of countries."

"That's it? Status? That's all they want?"

"Like I said, the political and regional status issue is pretty big in the Middle East—you know, the way they're always arguing who's closest to Uncle Satan," I replied. "Especially in the smaller Middle East potentates which, to be frank, could probably be taken over in a couple of hours by six well-armed guys in a Hummer."

She smiled, but looked skeptical, glancing down at her notes again. I couldn't help noticing her profile and her sweater in profile. Wow, Peter is one very lucky guy, I thought.

"Okay, well, I understand what you're doing, but..." She paused for a moment, apparently thinking through her options. "It's pretty lame."

I laughed out loud. I'm going to like working with this woman, I thought, even more than I'd expected to. "Sorry," I said, still chuckling despite the surprise in her face. "There aren't a whole lot of people up here who would say it flat out like that. It's refreshing. How is it lame?"

"Singling out an Arab country? A non-foreign aid recipient? Just for show?" She stopped, looked at me, and after a moment shrugged her shoulders with a grimace.

She had a point, I realized; it was lame. Not only was she the second person to tell me that, but worse, when she put it the way she did, it didn't even pass the smell test. This is the good thing about talking with new people every once in a while, I thought; they see right through you and don't swallow your bullshit so easily. I made a mental note to take this up with Weller. Not an urgent note, just a note. But how to respond?

"Show, as you call it, has tremendous value in that part of the world," I responded. "Policy, demonstrated by decisions like this, is often more important than action." Not bad, I thought, for having been completely unprepared for the question.

"Well, all right, that, yes, but Toby's got a few important constituents who always wonder what the Israelis think." Like that's a surprise, I thought. Who didn't, what with AIPAC so deep in everyone's shorts that there really weren't any Congressmen left you could call "pro-Arab"?

"Not a problem. First off, the Israelis are on board, and we've got people who can validate that." I'd have to get Weller to find those people, but I knew we could find somebody somewhere who could validate it before Conference—that was months away. "Since we're not putting it in the House bill, we don't need anything at this point." Now it was my turn to pause. "Although a private friendly chat with the Chairman during Conference would help."

Here it was, the purpose of the meeting. I needed to know if she'd be willing to help me despite her first instincts, not so much for this year's Conference—like I said, I had Will Richardson for that—but just to know. It would tell me what kind of staffer she could be and would have a big impact on my strategies with her going forward.

Most staffers in Washington are chickens, too afraid to do anything that might not be easy and obvious. "Greektown's in my boss's district, so we support the Greeks and hate the Turks no matter how stupid they are." "We get half a million from the Jewish community every election cycle, so we love Israel and wouldn't get caught dead helping Arabs." "We've got a state university campus in the district, so we're peace-loving human rights champions and hate all them dictators you're working for." Cut and dry, open and shut, life was all black and white for most Washington people. It was the *other* ones I was always in the hunt for.

Alexis was thinking, staring blankly at her notes, pen tapping slowly on her desk. I waited.

"Israel is definitely on board?"

"Yes." That I was sure of—Weller was very focused when he reported that Israel's government had no objection to this. The Israeli lobby, I was a hell of a lot less sure, but she hadn't asked that. So I made another mental note: Tom would need to find me a Big Jew—one of those political heavyweights, former Presidents of national Jewish groups, people like that—willing to support the amendment. It wouldn't be hard, since so many had moved to the far right in keeping with Israel's political leadership, and Tom had taken pains to cozy up with them. For now, though, I'd let it go if I could.

"And the democracy advocates?"

I laughed, impressed again. She wasn't letting anything sneak by. "There's nothing here to bite your boss in the ass. No disgruntled group of immigrants from the UAE living in your district. None of the district's major employers have problem contracts with them, and a few have some nice fat export markets and might even be grateful—I'll get you a list of those. And while no human rights group will ever say it supports a Middle East potentate, the UAE generally doesn't jail people wildly, has appointed women to the admittedly weak Parliament, and has all the power but doesn't use it to squash people. The democracy twinks don't pay much attention to them."

She laughed. "Hey, I said democracy *advocates*, not twinks."

"For the record, yes, you did. And off the record, we can have lunch some time to discuss why 'weenies' and 'twinks' are much more appropriate descriptors."

She laughed again. "I'll look forward to that. In the meantime, I need to talk this through with the Congressman, but I think we can probably do something private with the Chairman when the time comes."

Ka-ching.

"Thanks. I appreciate it." I did, too. She'd taken the meeting; she'd listened seriously to my idea, talked it through with me rather than just taking it under advisement, and come to a decision. No muss, no fuss. The best kind of meeting you can have. At some point, if I couldn't get it resolved, I'd have to come back and tell Alexis about my Karen Jameson problem, that student locked away in a UAE jail, but for now, I'd gotten exactly what I wanted.

*   *   *

"Did you *have* to do that to Kevin?" Charlotte glared at me, stamping her foot for emphasis, hands on her hips. The effort was wasted, though, given the thin smile tugging at her lips. She was certainly annoyed, but not so much that was pissed at me; after all, she knew the game as well as I did.

"Honey, c'mon, I had the guy ask one lousy question," I replied, looking up at her from the floor. I was pretty defenseless, cereal bowl in one hand, spoon in the other, the *Post* splayed across my lap. Geez, I thought, what a whiner; I'd given him a question that he should have been happy with.

I'd gotten in late the night before, coming from a long dinner at Sam and Harry's with Michael and some Russian industrialists that he was hoping to rope in as clients. At least, "industrialists" was what they called themselves; they looked and acted more like the Russian mafia and seemed unimpressed with our careful explanations that no matter how much they paid us, and whether or not they paid it in cash, we wouldn't be able to promise that the U.S. Government would provide loan guarantees for the crazy hotel-and-train project they were promoting for the southern Caucasus. As far as I'd been able to tell, they were looking for us to tell them how to buy enough members of Congress to secure what they wanted; but in our brief bathroom conversation, Michael refused to let me explain that, ever since Jack Abramoff scampered off to minimum security prison, we're back to the old ways of doing things, where you "rent" members of Congress through political donations rather than purchase them outright.

Charlotte, in the meantime, had used the free evening for dinner with Kevin, so they could catch up over old times and complain about new ones. Apparently I was one of Kevin's complaints.

"You realize that, if he'd had any balls, he would have told me to fuck off, right?" Then again, I thought, I only go to him because I know he's basically a eunuch.

"He told me that you browbeat him into it," she continued, stamping the foot again. She was still smiling, though.

"Sweetie, I'd hardly call it browbeating, and besides it was three and a half weeks ago," I answered, "so what's his problem now?"

"The three meetings he's had since the hearing. Two visitors to his office, one from Shaddock Mills, and one from GE—which I didn't know, but is the biggest employer in his district." Holy shit, I thought. "And then, an invitation to meet with a national security staffer on Cheney's staff."

"Whoa." That was one hell of a breadcrumb I'd thrown out.

She broke into a large grin. "Is that the best you can do? You sent up a trial balloon, Kevin gets smacked around by someone on Cheney's staff, and 'Whoa' is all you've got?"

"Shit," I continued, realizing as I said it that it wasn't much of an improvement. I looked up at her. "I set something off here, didn't I?"

"Uh, yeah," she responded. "At least Kevin thinks you did."

"What did he tell them all?"

"Nothing," she said. "He told them it was an issue of interest to the Congressman. They spent an hour telling him what a vital, strategic ally Kazakhstan is and how important they are to U.S. security interests in the region."

"GE?"

"Yeah, he picked up on that too," she laughed. "Their answer was a rather glum 'commercial *and* security interests' in the region."

"Is Kevin okay?"

"Yes, but." She paused. "Leave him alone for the rest of the year, will you? You totally flipped him out, and if his boss ever knew all this, Kevin would be screwed."

Oh, great, I thought, he's too stupid to tell his boss.

I glanced down at my wilted Special K for a moment, trying to decide how to phrase my answer. Using people was the nature of the business in Washington—the rule being, you use *everybody*—and I couldn't just drop people randomly off the list because they were my friends, or Charlotte's friends, or both. One of my skills was knowing how far I could or couldn't go, and even before this, I'd had Kevin down for just that one lousy favor all year—I'd already checked him off the list.

Besides, I smiled to myself, I value my life, along with my marriage, so I'd best let this one go.

"Okay," I said quietly. I dipped my spoon into the bowl and took a large spoonful of soggy cereal. Chewing on it more for show than because I needed to, I swallowed after a few moments. "I'll leave him alone." Pause. "For the rest of the year."

She'd started to turn after "alone," heading back to the kitchen to get her coffee. She stopped, glaring back at me for a moment, and smiled again. "Thanks." Turning, she walked out of the room.

* * *

Wellington was already at QC's when I arrived, and had a table. I needed to pick his brain and had arranged to meet for drinks somewhere away from the office.

I'd picked QC's to ensure us a little privacy: Michael would never be caught dead in a bar like this one, surrounded by Washington's young professionals and wannabees, the nubile young women and their ruddy male pursuers, joking, laughing, drinking, talking, and drinking some more in a sea of hormones, engaged in Washington's second most vital industry, the endless circle of lust, sex, and occasionally, love that bursts through the city and feeds a never-ending loop of coupling and decoupling, real and imagined, legal and illicit. Around 5:30 p.m. every weekday, bars all across Washington fill up as they undergo the nightly shift from watering hole to meat market. For the younger set in offices anywhere near Connecticut and L, QC's is the place to be.

Of course, Weller normally wouldn't be caught dead in place like this either and was here only thanks to my insistence on this location. With his full head of white hair and his patrician manner, he looked utterly lost amidst the crowd. His glare was appropriately baleful as I sat, so I assumed he had been waiting for some time—several minutes at least, an eternity for him in such a place. "Draw in any babes yet, Wellster?" I smiled at him.

"Please," he groaned, "these girls are my granddaughter's age. And they're all drinking like fish." Wellington was another of Washington's many recovered, or as he would have said recovering, "since you never really recover," alcoholics. Somewhere around 20 percent of official Washington by my guess, at least in his age cohort. My generation had gotten it down to about 15 percent or so. The other 5 percent were all serious drug users, but at least we had the alcoholism rates down.

"Speaking of drinking—" I looked around for the waitress, because I needed a drink at this point. She was across the jam-packed room, delivering a trayful of drinks to a particularly boisterous crew, ducking forward and back from the table, getting a drink in and herself safely back out again just before an unconscious boob waved a hand in her face or stood up and knocked her over. Lori? Linda? Not that it mattered: I went there often enough for lunch that the waitresses knew me and tipped well enough that they remembered my drink, Johnny Walker Black and water. I caught her eye and waved. She nodded briefly and then ducked back in under an arm to deliver someone else's drink.

"So, this is fun." It was Wellington, taking a slow sip from his iced tea and continuing to stare at me.

I looked at him for a moment. This wasn't going to be easy, but I needed to get some advice *and* to slap him around a little over our UAE amendment. With his patrician look and his stories about the grand old days of American foreign policy, Wellington was the epitome of the old-style lobbyist. But for all the crap I gave him, he was a mentor of sorts, someone I could trust, someone I could talk to, especially about Michael. And I was going to need a tremendous amount of help dealing with Michael.

"My client, the Dungan. I need to know what you think."

I had him. Wellington's eyes narrowed just a touch, and he brought one hand to his chin. They must train them that way in State Department School or something—they all do it; usually it's a way of saying, "I am thinking—please do not disturb me—I have to remember the official policy position on this issue," but tonight it was sheer surprise. This didn't seem to be what he'd been expecting.

"You've kept them to yourself, haven't talked about them much." He looked up at me. "And Michael doesn't talk about them at all."

Well, that was news. Michael must still be pissed at me, despite his denials, I thought. He used Weller the same way I did, as a sounding board, because Wellington knew every story in Washington and always saw something you'd missed.

"Start at the beginning."

I told him, the whole story, from the call from Belinda, Harry's handoff in his outer office, to the conversation over drinks at the Willard, the fight with Michael, the Chicago trip, the question Kevin asked for me, and the results, three meetings beating him up on Kazakhstan. By the time I finished, Weller was staring down at his iced tea.

"Something's wrong," he said.

"Yeah, I know, Michael's still planning to kill me."

"No ... well, yes but..." he stumbled. He looked off toward the door, recapitulating the story in his head, tapping his finger in the air as if counting the steps. "That's not what I mean. There's something wrong with their story."

"Wellington." I paused, staring at him, waiting until I had his attention. "We work for Ernest Koliba. We take money from a completely ineffective group of Greek-Americans that only hired us so that they can tell their members they're fighting the good fight against those Turkish bastards. Of course there's something wrong with their story. That's the business, for Chrissakes."

He looked over his glasses at me. "This is different."

"They're not trying to overthrow the government. They're not opposed to U.S. policy. They're not looking for anything but some statement of support for internal freedoms within Kazakhstan. They want some lousy report language. Jesus." To slow myself down, I reached for my scotch, but it was nowhere to be seen. Shit, I thought, it's Lori—Lori's the slow one. "Besides, that's not my question—I want to know what you think about Michael's reaction."

"Well then, junior, you're asking the wrong question." He leaned in at me, and I leaned back, surprised; that was totally unexpected. "If you can't convince me that they're clean, that there's something more that they want for $360,000—you're not going to convince me there's not something *wrong* here. And that means you've got Michael risking his business on a deal he doesn't understand."

My scotch arrived, and I seized on the distraction to look up. "Thanks, Lori," I smiled, and she smiled back. At least I was right about something.

Weller wasn't letting me off the hook. "What's Harry get out of this?"

"Nothing." My eyes narrowed instinctively—he was entering dangerous turf. A lot of people had gone down in recent years for cutting deals with family members, or best friends. That wasn't the way I played the game. "Harry gets nothing out of this."

Weller shook his head and sighed. "I don't mean money, you idiot. I mean, what does he get out of it? Why'd they go to him? Who does he know? What's this Dungan mean to him?"

My breathing sped up, and I could feel my frustration building. I wasn't getting what I needed here. "I said nothing—he's got nothing in play here.

He turned them over to me and walked away. He was helping me out." I could feel the red in my face and the tension in my voice, but I didn't like where this was going at all. Harry hasn't asked for anything, I told myself.

Yet.

"Hey, lighten up. Maybe you're right. Maybe he's got nothing in play." Weller was using his calming voice, the senior statesman voice developed over the decades. Even though I recognized it, it was working, the tension releasing, except for the small knot in the pit of my stomach.

Weller took a long sip from his iced tea. Scanning my face, he continued. "So, what else is happening?"

A sense of relief washed over me: he'd just given me an out. "Oh, thanks for the reminder. We've got some serious problems with the UAE amendment." That got his attention. "First off, there's the story we're using to sell the amendment—it's not good enough. And we've got to get some kid out of jail."

"Jail?"

"You remember, the one named at the Rice hearing, Karen Jameson, that student arrested while walking through the lobby of the Hilton," I answered. "Her parents are raising holy hell in Congress. You've gotta talk to Fawzi about her, to see how we can get her released, or at least get me some more information about what she's supposed to have done." I lifted my Scotch, but stopped. "I need something to work with, the sooner the better."

"People in dragnets are seldom just caught up," he smiled thinly. Gotta love ex-spooks; they never rattle. "But I'll look into her case." He looked down, swirling his iced tea. That was all he was ready to tell me.

"And the story?"

"What's wrong with it?"

"I tried it out, on a skeptic. It doesn't fly." I took a gulp from my glass and grimaced. That's right, I thought; he's drinking the iced tea. "It doesn't hold up, the idea we're going through all this rigmarole because it makes them feel good. People aren't buying it."

"Who's not buying it?"

"People. People on the Hill. Me people: I don't buy it. It sounds stupid when I say it, and as two different people said to me, it's lame. They've got to have a better reason than that."

"I've told you all that I can." That's a strange way to put it, I thought. I looked over at him, at his now poker face, the "that's-all-you're-gonna-get-so-whaddaya-gonna-do-about-it?" face. No wonder I like Weller,

I thought, he doesn't bullshit around telling you a load of crap, some new story to cover up the one that just fell apart. He just leads you to water to see if you'll drink.

"You got someone else who can give me more?"

His face quivered. Gotcha. "Well," he said, glancing down into his empty iced tea glass, as if maybe there was someone down there, "well, I might have someone…"

I waited. Nothing. Those last bits of melting ice must be tremendously interesting, I thought. "Fawzi?"

He looked up. "Fawzi. But he's back in the UAE. How soon do you need this?"

"Soon," I repeated, "at least in terms of talking to Fawzi. It's not just that I need the information. I need to know if the story's any good and how I can spin it."

"I'll set something up." He reached behind him for his coat and then looked at me, waiting. I nodded. He stood, ready to go, suddenly eager to get away it seemed, and then stopped. "The Kazakh thing. Kazakhstan's not a country to be playing games with. There's too much going on there: they're all over the War on Terror, they're stable, and they're friendlies. To top it off, they have Shaddock Mills working for them, and those guys own people all over State and the White House as well as the Hill. And that's not even counting the oil companies out there working on their behalf."

None of this was news to me. "Jesus, Weller, all they want is some lousy statement putting Congress on support of human rights in Kazakhstan." Looking away for a moment, I waved to Lori for the check. "You know, 'don't oppress the little beebles,' shit like that. It's a simple gig."

"That's why I'm worried." Wellington grimaced. "It's too simple a gig."

The knot in my stomach tightened.

* * *

The following Tuesday, I arrived at 419 Dirksen, the Senate Foreign Relations Committee hearing room, somewhere about forty minutes after the hearing had started. Michelle had saved me a seat, and luckily enough, the people standing by the back walls of the room had let her. I smiled a "thanks" to her, but she was clearly somewhat put out. I looked at her quizzically, and she leaned in to me.

"Nice of you to make an appearance," she whispered.

"Sorry, delayed at lunch." Sorry? Well, not really, since I'd been on a working lunch and knew she was here. I wasn't sure what her problem was, until she reached over and dumped a pile of five thick statements, each from one of the witnesses, onto my lap. I glanced over with a smile and, as I tuned in to the questioning, began flipping through the statements for anything vaguely relevant to our clients.

This was a reasonably important hearing, the annual military aid hearing, and I was actually sorry my lunch had gone long. This was one of the few hearings every year where everyone involved in getting or giving military aid showed up, so you could pick up some decent information from the gathering crowd—rumors about who was trying to earmark money for their clients, what countries the Administration was most focused on helping out this year, etc. In the old days, it was a great opportunity for picking up important pieces in the puzzle of what the Administration was up to; these days, post 9/11, it's only important in learning about the "open" programs, as opposed to the newer and much, much bigger programs hidden throughout the DOD budget in the War on Terror.

Above all else, 9/11's biggest effect on government was the dramatic increase in Department of Defense involvement and control of foreign policy in response to the dramatically changed threat map of the globe. Obviously, the collapse of the Soviet Union had made such a change, but that was in creating an absence—an absence of threat. 9/11 was the opposite— lots of threat, spread across the globe, in a form we were totally unprepared for, and the Pentagon ran itself ragged trying to respond. The results had been varied: base agreements, secret prisons, extraordinary renditions, etc., but the money had all been very, very green, and there'd been lots of it flowing. The thing was, just like all those NSA folks listening in on our phone calls, it was all classified. So nobody knew how much, for what, or where.

That made most of us spend hearings like these thinking, "Gee, if they're spending $20 million openly in North Africa, how much are they slipping under the table?" Still, the questions Senators asked could tell you a lot about what Committee members wanted to do and why, even if the answers weren't worth much anymore.

Like any Congressional hearing, though, to get to the questions you had to get through the testimony. And as the pile on my lap quickly reminded me, this was a particularly boring set of witnesses, five of them fighting

each other to find the most stultifying way to describe U.S. military assistance policy around the globe. State and DOD officials are truly masters at
taking a long time to say absolutely nothing, and today was no exception.
They'd probably only gotten to the Q&A in the last ten minutes or so.

Poor Michelle. I almost felt bad for her. Almost.

"Mr. Secretary, I'd like to turn to a part of the world that has a lower profile
than some of those you've been focusing on." That was an interesting
opening ploy—kind of like telling the guy, "I have a question you're not
prepared for." I looked up from my reading and leaned out into the aisle—
it was Sen. Burlingame, Republican of Illinois. "You are no doubt aware
of the case of Karen Jameson, the University of Illinois student currently
being held in a prison in the Middle East?"

Oh, shit, I thought, that's right. Rep. Fairchild, the one who went after
the Secretary Rice in the House hearing, he was from Illinois too. As I
shifted, trying to get a better look at the crowd, Michelle glanced up from
her doodling with a quizzical look. "What's up?"

"Nothing," I replied quietly. "Just checking for her parents."

"Whose parents?"

Damned kids, scarcely ever listened to the fucking hearings. Always
drove me crazy, but I could yell at them all day long and they'd still end
up doodling, or reading, or doing Sudoku. I shook my head in annoyance,
refusing to go through that argument for the umpteenth time.

And there they were. Third row, on the right side of the hearing room,
the mother leaning on her husband, her shoulders shaking ever so slightly.
They were serious about this, and they knew what they were doing. The
first time they showed up it was that early House hearing with the Secretary of State, so they'd get on TV. This time, they were showing up in a
more focused venue, indicating their plans for anyone paying attention:
they were seriously working the process to put pressure on the UAE. Either
these people were smart, or they'd hired someone very, very good.

Well, I thought, at least I've got Weller working on it.

The Pentagon and State Department witnesses were both leaning back,
listening to an aide who'd come up between them from out of the third row
and was whispering furiously. I could see the Pentagon witness's face, and he
looked completely baffled—whatever he was being told was entirely new to
him. That, combined with the fact that the only guy who could explain it to
him had been sitting in the third row, meant that the administration wasn't

taking this seriously. That is something we're going to have to fix, I told myself.

It was the State Department witness, Under Secretary Paul Brownley, who replied. "If I might answer this, Senator, I believe that this is a question that relates more to the Emirates' internal judicial process and to the War on Terror than to our military relationship with the country."

"We may have a disagreement on that, Mr. Secretary, but please, I look forward to your response." He wasn't letting the Pentagon off that easy.

"As you may know, Senator, the State Department has spoken with the Government of the UAE to discuss the conditions under which Karen..." Here he paused for a moment, glancing down to where he'd scrawled her name. "Jameson, Karen Jameson, is being held. We have also requested the opportunity to review the evidence in this case. As you know, Senator, she has been detained for aiding and abetting a terrorism suspect, and the Government has indicated that they believe she was affiliated with a member of Al Qaeda." He paused, thinking he'd hit a nerve: no one wanted to be caught supporting someone affiliated with Al Qaeda. "We are continuing to track this case, and we are continuing to urge the government to ensure that she is treated fairly and that justice is served."

The Senator shook his white mane, glanced down at his notes, and then put them aside. "Well, Mr. Secretary, I guess I would be a little concerned about the idea that Karen Jameson was affiliated with Al Qaeda if she had been in the country more than ten hours when she was summarily dragged off to jail, and if there was anything that connected her to the suspect other than the fact that she walked by him passing through the lobby of her hotel when the police stormed the place and arrested everyone there."

"Senator, I..."

"No, no, Mr. Secretary, we are under the five-minute rule, and I believe that I lost one or two while you consulted with staff. So perhaps I will get right to the point." Again he paused, this time looking over at the Jamesons before continuing. "I believe that the problem in your answer is the claim that the Department wants Karen Jameson treated fairly. The way that she was arrested was patently unfair. The judicial procedures that have taken place so far—justifying the government's decision to keep everyone arrested that day in prison pending trials that may be two years off—are patently unfair. There are a broad range of citizens who were mistreated that day and are still being mistreated. Only one of them is a citizen of the United States, however, so there is only one case on which I expect prompt, firm action by the Department. That is the case of Karen Jameson. Otherwise, this Congress may need to act in some way, Mr. Secretary, to ensure that the Government is paying attention."

Burlingame glanced down at his notes again and looked up, directly at the Jamesons. He breathed in deeply through his nostrils and then breathed out, another of his trademarked moves. "I believe my time has expired."

Chapter 9

"Ed, could I chat with you for a moment?"

He caught me looking down at my cold, soggy Eggs Benedict. That I'm not going to miss, I thought, unlike the tawny beauty sitting next to me. I took one long last look at her as I turned to get out of my chair.

I'd had more luck than usual this morning, as Harry's lead defense guy, Scott Suddaford, caught me coming in the door, with a quick question about DOD Approps. He'd been chatting with my tablemate, fellow House staffer Mary Anne Corrigan, at the time, and well, I hadn't seen any reason to move on. Now, though, it was time for Harry and me to play out our little game.

Ignoring Uncle Harry for just a moment, I said, "Delightful to meet you, Mary Anne. I hope we can catch up again soon." She smiled up at me in that dazzling way I was already learning to like.

Ah, what better way could there be to start a long and tedious day than with a 7:30 a.m. fundraiser? Fundraising never stops in Washington, and as more and more of them get scheduled, they more and more often pop up in the early morning hours. For me especially, let in free to any of Harry's fundraisers I wanted to go to, there was seldom anything pleasant about hanging out with a bunch of suits, mostly from the defense industries, first thing in the morning, when they were all "on" and I was still shaking the sleep out of my eyes. But I'd worked it out with Harry in advance, since

Sen. Joseph Belkin was also attending this event, that we would corner him to begin the process of nailing down his support for our MNNA amendment. Getting to sit with Mary Anne for forty-five minutes was just a bonus.

Following Harry over toward the head table, I saw Belkin standing by his chair, waiting. He must have tried to get away, I thought, and Harry must have stopped him. Good thing—this was my best shot at the guy without going through the Gates of Hell, better known as Raymonda Clayton, ex-girlfriend extraordinaire. I knew that avoiding her was the only way I was going to get Belkin on board.

Belkin recognized me in that special way that politicians have, as someone he'd met more than once but not someone important enough to remember. As he glanced down to my name tag, I said, "Ed Matthews." I slept with your Foreign Ops staff director for several years. "From Michael McPherson & Associates."

"Yes, of course, Ed, so good to see you," he said, smiling but only a little. I had him a little bit confused, looking as if my introduction didn't match up with the scraps of me buried in his memory. With Harry to hide behind, I took that as a good thing.

"As I was telling you, Joseph," Harry said, leaning in to Belkin and taking his arm, "Ed has a very important issue that I suggested he talk with you about." He looked over at me and nodded.

"Yes, sir," I responded quietly, just for the three of us, "it's a request from our ally, the United Arab Emirates, to be added to the list of Major Non-NATO Allies."

Belkin looked at Harry quizzically.

Harry said, "We'll have to discuss it when we have time in Paris."

What the fuck?

He continued, "It's too bad you have to rush now, Joseph, but this is a very important issue. You need to be briefed, and Ed here is the man to walk you through the entire procedure."

"Well, uh, that sounds good," Belkin replied. "We'll catch up in Paris, then, during the Air Show?"

The Air Show? The biennial Paris Air Show, held in late June, was one of the world's leading arms bazaars and absolutely the biggest boondoggle any Congressman could take. Not only was I not planning to go to the Air Show, not only was every flight to Paris that week and every hotel room within a fifty-mile radius booked by now, but the Air Show came dead in the middle of my busiest month, June, when the House State/ Foreign Operations Subcommittee bill was always moving, and the Senate bill often was. I couldn't possibly go to the Air Show.

"Yes, we will indeed, right, Ed?" Harry replied, pointing to me.

I was stuck. "Yes, Senator," you sonofabitch, "we can talk then."

As Belkin headed for the door, Harry leaned closer. "It's too crowded here to have that kind of conversation."

I took his arm and smiled for anyone who might have been looking before quietly tearing into him. "Jesus, Harry, I can't just run off to Paris. It's June—the bills are moving. What am I going to tell Michael? Hell, what am I going to tell Charlotte?"

"She should come along after we're done," he responded, "it's a wonderful time to see Paris—June? Perfect in Paris." He smiled.

"Gimme a break, Harry—in the middle of June?" It was bad enough I'd be heading to Paris in June, but there's no way that Charlotte and I could make it a vacation: it would be at least as hard for her to get out of town then, if not more so since she didn't have a business reason to be there.

So I'd be alone in the world's most romantic city, right when it's the most ... romantic.

"Michael will be fine with it too. It's one of his clients and the only way to get this amendment you're looking for," he continued. "Besides, I have a friend coming who needs a traveling companion. I think you met her? Mary Anne Corrigan?"

I turned to look at the table and saw Mary Anne leaning forward, telling a story while the men surrounding her sat rapt in attention, some maybe even listening to her. Scott Suddaford, though, he was looking directly at us. So he'd set this up, and she didn't know. Goddammit, I thought, I've been had.

"Son," Harry said, making me cringe—it was never good when Harry called me "son." "I need your help on this one, and you've asked for mine. I think it's only fair, don't you? After all I've done?"

* * *

"The budget is a joke, you know that. There's no way the Committee will fund foreign aid levels like that." Roger was in lecture mode, standing by his window, looking out to see who might be approaching the rear door of Dirksen, the one facing Union Station. I noticed the sag in his pants, his shirttail hanging down over his belt. For all he looked a sloppy dresser, though, it was a simple fact that nothing ever looked good on him. "There's far too much money in the President's Request, and we're deeply cutting it. So your goal has to be protecting those levels for your clients."

I'd been in and out of Roger's office since the beginning of the year, but this was my first scheduled meeting with him, the one where we'd reviewed the clients and I'd tell him what I needed. I always saved Roger for the last of these meetings for one simple reason: he was the guy I needed to give me things I just couldn't get from anyone else.

So far, I've been doing okay, I thought as I looked at him skeptically. At least this year it's not like I'm desperate, just needy.

Roger, hands in his pocket, paused in his ramble. My turn. "Great, so our big selling point for the year is to tell the clients, 'hire Michael McPherson and he'll get you less than the President wants.'" I laughed.

Roger turned, blinked several times, and peered at me through narrowed eyes. We were friends, so I could razz him, but he was Michael's friend too, having worked closely with him when Michael was at State and Roger staff director to a Senate subcommittee overseeing State Department funding. He knew from many long nights with Michael what a lousy business this was, how clueless and unreasonable the clients could be, and how hard it was just to stand in place. So he was vulnerable to this, and he bit.

First, though, he was going to make me wait. His mouth twitched, one of the more unappealing "tells" in Washington, and I saw a glimmer in his eyes that said he was caving just as he turned back to look out the window. A heavy sigh, his slim shoulders rising slowly on the inhale before a long, slow exhale. Jeez, I caught myself thinking, the theatrics these people put me through. Turning back to me, hands still in his pockets, he looked to the door as if hoping someone would arrive to rescue him—or maybe that I would take the hint and leave. Another pause. "So what do you want? What's the ask?"

Well, finally, we were getting to the point. "Okay, so let's start by leaving aside Koliba, right?"

He snorted, walking to his desk and sitting down. Reaching to his right into a drawer, he drew out a legal pad and peered at me over his glasses. "Sure." He shook his head as he looked down to scratch out a note on the page.

"So there's the UAE thing. We need ..."

"The UAE ... *thing?*" he asked, looking up again, somehow sounding out the italics.

"Yeah, you know, MNNA, Major Non-NATO Ally, for Chrissakes." I shook my head; this wasn't something I should have to go through with him. "What, like, you forgot?"

"The prime subcontractor of the equipment to be provided under MNNA, the ARCHON, is Coherence Electronics, based, you may recall," pausing for effect, peering some more—he was killing me with the peering—"in Lansing, Michigan, and made up mostly of constituents of the Honorable Senator Francis T. Johnson." He pushed his glasses back up his nose and, leaning back, put his pen down. Oops. I'd forgotten this was a constituent issue.

"Yes, yes, you're right, and Coherence's CEO, Robert Chester, is also campaign chairman for the Honorable Senator in the last campaign, I know, I know." God, I didn't need this, and from Roger of all people. "What, you think I don't take this seriously?"

"I'm not sure you take anything seriously anymore." Ouch, I thought.

Blinking furiously, Roger opened his center drawer and drew out a pack of Marlboros and a box of safety matches. Shit, I thought, I've *really* pissed him off; Roger only smoked when there was something wrong. And I'd never seen him smoke in his office.

I waited for him to pull out a cigarette and light it. Throughout, he watched me, glancing down at his cigarette only long enough to light it. I was surprised that he could find the tip through all the blinking. I thought, too, that maybe he was right, at least about me.

Truth be told, Roger was critical to our getting the UAE business, at least based on scattered comments that Michael and Weller had exchanged with me over the last year or so. It would have made sense: for all Coherence might have been a constituent, Sen. Johnson could never have gotten the MNNA amendment through on his own. So maybe he'd outsourced it, convincing Coherence that the UAE needed a lobbyist to make this work. It made sense in that crazy way that only applies in Washington.

But I'd never know for sure and was pretty certain I didn't want to.

"Okay, so, to begin again, our first priority is the MNNA amendment for the United Arab Emirates." I paused and made a face at him as if to say, "better?" He snorted, which I took as a "yes." "I'm working with Sen.

Fuller"—I always called Harry "Sen. Fuller" when talking to anyone outside the company—"to convince Sen. Belkin to offer the amendment in the
bill." I decided to leave out the Paris part; I was still coming to grips with
it in my own mind and didn't need Roger giving me shit.

"Belkin?" he asked, laughing. "Raymonda's Belkin?"

Oops. I'd forgotten: he knew me and Raymonda in the "good old days"
when we were dating and the miserable ones when it was falling apart.

"Yes," I replied. "Now maybe you can understand my attitude. Raymonda's going to rip me a new one when she finds out."

Roger laughed, exhaling a lung load of smoke at me. "She doesn't
know?" Coughing through his laughter, he opened his drawer again and
drew out his ashtray. Holding the cigarette loosely in his fingers, he tapped
it precisely on the corner, once, twice. I sat quietly and waited. "You are so
dead meat," he said, smiling at me.

"Like I don't know that?" I asked him. He was right; she was absolutely
going to kill me when I told her that her boss was going to help *me*. But
there was nothing I could do about that, and I didn't need his ragging me
about it. "What are you busting my balls for?"

Leaning his head back, he inhaled deeply and slowly released a long trail
of smoke. "Because at some point," pausing here for another inhale, "we're
going to end up talking about Koliba." Another long pause for effect, and
this time I didn't have anything to say.

He was right, of course; I couldn't figure out the Koliba thing without
him. I had an idea, but I needed to lead up to it. So finally, putting on my
best car-salesman voice, I said, "Yes, but just for you, today only, I'm willing to let you throw me out of the room if you don't like what I have to say."

That got a rise out of him, leaning his head back to cough out a wet,
hacking laugh. Jesus, he'd been smoking way too much recently. But at
least I'd finally gotten him laughing with me, not at me. Maybe I could
get somewhere.

* * *

About thirty minutes later, once we'd haggled our way through the
strategy on the MNNA amendment and a first cut at the Dungan—he'd
agreed to look at some report language—it was time. It had all come with
a tremendous amount of whining and complaining about my asking for
too much, my not realizing what a tremendous amount I was making him

carry, my failure to recognize that he needed to be able to accomplish a few things for other people, including constituents, yutta yutta yutta, blah blah blah. But that was a standard part of the game, so I ignored it while pretending to be sympathetic.

It was time to try for something that might keep Koliba and his cronies happy. When Tom and Michael had agreed to convince Gangaran to visit Washington for the reception I'd taken Eleanor to, it was in exchange for me coming up with something legislative that we could give Koliba to show we were accomplishing something. I had developed an idea that just might work. It was totally out of the box, but those were often the best kind. It was also something that we could probably sneak through because it wouldn't be written specifically for Koliba, just something he could benefit from if Golongo stopped screwing around with civil liberties.

"Okay, so that leaves Koliba," I began. Roger blinked several times in rapid succession, and then his face took on a blank look, another tell, his standard approach when he was preparing to blow someone out of the water. I waited for just a moment and continued, "And you're obviously not going to do anything to help him, so we're done."

Roger waited, watching me. We both sat still, neither moving, each waiting for the other to go first. Roger's left eye twitched, several times. "That's it?"

"Well, look, I know your boss won't stick his neck out for a dictator, so I'm not stupid enough to ask you to do something for Koliba." He looked somewhat relieved, but still guarded—he was waiting for the other shoe to drop. "We'll have report language to fight against, especially on the House side, but I'm not asking for help on this one. Like I told Michael, 'we're done, we're fucked.' Michael's fucked."

Roger leaned forward at this, looking me over. "That's what you've got? 'We're *fucked?*' No ideas on how to move anything?" He tapped the cigarette twice more on that same corner of the ashtray. "You guys never give up, at least not this early in the year. You got nothing?"

"Well, shit," I said, looking off to my left out the window, trying to look simultaneously skeptical and put upon, like it was Roger's fault for bringing it up, "I've got an idea."

Now it was Roger's turn to look put upon. With his free hand, he futzed with his glasses, straightening them unnecessarily. Two blinks. "Ah, an idea. Just came to you, no doubt."

"No, it didn't. And it helps all of Africa," one of Roger's weak spots, "and not just Koliba. But it may be too nuts to use."

"I'll bite."

"It's a simple amendment, and it's good for the environment." Roger looked skeptical. "No, seriously, it's actually sort of good for the environment."

"Oh, well," he jumped in, leaning forward, "if it's 'actually sort of,' then that's different."

One of the problems with winging a meeting like this was that I always ended up saying something like that. I grimaced. "Look, give me a second to explain. Africa never gets anything for military aid, right?" Roger blinked, just once this time. He was giving me a chance. "And one of the many ways in which the Africans are getting screwed is overfishing off the coasts, European and Asian factory ships sucking all the fish out of African waters. And they can't do anything about it—they have virtually no navies."

"So you want us to give Koliba a navy."

"No, not *give* him a navy." I shook my head and then stopped. "Well, yes, but the amendment's not *for* Koliba. It's for African countries. If Koliba shapes up, he'll get some when they finally dole it out. If not, it's not our fault—we set aside the money."

"So what are we doing?"

"We earmark $15 million for coastal fisheries protection in Africa." I smiled at him. "Your boss should like that—he's always worried about the Georges Banks, and overfishing in general. You worry that the Africans get screwed every which way from Sunday. Here's something you can both do about it."

"Fisheries? How is that defense spending?"

"Every country in the region has their Navy, such as it is, running coastal protection—so it's military spending. Everybody agrees that the region's being stripped of fish, including all the enviros, so you don't have them breathing down your neck for putting more guns into Africa. And if past foreign aid earmarks are any precedent, the Pentagon will likely squawk like crazy while you're moving the bill, but in the end they'll swallow it because you're not taking money away. You're just shifting it. Besides, since these navies are so pitiful, the Pentagon will be able to use the money to sell some of their retired Navy ships. Navy shipyards will do maintenance and repair work on them, sucking up half the cash, and the Africans will think they're getting serious 'warships,' since they come from the Yew-nited States Navy."

"The enviros are going to buy this?"

"Totally." I grinned; this was the real trick to the whole idea. "I Googled looking for environmental problems in Africa and found a report a couple years back by some guy at UC Berkeley—said the EU fishing fleets, especially Spain's, are wiping out African fish stocks, leading to greater dependence on land animals—including endangered ones—for food. It's perfect, something to wave at the State and DOD dorks when they lobby you on the bill. And if we make the focus the French instead of the Spanish, we've got pretty much the perfect amendment."

Roger snorted; like most people in Congress, he loved to ding the French, not because of Iraq or any of the more recent stuff, but just because. "And Koliba's navy?"

"Half the size of his neighbors, both of whom get all their military equipment from France, not us." I smiled. "Koliba would love this money."

Roger paused, staring at me. No blinking; he didn't hate it, and he was thinking seriously about it, his mind racing, likely trying to find something wrong with the idea. Glancing down, he reached for the ashtray, crushing his cigarette daintily against the edge and then emptying it in the wastebasket to the left of his desk, with a single bang against the edge of the basket. He opened the drawer, returning the ashtray to its proper place. Straightening, he settled deeply in his seat, pushing his glasses back against his nose and then crossing his hands. It was his traditional signal that our meeting was coming to a close.

As I began to gather up my papers, he said, "Where do you come up with this crap?"

* * *

"The talk to the State losers go well?" Michael was leaning back in the booth, lit cigar in one hand, full glass of some $125 Bordeaux in the other. He was awfully relaxed, considering the miserable dinner we had ahead of us.

Tonight was our once-a-year business dinner with Philip Galsworthy, my Senate Foreign Relations Committee contact from the majority staff. Philip's occasional appearances with Kevin at our house for dinner were totally because of Kevin, not Philip, but I always needed to keep a close eye on him because he tended to attack our clients. Philip was one of those staffers who figured that any Third World country willing to waste a few hundred thousand on a lobbyist had to have something to hide, a condition made worse by the fact that he just plain hated Michael. I never learned what set them at odds, but it must have been major, because it was a grudge that never went away, and every year Philip seemed to set his sights on one of our luckless clients.

The good news was that Philip couldn't resist fine wines and also couldn't hold his alcohol, a bad combination for someone who gets lobbied. The more he drank, the more he talked. So every year, as if in penance for whatever he'd done, Michael dragged himself out for a lavish meal with Philip to sound him out, a ridiculously expensive dinner complete with outrageously priced French red wines. Michael and Philip would drink their way through three bottles or so, while I kept notes and drank just enough to avoid being pissed about missing out on the good stuff.

Hell, in some ways, it was just a long night of drinking with some food sprinkled in, because both Philip and Michael were drunk as lords by the end of the night. But it was always fun, because the moron—Philip, that is—gave away everything he planned.

At the moment, though, while waiting for Philip to arrive, I was drinking Pellegrino. Last thing I wanted to do was get ahead of him, even if it would take less than an hour for him to lap me.

"The talk went fine." I'd spent a couple hours in the morning at the State Department's Foreign Service Institute, explaining the lobbying business to this year's class of Congressional Liaison Officers, the latest lambs to the slaughter, so to speak. No one ever understood less about Congress than the U.S. State Department, making it a classic no-win job for the poor bastards sent out to "liaise" on the Department's behalf. I always offered to speak, though, in case one of them might later move to a job more useful to me, something that happened every couple of years of so.

I shook my head. "As usual, they're eager but clueless. The only ones who bugged me were two guys who couldn't deal with the idea that Congress 'interferes' in foreign policy."

"Hah!" Michael roared, with the kind of rapacious grin that would scare children and small animals. He raised his glass and drank deeply. "They'll be chewed up and spit out within a couple of weeks."

"Yeah," I agreed. In my mind's eye, I could see one of them, a thin little weasel headed for the Asia Bureau. Just wouldn't shut up about Presidential prerogatives. "I'm thinking of telling Peter Chase about one of them, so he can show the guy Congress's role in the making of foreign policy."

"Ha-ha-ha!" Michael, his round face turning a bright red, slapped the table, just as I felt a hand on my shoulder.

"Sorry I'm late, gents. The Senator needed something immediately." Philip stood looking down on us, a self-congratulatory grin on his face. "You know how it is."

"No problem, Philip," I said. Never Phil—God, he hated Phil.

"Looks like I've been missing some amusement."

Michael, slightly out of breath and still chuckling over the thought of Peter tearing into a novice State Department lobbyist, pointed to me as he said, "He has a great idea."

Sliding over so that Philip could join us, I recounted the story about my talk, the unfortunate questioner, and my plans for him. We both knew this was a great way to start the conversation, since Philip was a former FSO himself, and like the vast majority of former Department denizens now working on the Hill, he detested State and all it stood for. Not disliked, or disapproved of, or simply had problems with, but detested. It had something to do with the very concept of diplomacy, in which the whole point of your job was to reach agreement with people, not smash them into the dirt or otherwise defeat them every time you disagreed. Some people just weren't made to be diplomatic, either because they were naturally confrontational or, more often, because they thought that, while it was okay for people to disagree with them on occasion, in the end people should just have recognized that they were right. Those types generally got out of State as fast as they could, and many raced right to the Hill so they could ram their personal beliefs down the Department's throat. Philip was one of them.

"Wonderful, wonderful," Philip crowed. He'd poured himself a glass of wine immediately after sitting and raised it in toast to me. "Send him to me! Really, send him to me!"

No way, I thought; I could be an asshole on occasion but I was never a dick. "Sure," I said with a smile. Peter's torments will be quite enough, thank you very much. I reached for my wine glass and hid behind a long, slow sip while waiting for Michael to change the topic.

"So, Philip," he began, picking up on my cue, "how are things looking for legislation this year? Going to get anything interesting through the Senate Floor?"

The Senate Foreign Relations Committee was notorious for its inability to get much of anything on foreign aid considered by the full Senate. Their minimalist legislative efforts seldom went anywhere, because every Administration from Clinton could count on the fact that the Appropriations Committee's bill would include any essential foreign aid legislation, making the SFRC unnecessary. This year, with Chairman Biden running for President and thereby constantly on the road, there was even less than usual going on. But even that wouldn't stop the Committee staff from trying, if nothing else so that at the end of the year they could beg the Appropriations Committee to sneak a few of their ideas into the appropriations bill.

"Well, the Committee isn't that concerned about getting bills into law. We simply want to ensure that our policy prescriptions set the frame within which the funding is done. Especially on the most critical issues, like your charming Mr. Koliba."

And so it began.

* * *

"Jesus, what a putz."

It was two and a half hours later, and Michael and I were outside the restaurant, watching Philip waddle back to his car. I was thinking how wonderful it would be if the Maryland State Police came across him driving home, and at the same time thinking I was going to have to give Michael a lift to his house. The man had a hollow leg, but we'd gone through four bottles of Bordeaux and I'd been holding back.

"Well, yeah, and the sky is blue. So how bad is it?"

"I don't know, Michael," I said. "I think you're drunk as shit."

He laughed. "Asshole. I mean Philip's plan."

Philip's plan. Like you could even call it that. "It's too easy. He has the Committee pass a bill prohibiting any U.S. government funds from being spent on Koliba next year and sends it to the Floor. He thinks he can follow it up with provisions in each of the appropriations bills—Foreign Ops and the DOD bill. Problem is, as soon as his Committee approves a foreign aid bill with a provision prohibiting DOD spending, they're absolutely *begging* for the Senate Armed Services Committee Chairman to wipe up the floor with him: he'll have violated every jurisdictional rule in the book. They'll slap him so hard he won't know what's happening.

"Then, when we get to Approps, we just add exceptions," I continued. "In Foreign Ops it's the 'other than NGOs' exception"—nongovernmental organizations, like CARE, Oxfam, and everyone else Angelina Jolie liked to hang out with—"that's the only way they get economic aid now anyway. In DOD, we add a national security waiver, 'except as determined to be in the national security by the President,' or some such. Easy." Too easy, in fact—I liked a challenge, and this was gonna be like shooting ducks in a barrel. I was actually kind of bummed; Philip, for all I disliked him, usually gave me some of my best strategic challenges.

Michael belched, one of those disgusting wet ones that come with too much booze. "That's what I thought." He looked over at me, blurry eyes seeming to look past my face. "But what do I know? I'm drunk as shit."

My turn to laugh. I took Michael by the elbow. "C'mon, chief. I'll drive you home and catch a cab back. Gimme the keys." I'd learned years ago that Michael would never take a cab back to Bethesda, but he'd let me drive him home in his car. With my cell phone, I could have a cab there waiting to bring me back downtown. Holding the door for Michael, I glanced at my watch; with a little luck, I'd be home in time for Jon Stewart.

Chapter 10

A couple of weeks later, I stopped by the offices of Rep. Toby Kelton again to see Alexis. I'd let some time go by since our first meeting, so she could settle in a little more before I actually asked for something I needed. Today, I needed something. Another test.

It was only a couple of minutes before I heard the door open behind me. Turning, I saw Alexis lean out. "Come on back," she said with a smile.

Taking the door, I followed her through the dark cubby-like mini-hallway into the rear office, and followed her to her desk, one of the two by the long window facing the Capitol Building. Like all House offices, Rep. Kelton's is hopelessly cramped, with this room that once served as a single office carved up into a tiny cubicle farm, three by two running down the center of the room, reached by clinging to the walls on either side as one steps over binders, piles of papers, boxes of correspondence, and other paraphernalia.

She waited for a moment before getting the meeting going. "So what can I do for you?"

I smiled. Straight to business. "The Foreign Ops Bill." The annual State/Foreign Aid Appropriations Bill, the one funding the year's State Department and foreign aid funding. "The majority staff has completed a draft of the mark-up notes, and I think they've turned a copy over to the minority. I was curious if maybe I could Xerox a few copies for you in exchange for keeping one—once you land your copy."

She laughed, leaning her head back and shaking it with a look of surprise. "And how am I supposed to get a copy?"

"Well, that depends," I responded and stopped. I sat still for a moment. "You're not the type to kill a guy with a good idea, are you?"

She turned toward her desk and began rifling through a pile of papers on her right. "This can't be good," she said, more to her desk than to me. She pulled out a folder and opened it. From where I sat, it looked like a list, perhaps of names.

I waited.

She turned to look at me. "Toby and I had a conversation about you, and we decided that you had one thing going for you." She tilted her head with a quizzical look and continued. "We talked about how, when I was back in the HFAC office, in that do-nothing job, Eleanor used to point something out to us: you always treated us like people, not doorknobs. You often asked for crazy things, but you always treated people with respect. Toby and I agreed that ought to count for something."

I kind of shrugged, thinking once again that simple politeness, with a little drop of thoughtfulness, was one of those things nobody ever taught you in Lobbyist School but was a more powerful tool than just about anything else. People liked me because I was a nice guy. Who'd-a thought? A nice-guy lobbyist.

"My momma done raised me good," I drawled in my generally unconvincing southern accent.

She laughed again. "So go ahead."

After a brief pause, I shot it all out, all at once, in a single breath. "You find the staff director, remind him you're a rookie, bat your eyelashes, tell him you don't even know how to read mark-up notes, bat your eyelashes some more, and say, 'please' with that big beautiful smile you've got. I assure you he'll turn it over."

Her eyes thinned. "You've got balls."

"I said I'd never lie to you. From this guy, it's the only way to get a copy, and you're the only Subcommittee staffer who can pull it off." I paused for a moment, to let that sink in. "You've seen him at the hearings, with your questions. You know it's true. Maybe it sucks, but it's true."

She was still looking at me, eyes still lidded. At first she didn't move, but after a moment, she turned to point at the office Xerox machine and said, "So you're going to copy it on that thing? You crazy?"

I smiled. Xeroxing—the simplest way to earn your way into the heart of a Congressional staffer. Their offices are plagued with crotchety old copying machines, aged, broken-down beasts that can be trusted for a copy or two, but never for ten copies of a draft bill. "Kinko's, 7th and D, NW. I'll have it back within the hour."

She laughed again and turned back to the papers on her desk. "It's true what they all say about you: you never leave a meeting without asking for something, and you've always got an answer." Running her fingers down the sheet in the open folder, she looked just a little bit triumphant as she turned to me. "Looks like I'll need six copies—no, wait, I need an extra one for the boss, don't I?"

I nodded.

"I'll call you when I have the notes."

* * *

The Ambassador waited, seething in his chair, alternating stares between me and his staff. He had work to do, and he was being kept waiting.

Two members of his staff were already in the room, his DCM Shaikh Mohamed and the Second Secretary. Each sat silently in his chair, looking blankly around the room, trying to avoid looking at me, and surely avoiding the gaze of His Excellency. As always in his traditional *dishdasha*, the DCM sat in the chair closest to the Ambassador's desk, while the younger diplomat was along the wall, off to my left and almost out of my vision.

I sat quietly in my place of honor, the chair directly in front of the Ambassador's oversized desk, hands crossed over my notebook. While at Kinko's Xeroxing Alexis's copies, I'd been able to confirm as expected that the MNNA amendment was not included in the mark-up notes. I decided to go straight to the Embassy and report the news, ripping that bandage off all at once rather than sitting around worrying about how the Ambassador would respond. With luck, I had thought, he might not even be there.

I had found on arrival at the Embassy that the Ambassador was indeed in his office and, after I had given Shaikh Mohamed a copy of the bill and informed him that the UAE's MNNA amendment was nowhere to be found, was told His Excellency wanted to see me. Now, along with the others, I waited.

The Ambassador muttered something incomprehensible in Arabic to his senior advisor, to which the DCM responded, *"Mish mumkin."* 'Impossible,' I thought, what would be impossible? The First Secretary too scared to come in? Caught on a phone call? Didn't hear about the meeting? Now *that* would have been impossible; the Ambassador had screamed into the phone and then, when his secretary came into the room, screamed at her too, demanding that the staff come to his office. They probably heard him in the building next door.

I wasn't surprised by the circumstances, but not happy about it either. Ever since Weller had promised the Ambassador that our amendment would be in the House bill, I'd known we were in for trouble when it didn't show up. But one can never tell what form client trouble will take, with options ranging from threats of a firing (the least likely case here, since the Minister of Defense had hired us, not the Ambassador); rabid reporting by cable back to the Government about our utter incompetence as lobbyists (a virtual certainty, often even when we succeeded); or simply a dressing down and demand that we do better next time. It looked like I was in for the full treatment, the whole "you FAILED, you infidel," probably minus any direct reference to the infidel part, but implied in there somehow I was certain.

The door opened again, and with an "*Asef,* Your Excellency," an 'I'm sorry,' the First Secretary made his entrance. Glancing at me with the slightest smile playing on his lips, he walked past the Second Secretary to take one empty chair, closer to the Ambassador without being as close as the number two, the Deputy Chief of Mission. Even in the simplest meetings, rank and privilege rule in this world.

"Mr. Matthews has reported," the Ambassador began, looking balefully at me while speaking to his staff, "on the failure of his company to secure the Major Non-NATO Ally legislation in the House appropriations bill. This legislation is exceedingly important to our country, and as you all know, it is a personal priority of the Minister of Defense and his staff. Mr. Matthews has come to explain to us how this failure has occurred and what they intend to do."

"Thank you, Mr. Ambassador," I began. It's a very good idea to always begin a conversation with a Middle Eastern Ambassador by thanking him, regardless of what he's just said to you. "I must say, though, sir, that with all due respect we have not failed at this point."

Rising to his feet, he slammed his open palm on the desk. "*WHAT?*"

Oops. It's also a very good idea to never tell a Middle East Ambassador that he's wrong. Never, ever.

He turned to the DCM, yelling, "Didn't Mr. Wellington tell us right here that their entire plan was to get this amendment in the House bill? Did he not? Did he?"

"Of course, Excellency." Shaikh Mohamed shook his head. "We were right in this room, as was Mr. Matthews."

"You see?" the Ambassador said to me, his right hand extended toward the DCM. "You see? You have no explanation other than that? Nothing?"

"My apologies, sir," I replied, "I did not mean to imply that Mr. Wellington did not say that to you. You are correct—he did."

From the corner of my eye, I could see the Second Secretary furiously scribbling. This would make a wonderful memo back to the Palace.

"So he LIED to me? Mr. Wellington was lying, is that it?"

"No, sir, he would never lie to Your Excellency."

"So, what then, he just didn't know what he was saying then, that's it?" Coming out from behind the desk, he came right over to my chair, looming over me. This was the full show. "So he came here to talk to me without knowing that he could not do this?"

"Well, sir..."

"You know how important this is to our country. We are a critical ally of the United States in the region, and we are among the region's most helpful countries in terms of defense matters. If we had known that you could not accomplish this important mission," he continued, spinning around and heading back behind his desk, "I would have undertaken the effort myself without your supposed assistance."

Ah, so there we were at the nub of the meeting, actually a good ten or fifteen minutes sooner than I'd expected: this was Wellington's failure, our company's failure, not the Ambassador's failure. And everyone else was in the room to hear, and to report to officials back home, that it was everyone's failure but the Ambassador's. The DCM would call one of his cousins in the royal family, and the First Secretary his senior Foreign Ministry officials, while the Second Secretary would write a long and detailed memorandum that all of them would send to every source they could think of. Oy.

"Now, instead," he said, "I must find a way to convince America's President and the Secretary of State that they must find another way, because Mr. Wellington and Michael McPherson & Associates have failed to win this legislation."

Oh, God, just what we need, I thought, the State Department getting ragged over this by an incompetent Ambassador. We'll have to push him off that.

"But Mr. Ambassador, we will be able to ..."

"You will be able to what? You have done nothing so far. You have accomplished nothing. Yet you wish for us to allow you to pursue the effort on your own? Is that it?"

"Mr. Ambassador, Wellington has assured me ..."

"Mr. Wellington, yes, and where is Mr. Wellington this afternoon?"

Goddammit. I'd told myself not to mention him, but it just slipped out. Now I'd have to go through the "if only he were here" shtick I'd been hoping to duck.

"Well, as you know, Mr. Ambassador..."

"Yes," he said, smiling as he turned to the DCM, "as I know so very well, he is in Geneva at this time and not here to assist our country."

"Sir, really, it isn't like that..."

Shaikh Mohamed drew his breath in quickly. Yeah, you're right, bud, I thought, I put my dick in a wringer this time.

"*WHAT*!" the Ambassador shouted again. "I suppose that *I* am lying now, is that it, Mr. Matthews?"

* * *

Two hours later, I sat in a small bar a few blocks from the UAE Embassy. It was still relatively early in the day, but I needed the scotch and water that Fawzi had procured. After leaving the Embassy, I called him on my cell, and we met up here. As military attaché responding to the Defense Minister, he hadn't been invited to the scream fest, and we were meeting for a debrief.

"I am sorry, my friend."

"You have nothing to be sorry for, Colonel," I replied. Fawzi looked at me with his sad face, the one where his omnipresent smirk was almost hidden away. A cloud of smoke oozed from his nose and worked its way up along the sides of his face. "It's Wellington who got me into this, as you know."

Fawzi laughed and, picking a tiny bit of tobacco from his teeth, responded in his smoky, rasping voice, "Yes, I have already spoken to him this evening. When you brought my copy of the bill and told me that you were unwilling to wake him, I decided that *someone* needed to ruin his baby sleep. I couldn't resist." He smiled broadly now; Wellington has long complained about how terribly he sleeps when he travels, and being woken at two o'clock in the morning would mean he was up the rest of the night. Fawzi had traveled with him to Europe and the Gulf many times, so he surely knew this.

"Perhaps next time he will listen to your strategy," he continued, releasing a long, slow stream of smoke, his grayish, toothy smile barely visible in the cloud.

"Oh, I doubt it very much, Colonel," I responded with a smile. "But I appreciate your willingness to test his resolve."

"So the Ambassador is satisfied now?" he asked, getting to the point of my return visit.

"Yes, sir," I laughed quietly at the memory. Another forty-five minutes of failure and disaster, doom and gloom, and all our fault. If only the Embassy had been allowed to do this without our interference, etc., etc. "The blame has been very clearly placed on us, and by now the Second Secretary is working diligently on the memo that will detail this, and the rest of them are making calls home to make the point as well."

"Well, I called the Minister immediately after you left earlier, of course," he said. He picked at another bit of tobacco, while tapping with his other thumb on the unfiltered *Gauloise*, as if to make it stop. "His Excellency asked me to express his personal appreciation for your work."

"Thank you, sir," I replied, warming up a little. A wonderfully thoughtful guy, the Minister. "Good of him to remember me."

"Don't be silly. He also expressed his appreciation for your willingness to take the blame for Wellington while he is traveling for us."

Traveling for you? That was news to me. I wondered what his contract extended to that would take him to Geneva. "It was nothing, Colonel. Besides, my friend Wellington might have had more difficulty sitting through the Ambassador's performance," at which Fawzi laughed in mid-drag, spraying a lungful of fetid smoke in my face, "depriving him of the opportunity to fully vent his anger. So perhaps this way is better for all of us."

It took Fawzi a few moments to recover from his coughing fit, and his furious nodding in agreement with me probably didn't help. "You are so very right," he finally said, coughing slightly again. "You are right. Tomorrow morning I will see the Ambassador and will get a better sense of it. But I am sure you are right."

* * *

"Mr. Chairman, I would like to review that report language if I could, as well as the later report language on refugees from Famagusta."

It was Rep. Kelton, Alexis's boss, chiming in right on cue to ask if he could review draft report language on Greece and Famagusta before the draft report was published. This was the favor he'd promised to Michael. Alexis had stepped up and crouched behind him at the Members' table just as that section of the bill was being closed, and slipped him a note asking that he make the request. For a rookie, she was a damned fast learner—her timing so far in this mark-up was quite impressive.

The trick with Appropriations Subcommittee mark-ups was that they didn't work off a copy of the actual bill and report, but off "mark-up notes," the semiofficial terms for a set of Xeroxed pages that provide precious little detail on what the Committee was actually proposing. For provisions included in the bill from year to year, that was fine, but for the new stuff, and especially for the stuff we lobbyists were sneaking into the bill, it was critical that someone reviewed the actual text of what was going in before the draft was "written"—also a lie, since it had been written and preprinted a month or so before, but was hidden in the Chairman's office. No Chairman would be so stupid as to go into a mark-up without knowing precisely what he or she wanted to come out with, but that, of course, didn't mean he or she actually had to share it with everyone in the room.

On the one hand, you had to look at it from the Chairman's point of view. Circulate the text in advance, and we lobbyists, piranhas that we were, would all try to rewrite the whole freaking bill. Only by drafting (and hiding) the text ahead of time could the Chairman have any semblance of control over the final product.

On the other hand, I was getting paid by my boss—and we the company by our clients—to put *exactly* what we want into the bill, word for word. So it was a tug of war.

The best way to be sure you'd won was to have a Subcommittee member ask to review the text before the report went to the full Committee. Not an easy thing to do, since most of the Members didn't even know what was in the bill, let alone what they were being asked to "review"—i.e., to have their staffs review.

In this case, Michael had gone to Kelton directly; he'd caught him in the hall on his way to a House Floor vote, another of the better lobbyist tricks of the trade.

"I'm sure the staff will be able to accommodate that on the Greece language," the Chairman responded from the end of the long oblong table. Smart answer: we'll go along, but only on the Greece language, not the whole report. Even then, all they'd let her do would be to look at the language, not make a photocopy of it, but with the original language I'd handed to her to compare it against, that would be good enough. Not that it was a big deal; we mainly wanted to be sure they hadn't spelled Famagusta with two *g*s or do anything else that would give the client a reason to be pissed off.

Alexis, sitting directly behind Kelton, glanced up at me. I smiled ever so slightly and nodded imperceptibly. She looked away and waited.

"That will be fine, Mr. Chairman," Rep. Kelton responded. "I appreciate your willingness to accommodate my concerns."

Ever so polite, these meetings. There was always an undercurrent of tremendous tension, a sense of foreboding among most of us in the room, that something would certainly go terribly wrong, but the discussions were—most often—the essence of civility. Very few junior members of the House got onto the Appropriations Committee, along with very few firebrands—the appropriators were generally smarter, more substantive, and politically savvier than their peers. They were being put in control of the money, after all, and their votes shaped the most important legislation the government passed every year: how much did we spend, and who did we spend it on? Unlike most other bills the appropriations bills had to pass every year, because if they didn't, the agencies they funded would shut down. As a result, the leadership of both parties had always been careful about whom they put on Appropriations, and how much they made people go through before they got there. It didn't always work: convicted felon Duke Cunningham ended up on Approps, to name but one. But they tried.

"Let's move on to the Agency for International Development section of the bill," the Chairman said, and countless pages turned in unison as Members, staff, and lobbyists all turned the page at the same time.

* * *

Sitting in my office later that night, I reached deep into my bottom left-hand drawer for the Johnny Walker Black I kept stashed away. Charlotte had told me she would be working late again, a Committee hearing coming up soon or some such, so I figured I might as well get some work done before heading back to our empty apartment. I poured myself a double or so, dropped in a couple ice cubes from my water glass, and then added a little of the water. Sacrilege, I thought, adding water to Johnny Walker Black, but I didn't care; it was my drink.

I'd been reading and editing some of the weekly reports, the long missives to our clients that detailed every critical—or even vaguely interesting—bit of news from that week in the Congress. Some weeks we had to hunt for news, a Budget Committee hearing on the defense portions of the Budget, for example, which had zero impact on our clients but provided filler when nothing else was going on. At other times, when the foreign aid committees were active, identical Budget Committee hearings went ignored—we didn't need them. The reports were long, tedious, and scarcely readable, but they proved that we were out there, keeping the clients' interests in mind, watching out for the bad stuff, promoting the good, so we prepared them religiously.

I'd just finished the report for the Dungan, which I cobbled together from the other reports that Michelle had prepared, adding in a couple of small tidbits specific to the client. I didn't usually add a whole lot to these reports, as Michelle was actually a pretty good writer. I gave extra attention to the Dungan report, though, in part because I was writing them for two audiences: for Bao and Charlie, but also for Kincaid and Hendrickson. On the one hand, I tried keeping the writing relatively simple and thus easily translatable to Bao, and on the other I needed to demonstrate enough sophistication that we'd impress our lawyer friends.

The heavy editing done, I could afford the drink. We were far enough into the year and were doing pretty well in getting what we needed for the clients, but I needed to walk through it all carefully to make sure there wasn't anything I'd forgotten, or unforeseen obstacles in the weeks and months ahead. It was still a guessing game, but the guesses were far more informed this late in the year than when you're mapping everything out in January.

As of this point, we had the strategy for our UAE amendment in hand: use Belkin to get it into the Senate bill for us, and use Will Richardson to make sure it survived Conference at the end of the year. I had no idea yet if Sen. Belkin would agree to do it, but couldn't move until Uncle Harry got me in front of him in Paris. Paris, I thought, what a crazy mess that's going to be.

The whole Koliba gig was where one would expect it, with everyone on the Hill excoriating the guy, saying all kinds of terrible stuff about him, but so far the Committees were doing nothing more than the standard ineffectual report language about human rights. We'd scoped out the most serious attack, the Senate-side prohibition amendment Philip Galsworthy and Franklin Wallingford were pushing, and were positioned to defeat that one outright.

I sat back and allowed myself a broad grin. Beating those two idiots looked like it was going to be our biggest victory of the year, since the real business of Washington lobbying was more often stopping people from screwing you than about doing something positive for your clients. Getting someone some extra money was always nice, but stopping the other side from taking away every dime the President was planning to give them, *that* was a serious victory.

In addition to all that, I'd even sold my Africa military aid amendment, the $15 million earmark, which would be hidden in plain sight in the Senate Foreign Ops bill. Another win for Koliba, when everyone thought they were screwing him. I was actually getting a lot done this year, more than I'd expected.

Holding tight to my scotch, I stood up and, leaning against the window, looked down to watch the traffic rolling along Connecticut Avenue. This time of night on days when Congress was still in session, there was still a lot of traffic, even at 9:00 p.m. But the city ebbed and flowed with the presence of the Congress, lobbyists, and their minions scattered in offices well into the evenings, watching late Floor debates, follow up on meetings, prepping the next day's agendas. Who out there, I wondered, is working against us? There was always someone on the other side of every issue, working his or her own brand of magic to undo everything I spent my time on. It was a bad way for a superpower to run foreign policy, I had to admit; hell, it was a bad way to run government, dueling lobbyists taking money in exchange for shaping, or reshaping, the policies and programs of the U.S.

Government. It was innate to the system, though, so deeply ingrained that I couldn't imagine it any other way.

That blue Cadillac, maybe that was someone from Shaddock Mills. No, more likely the gray Mercedes, or even the Beemer convertible; those bastards made serious money. And that Volvo station wagon, the beige one with the banged-up hood, that one was probably a human rights weenie who hated Koliba with all his might.

Laughing, I turned back to my desk. Three clients done—that left my report language on the Dungan, the easiest work we had all year. There was little going on in the open to this point, but there seemed to be lots behind the scenes: I received a call from Will Richardson that, after he'd dropped my one-minute into the *Record*, he'd also gotten a call from the Vice President's office, a friendlier one than Kevin had gotten but still enough to make him notice. He was pretty annoyed with me, because no one in Congress liked showing up on Cheney's radar—no one knew what that meant and how deep the radar might penetrate. But in the end he shrugged it off.

So far, though, while I had talked to some people about report language, I hadn't been trying very hard because I hadn't figured out who was who in this fight and what strategy was going to be best. Two calls coming out of Cheney's office, the nation's official black hole, didn't tell me much. Not that I was worried—I could do report language with my eyes closed, and with as inoffensive a client as the Dungan, I knew I could sneak something through somewhere. Maybe too easily, I thought, but that's what makes the business fun.

I smiled to myself and, rising from the desk, reached for my coat.

Chapter 11

The ringing doorbell woke me, and I glanced at the clock: 8:00 a.m. What the fuck?

"*Un instant, s'il vous plait*," I called as I crawled off the small daybed looking for my robe. Slowly coming aware, I noticed sounds from the bathroom—a hair dryer this early?—as I belted it and headed to the door. Mary Anne is up already, I thought. Strange.

"*Bonjour, monsieur*," the waiter sang to me as he angled the room-service cart in through the door. The tray was crammed with food, enough for three or four of us, several dishes under their metallic covers, a muffin basket, two coffee pots, more dishes than Mary Anne and I could ever eat. She ate like a bird, for Chrissakes. Carefully arranging the table, our *garçon*, our fifty-year-old boy, handed me the check with a flourish and fiddled with the dishes while I tried to do some quick math in my head.

"Oh, sorry," Mary Anne said from the doorway. We both looked over, the *garçon* and I, pausing to stare just a little more than was polite. Tall, 5'10" or so, willowy, her blonde mane dried and brushed and her long legs visible below the just-long-enough towel that covered her torso, Mary Anne was just as stunning dripping wet as she was all dressed up and ready to go. I smiled despite my better instincts.

"Harry's coming by around ten o'clock, so I wanted to have something in case he's hungry." She smiled back at me and winked before turning back to continue working on herself. Like she needed it.

Harry's coming by around ten or so, I thought. Dear Uncle Harry, coming by my hotel suite around ten or so for a quickie. Jesus. It was one thing traveling to Paris the same time Harry was there with fellow Appropriations Committee members, shadowing them around the city so I could pick up a check or two, find tickets for the jazz venue they've all heard about, and run other errands, but renting a suite for his latest paramour was turning out to be a little over the top. Here we were, on the first morning of a four-day, three-night trip, and I'd have to duck out, leaving our suite open for Harry's assignation.

That was on top of the fact that the timing for this trip was completely insane, coming between the uneventful House passage of the State/Foreign Ops bill the week before and the expected Senate Subcommittee action on the bill the week after. It would be a critical mark-up for us, and I somehow had to figure out how to get whatever I succeeded in accomplishing with Sen. Belkin into the bill right away, and I had no idea how I was going to do that. So I was a little more stressed than one might expect, spending a weekend in Paris with lots of time on my hands.

While signing for the outrageous bill and getting our *garçon* out of the room, I wondered again about our strange setup. I'd gotten to know Mary Anne pretty well by now, given the breakfast fundraiser, the hours of traveling from Dulles to Paris, and especially over drinks in the hotel bar the night before, after the reception where I'd played chaperone while Harry pretended to be spending time with me, not her. She was obviously a sweetheart, bright, funny, and a pleasant travel companion. A Senate Transportation Committee staffer, Mary Anne was one of those rare people on Capitol Hill who wasn't trying to leverage her way up the totem pole. She was a receptionist, and a very good one, seldom if ever taxed in a job that called for a little bit of efficiency, a lot of polite chitchat, and a bright smile. She was making enough money to live, and meeting enough interesting men to eat, sleep, and travel well. On the one hand, most of them were married, but on the other, most of them were Senators, so the dozens of egotistical letches on Congressional staffs and Washington's lobbying elite knew to keep away— while the rest of us, the small fry, knew she was totally out of our league. She found herself a little bubble of a life that seemed to fit her well, and at this point was enjoying it enough to stick with it. After all, not every twenty-eight-year-old receptionist can afford a room at the Westin Paris.

So Mary Anne I didn't mind, but their schedule so far was a little intense. Belinda in Harry's office had somehow tracked down this Westin suite, probably from some defense contractor constituent or other who'd given up the room in exchange for something I didn't want to know about. Harry and Mary Anne had spent the prior afternoon, right after our arrival, in Harry's suite at the Ritz, followed by dinner with others on the CODEL— as any Congressional delegation is always called, boondoggle or not—and the obligatory U.S. Embassy reception for them. That was where I met up with the group. From there, Mary Anne and I headed our own way, coming back for drinks downstairs and the very separate beds in our suite. And now, eight hours later, Harry was planning to come in for a quickie. Why wasn't she staying with him and just keeping her clothes in my room, like I'd expected? It wasn't like the other Senators didn't know what was up; they all knew Harry. It doesn't make a whole lot of sense, I thought.

It suddenly hit me. Aunt Helen was flying in on day four of this trip, and Harry didn't want any of Mary Anne's *things* in his room. So he was keeping her at arm's length. I turned to the breakfast table and snagged a muffin from one of the baskets.

"You don't mind?"

Turning, I saw Mary Anne's head peeking out through the bathroom door. I mumbled through my muffin, a very moist blueberry. "What? All the food?"

She paused. "Ten o'clock, I mean." Oh, she was serious.

I finished chewing, thinking carefully. It sucked, let's face it, but that wouldn't have made me much of a team player, would it? "Mary Anne, I'm in Paris, just hanging out while occasionally talking to Harry and his buddies. It's not a tough gig."

"It's your suite." She was almost right—the company was paying for it. In point of fact, it was the need to find an off-the-books room for Mary Anne in Paris that had tipped the scales with Michael on my flying off to Paris with Harry's CODEL. After Brent Wilkes had pretty much screwed the pooch on renting rooms for Members of Congress with the rumors of his poker-and-hookers nights at America's most scandal-plagued hotel, the Watergate, we all had to get a lot more creative and a lot more careful with travel favors.

"Look," I replied, "there's something terribly high school about having to leave my hotel room so my traveling companion can get ... well, you know. And there's something terribly disturbing about leaving my hotel room so my *uncle* can." That part of it was actually *profoundly* disturbing, but I made it sound light, light enough so that she laughed. "But I think I can find my way to Nôtre Dame, or Saint-Germain, or hell, that sandwich joint at the end of the Île-St.-Louis. It's no biggie."

"Thanks." She was smiling at me. "I mean it." God, she could stop a train with that smile.

* * *

"Edward, my boy, so good to see you."

It was five o'clock, and we were gathering at the famed, highly overrated Hemingway Bar in Paris's Ritz Hotel. Harry seemed smaller somehow, a little lost in the dark, heavy room, less the wise elder statesman I'd trained myself to see and more the grasping, conniving politician I'd pretended not to. It was amazing what hours of walking the streets of Paris, leaving a sixty-seven-year-old man to cavort with someone who was becoming a friend, could do to your impressions of him.

Harry had arranged the meeting, asking his travel partner, the Honorable Sen. Joseph Belkin, to join us for that conversation promised in Washington. Belkin was more than the average Defense Appropriations Subcommittee colleague, for he and Harry were partners-in-crime in many of Harry's more egregious earmarks. Members of Congress see earmarks as a prerogative, but the various scandals spinning out of Duke Cunningham's outlandish greed made them more difficult to pursue. Senators, more visible than their House counterparts, seemed to be adapting to increased scrutiny by increased horse-trading, each agreeing to pursue some pet project or other in exchange for their colleagues doing the same. It wasn't a tremendously successful art, but better than getting caught writing your nephew's client into the State/Foreign Operations Appropriations bill. So here we were, looking to deal.

There was one enormous irony in this meeting, one that I had no intention of mentioning here or anywhere else: while Sen. Belkin was the only opportunity I had for getting the UAE its MNNA status, he was also the Senator most likely to oppose my efforts in support of the Dungan. As the Ranking Republican on his Subcommittee, he was the Administration's and, from past experience, especially the Vice President's lapdog on anything and everything related to foreign policy. The FEC Web site indicated that he also took buckets of money from Shaddock Mills, so he was doubly a problem for that client. But that's one thing about Washington that most people just don't get: someone who's your best friend on one amendment can be your greatest enemy on something else. It's just the nature of the business.

"Hello, Uncle Harry." He looked well, relaxed, happy. I couldn't help wondering how often Mary Anne had made him happy, or how many Viagra had given their lives that day in Harry's quest for eternal youth.

Sen. Belkin's arrival was just in time, as my mind was headed in a direction I seriously didn't want to go.

"Joseph, you remember my nephew Ed."

"Indeed," he lied, "delighted to see you again." Belkin's weak smile and troubled look indicated that he still wasn't sure, still hadn't made the connection between Raymonda and me. Ever since our break-up, I'd avoided his office like the plague—she took her vengeance seriously, so it was somewhere I couldn't even get a decent cup of coffee, let alone help with my clients. But like any good Senator, Belkin was happy to pretend for now, as was I: if I could get through this meeting and into the next one, with Raymonda, without him figuring out who I was, I might make it through this alive.

Of course, after this trade, I was going to have to find a way to know him, or at least his campaign committee chairman, a little better. I was figuring we'd need to raise about $25K for the guy's reelection, but that was something I'd work out with Michael later.

"Sit, sit," Harry waved us both to a table to the left of the door, seemingly the only place with any privacy, the one decent booth in the whole cramped bar. There were photos of Hemingway everywhere, from the framed *Life* magazine cover on the left as you entered, to the scattered hunter shots around the room. Rich, dark oak, simple in its way, but still decidedly overbearing in its Hemingway-was-here-ness. Climbing the two steps to our table, I looked back around at the few faces in the room. Good, I thought, almost no one here to see Harry's Ugly American act, and those that were looked to be Ugly Americans themselves.

"Harry tells me you have a problem, son."

I turned, surprised by Belkin's quick move to business. The waiter was still on his way, in that excruciating fashion the French have, even here at the Ritz, an undying need to demonstrate their disgust for everything American. I'd been hoping to get a drink or two into Belkin before we got down to the meat of it, but that wasn't meant to be. "Well," I started, "we do. We need a provision in State/Foreign Ops Approps, and I don't have a champion."

"It's hard for me," Harry intoned, reaching out to lightly touch Belkin's sleeve. "You understand."

Belkin didn't look over, staring at me instead. "Give me the story." He wasn't living up to his Casper Milquetoast reputation, and I was starting to worry a little. Harry had said this was a lock, but Joey wasn't making it look that way. A glance at Harry indicated that he was less worried; lifting his hand, he tried flagging down the waiter in a way more likely to add to our wait than shorten it.

"It's simple—DOD and the intel community want to give the UAE a particular air defense radar system, but they don't want anyone else to know about it because every Moslem state from Morocco on over to Pakistan will want one. So they need a way to do it quietly, and the only way they can see to do it is to have the UAE declared a Major Non-NATO Ally. It's a simple one-line amendment, in Foreign Ops."

"Israel?"

I tried to ignore Harry, but he was beginning to get more frantic. I was thinking that in another few seconds his arm waving would prove so disturbing to the mood of the place that the waiter was certain to stop by. Whatever his impact on the waiter, though, he was terribly distracting to me. "The Israelis don't care. DOD tells us they actually like the idea. But AIPAC has told DOD that they will oppose any sale of this system to any Arab country—if it's public."

"Waiter! Oh waiter!" Harry said, at which point I reached out to stop him. God forbid he yell "Gars-sown!" at the guy, because then we would *never* get drinks. Turning, I grimaced in mock embarrassment at the waiter. "*S'il vous plait, Monsieur. Il ne va pas arrêter,*" he will not stop, "*et je ne peut plus, eh…*"

The waiter grinned as he ambled our way. I turned back to Belkin.

"So what good does the amendment do you?" Belkin didn't skip a beat.

"Well, DOD has an 'extra' system they purchased. I don't know why, but they don't need it and they plan to declare it excess and give it to them using a classified reprogramming." I glanced at the waiter, who'd finally arrived. "Cognacs, gentlemen? Mr. Hemingway's preferred brand?" To my right, I could sense the waiter straighten up, the way Europeans do when Americans order something indecently expensive. *"Oui,"* I told him in response to their nods, *"ça va."*

"The Israelis won't claim it?"

"They already have something better," I replied. "I'm told it's two or three generations upstream." I made that part up, but it was an informed lie rather than an outright one: the Americans consistently sell Israeli technology that's several generations ahead of what they sell the Arab states, lest the Arabs be foolish enough to think they could use American weapons in attacks on Israel. Every once in a while, the Israelis drive the point home: on their way to Tunis in the 1980s to bomb the PLO, they'd shut down Egyptian antiaircraft systems as they passed by Egypt's coast. The screens just went black, and the Egyptians went a little loopy trying to figure out what was wrong. It all got lost in the news of the bombing, but the Izzies had made their point.

Belkin turned to Harry. "I'll need to talk to someone from Israel. And someone out of the SecDef's office." I nodded, and Harry nodded too.

"Why do it in the dark?"

Geez, he was a lot smarter than I gave him credit for. "You mean besides the AIPAC problem?" He nodded. "Afghanistan."

"What?"

"Well, we spent the last half of the 1980s arming every anti-Russian Afghan we could find to force the Soviets out of Afghanistan. Twenty years later, in the aftermath of 9/11, the same people who sent the weapons are sitting around waiting for just one of the Stingers to take down a civilian aircraft or, God forbid, a troop transport. Nobody wants their fingers on this sale because nobody wants to be in that same position twenty years from today." He was staring at me, as if waiting for something more. I shifted slightly. He wanted to know how he would escape without blame. "That's why this one is invisible—many hands in a completely opaque process with no one specific person to blame. You ask the Chairman for the Major Non-NATO Ally provision. It's in the Subcommittee draft with no name attached. DOD excesses the radar in a classified communication with a million signatures and no one author. It goes to a different Subcommittee—DOD—and they let it go. No muss, no fuss."

He was still waiting. This time there wasn't any more. I leaned forward and took a long sip from the cognac that had magically appeared. My God, that was smooth.

"Who would object?"

This question was to Harry, so seemingly his interrogation of me was complete. Harry and I had walked through all these questions before we left D.C., though, so Harry knew this one. "You would, Joseph." He smiled patronizingly at him. "You're the biggest pro-Israel Senator on the Committee. You're the guy everyone looks to on weapons systems like this. That's why we've come to you."

"What's my angle? Why would I do this?" Half what's-in-it-for-me, half how-do-I-explain-to-my-people-why-I'm-doing-this. Smart guy.

"9/11." The catchall, the rationale for half the crap that ends up in defense, homeland security, and foreign operations bills. Need a post office in East Buttcrack, Arkansas? 9/11, so the mail can be x-rayed right there where the Ozark loonies live. Need some economic aid for starving children in Ethiopia? 9/11, so that they won't become Al Qaeda recruits. Need more border-crossing staff along the Canadian border? 9/11, to keep America safe from the Middle Easterners the Canadians let in willy-nilly. "The UAE's one of the good guys in the Gulf," I continued, "and they need air defense. It's a straightforward argument, with the added benefit of being true." At least as much as the other bullshit amendments were.

"And how do I sleep at night when the system gets turned against us?"

"It's air defense, designed by us for us. We can turn it off from a distance if we want to and drop all the goodies we want all over them. And so can the Israelis."

His eyes tracked mine, watching me closely to see how much was true, how much wasn't. It was all true, and I was totally comfortable selling him this idea. The amendment was a tough sell, but only because of the politics and of everyone being chickenshit about getting caught with their pants down, not because of the rationale behind it. It was a good amendment. For once.

He turned to Harry. "We should discuss this a little."

Harry looked at me, and I nodded. Time for me to leave them alone, he was saying, so Harry could hear what Belkin wanted in return. This would be a straight trade: Belkin does my amendment, and Harry does his. And nobody wanted me around when they cut that deal.

But I still had one problem.

"Senator, one last thing. The bill is going to be marked up very soon— they're threatening to move it next week." I looked from Belkin to Harry, who was stone-faced, and back to Belkin. "It would need to be added to the bill very quickly."

The slightest smile tugged at Belkin's lips, but it was Harry who spoke first. "It's already in the bill."

"Hmm?"

"I've already secured the Chairman's agreement to put it in the draft bill," Belkin continued. "This meeting was to determine if we should take it back out."

Again my look went from Belkin to Harry and back to Belkin. This was a surprise; Harry had done it again. Saved me a hell of a lot of trouble, but wasn't Harry's usual way of operating.

Then again, this was my first time playing at this level. Maybe it *was* his way of operating.

"Thanks for listening, Senator." Discretion being the better part, etc., etc., I quickly downed the rest of my cognac, way too fast given how good it was. I rose and turned to walk away, and then turned back. "I appreciate all your help and your willingness to listen. Have a great rest of the trip."

On my way out, I snagged the waiter again. I paid him in cash for the brandies consumed so far, along with enough for another round for the Senators just in case, and a nice tip on top of that. It was the only way to be sure that the asshole would treat them well from here on out. It meant leaving without a receipt, but that was okay—given what I'd gotten out of the meeting, I didn't mind eating the cost. Besides, I really didn't want any kind of record that this conversation even took place.

* * *

"Mr. Minister, this is a tremendously important request," I said, "or else we wouldn't be wasting your time on it."

From drinks with Harry, I headed across to the *George V*, where our UAE client—the real one, the one who signed the checks, His Excellency Hassan al-Farouk—had agreed to a brief meeting before his next reception with yet another element of the global military-industrial complex. The time of Defense Ministers at the Paris Air Show was like gold, and especially for those from the wealthy emirates in the Persian Gulf. They bought military gear more than anyone else and could always afford the newest and shiniest. Everyone wanted their time.

Ironically, I hadn't told the Minister or Col. Fawzi, who was also here, about the meeting with Sen. Belkin I'd just been through. They would have wanted to meet with him, talk to him about the amendment, and tell him how important it all was. But given the fact that we were moving this amendment entirely in the background, under the table, they'd just spook Belkin and we might lose the whole thing.

So I just never mentioned it.

This meeting, though, I needed, if not here in Paris then pretty much anywhere as long as it was sometime soon. With Belkin on board, our Major Non-NATO Ally amendment was well on its way, but I still had the problem of Karen Jameson, the unfortunate idiot who'd gotten herself captured in an antiterrorist police round-up in the local Hilton and was now rotting in some jail. Or if you believe the police, the young terrorist recruit who'd been captured along with her coconspirators—and would be rotting in some jail for a very long time.

When Weller had told Fawzi I needed more details on Jameson's imprisonment, he ducked a discussion and instead set up this meeting. That in itself was a bad sign, meaning that the issue was so sensitive Fawzi didn't want to talk about it.

Me, I wasn't so much worried about who was telling the truth as I was about when they would release the girl. Disgusting though it might be, I just needed yet another foreign government client to kowtow to Congress. Ever since the end of the Cold War, nations around the globe have bristled at the pressures that America puts on them, to vote a certain way in the United Nations, to support blindly our determination of countries that merit the imposition of economic sanctions, and even to join us in invasions halfway around the world, as El Salvador did in Iraq when CAFTA was pending. Less visible, though, are Congressional interventions, where individual members of the House and Senate hold up legislation in order to get a highway redirected away from the cemetery that holds some constituent's ancestors, to pressure a government to issue licenses for a new casino financed by a company in the district, or to get some kid or other released from prison. It happened all the time in Washington. It was ugly, but it was a fact of life.

"Well, as you know, it was the police who arrested this girl, not the military," the Minister replied. He looked over to Fawzi, who was smiling down us, wreathed in smoke, having gotten an unplanned trip to Paris out of this problem when Weller had convinced the Minister to meet with me. Fawzi was in a good mood—he liked Paris, and being here during the Air Show meant a whole lot of defense companies were pursuing him around town, trying to get the Minister to visit their displays. "My cousin Moustafa"—Minister of the Interior, someone we had absolutely no connection with—"is the person you need to speak with."

"Yes, sir, I understand," I replied with the slightest smile on my lips. Nice try, I thought, but you can't get off that easily. "But this is an issue that will primarily affect you and the Ministry of Defense, not the Interior Ministry. We are deeply concerned that we will not be able to get the Major Non-NATO Ally status approved if she remains in jail."

The Minister stiffened, and his face flushed just a touch. My God, I thought, this guy's charismatic. He was built like a bull, thinning brown hair crowning his round olive-skinned face, dressed in a leather bomber jacket that showed just enough wear to be fashionable, an open-collared shirt, and dark blue slacks. No insignias, nothing that would indicate he was in the military, but a bearing and air that demanded respect. Watching him walk through the hotel lobby or at the receptions where I'd seen him in Washington, you could tell at a glance that he was someone important. Sitting here alone in front of him, seeing him beginning to anger over something I'd said, was significantly more intimidating.

"This is very important to our country, and to our relationship with the United States," he said, looking again over at Fawzi and then back at me. "There is no comparison between these two issues."

I raised my hands, a sign of supplication, and my voice caught for a moment before I responded. "You are absolutely correct, Mr. Minister. This is a much less important matter." I paused, trying to decide how to go back at it. "It is not something that anyone sensible would compare, or would link together. But I fear that our Congress is seldom very sensible." I shrugged and smiled just slightly.

He leaned forward to me, his face stern at first, but as he paused I could see the slightest twinkle in his eyes. Jabbing a finger at me, he said, "You are right, my friend. They are not sensible at all." Turning to Fawzi, he laughed and, with a shrug of regret, slid back in his seat.

Fawzi laughed too, beginning just after the Minister, but he laughed. Reaching into his pocket for a fresh cancer stick, he coughed through his laughter and said to me, nodding as he did, "Perhaps if the Minister could ask his cousin about this girl's case?"

That was all I was going to get, but it was a whole lot better than nothing. "That would be excellent," I said.

* * *

At ten o'clock the following morning, I sat in the outer room of my suite, the day bed made up, coffee on the table, the *International Herald Tribune* in hand, catching up on some news. The room was cold, the way I like it for sleeping, so I had a robe wrapped around me and was crouched on an end of the sofa. I was most of the way through a basket of pastries and looking forward to a nice quiet morning when the door to Mary Anne's room opened. As I looked up, my heart skipped.

Raw male lust has always been such a curious animal. I'd spent three days with Mary Anne so far, three days ducking in and out of the room and traveling with her and Harry to various meetings, receptions, lunches, and dinners. She'd been resplendent every time, stunning in her ability to dress the part, the casual but perfectly tailored skirt and jacket, the formal evening dress, the Dior pantsuit. I'd been checking her out a lot, sure, but there'd not been a moment when I'd been thinking, "I want her"—never a flicker. And now here she was, in the top half of some oversized Victoria's Secret pajamas and unrecognizably fluffy slippers, hair in shambles, and the sleep still being rubbed from her eyes. I couldn't look away.

"Good morning," I said, just to say something.

"Hi," she replied, smiling. She stopped and stared back. She caught me. "So where's Harry?"

"They're meeting with the Mayor this morning." She came closer to the table, still smiling. "You know Harry. He loves meeting celebrities in those magnificent old palaces. He's even staying for the lunch."

"Yes, that's Harry. A sucker for a good show."

"Hmm," she said, playing with a croissant she'd picked up. I was trying not to stare, but losing that battle, and she was looking playful. "You know, Harry's sixty-four years old this month."

"Well, sixty-seven, actually," I replied.

Laughing, she came around the table and fed me one end of the croissant. Jesus Christ Almighty, I thought, chewing, you're screwing my uncle, I'm a married man, and you're a stunningly beautiful woman, and I'm tired of running out of this room so that my old fuck of an uncle can get laid. By the time I'd gotten that convoluted sentence through my head, I'd gulped down the bit of croissant, she'd brought her lips to mine and was kissing me, and I was kissing her back.

The first time moved quickly, very quickly, as suddenly her nightshirt was gone, and we were on the floor, my robe open, my pajama pants off somewhere, and our two bodies entwined. I could feel a need in her, a need for what I couldn't tell, perhaps someone younger than a Senator, perhaps someone who didn't expect anything from her, perhaps just some fun. And the need in me was palpable, as undefined as hers, but palpable. Her body shimmered in the morning light, above me, her long hair trailing across her arms and breast, her narrow waist and hips rotating on me before I realized I was inside her. And then it was over.

The second time was slower, much slower, from the start as she led me by the hand across into the bedroom through the playing and toying with each other as we waited for me to recover. We took the time to enjoy ourselves—I to luxuriate in the feel of her skin against mine, in the softness hiding in the lithe tightness of her belly, her thighs, the delicate curve of her ass. We were so much more careful this time to enjoy the pleasure of it, to run my fingers along her legs, to taste the salt in the budding sweat along her shoulder, to feel the lightness of her touch as she played with my cock. And there was time for thinking, time for the guilt, for the power of the betrayal to be driven home much as I was driving into her, betrayal, betrayal, be-TRAY-ALLLLLL. It wasn't enough to stop me, only enough to make it hurt as I came, hurt, deep, buried inside me, a pain that I did not recognize other than as hurt.

As I lay in her arms, sweat rolling off me, I thought, why am I here and what am I doing?

Feeling her fingers sliding aimlessly along my spine, my eyes drifted open for a moment to the lingering slope of her belly as it wound down toward her crotch. But then again, I thought, it's not so terribly bad a place to be.

* * *

Charles de Gaulle is a lousy airport to get in and out of, even if you're just out there picking someone up. It's that much worse in a blinding Paris rainstorm.

I'd arrived an hour early for Aunt Helen's 8:20 a.m. scheduled arrival from Dulles, if for no other reason than a driving need to be up and out before Mary Anne woke up. The headwinds are unpredictable over long distances, I'd told myself, so sometimes the flights are early, sometimes hours late. I was eager to end this trip, eager to get away from Harry and Mary Anne. And this was the most delicate part of the journey, with Helen arriving today and Mary Anne not headed back to Washington until the next morning.

Helen surfaced out of Customs by around nine fifteen, shortly after my fourth *café au lait*. She had that haggard look of overnight flights, too few hours to get a reasonable amount of sleep, and stared at me as if not recognizing my face at first. After a few seconds, she managed a wan smile.

"Hello, Edward."

"Welcome to Paris, Aunt Helen." I leaned in to kiss her lightly and reached to take her carry-on. Stepping around her, I took the handle of the suitcase rolling behind her as well, but she held on, resisting for a moment, seemingly unwilling to give it up. "I got it," I told her. As I took it from her, she straightened, relieved of the weight, regal again in her bearing, the Senator's wife redux. But looking askance at me, she continued on without comment in the general direction of the cabs. She must be very tired, I thought; she usually travels better than this.

The cab ride was no better. The rain was worse, if anything, and the traffic out of Charles de Gaulle crawling in toward the city. Looking left out my window, there was little to see beyond the sheets of rain, the cars in shadow flinging more water our way, their headlights wasted in the dismal day. Mary Anne's smile glimmered back at me in the glass, the long slow curve of her back mirrored in the stream of water blown down and across the window by the wind and rain. Shaking myself to break the image, I looked over to Helen, but she seemed similarly lost in thought: she stared ahead without seeing, eyes open but glazed, her face long and drawn.

"Are you all right?" I asked. "You look like it was a tough flight."

She stirred, her left eyebrow rising ever so slightly, her body, slouched down in the seat, shifting from one uncomfortable-looking position to another. "The flight was fine." She turned away, looking out the window now, or perhaps at it.

I turned back to my own window and again watched the cars, the rain, the backwash flying up at us. I was troubled, but there seemed nothing to do.

Rain, cars, backwash, cars, rain, backwash. The minutes ticked by.

"You don't have to do everything he asks for, Eddie."

I roused, surprised. "What? Sorry, I ..."

"The girl." She continued staring out her window, and my breath caught. "In your suite. I called yesterday to check about this morning—she answered. The girl he brought."

Oh good God almighty.

"He's your uncle, Eddie, and he's a Senator. But I'm your aunt, your mother's sister." She paused, looking down at the floor of the cab. "This isn't an easy life, and I get through it knowing that my secrets are my own." She looked over at me. "But that doesn't work with you, Eddie, when you're one of the secrets. That doesn't work at all."

Oh good holy Christ almighty. She knew. "Helen, I ..."

"Please. Don't try to explain." She turned, just her head this time, her body still facing away from me toward the window. "And don't say you're sorry." She looked away again. "I just wanted to say, you don't have to do everything he asks you to."

Rain, cars, backwash, cars, rain, backwash, and the unending sound of the wiper blades. We said nothing more on the way into town.

* * *

At six forty-five the next morning, I stood alone on the Pont St.-Louis, watching the Seine flow by at its glacial pace. I'd hardly slept, slipping out of Mary Anne's bed—my bed, dammit, just with Mary Anne in it—and wandering back to the couch, where I spent most of the night staring out the window, thoughts of Helen's comments keeping me from sleep.

What am I doing? I asked myself. I'd gotten what I needed from this trip, but at what cost?

Between Harry, Helen, and especially Charlotte, I'd betrayed everyone I cared about on this trip. With Mary Anne I found a couple of days of mindless physical pleasure, entirely tainted by the betrayal and my imminent return home to my wife. There were still so many options for things to go even worse: while Helen knew about Mary Anne's presence in Paris, Charlotte did not, and I didn't need her finding out that I'd shared a suite with Mary Anne, let alone that I'd helped Harry get a little on the side. And God forbid Helen or Charlotte ever figured out that I was getting a little of my own as well.

With a shiver that came from more than the chill off the water, I looked down into the slow, lumbering river, and it was Belkin's face I saw looking back at me. The whole trip was built around that drink with Belkin, that chance to talk him into whatever trade he made with Harry. From there on, I supposed, the rest of it was easy, so easy that it had come naturally to me, slipping over from my professional life into the narrow, walled-in social life that living in Washington permitted. My personal life was merging into the professional, becoming a part of the cheap and tawdry games that made up the everyday life of being a lobbyist. Lying was so natural now, I thought, that the biggest surprise of the trip was when Helen caught me with my pants down—but even she didn't realize that my pants were off, not just down, and I'd been cheating in more ways than she knew.

Watching a single branch weave its way down the river, I thought about all the games I had going, how suddenly they were me and I was turning into them. I was using everyone I knew, just like Eleanor told me I needed to so long ago, just like I always thought I never would. Worst of all, standing on that bridge I could tell that I scarcely even felt it anymore. At some point, I thought, some of this has got to start rolling back in my direction.

Chapter 12

Of course, I didn't expect it to start going to shit as fast as it did.

Late Monday night after my return from Paris, I buried myself in the living room sofa, working my way through the masses of emails that had accumulated while I was out of the country. I hadn't been able to sleep, not so much from the jet lag as from the strange sensation of lying next to Charlotte, knowing I'd betrayed her, my mind spinning at the contradictory thoughts that cheating on her wasn't something I'd do while simultaneously something I'd thoroughly enjoyed. I'd tossed and turned for a while, but sleep wouldn't come. Afraid to wake her and eager to clear my head, I'd taken out my laptop and settled in.

Most of the e-mail was spam, along with the many political e-mail newsletters I subscribed to. Occasionally there was some actual business, but nothing serious enough to get excited about.

By 2:30 a.m., I'd deleted most of the spam, answered the serious stuff, and was ready to turn to those emails that looked like jokes from friends, the semi-spam that, as a lobbyist, I couldn't ignore despite my fervent desire to get my name removed from their lists. The same staffer who was including me on the stupid crap he sent routinely would also include me when he had something important to share, so I was stuck with the crap.

I decided to start with an e-mail from Peter, entitled, "the good news is…" It took a good forty-five seconds to download over the wireless, ensuring that it included photos if not a small video file. Opening it took another half minute, all with my laptop waiting, waiting for the file, while I scratched furiously at the back of my head with two hands to wake myself up.

As the file opened, the text showed up first, followed almost line by line by the first photograph, slowly filling in. The message was short: "... she doesn't name the Member. The bad news is, she gives his member a name."

He had me. Like the vast majority of Washington, I was a total gossip hound, not just because the stories were usually so juicy, but because half the time I'd met the offender: the indicted Congressman, the lobbyist who used his upscale restaurant as a feeding trough for House and Senate Republicans, the staffer who'd had her salary reduced her final year on the Hill so that she could sneak under the mandatory one-year lobbying prohibition for staffers over a certain pay level.

The first photo was a strange shot, a couple from the back—he in a dark blue suit, she in red, cut very low in the back, his right hand prominently clutching her ass. The skirt was askew, as if he'd been rubbing her with some vigor, but that was about it.

Picture number two, again from the back, this time with her facing him, one leg wrapped around him and his arms holding her close. Her face was shadowed, partly by his head and partly from the tight cropping of the shot from the top. She was kissing him, her head tilted to the side, thick brown hair flowing across his shoulder and, very obviously, her one visible eye staring straight at the camera.

The third shot looked to be more from a cell phone camera, grainier, lower quality but with much higher content value. The shot was of guy, the same guy from the cut and style of his hair, lying face down on a bed, naked, his head turned away from the camera, his left arm trailing back across the sheets. Just out of reach, a bra hung on the bedpost; the red dress hung limply from a lamp on the bedside table. The light from the lamp glinted on the big, ugly ring on his hand.

Fuck, I thought. The big ugly ring on his finger.

Copying the image, I opened it in my photo editor and blew it up. Like most cell phone photos, it bitmapped, the image disappearing into a haze of dots as I enlarged it. I went back to the e-mail and checked the two others. In the first, where his hand was on her ass, there it was again. I copied this photo, opened it, and closed in on the ring. Just as I feared—it was Will Richardson's big ugly goddamned Yale class ring.

At least, I had to assume it was Will's. Peter capitalized Member, meaning a member of the House, and wouldn't just send this around unless it had something interesting in it. And the hairstyle was his, a fairly typical blow-dried congressman look that wasn't unique to Will but combined with the ring enough to know it was him. But so what? Will Richardson getting laid? That wasn't news; that was an everyday occurrence. Still, something was wrong—her looking at the camera, her shot of him in bed with the ring, the whole thing.

Returning to the e-mail, I scrolled to the very bottom to find the rest of Peter's message. "Can you tell who this is? Check out KitchyKoo2 at MySpace—she's got a whole story about him. Let me know what you find."

I'd always been the Google guru among my friends, especially the ones who never got off the Hill. For all that Congress runs technology policy and supposedly funds cutting-edge research, the Hill is like one humongous dinosaur when it comes to understanding how anything works. They all carry Blackberries, but mostly as symbols of power and importance, and they all have shiny new computers, but the vast majority have no idea how anything more complicated than e-mail even works.

And MySpace, Jesus, seriously, who could be stupid enough to have a MySpace page in Washington after all the scandals? Not that I wanted to know what Peter was doing finding the MySpace pages of pretty young things who screwed Congressmen and shot photos of it. But this was Will, and I needed to know what the hell was going on.

I started by on KitchyKoo2's profile page, but focused on her "Friends," the hundreds of fellow idiots who spilled their lives all over the site. Running through the posts that had been left, I clicked on the photos of women who'd sent messages with a personal touch to them. After about ten, I found the first common denominator, Wellesley College; that took a little over half an hour, but after that, I quickly cross-linked through six other Wellesley alumnae, all linked to her page. Their pages were relatively tame, and their postings to KitchyKoo2 made her seem the slut in the crowd— all the way from "you're wild, girl," to "OMG—that's disGUSTing!" More importantly, though, their Wellesley pages all included group shots in which one other girl showed up whose page *wasn't* linked to KitchyKoo2, some kid named Jean Chamberlain.

Googling "House," "Committee," and "Jean Chamberlain," I found one reference in House Committee pages, a cached file showing her working for the Energy and Commerce Committee, the front office staff from the looks of it. But the current page didn't include her. She'd moved on.

She was Jean Chamberlain, former House staffer, but what was she doing?

From there it was comparatively easy. She was listed in the online White Pages, so I knew where she lived. Next stop was the Federal Election Commission Web site, where she popped right up at that address as a donor to Will. Only to Will. Running through his donor list, I found two other women who'd made political donations to him and listed the same home address. This is getting worse all the time, I thought.

All three women showed as employees of General Micronics, a small Beltway Bandit-style defense contractor based out of western Maryland. The company's Web site indicated that it had annual sales of around $75 million, including a contract in the area of microrobotics. Pulling up the last two years of DOD Approps bill off Thomas, the Library of Congress Web site, I found two earmarks in the area of microrobotics, one for $6 million two years before and one for $18 million in the current year's law. Both originated in the House, so both could have been put in by Richardson. I wondered what number they were working on for this year.

With all this data in hand, I went back to MySpace, where she'd conveniently maintained a blog; the story all came together very neatly. From recent references, it looked like Will was her landlord, and going back to the earliest references I could find, she'd been in the apartment a little over two years. She'd started by talking about how important he was, a senior Member of Congress, what an impressive guy, manly, yutta yutta. By June, she was having sex with a Washington bigwig, no name of course, no longer any indication that it was her landlord, but by July she was back making little jokes about her rent. By early August, one of her classmates from college moved in, and KitchyKoo2 soon reported that she was "hanging" with the bigwig too.

I opened another window and went to Thomas.gov, the Library of Congress Web site, in search of the Defense bill from that year. The House Appropriations Committee hadn't reported it out until September—plenty of time for KK2 or her friend to have made a deal with Richardson for that first earmark.

Another old college friend moved in during November of that same year, and KitchyKoo2 soon reported that she was hooking up with the bigwig as well. God, I'm getting old, I thought; routinely hooking up didn't exist back in my day, at least not in this public sharesies kind of way. Will's getting a live-at-home three-way over the next ten months, though, did explain the tripling of the first year's earmark.

But that wasn't the worst of it: KitchyKoo2's blog postings, each date stamped, were getting sloppier, and she talked about hearings that she'd gone to just so she could see her lover, scattering dozens of clues about when his Committee was meeting and sometimes even the building the hearing was in. There was the name she'd given his member, his "ICBM" she called it, complaining about the boxes of "missile silos" they had to keep in the house because Will never brought his own rubbers. With several of that kind of hint, pointing the reader toward Congress's defense committees, any decent reporter with a whole lot more time than I had could easily track back through this, even without recognizing the class ring. And if Peter was e-mailing me the photos, that meant it was only a matter of time until someone else would be able to put it all together.

Looking over at the clock, it was 4:40 a.m. I still hadn't slept, and this was a busy week. I yawned and looked back down at the screen. I had to give Will one thing—this woman and her friends were *hot*. I wonder if it'll have been worth it after the media destroys his career, I thought. I wonder if he'll care.

* * *

"Jesus, was that *you?*"

Alarm bells began going off in my head—loud ones. Roger, looking down the small pile of papers he kept on his desk, was moving them randomly from one side to the other, looking nonplussed and blinking like a demon.

"What's that supposed to mean?"

"Well, damn," he replied, still avoiding my eyes, "you know I work a lot into that bill, and I can't always keep track of all of them. I depend on you guys to keep me up to speed on items you're working."

"Bullshit. You throw me back out the door if I come back to check up on you." God, wasn't that the truth. "Don't hover," he'd say, "stop playing mother hen." That was on his good days. On his bad days, he'd be threatening our amendment just out of spite.

"That's a load of crap."

"So what's the status of the amendment? Is it in the bill?"

Roger paused and then looked up at me for the first time. "It was."

"Was?"

"I couldn't remember why I'd asked for it." He looked down again, moving the same papers from the right to the left this time. "So I told them to take it out."

"Well, have them put the fucking thing back in again."

"I can't. They'll know a lobbyist showed up and talked me into it. They'll ask questions." He looked back at me again, his face barely recognizable behind the tics. "You know better than I that this amendment can't survive a whole lot of questions."

Well, he was sure as shit right about that. The whole fucking amendment was a sham, an amendment earmarking $15 million in military aid for Africa for coastal biodiversity and sustainability programs, all so that maybe Koliba could sneak in under the radar and qualify for some military aid funding. It was a long shot, but it was the only shot we had. Thanks to Roger, I'd succeeded in sneaking it into the bill without anyone being the wiser.

And, now thanks to Roger, because I didn't "hover," it got snuck right back out of the bill again.

"So what the fuck am I supposed to do?"

"You'll, uh, have to find another sponsor." He grimaced a little, and his jaw twitched. Glancing to his left for a moment, he looked quickly back at me. He was getting angry.

I was furious. "Are you *fucking* crazy? Another sponsor? The fucking mark-up is next week, you asshole!"

I could feel myself sliding quickly over the edge and took a deep breath. I wasn't getting through a sentence without the word "fuck" in it, and I wasn't just saying it—I was pretty much spitting them at Roger. "Fuck," in and of itself, isn't that big a deal in Washington—despite all the polite appearances on television and in visits by constituents, most people in Washington curse like stevedores. In a town where speech is one's only weapon, the effective use of the most power-packed words in the English language is a critical skill. Roger wasn't like that, but even he was used to getting it thrown at him every once in a while.

So it wasn't the fact that I was cursing Roger, it was how serious I was about it. Even if he had screwed this up royally, Roger was still the one on the inside and I was still, as I always would be, the one on the outside. So

I needed to slow down a little, take it down a notch, or I might get myself in a heap of trouble.

I turned around, looking for his guest chair. Walking to the corner, I leaned down and grasped the chairs' arms. Squeezing my hands as tight as I could, I leaned there, breathing in, breathing out, slow myself down, breathing in, breathing out, again, again. After eight or so breaths, I picked it up, brought it toward his desk, and took a seat. I could feel my anger beginning to dissipate. Settling in, shifting a little back and forth as if that might help the wooden seat accommodate me somehow, I looked over at him. I waited for a few moments, as did he, blinking quickly but the grimace gone, and I felt the mood in the air shifting around us.

"Got any ideas who I can get at this late date?"

"Is that an apology?" he replied.

"Let's call it a recognition," I said, "of going too far, perhaps, in expressing my concerns about the amendment we agreed to. We. Agreed. To." I let that hang for a moment and then continued, "And yes, Going. Too. Far."

"Yeah, well, you're full of shit," he answered.

I smiled; he was getting past it if he swore.

"Sorry," he said.

I breathed in again, deeply and let it out. "I needed a challenge this year anyway. Everything's been going along too easy." I smiled over at him and started thinking: who the hell was I going to get? I'd already used my one shot at Uncle Harry, and besides, this amendment would be way too transparent for that avenue—it would so obviously trace back to me and our clients that it could start some serious trouble for Harry. Not only would it be stupid to take it to him, but he'd figure that out on his own and refuse to do it anyway. So I'd have to find another route.

He snorted and shook his head. "You enjoy this business way too much."

Well, that was certainly true. But this wasn't the time for that discussion. "Maybe, but right now I have to find a new sponsor. I still haven't heard any ideas out of you."

"You'll have to talk to Peter." He looked over at me, his face a little grim. "I've got nothing."

* * *

"Khhhhor Fakkan." Fawzi coughed as he said it, the heavily aspirated *kh* of the Arabic pronunciation catching in his much-abused throat.

That can't be right, I thought, glancing unbelievingly at Wellington. "Wait. Whore Fuckin?"

"No, my friend," Fawzi laughed through another uncontrollable cough. I'd caught him on the inhale, which was cruel, but I'd been too surprised to notice. "It is KHHHHor Fakkan, Khor Fakkan, our country's most important port."

"Well, it sounds a whole lot more like 'Whore Fuckin' when an American says it." I turned to Weller. "You're just getting around to telling me this? Are you crazy?"

Well, this was certainly turning into just a wonderful day, first with the Richardson photo shoot, then Roger, and now this. Wellington, Fawzi, and I were off to the edge of a busy Moroccan Embassy reception, on the back lawn behind the Ambassador's residence. The location was beautiful, in a quiet northwest Washington neighborhood close to the Rock Creek Parkway, and the sun was still up, that summer sun in Washington on a day that was mercifully warm instead of the more typical hot, humid, and disgusting. In Paris, I'd had no time alone with Fawzi, so I'd never been able to quiz him on the amendment. So this was the "meeting" with him that Weller had promised me, held here at an outdoor reception presumably to avoid the inevitable microphones and other, more esoteric listening devices that would be found in Fawzi's office, the Embassy, his car, his home, and pretty much anywhere else he frequented.

Of course, the Moroccan residence was probably miked too, but I'd always assumed it was still a bitch to record a conversation out of the air in locations like this, crowded parties with people who knew to avoid words like "classified," "missile defense system," or "I had lunch with Ayman Zawahiri last week."

"Khor Fakkan is the primary shipping port of the Emirates and is tremendously important for trade in the Arabian Gulf," Fawzi continued. "This is not a joke, my friend."

"Guys," I replied, raising an arm in frustration. I took a drink of my scotch and water and turned to Fawzi. "My friend, *you* have to understand. If I'd mentioned this at the beginning, when I first started to lobby for MNNA status, it would have been a throwaway—'oh, and wait 'til you hear this, the place they're defending is called—I'm not kidding—Whore Fuckin.' That's simple—we all laugh, it's stupid but funny, and we go away. Now, when we're 90 percent of the way there but the amendment could still blow up in our faces, I'm supposed to go tell them that oh, by the way, if it comes out they'll hear no end of it in the blogosphere because they're defending a place called Whore Fuckin."

There was a long pause, Weller and Fawzi first looking at me, at each other, and then at me again. "But Ed, I have to say, that is, well, just stupid." Weller had his stern face on. He just didn't get it.

"Of course it's stupid," I replied, "but this is what American politics has descended to, whether it's Swift-boating Presidential candidates or making up funny mispronunciations of foreign ports. The people who listen breathlessly to news about Lindsay Lohan and Paris Hilton are the same people who listen to Rush Limbaugh, or Hannity and Colmes and all those other talk radio morons. It's stupid, but it's our world.

"So again, guys," I continued, "are you crazy?"

They looked at each other for a long moment, and Weller turned to me. "I'm sorry. I know this place. I know it as Khor Fakkan, the most important port in the UAE. I would never have seen this problem."

"That's why you bring me in at the beginning," I said, "not the end."

Fawzi put his right hand on my shoulder. "How bad is it, my friend?"

I turned to my right, looking into the crowd to see who else was there. "My friend," my ass, I thought. "It will be fine. I'll figure something out." Turning back to Weller, I continued, "Don't do this next time, okay?"

He smiled. "Sorry."

"I need another drink," I responded. Looking down at my glass, I saw that it was still half-full. Looking up at Fawzi, I smiled, drained the glass, and repeated, "I need another drink. Nice chatting with you." With a glance at Weller, I said, "Don't do that again," and turned to leave, shaking my head as I searched out the closest bar, mercifully set more than halfway across the wide lawn. You two idiots, two old secret agents playing your secret games.

As I strode away, Fawzi called after me. "Ed. Ed!"

I turned back to face them, but stayed where I was.

"That girl you asked about." He smiled grimly. Smiles are never good at time like this, I thought. Must be more bad news. "The boss says he cannot help. The other boss would not agree."

Shit. So the Minister of Defense asked the Minister of Interior, who said no. So Karen Jameson is still in jail, and they're telling me she's going to stay there. Swell.

The day was just getting better and better.

* * *

As I crossed the lawn, I could see my friend and former client Mourad over by the entrance to the Residence. Ever the graceful host, and here, at his Ambassador's Residence, forced into that role, he was talking with a small crowd of Congressional staffers, including Peter Chase. Mourad and Peter had always been thick as thieves, even back when we had Morocco as a client and I was supposed to be the one selling Peter on our amendments. But Peter was the last person I wanted to see at this point, so I tried to ignore them until they waved.

I waved back to them and then pointed two fingers, first at them, back and forth between them, and then at my eyes. Mourad laughed and waved me over, but I held up my empty, shook the glass, and pointed once more, this time to the bar. Seeming to excuse himself from Peter, he headed in my direction, catching up with me as I arrived in line by the bar.

"Where is your good wife?" he asked, looking around me. Unlike most American hosts, he was actually curious where she was; Arabs are like that, seldom just spouting the niceties, usually meaning them.

"She sends her regrets, to you but especially to Halima," I responded with a smile. "She's working late this evening. They have a bill on the Floor tomorrow."

"Halima will be sorry to have missed her," he said.

"Johnny Walker Black and water," I told the waiter. Loved those Embassy receptions, always putting out the good stuff.

"Have you spoken with my friend from the Ministry yet?"

"Ah, no, I almost forgot," I said, kicking myself. For all I liked seeing Mourad again, talking to his friend was the reason I'd come. My conversation with Weller and Fawzi had pushed it out of my head. "Does he have much to tell me?"

"He's hoping you have something to tell him," Mourad replied. "He says there's nothing going on with the Dungan, and nothing new in U.S.-Kazakh relations except for the upcoming elections. We're all expecting Nazarbayev's party to get around 106 percent of the vote. Your government won't be very happy, but like the Europeans, they won't make much noise."

Kazakhstan's lower house of Parliament had been dissolved for snap elections earlier in the month, just before I'd headed off to Paris. We all knew what to expect—typical former Soviet republic stuff, gotta have elections because the West says so, but gotta stuff the ballots so no one else has a prayer of even looking good. God forbid the dictator look at all weak to his beebles. Like Mourad said, Nazarbayev's party would almost surely win the vast majority of contested seats, a virtual impossibility in any free election, but something quite common in that particular region.

This was good news at least: there was nothing like a dictator acting dictatorial to ease the way for some report language like I wanted for the Dungan.

"Other than that, there's an oil pipeline deal that a bunch of American firms are fighting over with the Europeans. It looks like one of those cases where you've both got government financing, and it will probably be the one with the biggest checkbook"—payoffs, he was saying—"who wins." Mourad shrugged. "We still don't get it, why they hired you. But come along, he's in the Residence and very eager to meet."

* * *

Hours later, I sat on the floor at home, my back to the sofa. Charlotte was still on the Hill, but had called to say she'd be home soon. A bottle of Merlot was to my left, a half-empty glass to my right and an empty one for Charlotte just beyond that, and my laptop open on my lap as I followed up on my earlier KitchyKoo2 research and the few small tidbits I'd gleaned from that evening's event.

It was a busy but useful reception. Mourad was right; his friend had nothing new to report, something I took as a good sign: while they were looking for what was wrong with my client, I was comfortable enough with Bao and with Kincaid's explanations and had seen our firm hired to do less than this. Nothing short of a smoking gun could convince me that they were anything but on the up-and-up.

The UAE news was less helpful. The first thing I'd done on getting home, of course, was to Google "Khor Fakkan." They weren't lying: according to Wikipedia, it was a major port in the UAE. Jesus, I thought, they couldn't have named it like Port El Araby, or Mohamed's Port, or something? Crap.

Of course, maybe I could use the Wikipedia entry. Maybe if I print out copies, I thought as I reread it, and give those to people… I wouldn't even have to say the name, just hand them out… That might work.

Shaking my head, I turned back to the budding Richardson fiasco. Here I was somewhat conflicted: on the one hand, Will was my friend, so I found the whole thing terribly disturbing. On the other, Will was the go-to House supporter for my UAE amendment, the person I'd set up to help us out in Congress. If he was thrown out of the House for these shenanigans, that strategy would go down the toilet—for that reason I was totally pissed.

At around 10:30 p.m., as I was turning back to the FEC Web site to cross-check more General Micronics contributions, Charlotte came in, looking tired but relaxed—must have been a good night, I thought. "Hey, Sweetie," I called out, reaching for my glass.

"Hi, babe." She hung her coat on the rack by the door and headed for the kitchen.

"Long night? How'd it go?"

"Not bad. The bill passed, so the boss is happy." I could hear water running in the sink, and waited. In a few moments, she came out through the dining room, a glass of water in one hand, an empty wine glass in the other. "He'll be in a good mood for at least a week, the asshole."

"I've got a glass for you here," I said, holding it up.

She smiled, turning to leave the one she had on the dining room table. "Fill 'er up."

Holding it up so she could see while I poured, I said, "By the way, Sweetie, men are ruled by their dicks." Not to shock her, just to beat her to it.

Instinctively, I knew I had to get ahead of Charlotte on this story, lay out the worst of it before she started quizzing me for details like it had been me. This time it hadn't, but I was still raw around her following my return from Paris, and I wasn't ready to go through an extended interrogation. My guilt was still riding too close to the surface.

Charlotte came from the school that said men are basically just idiots, running through their lives asking their dicks for advice about just about every decision they made, from the little ones—"should I ask the librarian, or the hot blonde reading over at that table?"—to the big ones —"should I lie to my clients? sell my soul to the devil? give away national security secrets in exchange for a contract?" Mostly she was right, of course; I mean, let's face it, I'd always ask the hot blonde at the table whatever question I had, and why not? The librarian wasn't going to refuse to answer if she knew I'd asked the hot blonde first.

Sometimes we'd be watching TV, some cheese ball movie on the Lifetime channel or something, the kind that says, "I must really love my wife to sit through this drek," and some guy would do something phenomenally mean, or stupid, or guy-like to the heroine, and I'd get a smack on the arm while Charlotte called out, "What is *wrong* with you guys?" Like I ever beat a woman, or had four wives, or ran off with the fifteen-year-old babysitter. I swear—it's a good thing I don't bruise easy.

"So do you want to explain that comment?"

I went through the whole story with her, starting with the e-mail from Peter and the realization that it was Richardson, through my own research tracking down what company was involved and how bad it was. I skipped through a lot of it—Charlotte hated the Web and wasn't going to tolerate surfing through dozens of pages to see every little tidbit go by—but got her all the way through to the two women and their earmarks.

"Jesus Christ," she said, "you guys. Ruled by your dicks."

I laughed, for a brief moment completely at ease with her, the first since my return from Paris. I looked back down at the screen, just for something to look at.

All of this, I thought, all this you put at risk so you could fuck some twenty-eight-year-old you don't care about? Jesus, you're an idiot.

"So, what, he's hung like a horse?"

I laughed, loud and long, in a rush of relief. I paused for a second before responding. "No, it seems to be the power thing. There's no sense in what she writes that he's some stud among studs. It seems to be all about him being important, having the power. Like that ugly stump Kissinger said, it's the ultimate aphrodisiac."

"I've often wondered how much that toad actually got laid," she said, rising to her feet and heading for the hall. "I'm going to change."

"Love ya," I said, returning to the screen. I do, I said to myself, my God, I really do, and I'm sorry.

"Ditto," I heard her say as she headed down the hall.

I sat still for a few moments as she receded, my eyes unable to focus on the screen before me. What was I looking for? Maybe her friends' pages, maybe they'd have more of the story. Yeah, I thought, I should check those. Anything to stop thinking about Charlotte and Mary Anne Corrigan.

I shook my head as if to clear the cobwebs and forced myself to focus.

This was going to be ugly, very, very ugly. It was Randy "Duke" Cunningham all over again, except in reverse—instead of living rent free on a boat owned by a lobbyist, Will rented his house out to hot young lobbyists and traded earmarks for sex. How long could he last? If Peter had asked me for help on this, he'd probably passed it on to others, and there was still whoever gave it to Peter. The net result? It would break sometime soon, and when it did the House would be turned upside down watching this poor bastard go down very fast and very hard, and the public up in arms again—at least for a couple of months—about corruption and earmarks.

There were all sorts of dangers in that, starting with the problem of my UAE MNNA amendment, which just lost its House-side Conference support. In Washington, though, dangers always came with opportunities too. At this point, I just wasn't sure which were which.

Chapter 13

"This is *BULLSHIT!*"

Rage is a powerful tool in Washington, but seldom wielded effectively. Rep. Dave Obey of Wisconsin was one of Congress's rage masters, a cranky and generally unpleasant person under the best of circumstances, but a star at exploding in rage when the moment was right: at 3:00 a.m. in the middle of a Foreign Ops Approps conference, or in the middle of a mark-up when things weren't going exactly his way. Younger, less experienced Members quaked in the face of a classic Obey eruption; the more seasoned among them glanced at their watches and placed bets on how long he'd keep it going. In the late 1980s, he once spent over an hour in the wee hours of the morning spitting nails about an African despot who had mistakenly been lauded in the prior year's Committee Report. It was classic Obey, somewhat remarkable for its length but otherwise a perfectly normal performance.

Raymonda, my former lover and the current minority staff director for Sen. Belkin, was once again giving me a private demonstration of her own special skills at rage in response to my story about Paris and *her* Senator. Curt by nature, always testy under even the best of circumstances, fiercely protective of her boss and especially outraged whenever anyone (like me this time) went around her to get the boss to agree to something, she was an explosion waiting to happen.

The trick was to understand her style and sit through it. Ray tended to blow early, with a vicious bitterness designed to knock you right back out the door you'd come in through. She was made for the one hundred-yard dash, not the mile, so after a massive, volcanic explosion she'd peter out after five or ten minutes. I figured this one would go closer to her ten-minute limit, since I'd given her no warning at all about my plans for Paris, and she could only take that as a betrayal. Problem was, I couldn't have told her ahead of time; she would have killed the deal. So here I was, paying my penance.

"Those fucking Emirates aren't worth the sand they shit in," she continued, an image I tried to conjure up while letting her continue to blow off steam. "There's not a decent democracy among them, they oppress women all get out, and they aren't fucking trustworthy when it comes to national security. We can't just give them our best assets like this—they're not fucking trustworthy."

"In the time since 9/11, they've been incredibly helpful," I ventured.

"I'm tired of all you *assholes* citing 9/11 as if it's the answer to everything!" she cried. "Americans *died* on 9/11, you prick!"

As if politicians like her boss—God, especially her boss—weren't the first people in the country running out to use 9/11 as an excuse for every crazy-ass spending idea they ever had. From the subways in Washington, D.C., to the ports in Los Angeles, from the Florida panhandle to the eastern mountains in Washington state, 9/11 was the rallying cry for spending, spending, spending. And, praise the Lord, every Senator and Member of the House was out there day after day, toiling in the fields, saving us from the evil terrorist bastards who wanted to destroy the American way of life. Of course, sometimes they were, and some programs had use, but puh-lease, it was mostly just crap designed to push more Federal dollars back to their constituents. And much of it, as with all government spending, was simply pissed away.

As I listened, my mind wandered to the various directions she might take this conversation. My friend Ginger the dog from all those old *Far Side* cartoons was back: "blah blah blah Emirates, blah blah blah Arabs," while I mentally ran through ways to escape from her ranting, reviewing each against her likely reactions. Of course, the Ginger strategy was probably one of the main reasons my relationship with Raymonda lasted as long as it did: when she finally broke it off, telling me she couldn't take all the arguments anymore, I didn't feel like we'd argued all that much. Maybe I just hadn't been paying close attention. Today was no different.

Tuning back in, I heard Ray say something more about the UAE Government's oppression of women, and I tuned right back out again. Jesus, that old shibboleth. I couldn't for the life of me tell where she thought she'd get with that idea; the whole "oppress women" thing is a purely Democratic argument that doesn't even fly with most of *them*. Hearing it roll off her tongue when she worked for a Republican New York Senator born and bred amidst the horsey set out in Nassau County near Belmont Park was laughable—except for the fact that a laugh at this moment could have cost me my life, since steam was still coming out of her ears.

News Flash: Traditional Arab Societies Oppress Women! Film at 11:00! *Of course* they oppress women; it's in the nature of traditional societies all around the globe. The question isn't whether—it's what are they doing about it and what direction are they heading in? More or less? Better conditions or worse? All this black-and-white, either-or debate that dominates Washington these days is one of the main things killing the body politic. As if any of these idiots in Congress, let alone the boobs we send to the White House, have the right answers for everything. Smartest thing the founders ever did, separation of powers: since all three arms of government have equal tendencies toward stupidity, divide their powers and the moderate middle will conquer.

Ray was still going strong, and I noticed that she was focusing now on the whole "untrustworthy Arabs" part. This was a little more sensible, the whole Afghanistan thing again that I'd talked about with her boss in Paris. "The leaders in these countries turn over like flies, and weapons we provide them today will end up in Afghanistan or Somalia before you can say Abdul Robinson."

"Jesus, it's MNNA status, Raymonda," I replied. "We're not talking about F-16s here. We're talking about them being at the back of the line for the bits of shit that roll through the process after the Reserves, the states, the Israelis, the Egyptians, and about ten other countries that go over the cache with fine toothcombs. This is mostly just a political statement." Sort of. That was as close as I ever wanted to come to a direct lie, but she was starting to get to me.

"Politically, they *SUCK*!" Ooh, I thought, I'm wrong. She's starting to fade pretty early this time. "You suck" was the weakest argument I'd hear in Washington, even if it was the best shorthand for how our two major political parties see each other. Raymonda using it here meant that she was running out of steam.

"Ray, they are not a democracy. They are not the leading promoter of human rights in the region. They are not the most critical nation to U.S. interests in the region. But they want MNNA status as a symbol of the relationship, and Sen. Belkin agrees." That was dangerous, telling her what her boss thought. It could start her off on another explosion, depending on whether he'd told her about the Paris agreement or not.

"Fuck you." Nice and quiet—it meant he'd told her there was no backing out of this deal. "I know what the Senator plans to push in Committee. MNNA status for the UAE, for the life of the bill."

That meant one year, the term of all appropriations bills. It was the perfect solution, the one I'd been hoping for. This way, Ray would think she screwed me, but I would get what I needed: MNNA status long enough to ship the radar system they wanted. But I needed to be shocked and outraged, so she wouldn't know I was okay with it. "Wait, Ray, Sen. Belkin didn't say anything about having the authority for one year. That could kill the deal."

"I have convinced him of the importance that this be a provisional authority," she replied, steely eyed as she glared down at me. "And it's the only deal he's offering."

"Goddammit, Raymonda, that's going to kill us with our client."

"Like I give a shit about you and your client." Smiling at me briefly, she looked down at her desk and grasped a random memo. Starting to read without looking back at me, she continued, "Are we done?"

"I'm going to have to take this back," I began.

"We're done," she said. "And that's the deal. Goodbye."

* * *

From behind his desk, his body turned sideways, Weller played with his pen, twirling it between his fingers, a nervous habit. "Can we fix it in conference?"

"Fix it? Weller, they wanted one system. They can probably get it shipped thirty days after the bill's signed into law. There's nothing to fix."

He sighed and glanced out the window. "Yes, but the Minister has decided he likes the idea of being a Major Non-NATO Ally."

"Jesus Christ Almighty, Weller, don't fuck this up for me. I used Harry for this, and he's never put himself on the line for me like this." It was true; more importantly, I couldn't go back to him to ask him to redo the deal. I swear—it wasn't always just the clients who were clueless. "You tell him that this year we can only get one year's authority. *Next* year, we'll make it permanent."

"Hmm." He was still looking out the window. Turning his head, he said, "I guess that means they'll need us next year, won't they?"

"There you go."

Turning to walk out of his office, I stopped, looking back for a moment. "Didn't you say Fawzi was being rotated out of Washington at the end of the year, and wasn't happy about it?"

"Yes," Weller drawled as recognition began to dawn.

"Well, he just got his ticket to stay two more years—we can't do it without his intel contacts."

Weller was up from his desk at a speed that belied his seventy-three years. "I think I'll take a ride over to the military mission office. You haven't told anyone, have you?"

* * *

As Weller pushed by me, I headed down the hall in the other direction, toward Michelle's office. I needed to make sure she was the next one to hear the news, or there would be hell to pay. There was gonna be hell to pay anyway, but I was getting used to that. Somehow Michelle was starting to remind me of Raymonda.

"We're all set on the MNNA amendment," I said from the doorway, one hand on each lintel, leaning a little so as to appear relaxed.

"*What?*" she responded. She was sitting at her desk, her hands now frozen in place above her keyboard. In the dim light, I thought I could see the blood rising in her face. "How? I thought we still had to talk to Belkin's staff director, Roberta or whatever."

"I stopped by earlier this afternoon, and she agreed to it."

"Goddammit, why wasn't I there?" She stood, placing her hands on her hips and staring at me. "The UAE is my client, dammit. I thought after your Paris junket that you were going to stop going it alone on this."

"Hey, gimme a break—it's not like it was a fun fucking meeting." God, she'd set me off again. I couldn't put a finger on it, but it was getting to the point where every time I talked to her I got pissed. "Raymonda"—emphasizing it a little more than needed to remind her of the name—"ripped me a new asshole, thank you very much, so you didn't miss anything."

She wasn't buying it. "I missed participating in the deal you made." Well, okay, she had a point there. "And I missed a chance to learn something about how you operate." Okay, well, when she put it like that, it made some sense.

Looking down at her desk, she continued. "So the deal is what exactly?"

"MNNA status for the length of the bill—one year."

"One year! The Senator agreed to the provision as written! I could have done better than one year. Jesus, I can't believe you bit on that." She stormed out from behind her desk, coming straight at me. "I need to talk to Welly so he and I can fix this."

Now I remembered why I didn't take her with me. She was an arguer, not just with me but with everyone, and she had no sense of the subtleties of Washington. The main reason I always asked for more than needed was so that I could give a little and still come away a winner. Members and staffers hated to say "no" to any request, and if I could make them feel like by giving me what I wanted they still had to say "no" to me— or in Raymonda's case, *got* to say "no"—that only ensured that they'd fight all the harder for the compromise. This approach was especially important since I was always on the outside looking in, with clients who weren't voters but rather foreign governments looking for some form of handout.

"He's not here. He went to tell Fawzi."

She stopped right in front of me. "So you told him first?"

"He's between here and the elevator." Boy, that was lame. I knew it even as it was coming out of my mouth.

"And he just ran off to the client?"

"He always talks to Fawzi alone. You know that. It's an intel thing." At least that was true; I seldom saw Fawzi except at Embassy receptions and the like, or when Weller was out of town and something needed to be brought by his office. Weller loved talking to him alone, and for all I knew they used the Cone of Silence to make sure the NSA wasn't listening in.

"I will talk to him tomorrow about meeting with the Ambassador to inform the government, as opposed to the Defense Ministry." Helloo-oo, I thought, in most of these tiny countries, the Defense Ministry is the government, but decided discretion was definitely the better part of valor on that one. "And I'll talk to him about fixing this so it's the amendment we're supposed to get."

"Michelle." There were so many things wrong with that sentence, the worst of them being the assumption that we were *supposed* to get anything. We're lobbyists, I thought, and a small-potatoes firm at that; we only get what we beg for, and all of it can be taken away at any moment. "We'll take what we got and live with it. That's my job, deciding what's gettable for all the clients, and this is the best we'll get."

"Jesus, you act like I don't know anything."

"It's not that." It probably is, though, I thought; the biggest button of mine she keeps pushing is this idea that she knows the system and there's nothing I can teach her. "This is one of the things you have to learn: it sometimes works out this way. Michael talks to certain Members alone. I talk to certain staff alone. It's the only way to do it—most of them don't like to cut deals with witnesses present."

"She didn't cut you a deal. She screwed you."

Well, yeah, but that was the plan. And it was way too much to explain to Michelle.

"I need to finish this memo before the mark-up," she said, turning back to her computer and beginning to type. At least she didn't just tell me to fuck off, I thought, or walk across the room and slug me, so I guess I'm coming out of it okay.

As I walked out, I wondered if there was any way to rescue a professional working relationship with her, and whether it was worth the trouble.

* * *

Three days later, I stood nervously in the outer lobby of Sen. Jacob Colbert, the junior Senator from New Jersey and another of those East Coast Republicans with a decent environmental record. Colbert's offices lie on the first floor of the Hart Senate Office Building, a soulless, modernist building whose only saving grace is the massive Calder sculpture in the six-story lobby. The large office lobby space, with its two receptionists and their constantly ringing phones, its television tuned continually to Senate Floor proceedings, and its standard issue office furniture, mocked the smaller, squatter offices of the Russell and Dirksen Buildings—the older ones, the ones with character—in a way that belied the larger size that gave Hart offices their limited appeal.

I was here to save my African coastal fisheries amendment, and Jacob Colbert seemed as good a prospect as I was going to find. A former State Senator in New Jersey, Jacob Colbert had built a career around protecting the New Jersey shore and leveraged that into a U.S. Senate win in 2000 and reelection in 2006. He didn't have much of a foreign policy focus, other than the obligatory participation in Iraq, Iranian nukes, and Middle East peace debates that everyone had to be part of. But if Peter was right, his defense and foreign policy staffer, a young woman by the name of Erin Monaghan, was eager to get her boss more focused on international environmental issues, especially around the foreign aid bill.

"Mr. Matthews?" a small voice said from behind me.

I turned, and the words "young" and "not a player" came immediately to mind. In D.C., you learned to trust intuitive responses, because they represented your animal instincts rearing their ugly—but by and large useful—heads. I couldn't have told you how many times I'd been walking the halls in a Senate or House office building, going about my business, and suddenly felt "danger" bells ringing in my head, only to turn and see the one person in Congress I didn't want to run into that day coming down the hall toward me. Sometimes, it was even in time to get away, but regardless it was a sense that seldom let me down.

By young, I mean she was *really* young, both physically and, from the deer-in-the-headlights look in her eyes, professionally as well. And by "not a player," well, she was pretty enough and dressed quite professionally, but that wasn't the criteria that made a player. There was a look, not so much one's clothes or appearance, but attitude, carriage, in the way somebody walked, in her ability to meet your gaze without looking away, in the level of comfort in the way she exhibited, just in the way she stood. It was all a mix of factors, indefinable and subconscious, that created snap judgments a real Washingtonian trusted implicitly. And this girl, well, she wasn't a player. No, sirroonie.

"Hi, Erin, Ed Matthews. Peter Chase sent me, told me that I should speak with you." I gave her my trust-me face, the one vacuum-cleaner salesmen used to use as they tried to inveigle their way through someone's front door.

"Peter sent you?" A light glow came to her cheeks, accompanied by a shy smile. Goddammit, I thought, if that sonofabitch is using me to get in this girl's pants, I will absolutely kill him.

"Yes, he spoke very highly of you," I replied. The blush deepened. Shit. I continued anyway; I had no choice. "We have an important amendment we're working on, and he thought you'd be interested. It involves biodiversity in Africa."

"Biodiversity is an area where the Senator has a strong interest."

"Well, I think you're being a little modest," I replied. I looked over to the receptionist with a smile, to draw her into the conversation, create that undercurrent of a "we" in my words. "The Senator's record on environmental and sustainability issues is pretty stellar and predates his time here in Washington."

Erin took the bait. Looking down, she said, "Have you worked with our office before?"

Well, that question showed some smarts; it's a way of saying, "is there somewhere I can validate your credibility?"

"No, I haven't had the opportunity. But Peter felt that this amendment is one the Senator would want to support. Do you have a few minutes now, or should I come back?"

"Why don't we sit here for a second?" The tentative yes: I won't throw you out, but then again I'm not letting you in either.

"Thanks." I took the end of the couch facing away from the door, so I wouldn't be distracted by it opening and closing as constituents and tourists floated in and out. She sat at the far end, again indicating her uncertainty. She wasn't sure about me yet.

My mind raced. I had prepped Peter for a phone call from her, pitching the amendment to him in the way I knew he'd want to hear it: protecting what remains of the badly depleted fisheries off the coasts of Africa, through the development of greater indigenous capacity to monitor and protect the stocks. But I knew Peter ahead of time, so I knew that he would respond equally well to the two parts of that argument: one, that we have to do what we could to protect them, and two, that the locals had to be trained to be able to protect the fisheries over the long term, "capacity-building" in Washington-speak. This kid I didn't know from Adam, so I wasn't sure what argument was going to work.

Worse, now that I knew Peter was trying to get her into the sack, I couldn't be sure what Peter would be talking about when he had her on the phone.

I decided to lead with coastal protection—the Senator's biggest achievements had been in fighting oil and gas drilling off the coast of New Jersey, so maybe I could spin out from that.

"I appreciate the time, and I'll try to make this quick." She smiled and nodded. A standard opening, pawn to Queen's 4 so to speak, but well received. "As you know, coastal protection is a global problem, whether it's protecting the New Jersey coast from oil platforms and their inevitable oil spills, or protecting Florida's southern coast from drug runners, or protecting the fisheries stocks off the coasts of Europe and Africa from being completely depleted by massive overfishing from South Korea, Russia, France, Spain, and other industrialized countries."

She was scribbling on her note pad—"S Korea Russia France Spain." I let her finish and went on.

"We're hoping to bring some resources to bear in one of those cases—Africa—to help African nations defend their own waters. We're looking to direct $15 million from the Administration's military aid budget to support biodiversity programs in Africa by building Africa's own coast guards and navies, so they can better protect those fisheries from, well, predators—there's nothing else to call them, predators."

"$15 million," she scribbled.

"We're not adding money to the budget"—Colbert was also something of a budget hawk—"we're just directing the funds to be spent in Africa on biodiversity."

"Fifteen million seems to be a lot."

Fifteen million dollars in Washington is sort of like spitting into the Atlantic, I thought. Just another sign of how junior she was.

"Well, you have to remember that the military aid budget is well over $4 billion total, so this is a pretty small percentage of that." True, as far as it went—with Israel getting $2 billion-plus a year, and Egypt getting $1 billion-plus, I was talking about a much smaller "rest of the world" budget that this money would be taken from. And $15 million in military aid for Africa was actually a lot more than normal, since after Israel and Egypt there was a whole list of countries that got some serious cash, starting with Pakistan, Turkey, Jordan, Morocco, and Tunisia, leaving scraps for the rest of the world. But I didn't expect her to pick up on that, and she didn't. That gave me another important clue about her: she's his foreign aid staffer, but doesn't know the foreign aid budget. Not uncommon, actually, among Congressional staffers, just another factor to keep in mind.

"Has anything like this ever been done?"

"Congress has a long history of making such recommendations in legislation," I replied. When they made it in legislation, of course, it was no longer a recommendation—it was a mandate. And the administration, all administrations, *hated* earmarks like this with a passion. But she hadn't asked me that.

"So what are you looking for the Senator to do?" Another good sign, focusing early on what I wanted out of her, not just my story. Problem was, I'd come here asking for her to try to squeeze it into the bill before the Committee considered it the next week; talking with her, I knew she'd never be ready to move that quickly. I made a snap decision.

"We'd like the Senator to consider offering it as a friendly amendment when the bill is on the Senate Floor."

She looked confused and seriously taken aback. "But if Peter supports the amendment, I don't ..."

"Here's Peter's problem." I slid along the couch toward her a little and lowered my voice, like it was a secret. "His appropriations guy forgot to request the amendment in the bill, and now it's too late even for his office to seek additional amendments." That was as close to a bald-faced lie as I ever wanted to get, since the Senate Majority Leader can move mountains if he wants to. Peter had agreed to confirm this story if she asked; it gave him a rare opportunity to get a dig in at Roger. The two of them had an unhealthy competition going on, both very active on foreign aid bills and highly effective despite not being on the Subcommittee staff. Roger was far better at the details and the process, but Peter always better positioned, working in offices like the Majority Leader's.

I reminded myself to tell Roger how I'd pitched it; if he found out from Peter, it would be another black mark in their unending struggle, and that one would be my fault.

"I know it sounds crazy, given who he works for, but it's true. He's totally stuck, and you're the only person he could think of who can help us all out."

Looking me in the eye, she sat perfectly still for a few moments, waiting for me to give it away, maybe waiting for me to roll my eyes and say, "just kidding, it's all bullshit," or maybe just for me to break out into an uncontrolled sweat. Thing is, after a few hundred of these kinds of meetings, you can do them in your sleep and pretty much without any shame.

"Do you have any background material I can read?"

Gotcha. "Not with me right now. I just happened to be talking about this with Peter, and when he said you were the person I needed to see"—

here she blushed again, and I knew I had her—"I came straight over. I could pull something together and bring it by tomorrow." I tried to remember all the materials I'd Googled while planning out this amendment, the stuff I never needed with Roger because he bought the amendment straight out, and figured that, with a little work, I could have a decent package together by morning. If I hustled.

"I'll review it all and get back to you. And we'll definitely consider it." She glanced down at her notes for a moment. "It's definitely an area of importance for the Senator."

I stood, recognizing the end of the meeting. "Thanks. I appreciate it, and I really appreciate your coming out with no advance warning to talk to me." As she got up from the couch, straightening her skirt, I reached out to shake her hand. "I'll tell Peter, and I'll drop those materials by tomorrow."

As I turned to leave, she said, "Oh, I forgot. What will the Administration say?"

I turned back, surprised, and looked intently at her face. That was either the question of a real pro, hoping to catch me off guard, or just what she said it was, something she forgot. From her face, I couldn't tell.

"They'll oppose it. They oppose any Congressional limitation on how they spend their military aid." That was certainly true, and it wasn't just the current crop in the White House and the halls of the Pentagon; it was every Administration since the dawn of time. "That's one of the reasons that the fisheries off Africa have been so devastated. Even in the '80s and '90s the Defense Department knew Congress was concerned about this, and they've ignored it. So they'll oppose it, but probably not too vigorously— they worry much more about people who try to take away their money than people who tell them how to spend it."

She smiled at that. "Okay, that makes sense. Thanks again for coming." As she turned back to her office, I thought, I still can't tell if she held that question; I'll have to keep an eye on her.

Glancing at the receptionist, I said, "Thanks," before turning to the door and heading out.

* * *

"Senator," Tom tried again, "this is an important country, one that's vital to America's interests in that part of the world."

Good God, I thought, he may be my senior colleague, but I may just have to take a baseball bat to the man anyway. He was just so clueless.

It was Monday of the following week, two days before the Senate mark-up, and here I was babysitting Tom as he tried to sell Koliba to Sen. Cory VanderMeer, third-ranking member on the Republican side of the Foreign Operations Subcommittee, and another of Tom's wingnut right-wingers. VanderMeer was one of those who got into Foreign Ops because of the opportunity to push Jesus around the globe, a Mississippi Senator with a deep Christian bent and a former missionary to boot. He was typical of the kind of far-right Republicans who were Tom's bread-and-butter. But even he, we were finding, was smarter than to side with Koliba.

"Tom, my friend, that dog just won't hunt," he said, dragging out the most tired Southernism there was in Washington, but one that somehow still worked. "I can't put myself on the line for a despot."

"But sir, the President is a good friend..."

"Tom, Tom," VanderMeer interjected, raising his hand to wave off Tom's efforts, "I'm serious. I can't help you on this one."

Tom looked crestfallen, like that kid in the old movie who got bunny pajamas instead of a BB rifle. I was struggling to keep a straight face, what with how incredibly stupid it was of us to come in here and try this.

"Is there something else I can help you out with?" You had to love Senators; like I said, they just *hated* saying no.

I counted to five before saying anything, but when Tom just sat there, I decided to jump in.

"Well, Senator, there is one other client." Tom looked at me in surprise, but didn't stop me. "As you may know, we represent the Dungan-American Friendship Society, which promotes closer ties between the U.S. and the Dungan people of Kazakhstan. You may know that, while Kazakhstan is an important ally in the War on Terror"—I always had to throw that in with Republicans—"the government has been less than supportive of some basic human rights, including freedom of religion."

As I continued with the spiel, I found myself a little surprised at how easy it was for me to play this one, something I'd thought earlier in the year was like dancing with the devil. It was where the client found most resonance, and it would only help to have yet another Republican chiming in on our Dungan report language.

VanderMeer listened for another couple of minutes without interrupting and, when I was finished, said, "Now this is something I can get behind." Ka-ching! "I want you to work with Allison here"—the staffer in the meeting, his Deputy Chief of Staff instead of his foreign policy person, probably more an indication of how he viewed Tom than of how he thought of the bill in question—"on an amendment that we can push in Committee."

Whoops. I wasn't looking for an amendment, just some support for my report language. I smiled over at Allison and nodded, all the while thinking how I might talk her back from an amendment.

VanderMeer scooched forward in his chair and pointed at me. "This entire region of Central Asia, the 'Stans' people call them, it's an area that has never heard the word of God. It's time they do, and I'm happy to help make that happen."

Oy, I thought. I could feel my face kind of freeze up, while an image of Bao's smiling visage rose slowly in my mind's eye. Be careful what you wish for, I told myself. It might just come true.

Chapter 14

"Who's the fucking Queen of Sheba up there?" a voice behind me mumbled.

I laughed. It was pretty much what I'd been thinking, although not nearly so colorfully. Besides, I knew who it was: Michelle.

Washington will drive you crazy sometimes, going from its usual slow Southern crawl into a day at the races in no time. In a normal world, the Congressional process would consider bills in some semblance of order, with the bills authorizing the spending of money finished before the bills that actually spend it come up. And the House would act, followed by the Senate, with a little time in between each so everyone could get organized for the next step. For us on the outside, that made the process bearable and gave us the time to respond to one Committee's actions before racing on to the next. It gave us time to *breathe*.

Not this year: we'd had no action on foreign aid at all until the beginning of June, but from there on it had been insane. The House Subcommittee, Committee, and Floor had all passed the State/Foreign Operations Appropriations Bill within the first three weeks of the month. The Senate decided to skip Subcommittee and move straight to a full Committee markup, which was scheduled for the following day. Here it was June 27, and we were sitting in one of Congress's most cramped hearing rooms, S-116 in the Capitol Building, waiting for the Senate Foreign Relations Committee to start marking up its own batch of foreign aid bills. Most of these wouldn't ever see the light of day, and the entire hearing was little more than a feeble attempt to demonstrate the Committee's alleged relevance. But buried in that pile of bills, there was one on Ernest Koliba.

So on a day when we should have been out tying up loose ends on Approps, we were stuck listening to the Foreign Relations Committee.

Michelle was at the front of the room by the dais, greeting several of the Senators. Daughter of a former Democratic National Committee chairman, she was well known in senior Democratic Party circles, and one doesn't get much more senior than former Presidential candidate John Kerry and Presidential-Wannabe-Ain't-Never-Gonna-Happen Chris Dodd. Smiling and chatting amiably, she looked utterly in her element, one of the rare times I'd seen her like that.

Had I played my cards differently, I thought, maybe I could be up there with her. Back in my youth, though, instead of hanging out with my Democratic Party powerhouse like Michelle and her dad, I'd avoided Uncle Harry like the plague. He was a glad-hander, a big, gruff, smiling old goat who was always looking past you to the next constituent, or donor, or dignitary, never *there* with you. Now that I was in the business, I forgave him that, but as a kid it just rubbed me raw.

So she was an insider and I played around the edges. I didn't mind; it was never the way I wanted to do the business—at least, not until I'd stumbled into my Dungan client earlier this year. Now, I thought, now might be a good time to have those kinds of connections and a little more experience working them. At least Harry wouldn't seem so mysterious.

As she strolled back toward the seat I'd saved, Michelle was radiant in the afterglow of her chance meeting with the Senators. The people around us were watching, wondering, looking at her come down the aisle in her semi-trance. They didn't know her or know why she was important, or even whether she was important; they only knew that she talked and laughed and joked with Senators, so she must be someone, and they wondered who she was. It wasn't the person I wanted to be, but as she stepped over me to get to her seat, she was the one people were noticing.

Is this why I can't stand her? I wondered. Is this why she grates me like she does? Because she enjoys this sliver of life? Or is it just that she thinks this is the way every day is supposed to be?

"The Committee will come to order," the Chairman called, with a single, sharp bang of his gavel.

Settling back in my seat, I felt disturbed by my reaction to Michelle's display and, as the Committee got going in earnest, silently played through my interactions with her since she'd joined the firm. It wasn't so much our periodic arguments—like the recent Belkin Paris trip fight we had—for we always got over those and moved warily on. It was more the entire way she'd arrived at the firm and the way she saw her role. She'd arrived as royalty, even in our first meeting, an "interview" arranged by Michael despite the fact that Weller had already promised her the job. I knew from the moment we met that she would be trouble: she was primarily interested in all the lobbying she'd be doing, in exactly how much freedom she would have in her interactions with the Embassy and with the Congress, and in who would be backing her up with written materials and research. That alone was enough to flip me out, given that I'd spent my first two years with Michael serving as his writer/driver, among other menial duties, and had worked my way up. But it hadn't just been that, I thought, there was more than simple resentment to it.

At least that was what I'd been telling myself. But was it true?

Glancing at her, I saw that she was still basking in the conversation. I'd no idea of what they'd spoken, and she was dutifully taking notes of the Committee's deliberations, so it wasn't as if she were starstruck. No, she was in some new zone I'd never seen before. Feeling my gaze, she looked over at me briefly and smiled, raising her eyebrows to ask if there was anything I needed. I shook my head no.

So if this is her comfort zone, I wondered, why does every encounter I have with her feel like fingernails on a chalkboard?

She leaned in to me and whispered, "Chris wants me to tell Michael he says hello."

Chris? Chris Dodd?

Then again, there was that whole stuck-up, privileged bitch thing she had going. Maybe that's it, I thought, turning back toward the dais.

* * *

"Mr. Chairman, I would like to speak in support of the bill regarding the reprehensible Ernest Koliba."

I winced at that; somehow the gall of Senator Newman denouncing him as "reprehensible" right off the bat gave the discussion just a little extra edge.

While Newman continued, discussing Koliba's antics over the last year in some detail, I thumbed out a four-word message on my Crackberry, "Newman bill debate begun," and sent it off to Roger. With the device on silent, I watched the screen, waiting for his response.

"Im in mtg. All fnds?"

Jesus, the man needed to take a typing course. He wasn't even working off a Blackberry, since he simply couldn't tolerate them, but rather off his desktop computer and its standard keyboard. Earlier I'd stopped by his office to open up a chat window on his desktop—something else he was incapable of doing—and set it to beep loudly whenever I sent a note. Then I'd sent a "Test" note to him, to get the chat started so that he wouldn't even have to accept it. Even then, I thought, "Im in mtg" was the best he could do.

"Don't know," I thumbed. "Newman still talking. More to follow."

That probably wouldn't satisfy him, but it was the best I had at this point. He told me he wanted to know the moment it was brought up, but of course at this point he was probably cursing at his computer about my stupidity at contacting him before I even knew what the amendment was.

Michelle elbowed me, and I tuned back in to Newman's droning voice.

"... and as you know, I serve not only on this Committee and on the Defense Subcommittee of the Committee on Appropriations, where there are also funds that are increasingly spent in foreign countries in response to the War on Terrorism. Those funds do not receive the oversight that this Committee provides in terms of critical foreign policy issues, especially in the areas of democracy and respect for human rights. For that reason, and because President Koliba's actions are, Mr. Chairman, simply beyond the pale of what this Committee deems acceptable, I believe that we must condition all U.S. Government funding to that country, and not just the funds covered in the foreign aid bill. My amendment, therefore, would prohibit the spending of any U.S. funds to support the Koliba government ..."

I'd begun thumbing with the words "prohibit the spending," and completed the quote before sending the e-mail off to Roger.

His reply was almost immediate. "Postive?"

"It's a quote. Newman amendment: prohibit spending of any U.S. funds to support Koliba government." Sending it twice should satisfy him.

"Aprved?"

"Not yet," I typed in reply. "Jeez, give me a minute here."

Nothing. I smiled, seeing him in my mind's eye, staring at his computer screen, setting and resetting his glasses in place as he tried to think of a good response. This was one of those times when being one of the few folks in Washington who never swore in anger put him at a disadvantage.

I thought about sharing the exchange with Michelle, but thought better of it. It's bad form to joke around at a Committee hearing, especially when the Committee is in fevered debate on how best to screw your client. And, boy, were they taking off after Koliba; there wasn't a single voice on the Committee willing to stand up for the man. Even the Committee's Ranking Republican, Richard Lugar, reelected in 2006 into what had to be like his 312th term as the senior Senator from Indiana, was overcoming his usual willingness to allow the Administration to do almost anything they wanted and letting his disgust with Koliba's human rights record carry the day. After extended discussion, the legislation was approved on a voice vote, with several more voices chiming in than usual.

"Passed," I typed. "Voice vote. No objections. Tell them Newman did it. Go."

"Ill go wn redy."

I'll go when I'm ready? Chances are, he'd gotten up out of his chair right after sending that and headed directly over to the Armed Services Committee offices to be the first one in with the news. But that didn't mean he was going to let me get away with telling him what to do.

Roger, I thought, will always be Roger.

* * *

Leaving the room after the mark-up, I walked straight into Philip Galsworthy as I turned a sharp right out the door.

"Michael couldn't be here?" he asked.

Ah, he was waiting for me. Bad form, Philip, mocking your enemies, at least before you've fully defeated them. Another Washington rule, especially for lobbyists but also true for staff: don't try to kill someone unless you can kill him utterly, totally dead. And sometimes, even the dead can come back to haunt you.

"No, he's out of town on business." Another not-quite-a-lie; Michael decided to work from the house that day and, after all, lived in Maryland. "We took particularly good notes for him, though—he'll hear just about every word."

"Yes, but I so wanted to hear his opinion of the day's proceedings," he continued, as if being solicitous.

Asshole, you just wanted to dance on his corpse. "I'm sure he'll regret the Committee's actions."

"Mmm," he murmured, like a cat with the mouse still caught in his teeth, not sure what to do next. I found it a profoundly disturbing moment, the corridor crowded with lobbyists and staff debating the morning's events, Philip much too close to me, his oily hair slicked down against his forehead, striving silently inside himself to find just the right insult, or perhaps the right *bon mot*, to dig the knife in further.

"Sorry," I interjected, "I have to run to a meeting." I slid to the left, edging two young women slightly backward, nodded in apology, and turned back to Philip as I moved into the gap I'd made. "I'll tell Michael we chatted."

He looked ready to respond at last, but I turned away, bolted into the crowd, and was gone.

* * *

"Oh, sweet Jesus, there it is," Charlotte said, bits of Special K falling from her lips as she read the headline. It was below the fold, with another Supreme Court ruling narrowing affirmative action taking up most of the top of the page.

"There's what?" I asked, mildly annoyed as I looked up from my end of the sofa. My copy of the *Post* was open to the Nationals' results. Having a decent baseball team in Washington was once again proving to be too much to ask for.

"Richardson," she said, "in full glory."

"Jesus, they used one of the photos?" I replied, rummaging through the various sections trying to find the story. I didn't need this right now.

Another small flurry of Special K flew. "No, you idiot, of course they didn't print the picture. They have the whole story, though. Listen."

Congress is bracing for yet another scandal this week, as Representative William E. Richardson, Democrat from Georgia, announced on the House Floor late yesterday that he had been served with a subpoena by the Justice Department. Justice sources, speaking on condition of anonymity, stated that the subpoena related to an ongoing investigation of Richardson's relationships with several female Congressional staffers and lobbyists renting rooms in a house he owns on Capitol Hill. The investigation, which is still in its early stages, focuses on allegations that Richardson has provided earmarks and other favors to the women and their employers in exchange for sex.

"Well, the investigation may be in its early stages," I said, "but they've got the whole damned story right there."

She smiled over at me, seductively. "I love this town. They know how to prioritize the news, and being on the inside we get to know it before anyone else."

I smiled back at her. Despite myself, and my friendship with Will, this was fun. "How long 'til he resigns?"

She leaned back and laughed. "Well, at least his tenants weren't minors."

"Yeah, and none of the *she*'s was a he." I paused, walking through Richardson's committees and caucuses in my mind. "Besides, he's not on any of those, 'Hey I Swear I'm Not a Pedophile' caucuses, like that asshole Foley from Florida a few years back."

She lowered the paper again. "True. It didn't happen with Congressional pages, either, or somewhere in the Capitol complex. How long did Foley last? A week?"

"More like forty-eight hours, but this is more about the money and the lobbyists than the sex," I said, "more of a Cunningham. And he lasted something like seven months, right?"

She leaned her head back, the line of her neck a slight parabola. Her narrowed eyes and the slightest bob in her chin implied she was counting. "Five," she said finally, with a sharp nod. "June to November." Satisfied, she turned back to the paper.

"So at this point," I agreed, "there's more likelihood people will believe it right off the bat, he's got...?"

"Three months, max. In the meantime?" She looked up from the paper and smiled at me. "Dead man walking."

* * *

The Senate State/Foreign Ops mark-up began later that same day, promptly at 2:30 p.m. At least, that's when the gavel first hit the table calling the Subcommittee to order. It took another ten minutes of Subcommittee members chitchatting and showboating to get the actual mark-up started, and sure, the meeting was scheduled for two o'clock, not two thirty, but nonetheless, it got off promptly at two thirty. Ish. Sort of.

In the run-up to the meeting, I'd been hanging out by the doorway, pretending to stretch my legs. Michelle held my seat over by the window looking out onto the Capitol lawn, but I had a few last-minute tidbits for staff and could only catch them as they came in the door. Most importantly, I needed to talk to Roger—I hadn't yet told him about my lack of progress on the coastal fisheries amendment and the need to push it to the Floor. Roger hated worrying about Floor amendments, which were much trickier to slip into a bill. Just another opportunity for him to bite my head off, I thought, hearing his reedy voice rolling down the hallway toward me.

As he came closer, several of us stepped forward at once. We were like street beggars, groveling for change. Roger's attention was caught first by one of my fellow gypsies, as he stopped briefly to refuse her request. Before I could interrupt, he turned to me and asked, "Who's carrying it?"

I stammered in reply. "I, well, she's, I, uh…" I stopped to catch my breath, looking around momentarily as if for support. There was no one there. "Not today," I said, turning back to face Roger. "It's not going to happen until the Floor."

"What?" His eyes grew large behind his glasses, and a flurry of blinking and twitches were visible before he turned to scuttle away. Over his shoulder, he called out, "That's ridiculous. That's a bad idea."

So was taking the amendment out of the bill, you boob. "Sorry, Roger, there's nothing I can do."

"Tell me about it."

While Roger was still getting settled, Sen. VanderMeer arrived, pausing momentarily to squeeze my arm as he headed into the room. I smiled, and pointed Tom out, over on the other side of the room. VanderMeer gave him a little wave on his way to the table.

I hadn't wanted Tom at the mark-up, given how badly he usually took these committees' open assaults on Koliba, but VanderMeer's interest in helping out with the Dungan mandated bringing him along. I might get an acknowledgment out of the Senator, but action, that was more likely to come if VanderMeer knew that Tom was watching over him.

It was a long, slow slog, two and a half hours of listening to blather, before we got to the discussion on Kazakhstan. That was normal; the Central Asia portion of the bill was buried in Section 6, the butt-end "General Provisions," little snippets of legislation tacked on either to keep the

Administration honest by making them send a bunch of useless reports up to Congress or, more often, to keep various interest groups happy. Like us.

"Mr. Chairman," VanderMeer intoned with his serious voice, "I have a concern about the provision in the bill referring to Kazakhstan, Section 678, and whether we need to further restrict our assistance to that country given their abhorrent disregard for religious and ethnic freedoms."

At those last words, Sen. Belkin suddenly snapped to attention, while Raymonda, seated next to him at the table, stopped the conversation she was having with the junior staffer behind her and spun around to face VanderMeer.

Big alarm bells went off in my head. I'd expected them to question VanderMeer's amendment, but I hadn't expected them to freak out about it. Something was wrong here.

"Please proceed, Senator," the Chairman responded.

The next few minutes went by in something of a blur, for there was way too much going on all at once. After confirming that Michelle was taking rabid notes on the discussion, I focused on watching the room and tracking the varied reactions. First off, I thought I'd talked Allison out of the amendment, but she wasn't in the room and VanderMeer's foreign policy staffer was up by the table, kneeling next to the Senator feeding him notes and, during the debate, whispering arguments to him.

More important were the reactions of Raymonda and Sen. Belkin. After only a few moments of listening, Raymonda flipped her binder of talking points papers open to a specific section and plopped it in front of Belkin. In the ensuing debate, Belkin fiercely debated Kazakhstan and Nazarbayev, mostly reading from the notes but also throwing in a few shots off the top of his head.

Meanwhile, the crowd in the room was showing a lot of excitement too. Four undistinguished young guys in high-priced suits, who'd already struck me as out of place in this crowd and a couple of whom at least I'd assumed were working for Shaddock Mills, were set all atwitter by VanderMeer's move. Two rows ahead of me, on the other side of the room, I could see them stiffen, redden, and begin whispering furiously to one another. After some discussion, one bolted from the room, taking the cell phone from his pocket to dial as he went; a second began thumbing furiously on his own Blackberry; while the other two began taking notes. Maybe they're *all* working for Shaddock Mills, I thought.

It made no sense to me that there were talkers prepped against this, but Belkin's notes were good, a disturbing sign. The counterpoints he was making matched VanderMeer's arguments point by point. Either someone had been reading over his shoulder, or they'd spent a tremendous amount of time and energy murderboarding every argument that could be put forward. If that was true, someone was paying a boatload of money to prep for amendments that might not even get offered. It also meant that there was something serious to defend here, something I wasn't yet seeing. In this business, you didn't spend that kind of time and energy figuring out how to defend some dimbulb autocrat off in Central Asia. There was something more here, but for the life of me I couldn't tell what it was.

The debate ended when Belkin convinced VanderMeer that, at this critical time in the—you guessed it—War on Terror, approving such an amendment would not be in the interests of U.S. national security. He also promised to work with the Senator as the bill progressed, another of those Washington weasel ways of saying he was going to try to sweep it under the rug. VanderMeer, who hadn't intended to do anything until his meeting with Tom and me, looked surprised and seemed happy to back down from his colleague's assault. The meeting ended shortly thereafter.

Staying where I was, I watched the crowd disperse slowly out into the halls. The three guys in suits proceeded quickly into the exit, each working a cell or Blackberry as they headed out. Raymonda stood still by the table, watching the crowd as if trying to find someone or something. Luckily I'd never told her about my Dungan, or from her look she'd have been over in the corner beating me to a pulp. Roger, meanwhile, glared at me again as he left. The VanderMeer amendment? Or still just pissed about there being no Colbert amendment?

Something was very wrong.

Not a good place to be this late in the year.

* * *

In the hall after the mark-up, as the crowd slowly thinned, Mourad approached. He'd been in the back of the room, sitting between two human rights advocates who apparently didn't recognize him. For the liberal side of the aisle, Morocco was one of this year's bad guys, someone—whoever made these decisions from on high—having decided that once again Morocco's hold on the Western Sahara, one of the most pitiful and pitiless scraps of land on the planet, needed to be a high priority for Congressional debate and derision.

Mourad was there to monitor Congress's fruitless efforts to demand that Morocco straighten up and fly right. They weren't nearly as harassed as our client Koliba, of course, but being Moroccan Mourad actually took it worse than we did—for all the shit Congress heaped on our client, they were never talking about *me*.

"So they weren't too bad," I said to him as he walked over. "Not as bad as our guy got, anyway."

Mourad laughed. "Yes, my friend, President Koliba did not have his best day in that room today."

I shrugged. "It all could have been worse." The prohibition on aid to Koliba had passed as written, without any need for debate but with, as had been happening throughout the year, extended caterwauling about the evil nature of our client. It was, also as usual this year, the one bad result coming out of the day. "Other than Koliba, the day went well."

"Well, Koliba and the debate on Kazakhstan."

I grinned, and glanced quickly around to see if anyone was close. "I'm not sure what all that meant yet, but Belkin sure was on the warpath."

Mourad smiled. After a pause, glancing away to look at the dissipating crowd, he asked, "You have anything else major out there?"

He knows something, I thought; looking away was Mourad's "tell." "I'm not sure I know what you're asking."

"It is an environmental program, I think. For Africa."

Peter, I thought, Peter must have told him.

"Yes, it is," I said, smiling, "although I'm not sure this is the best place to discuss it. Perhaps I could come by the Embassy sometime. It would have to be a Senate Floor amendment at this point, so I have some time."

"I believe it is something we would have an interest in," he responded, looking me in the eye now, "from what I have heard."

"Well, between you, me, and Peter, yes, it is," I replied. Mourad raised an eyebrow. I'd been right. "But we should talk at the Embassy," I continued, looking around at the few stragglers remaining.

Mourad nodded. "Call Mrs. El Ayoubi to arrange a time."

"I will." Maybe, I added to myself; I'm not sure I need your help, my friend. Smiling, I turned to head on out.

* * *

At this stage of the process, my biggest problem was the fact that I had no idea what the hell was going on with regard to Kazakhstan and my little friends, the Dungan.

Luckily, there are ways to figure that kind of thing out in Washington. None of them are direct—like running up to your opponents and asking, "what the hell's going on?"—but they can be just as effective.

I wasted much of a morning later that week at a trade hearing pursuing one such strategy, all for the sake of a five-minute conversation.

"Would the gentlemen please take their seats so that the Subcommittee can bring the hearing to order?"

This was a little off my normal beat, the House Ways and Means Trade Subcommittee's annual shouting match on Canadian lumber. Not that I was staying for the whole thing—the hearing promised to go deep into the afternoon.

The large Ways and Means hearing room was packed. Many of the Members were off the dais or leaning over it, schmoozing with the occasional constituents and the oh-so-many lawyers that were present. Almost the entire Subcommittee appeared, since lumber was one of the biggest money trees a Trade Subcommittee member had to shake. Lots of Members meant lots of question-style statements about their deep concerns, their tremendous interests in the issue, the many years they'd fought for justice for America's lumber industry, yutta, yutta, yutta, blah, blah, blah. This was going to be a long day.

Canadian lumber is the *Jarndyce v. Jarndyce* of U.S. trade policy, a never-ending battle between two completely conflicting lumber economies over America's "dumping" laws, where only the lawyers and lobbyists make any money and both make it by the truckload. Every time the U.S. housing market slows, American timber owners stop feeding trees to their mill yards while the Canadians, looking to protect jobs, just keep cutting and shipping their wood to the U.S. When prices fall below the American market price, U.S. producers bring a dumping claim, and the lawyers and lobbyists get to work, for years at a time. It's thousands upon thousands of billable hours, and with so many possible clients wanting in on the game—U.S. lumber producers, timber owners, unions, and home builders, and similar groupings of Canadians—any trade lobbying firm that couldn't get a few years worth of this business just wasn't trying hard enough.

My target this day was near the front of the room, a little off to my left, his thick white hair gleaming, J. Riley MacGonagill, the old Kennedy Administration hand who'd been handling British Columbian lumber companies since the dawn of time. That wasn't why I was hoping to catch up with him at the hearing, of course; I was here to talk to him about his law firm—Shaddock Mills. Around MacGonagill was a sheaf of nameless, faceless lawyers from the firm, already a global legal powerhouse when they stumbled into the lumber game by convincing MacGonagill to join them. Off to his right, closer to the witness table, the blue-suited crowd representing American lumber, all stiff, solemn, and faceless, peering around the room to see what other firms might somehow have joined into this hunt. If you listened closely, you could almost hear the tick, tick, tick of the seconds, minutes, and hours of billable time creeping by. No wonder no one was in a hurry to get the hearing started.

Three panels on lumber today, the first made up of Administration witnesses, the other two of private witnesses. It was a scary prospect, what with most of the testimony coming from economists hired by one side or the other to argue their arcane case, arguing about how many thousands of board feet were being shipped, the inherent unfairness of Canada's long-term Tree Farm Licenses, insanely obscure academic jargon like the "Nordhaus effects test," etc., etc., incoherent bullshit that would go on and on for hours.

I figured I had about ten minutes, what with Chairman having made that first call to order and the Members still scattered around chatting up the various teams of lawyers. Folding my paper, I headed straight for MacGonagill.

"Hello, Riley," I said, holding out my hand. "It's been a couple of years."

He smiled broadly, his rheumy eyes twinkling, and took my hand in both of his, shaking it slowly. "Edward, my boy, what are you doing here?"

I'd met Riley when we'd landed a small contract for a Quebecois lobbying group, feeding at the lumber trough for almost three years while accomplishing, like everyone else in this particular game, absolutely nothing. I'd first seen him at one of the never-ending sessions when all the lobbyists on the Canadian side got together to discuss strategy, three or four people representing each firm, haggling pointlessly for hours over whose tactical moves were better than who else's, all the while amassing those hours to bill back to the client. Riley and I would inevitably find ourselves over by the coffee, standing around trying to ignore the foolishness, the only two in the room willing to admit that the whole thing was a sham. Not that it stopped us from billing the time, but at least we knew, right?

"Well, we like to keep an eye on past clients that might come back, and lumber just never seems to go away."

Riley smiled, looking at me expectantly.

"Okay," I said, laughing a little, "that's bullshit. I have a question about your firm."

He laughed and said, "Yes, I've been asked about you. They're wondering about this Dungeon group you're working with."

"Dungan," I said quietly, stepping in a little closer to him. One of the associates to Riley's right looked up from his seat, glancing at me and then at Riley. MacGonagill glared at him, so he ducked his head back into his notes. "So what's their take?"

"They're just curious," he said. "They'd never even heard of the client until someone over at the White House called them."

The White House? After what Eleanor told me, that would presumably be the Vice President's office, but who the fuck told *them*?

"I assume they're not worried."

He laughed quietly. "My boy," he said, "we don't worry about firms your size." Ouch, I thought; something of a blow to my pride. Still, it was a relief: while they seemed to be everywhere I was, and they certainly had prepped their Senate Committee people exceptionally well, it didn't sound like they were targeting me. From the sound of it, Shaddock Mills had us on their radar screen but weren't taking us very seriously.

"Not to worry, son," Riley continued, "I told them you're too smart to fuck with a major U.S. ally represented by a firm that's asshole buddies with the Veep." He put an arm around my shoulder. "You are too smart to do that, right?"

Chapter 15

August is a strange and ugly month in Washington. The streets are filled with tourists, despite the monstrously evil heat and humidity. Everyone and everything slows to a crawl, from the cabbies in their dilapidated old hacks, a.c. wheezing like an asthmatic smoker drawing his last breaths, to the pitiful softball teams struggling to keep playing through the damp, heavy air hanging over the National Mall. Late afternoon flights from National and Dulles Airports are subject to long delays when the almost inevitable thunderstorms roll through, drenching the city but never seeming to relieve the heat.

The August Recess, Congress's annual holiday from the beginning of the month through Labor Day, is a holdover from the days before air conditioning. Prior to the arrival of that glorious invention, it was deemed too hot to live and work in the District of Columbia, filled-in swamp that much of the city core is. This despite the fact that most Congressional buildings and rooms—such as the glorious old Supreme Court room on the first floor of the Capitol Building—are quite cool during the hottest of days, thanks to their thick stone walls. But apparently it was the going back and forth between home and office that was too much for the delicate Congressmen and Senators of those more genteel days, and the August Recess became the annual tradition it remains today.

Maybe it was still that problem of going back and forth from home to office. Or maybe the simple fact that, by the end of a long, hot July generally marked by ugly partisan debates over legislation designed more to "energize the base"—flag burning, estate taxes, the occasional renewals of the Voting Rights Act—than to actually accomplish anything meaningful, after a month like that everybody just needed to get the hell out of town so they could settle down, get themselves focused and organized, and come back to Washington ready for those few remaining months spent fighting over the things that really mattered: the money bills.

This year the House remained in session until deep into the night on Saturday, August 4, passing the FY 2008 Defense Appropriations Bill a little after 1:00 a.m. so that they wouldn't be heading home empty-handed with the country at war. As a result, the Recess didn't start off until the following morning, Sunday, the fifth, when it was launched with a bang, a front-page follow-up *Washington Post* story on Will Richardson. This one focused on an entirely new angle to me, reports of "house parties" that Will threw, small, intimate (in more ways than one) get-togethers where the Congressman and four of his dearest friends would gather with his five female tenants over a catered dinner to eat, drink, and cavort the night away. The story read like it had been leaked from the FBI in the apparent hopes of scaring participating Members of Congress to come forward—it was a standard trick in corruption cases. It included several sordid details, the choicest of which was the fact that one lobbyist tenant—immediately dubbed the Black Widow—apparently requested specific Members to be invited as her partner for the evening. No Member names were included in the article, launching a massive blast of rumors and unfounded allegations throughout the blogosphere.

It was a bad way to start the Recess, remembering as I did Will's invitation to join in one of those parties and how close I'd come to saying "yes." I never told Charlotte about that invite and couldn't tell her now—it would sound too much like I was coming clean before she heard something. Besides, at this point I had something much more serious I was hiding.

I must have read that story three times before heading off to the shower.

* * *

That Monday morning, I decided to try once more with Erin Monaghan to see if there was any progress to be made on my African coastal fisheries amendment.

I'd been back by Sen. Colbert's office twice since our first meeting, once when Erin wasn't around and once just before the mark-up when we chatted briefly. That time, I told her about all the effort I was making to find another Senator to support the amendment in Committee, telling her I was "doing everything I could" to get it into the bill. That, of course, meant nothing—in Washington, "yes" means "yes," "no" means "no," and "I'll do everything I can" means "no." It wasn't entirely a lie, for even though I knew when I said it that there was nothing I could do, I didn't actually tell her I was doing anything—so it was more of a way of avoiding the painful truth than a lie. And now that the mark-up was over, I needed to tell her my best hadn't been good enough and get her focused on moving it herself.

I lucked out when I got to Colbert's office; Erin was there and, true to the receptionist's promise, came "right out" about twenty minutes later.

She was preceded through the door to the back office by a large stack of binders and loose papers, all of which seemed on the verge of toppling as she chased them into the front room. Pausing, she righted the stack, and herself, before coming forward toward me.

"Can I help you with those?"

"Thanks, no," she responded, the pile balanced precariously as she freed her right hand, pushing her glasses back up her nose, before quickly sliding the hand back under her pile. She peered through her glasses at me, tilting her head slowly back to keep up with them as they slid again down her nose. Resisting the urge to push them back in place, I asked, "Have a few minutes to talk about the Committee mark-up?"

Glancing around, she saw that the couches were filled with constituents, most of them in shorts and sneakers—meaning real constituents, the voting kind, as opposed to the Washington reps for the State's largest employers. She looked back at me, trouble written all over her face, and said, "Let's go back to my desk."

Ducking ahead of her, I reached the door first, opening it quickly so she could sneak through with her pile. I followed her down the hall past the first sets of cubies and up the stairs. At the top, she turned an immediate left into her space, desk meticulously clean until she dumped her pile of binders on it before sitting. Coming around behind her, I glanced at the distant window and the many office spaces between here and there. This looked to be the worst positioned space on the floor. Not one of the more senior people in the office then, was she? Not that I hadn't guessed that already, but in cases like this, one always hoped to be proven wrong.

But I had to play the cards I'd been dealt. Colbert, and therefore Erin, was my only way out of the mess Roger had gotten me into.

"Looks like you're having a busy week." I began sympathetically, giving her the boy-I-understand-your-plight approach. It was the beginning of the Recess, so she should have been able to relax a little, but the mess on her desk implied that for her there would be no rest.

"Yeah, I'm really busy right now." She reached into the pile of papers and removed a folder. "I have a lot of appropriations issues taking my time, especially preparing for VA-HUD."

VA-HUD, Veterans Administration, Housing and Urban Development Appropriations Bill, one of the great cash cow bills for Congress, incredibly useful for grandstanding and partisan gimmickry. Everything bad about Washington, D.C., all rolled into one bill. "I didn't know that was one of your areas," I said.

"Well, yes, veterans, housing, urban affairs, environment, telecommunications, and women's issues," she replied, still looking down at the folder in her hand. After the briefest pause, she looked up at me and said, "Oh, and foreign policy and foreign aid, of course."

"Of course." Last on the list, and only remembered as a throwaway. Told me a little something about office priorities. And it sounded like I needed to focus on the environment side of the argument, since that at least was fourth on her list as opposed to an afterthought.

She was still looking at me.

"Well, like I told the receptionist, I wanted to update you on our environment and coastal fisheries amendment in Senate Foreign Ops." That might have been pushing the point, since biodiversity and environment are two very different topics, but what the hell, I thought. Looking grim, I said, "We couldn't make it work."

"Oh, that's too bad," she said, her hands crossed in her lap.

"So I'm afraid we need the Senator to step up to help us out during the Senate Floor debate," I said after a few moments. I waited.

"Yes, but I can't do anything right now," she said. "There's just so much else to work on."

"It's okay," I said, looking down at my hands. "Really, not a problem."

I looked up at her again. She was very young by Washington standards. Long, brown hair hung straight, the college look that most Washingtonians quickly shed. Clear blue eyes, open wide to look at me, seemingly without seeing much of anything. An innocent face, or more precisely, the face of a true innocent.

"You're right to focus on the immediate," I continued, nodding, "and you can't work an issue until the boss is ready to deal with it. I'm betting that it will be just before the bill gets to the Senate Floor."

"Yes." She brightened, straightening up in her chair, as if freed from a weight. "Yes, we have to focus on this," she reached out to pat the precarious pile on her desk, "before we can move on to the rest of the bills." She turned to me and put her hands on her lap. She didn't even know the stand-up-to-force-me-to-leave trick yet. "So. Maybe we can talk when Floor debate gets closer?"

"They're saying that's right after the Recess." I smiled. "First week in September." Meaning, I thought, now is the time to deal with it.

"Then definitely by the end of August," she replied. "I'll definitely get to it then."

Dammit, I thought. Rising from my seat, I smiled down at her. "End of August it is. I'll be away a lot of the month, but I'll check in with you as we get close to Labor Day. Is that okay?"

She smiled up at me. "That's great. Thanks."

As I approached the stairs, I turned one last time and took three copies of an article from the manila folder I was holding. "Let me leave you this, at least. Front-page story from the *Wall Street Journal* a few weeks back on this very problem: Europeans destroying African fish stocks." It had come as manna from heaven, the perfect cover for a crazy Senate Floor amendment, the right-winger's financial bible identifying the issue as important—but only if I could get her to pay attention to it.

"Wow," she said. After peering at it for a moment, she placed it atop the pile on her desk. Later, she was saying again.

Walking back down the stairs on my way out of the office, I had an image in my mind of a dark, twisting road in northern New Hampshire where I'd come up around a bend one night only to find the proverbial deer in my headlights. That day I was driving carefully because of the wet roads, and I'd had plenty of time to stop. This time, though, as my mind replayed the meeting with Erin, the image in my head had me running the deer down, over and over again.

* * *

"Well, that was certainly a most informative presentation, Ed." It was Hendrickson, throwing it out there like he couldn't think of anything else to say. I looked over at Charlie, who seemed similarly baffled, and smiled.

We were two weeks into the Recess, and here I was, in Chicago's finest vegetarian restaurant, not that I could tell. It was some Indian joint whose name I'd forgotten as soon as I walked in the door, since I knew I'd never be going back *there* again. I'd flown out to Chicago that morning: the 9:40 a.m. United flight out of National put me at O'Hare by ten forty-five, time enough to limo into town for a noon meeting.

The meeting, back at the Association's office, had been fairly routine if somewhat smaller than I'd expected—only the four players from that first Washington visit, Kincaid, Hendrickson, Bao, and Charlie. I surprised myself with my ability to talk for thirty minutes about what we'd been up to so far, outlining the Committee hearings, the personal meetings, the discussions, the drafting sessions, etc., etc. Kincaid, of course, spent the entire meeting on his Blackberry, glancing up every once in a while to throw me a grim smile, while Bao sat attentively, alternating between watching me and looking at my PowerPoint. I was pretty sure he couldn't read anything on the slides, but he was taking his native politeness seriously.

For me, the meeting's highpoint, of course, had been the presentation of the second check, the second $180K, the whole reason for my trip out here. We were just about six months into the contract, meaning it was time for that second payment; and in our business, you never trusted those to the mail when you could pick them up face-to-face. So here I was.

Much of lunch, which Kincaid bowed out of, was taken up with the simple pleasure of watching Bao in his element. The restaurant was Indian, but the spirit was the same, and Bao, despite the need for Charlie's translations, was having a wonderful time, charmed by the restaurant and charming its caring staff.

Watching them interact, it was more like Bao was visiting someone's home than eating in their restaurant. His ordering indicated a broad knowledge of Indian food and spices that the waiters and, subsequently, the chef clearly enjoyed, and resulted in our getting a meal not off the menu but from the various mixes and matches that they shared. As plate after plate arrived at the table, each with its own special garnish, Bao played with them all, bowing deeply to accept their offerings and then insisting that they share in the dishes. They did, in a custom totally unfamiliar to me, and returned to the kitchen to bring more of everything they sampled. I joined in the tastings, mostly the kind of vegetarian items carnivores like me never experienced, simply to be a part of this odd pageant. Over time, Bao began to serve me, mixing chutneys and vegetables in ways I never could have, creating little bursts of flavors completely foreign to my palate. I marveled at the choices, laughing out loud at many of them, and always asked for more. Bao's eyes would narrow as he peered at his plate; consulting a waiter, and sometimes Charlie, he would reach delicately among the many plates to choose another entirely new taste—and with a thin smile hand it to me expectantly, watching carefully as I ate.

Bao said something in his native tongue to Charlie, who told me, "You are most polite and friendly to share with us in this way."

"No, not at all. You are sharing your food with me."

Bao laughed at the translation, rolling out a response in his peculiar lilting voice. He waved an arm, to indicate our colleagues. "But you are sharing our *way* of eating," Charlie invoked for him. "It is rare among your people." Bao smiled at me.

"Thank you," I said, "I am honored." And I was. But as I leaned in to attempt a bow, I could see Hendrickson, his mostly untouched plate before him, looking grim.

That's okay, I thought, I have the check in my pocket.

Emerging from the restaurant after lunch, we turned right out the door and began walking back to the Association offices. Charlie moved ahead with Hendrickson, while Bao and I began walking slowly behind them. Bao leaned on my arm for support.

"You are most kind." I turned, surprised. It was from Bao.

"Yes," he continued, "I talk little English. You are most human." He smiled up at me, his wizened face in a wide, knowing smile, and I laughed.

"Thank you," I said, tipping my head down. "You are most interesting, and full of surprises."

Bao looked at me quizzically and called out to Charlie something I couldn't understand. Charlie stopped and asked, "What was that last thing you said?"

I repeated myself. Charlie nodded. "Surprises," he said to Bao, "surprises," and then again something in his own tongue.

"Sur-prises," Bao intoned. "Surrr-prises." He looked up at me with a broad smile. "Yes, surrrr-prises."

* * *

"I didn't expect to see you here."

Michelle stood in the doorway of my office. She had a point—I'd promised to be out of the office for two full weeks, and here I was, late on Wednesday of the second week, scouring through the piles of paper on my desk. I'd done my annual summer visit with my folks in Maine, and Charlotte hers in Minneapolis, after which we met up in New York for a few days. We'd flown back into D.C. earlier that afternoon, and after dropping everything off at the apartment, Charlotte headed to the Hill and me to the office. We each had a few things to get off our desks before life got back to normal.

"I was hoping to get in and out without anyone seeing me," I replied. "It's six o'clock—what about you?"

"Just cleaning up a few things I need done before they come back."

It was another of the curses of Washington, falling behind during the year while Congress is in session, especially on anything that wasn't tied directly into their schedule—amendments, report language, questions for Committee hearings. The rest of the company's work—identifying potential new clients to replace the one or two you lose every year, developing proposals, learning new areas of the business that could be sold somehow—that stuff all fell by the wayside until Congress got out of town. Then when they did, you were so tired and cranky and needing a vacation of your own that you didn't do much of anything for a week or so, and before you knew it the Recess was almost over and you'd produced nothing.

"Did I miss much?"

"Just Gangaran's comments," she replied. "Other than that, it's been quiet."

"Gangaran?"

She snorted in that way she had, the one that annoyed me so much. "Jeez, you've only been gone two weeks and you've already forgotten? Koliba's Vice President."

"I know who he is," I snapped, glancing down at my desk and continuing my hunt through the piles. Despite all the work we'd put into the reception for him, in truth Gangaran was even less important than the standard U.S. Vice President, having no authority at all. And that Committee report I was looking for had to be in there somewhere. "What did he say?"

"He told a press conference that Koliba's sacking of the Supreme Court last year had hurt the nation, and that the Justices needed to be reinstated."

I sat. "He said what?"

"Yeah, that was pretty much Tom's reaction." Michelle smiled at me. "He actually decided to get on a plane and fly over there. In August."

The Democratic—oops, just kidding—Republic of Golongo sits right on the equator. Hottest place on the planet. I smiled for a second at the thought of Tom sweating like a pig in that hideous heat and humidity before refocusing as I remembered what Michelle had said.

"Gangaran can't have said that," I told her. "He's a figurehead—he's nobody."

"AFP"—*Agence France Presse*, the French version of AP—"and the BBC were both there. It was in the *Times*. That's why I thought you'd have seen it."

Crap, I thought; comes from being married to someone who totally let go of the office when vacation was on. Charlotte always freaked out if I started talking about the clients while on vacation. Ruins the mood, she'd say; it's hard enough that we both work the system without carrying it with us wherever we go. Like it was that easy to give up.

That was how I often found myself sneaking off to the business center of the hotels we were staying in, Googling our clients or pulling up the *Post* and the *Times* Web sites. This time, though, I hadn't been doing that. Part of it, I thought, was coming from my parents' house, which was a buffer of sorts between Washington and vacation time with Charlotte. I got to New York thinking about the folks, and the family, rather than work. Part of it—a big part—was my continuing guilt over the affair with Mary Anne in Paris, and my inner need to somehow make up for that. I'd been on my best behavior and, of course, missed something important that had gone to shit. Ain't it always that way?

"So what next?"

"We don't know," Michelle responded, laughing. "Haven't heard much from Tom, especially since last time he called the receptionist dumped him into Welly's voice mail. You should hear it. It's hysterical." She walked over to my phone, turned it around, and dialed into voice mail. Dialing in the code and extension number, she skipped ahead to the saved messages.

"Received Monday, August 17, at ten-oh-four," the metallic voice said.

There was a pause, strong static, and then what sounded like it could have been a long sigh before I heard, "Oh, Wellington, this is tragic. I don't believe it. I've been dialing for hours and hours." It was Tom, deep distress apparent in his voice even over those long distances, with long pauses between each sentence. "I just don't believe it. I wanted to report on my m-mm-my-unh-mm-meetings, well, planned meetings, to talk about what's next." A very long pause. "I don't know what to say. This is tragic, really."

Tom had the technology sense of a rock and apparently never learned how to boop and beep his way out of our voice mail system; in Washington, he probably just would have hung up the phone and called back. Here, though, his voice rambled on and on, the way one does when trapped in voice mail with nothing to say, only much more distressed. He didn't tell us anything about the situation there—for one thing, it's safest to talk in code when talking about the clients from their own turf, but more to the point this time it just seemed like he was totally bummed by being out there alone. It got more depressed as he went, more down, more desperate for someone to talk to, with no way to get out from the machine. I looked up at Michelle, who had a broad grin on her face.

"You realize you're enjoying this just a little too much?"

"Yes," she said, "but I've been waiting for two days for someone I could play it back to. There's no one else around."

At least she was smart enough not to play it for the support staff.

* * *

"Edward, my boy, so very good to see you," Harry boomed from the front porch as we approached. He held up his scotch as if in toast, his thin, ashen white legs peeking out between his overlong shorts and his Docksiders. Those sticks are barely holding him up, I thought, realizing once again how much happier we'd all be if he'd wear long pants to these damned parties. A lifetime without exercise takes its toll. "And Charlotte, my dear, so wonderful to see you."

Charlotte smiled up at him, her fake smile, the one she used for people she couldn't stand. "Senator," she said, "a pleasure as always."

He laughed. "Please, please, my dear," he said, taking her hand and drawing her into a one-armed hug, "out here I'm Harry." Even for people like you, he seemed to be saying, even for you.

Over his shoulder, Charlotte made a face at me. She'd come to dislike Harry intensely over the years, she simply couldn't tolerate the fakery.

"Walter," Harry suddenly boomed, looking past Charlotte to the next group coming in. She looked over at me as he breezed past her, or through her, sliding her to the side so he could greet the next set of guests.

"What a dick," she said to me, turning to storm away.

"Okay," I laughed, following after her, "you can either hate him for paying attention to us, or for ignoring us, but not both."

"He's such a *politician*," she replied without looking back. I caught the screen door before it closed behind her, half-running after her as she breezed through the living room toward the back lawn where the party was. "We're family, dammit."

"Well, not on Harry's side," I said, almost running to keep up. She was moving, having gone out through the back hallway down to the kitchen. "We're on Helen's side of the family, and even then she doesn't see Mom all that much."

"Will you stop apologizing for the man?" She stopped, finally, just before heading out the back door. Poking a finger into my chest, she continued, "You're always apologizing for him, just like you apologize for the system. He's a dick."

"He's my uncle, Sweetie. And for Chrissakes, will you keep it down?"

This screen opened from the outside, and a woman I didn't recognize entered the room. While I didn't know her, her formal Ann Taylor look at this allegedly casual party told me she was one of us, one of the Washington tribe, out here to see and be seen rather than for the food or the relaxation. My first thought was about what she'd heard, but I couldn't read her face that well.

Charlotte could see mine, though, and must have sensed that I was more worried about what this woman had heard than about what she was saying. Sliding aside to let the woman through, she stormed out the door and into the party. I kept an eye on the woman a little too long, still not seeing her give anything away, before heading out onto the lawn. By that time, I'd lost Charlotte in the crowd.

I paused to get my bearings. Uncle Harry's back lawn ran up against the waters of the Chesapeake Bay, the bay to my right and the land running straight down for a couple of hundred yards. The house was set close to the water, the living room angled to face into the sunset, a gap cut in the pines to give that room the view's full effect. Here on the back steps, I could see the crab pots steaming just off the back corner of the house, the picnic tables covered with paper and bits of smashed crab shells where some of our fellow guests had already been eating. This party was a food- and boozefest, eating and drinking going on all day long and into the night. The bar by the crab tables, though, would be stocked only with ice-cold beer and scotch, which weren't what I was looking for.

Somewhat to the left, away from the water, I could see the steam tables set up for the roast beef, lamb, and other delicacies that Aunt Helen would have arranged. Harry would have been happy with just the crabs and beer, a traditional Maryland feast to remind his lobbying friends how much he was at home in this environment. Helen, though, was the better hostess, looking to feed her guests well rather than to drive home a political point.

There, just to the right of the steam tables, I saw Aunt Helen, elegant as ever in a smart summer dress, chatting with a couple who looked like a Brooks Brothers store had exploded on them. He was in one of those greens that no human who hadn't won the Masters should ever be seen in, and she, well, she had just the kind of skirt-blouse-sweater-tied-around-the-shoulders-just-so combination that said, "I don't work, I've never had to, and wouldn't soil my pretty little hands even if Biff lost ever single dime he inherited." Just like you'd see at pretty much every summer party in Washington.

As I walked over toward her, I could see that Helen was disengaging from her companions, pointing them toward the food. She took Green Jacket Man by the elbow as she came around him, and I marveled as always at her skill in getting rid of people without them even seeming to notice what was happening.

"Eddie, welcome," she said gently as I approached.

"Aunt Helen," I replied, grimacing slightly. As I got closer, I continued, "I'm sorry about Paris. Really, I am."

She shook her head with a sad smile. "No, Eddie, I'm sorry. I shouldn't have laid that on you. You have a job to do." She tilted her head to the side, the smile still in place, a deep sadness in her eyes.

"Not that way," I said. "You were right, Helen. There are things I don't have to do. And things I shouldn't do, ever." She looked over at me, and I could see a tear welling in one eye. "It won't happen again."

"Thank you, Eddie." She looked down at the grass, watching where she placed her shoes, as if the immaculate lawn might hide some pebble or other obstruction. "I appreciate it."

"I'm just sorry—that's all." I took her arm in mine and, turning her slightly, headed her toward the bar. The good one. The one where Uncle Harry's wine collection was on display for all of us to savor—at least some of it was. Generally, the "very good" wines were there, the lowest grade Harry drank. The excellent wines, well, those were still hidden away, down in the wine cellar. For a summer party, though, the "very good" wines would be just fine for me.

As we arrived at the bar, she stopped and looked me in the eye. The tear was still there, in her right eye, no bigger but still there. "It's done, Eddie." She smiled and wiped quickly at her eye as she turned to the bartender. "Now I think I could use a cranberry wine spritzer. I have a long day ahead of me, so I'll stick with that."

I flinched, thinking of the $45 Chardonnay she was corrupting with cranberry juice. Then again, long before she'd told me how little she noticed the difference between Harry's wines and the $10.99 supermarket variety. Maybe she was just enjoying the idea of ruining a fine wine.

While the bartender poured Helen her drink, I looked over the row of diverse reds and whites behind him, two of this, three or four of that, recognizing several from the occasional dinners at Harry's. He obviously bought his wines by the case, I thought, probably billing everything to his campaign war chest, and used the leftovers for his lawn parties. It made for so much nicer a lifestyle having enormous campaign accounts to subsidize your standard of living.

"Could I see that one?" I asked, pointing to a lone French wine that, if I was right, was surely out of place. "No, to the right. Yes, that one."

As he held it out to me, I turned to Helen and said, "This shouldn't be here. It's the Chateaux Margaux I gave him on his birthday last year. It was a four hundred dollar bottle then, and must be more by now."

The waiter started to take it back, but Helen reached out and took hold of it. He held it out for her, delicately, as she read the label. "1985." She looked at me.

"That's the one."

"Open it," she commanded to the bartender. She stopped his protestation with one finger in the air. "Open it, and keep it hidden behind those others, just for my nephew here. And whoever he chooses to share it with."

She smiled over at me and gave me a light kiss on the cheek before turning to rejoin her guests.

I watched her walk away, smiling. Turning back to the waiter, I asked him, "If you open it now, how long should I wait before that first glass?"

* * *

Twenty minutes later, wine in hand, I set off to find Charlotte in the crowd. She wasn't by the steam tables, where I'd looked for her while procuring myself a plateful of items that would go well with a Chateau Margaux. I was planning to surprise her with it and also to see how well the wine opened up over the course of the afternoon. It was already quite magnificent, thank you very much, but I expected it to get better as time went on.

As I crossed the lawn back toward the house, I caught sight of her in the crowd near the crab tables. Must have found someone interesting to talk to, I thought, since Charlotte—after trying it once or twice—wasn't into smashing steamed crabs into tiny pieces so you could hunt for little bits of crabmeat. Wasn't worth the time or energy, she'd said. I had to agree with her, except on those rare occasions when I was in the mood for drinking really cold beer; I'd figured out years before that the crab smashing part was all about keeping you at the table longer, so you could pump down an extra two or three beers over dinner.

"Ed," I heard from my left and looked over to see Roger hustling across the lawn toward me, a plate of food in one hand, a half-filled glass of iced tea in the other. I stopped to let him catch up to me, thinking as I watched that I didn't feel like conducting any business right now. His plate, which looked empty from afar, proved to be holding five asparagus, two shrimp, and a single slice of roast beef, each carefully separated from the others by a good inch of empty plate. Jesus, I thought, no wonder you're so thin and pasty.

I took a long sip of the wine and savored it. "What's up?"

He came to a halt in front of me and stared, his eyes big, his glasses for the moment askew. "What are you going to do?"

I shook my head. "About what?"

"Gangaran."

"Oh, that," I said, annoyed. This was still my vacation. "He's the duly elected vice president, and he can say what he wants. It doesn't change anything."

"You don't know?" He reached out as if to take my arm, the tea and ice sloshing back and forth in his glass. He stopped to let them settle before continuing.

"He's dead, Edward." He was serious. "This morning. Butchered in his home with his entire family."

"That's impossible. The house is guarded by Government troops."

"That's your real problem," he said. "They weren't there. Sometime last night, they were withdrawn to the barracks, and this morning a mob attacked the house, hacked everyone inside to death with machetes, and burned it to the ground. When the police got there, they just watched."

Oh, shit.

Chapter 16

"Hello?"

Tom's voice came through as a hollow echo, a thin warble over a sea of static. For the last minute or so, all we'd been able to hear was some kind of rumbling or crashing noise, like the sound of a car accident that never seemed to end, along with screeches that could be screaming and yelling, or maybe just a screwdriver dragged along the sides of a Cadillac. We'd thought we'd lost the call and been hoping we hadn't lost Tom, given the reports we'd been reading on the Web of widespread rioting, military deployments, and random violence following Gangaran's murder.

"Dammit," I said quietly, to no one in particular, pacing back and forth in the cramped space between Michael's desk and the wall. It was the Wednesday after Labor Day when the news first broke; we'd waited one full news cycle to see if anything else happened—like maybe a coup, which in this case would have been good news—before checking in with Tom on the ground in Golongo's capital, Kambala.

This is so Tom, I thought. Too cheap to buy or even rent a satellite phone, despite the fact that most of his clients were in Africa, where phone service still sucks even at its very best. I'd spent the last hour and a half sitting on the other side of Michael's desk, dialing Tom's hotel while debating with Michael how we were going to deal with Gangaran's murder, and finally getting through once only to get cut off almost immediately by the switchboard. The second time we'd gotten a line through, around 11:45 a.m. our time, 3:45 p.m. his, they'd found Tom in the hotel bar, where he faced the street sipping warm scotch while watching the world go by. Here we were, everything going to shit on Koliba, and we're talking to Tom from Golongo over what sounds like two Campbell's Soup cans connected by a six-thousand-mile string.

"We're still here, Tom," Michael responded, leaning in over the speaker. "What the hell was that?"

"Nothing. Really," he answered, and we looked at each other curiously.

"Sure didn't sound like nothing," I muttered, not loud enough for the low-grade speakerphone on Michael's desk, but loud enough for Michael and Weller. Michael grimaced and waved at me, to warn me off such risky comments. My first reaction was to give him the finger, but I held off, realizing that he was just as frazzled as I was, struggling to see ahead to how we'd fix this. He probably wasn't in much of a mood for more of my presumptions, I thought.

We were in a little bit of a bind here. Working for foreign governments, you get used to cryptic telephone conversations when traveling, although not for fear of the National Security Agency, which has bigger fish to fry than carp like us. No, it's your clients you worry about, listening in on what you say about them and potentially misinterpreting the slightest negative comment as a reason to fire you at a minimum or, at the other end of the scale, put you on trial. So open conversations like, "did Koliba kill Gangaran, or was it just bad luck?" weren't an option here. At the same time, we needed to know something of what was going on and what we should be saying. In situations like this, folks on the Hill were never interested in hearing us come in and repeat whatever Christiane Amanpour had breathlessly reported twenty minutes ago from her outpost in CNN's Cairo bureau.

Luck was on our side in that sense: while the UK and the French put live reporters on the ground in most African countries, CNN and Fox do all their initial reporting from three or four nations away, avoiding shots of the moderately lovely Christiane interviewing bleeding African demonstrators. Iraqis, sure, them she'd run to, but Africans are a different story. So to speak.

But we still needed *something* out of Tom, something we could use on the Hill, something that would keep us ahead of the reporters. It would have sounded stupid to anyone outside our little world, I knew, but lobbying was all about credibility, about being ahead of the game and knowing more about the issues than anyone else. So while we were primarily focused on covering our butts, there was a benefit that extended beyond the immediate problem here: if we walked Congressional halls as, "there go the guys who didn't know squat about what Koliba was doing," that wouldn't help *any* of our clients. We needed to know, and comments like "nothing, really," from Tom indicated that we wouldn't get the kind of details I'd been hoping for.

"It was just a few trucks rolling by," Tom said. After a pause, he continued, "Nothing out of the ordinary."

The video on cable news was showing only tanks in the streets, so it must have been another row of tanks rolling through. And "nothing out of the ordinary" implied that this had been going on all day.

"Have you been out much?" It was Weller, up off the couch and over near the phone. Nice question—lots of directions for Tom to go in.

"Not in the last couple of days. I've been hanging around the hotel since late Sunday, when I got back from the hills."

"The hills," I assumed, had to be the CIA listening post. It was the only possible place that would take an American out of the capital in that godforsaken country these days, especially as Koliba's intense military control of the capital city had given rise to popular unrest in the remainder of the country.

Weller leaned in closer. "How was the trip?"

"Great." There was a little hop in his voice at that, like we'd distracted him from his more immediate worries. "Everyone I saw was just incredibly happy to be there, and they think it's just a great country to be in."

I looked at Michael and made a "yeah, right" face. Terrific country to be in, I thought, a sham democracy on the edge of civil war even when there aren't tanks in the street.

Michael shook his head in disgust with me and leaned forward from his side of the desk again, starting to ask, "So they're happy..." But Weller stepped forward with his hand outstretched. Michael stopped.

"The hunting is good?" Weller asked.

There was another pause, and then Tom said, "What? I missed that. Sounded like two of you."

"It's me, Tom, Wellington. I said, the hunting is good?"

"That's what they tell me." Something rumbled again in the background, more quietly this time, as if a single vehicle were passing. We waited. As the sound subsided, Tom continued, "Very good, in fact. Gets better all the time."

"And were they expecting Mr. Hatfield catching up with Mr. McCoy that way?"

Nicely done, I thought; maybe it made sense for Weller to take over the conversation from Michael. To any American, those names immediately brought up images of never-ending feuds that, in the current circumstances, could only mean Koliba-Gangaran. To anyone else listening, though, especially someone who probably spoke French far better than English, hearing those names for the first time, without access to Google, would be utterly meaningless.

"They predicted it the way it happened," came Tom's voice echoing down the line. "But not for six or seven months at least. Not that they're worried—in the current environment, they said, Mr. Hatfield's the man."

Weller stood up straight and looked into Michael's eyes, triumph on his face. After a pause, he turned back toward his chair and sat back down. I decided that he must have heard all that he needed.

'Hunting' could only mean listening, at least in our lexicon, so apparently the folks at the CIA station were happy with the information they were getting and were comfortable that Koliba was in charge for the long haul. 'Getting more all the time,' well, that could spin several ways, but Weller probably had a clearer sense of what Tom was saying. The two of them kept their own secrets sometimes, from me at least if not from Michael, so Wellington must have felt he had something he could work with.

That didn't help me, though. I needed answers on what we could say about Koliba and when we'd know more.

"Hello? Still there?" It was Tom, talking into his soup can.

Looking at Michael, I gave him a sign to keep going, to get more information out of Tom. He nodded.

"We're here," he said. "How's the boss doing?"

"My meetings today have been canceled," he added, "but the Colonel's coming by the hotel tomorrow morning."

He could only mean Col. Thomas N'Gada, "Colonel N'Godawful" as he was known over at State, the scariest person I'd ever met—six feet tall, ramrod straight, that same blue-black skin that Gangaran had, and always in military dress. It wasn't his looks so much as his bearing that was scary; even in seeing him only two or three times, in Washington hotel lobbies during his rare "private" visits to the city, he always seemed like he had precious little time for fools like those around him and wanted to squash them like bugs. He ran the Ministry of the Interior, the agency in most countries that oversees the national police as well as the judicial system. You've never had a powerful dictator anywhere in the world without a strong Minister of the Interior, and N'Gada sometimes seemed to be setting new standards for how to quash internal dissent. He was one mean sonofabitch.

Tom, though, well, Tom was a very big fan of the Colonel, who was his main contact with the Government and the guy who made sure we got paid. So a meeting with him was a good thing, at least in Tom's eyes. N'Gada traveling the streets, well, that meant Koliba was absolutely in charge and not worried about his prospects.

Michael leaned into the phone. Glancing at Weller, as if to make sure he phrased it right, he paused and then asked, "Any idea if he'll be able to tell you anything about recent events?"

There was a long pause. "My sense is that it's their issue, not ours," he said in a thin, slow voice. "I, uh, don't think I'm going to ask."

Un-be-LIEV-able, I thought. Not our issue. I banged my head, hard, against Michael's bookcase, immediately regretting it.

"Thanks, Tom," Michael said. "When are you coming back?"

"I'll know more when I talk to the Colonel."

"We'll call tomorrow or the next day."

With a few more pleasantries, Michael and Tom closed the call. Weller sat unmoving in his chair, watching Michael and waiting. I was still pacing back and forth, trying to decide where we were and what the hell I was supposed to do next.

"At least Koliba's still in charge."

I turned around to look at Michael. "Is that the good news or the bad news?"

* * *

Roger looked at me. "That's all you've got?"

Biting down on the inside of my lip, I glanced for a moment at Michelle, who was trying to look innocent. This was only our first meeting of the day and one of our friendliest contacts on the Hill, but it took no time at all for us to feel like we were slogging up a hill of loose stones and mud, making no progress.

Still, I had to touch base with my key contacts. That was what they'd remember later, the fact that I came up there and faced them, not the fact that I had nothing to say.

Trick was, I still couldn't talk about the CIA listening post, but only about what we knew about what was happening in the streets and how the investigation of Gangaran's death was going. Weller had left right after the phone call, telling us he would first visit privately with friends on the Senate and House Intelligence Committees, telling them what he knew, and then head over to Fox News to talk a little on background about the situation on the ground. Wellington played both sides of the press, left and right, but Koliba being a dictator America supported rather than one it hated, Fox was the obvious choice over CNN for this set of leaks.

Me, though, I got to go to the Hill unarmed, dragging Michelle along for the experience and so that I'd have someone to commiserate with every time a staffer put me through the sausage grinder. I started out with Roger, who must have welcomed me on the assumption that we'd have some credible explanation as to what was happening. When he understood that I had nothing to report on the Vice President's death, he began blinking like a madman and demanded we get out of his office. "Don't come back before you can tell me why he had his Vice President hacked to death, and what he's going to do about it."

"Well, now, Roger, we don't know..."

At that, he started out from behind his desk, as if to throw me out the door bodily. I beat him to the door, with Michelle close behind me.

From there, we headed to see Peter in the Senate Majority Leader's office. This was a much more delicate meeting, since I told Roger he should bring Peter into the jurisdictional fight over Koliba a few weeks before, when the Senate Foreign Relations Committee approved its anti-Koliba bill. Going into this meeting, I wasn't sure if Peter would blame me for that, though, since I figured Roger would have wanted the credit for recognizing the jurisdictional problem.

"You sonofabitch," Peter began before we'd even gotten through the door, "you suckered me into helping out with this maniacal dictator, and now everybody's all over my ass wondering why I'm supporting Africa's biggest psycho murderer."

Wrong again, buckaroo.

The discussion went downhill from there, especially after my feeble "information dump" on what we knew. I promised I'd have more information later, having no idea how I'd fulfill that and shuffled out the door as soon as I could do so gracefully. As I left, he dropped a parting shot, telling me that I'd better have more information before showing up to the Koliba dinner I'd promised him—a dinner I'd forgotten about in the rush of events and was now seriously regretting.

Next was a long, slow walk to the House side of the Capitol, taking the underground tunnels just to stretch it out a little. We started with Kevin, Charlotte's friend on House Foreign Affairs, who generally refused to talk to me about Koliba but this time not only took a meeting when I showed up unannounced, but ranted at us for about thirty minutes about how the Committee would not take this outrage lying down and "that Koliba bastard" would finally be cut off at the knees. I took the route of least resistance: I kept quiet and listened. Wasn't going to change his mind anyway, not that day.

From Kevin, I headed off alone to meet with Alexis. I don't know why, but I thought the conversation would go better if I went in alone.

After asking if she was available, I stood waiting by the front desk, facing the door to the back office, pretending to read some of the local interest crap they'd left out for constituents. That way, I could see her coming through the door before she knew I was looking at her, and sure enough, she came through with a look more wary than usual.

"Hi," she started, stopping outside the door. She held it for a moment, as if not sure she was going to let it go. "Maybe I can guess why you're here."

I smiled, but not too much. "Maybe. Everybody else has."

The door slipped out of her fingers, but she remained standing, folding her arms across her chest, her omnipresent file pressed up against her dress. I wondered for a moment if she had this one file she kept on the corner of her desk, bringing it with her every time she stepped away. Maybe it gave her a little more confidence in the move from receptionist to staffer. Whatever, she held it now like a defensive shield.

"I just wanted to stop by," I began, "just to check in."

"Is it just my imagination, or is the guy a monster?" Despite the words, Alexis's tone made her seem more disappointed in *me* than angry about Koliba. This was another element of my life I'd gotten used to, people's tendency to judge you by your clients, but I was surprised this time, surprised by Alexis picking up on it so quickly.

"It's not clear what's happened, or what happens next."

"How do you do this?"

"What?" I responded.

"This, coming in here as if your client caught a cold or something." Her head tilting to the side, she was clearly more curious about my lobbying for such a client than about what the client had done. That threw me a little; her boss was anti-Koliba, but this wasn't about Koliba. It was the "how do you sleep at night?" question, but from one of my best contacts, not some schmuck staffer who hated my very existence like it usually was. This wasn't good, not good at all.

There was a long pause, as I struggled with what to say next.

The door behind me, the one to the Congressman's office, opened, and Toby Kelton strode out into the lobby. I spun around, knowing the only door behind me was his and backed up toward the sofa so he could pass. He stopped at the front desk and, seeing me there, looked surprised for a moment. "Jesus," he said, "you're not here to defend that asshole Koliba, are you?"

* * *

Throughout all this, I still had other clients to work on, and I still needed to find a way to get the coastal fisheries idea into the Senate bill. Most of all, I needed to get Erin Monaghan to get off her ass to put it in front of her boss. In normal circumstances, I'd have dropped the idea of working with Erin and moved on to Plan B, but I hadn't for the life of me been able to identify a Plan B—even before Koliba apparently decided to have his thugs slice and dice the Vice President into a kajillion pieces.

Which reminded me, as I walked slowly across the third-floor bridge toward her office, the cavernous Hart lobby off to my right, I also needed to find a way to tell Erin that the only client we had who could benefit from this amendment was Koliba.

The door to Sen. Colbert's office seemed particularly heavy as I drew it back. Entering the office, I queried the receptionist in front of me, "Hi, is Erin Monaghan in?"

"Can I tell her who's here?" she replied.

My first thought was "no, that'll give it away," but while that was still running through my head, the other receptionist beat me to it, responding, "I'll let Erin know that Mr. Matthews is here." I recognized her from my previous visits. "I *think*"—I could hear the italics, as she turned toward her phone—"she's in a meeting, but I'll check."

With her back to me, I couldn't hear what she was saying, but it took a lot longer than "Ed Matthews is here to see you" and involved a whole lot more back and forth. Erin obviously didn't want to meet with me, that I could tell, and they must have been disagreeing about what to tell me. Ah, well, I thought, maybe she'd pass along some information I could use.

The receptionist turned. "I'm sorry. She is in a meeting. She's wondering if there might be something you could leave for her, and she'll get back to you when she's able to focus on the Foreign Operations bill?"

Oh, God, I thought, that's a bad answer. Up to this point, she'd been ducking me with getting answers that worked out to, "try again later." This time, she was telling me to leave something—knowing I'd already left her everything there was—and she would get back to me. Read: Don't come back. She was blowing me off. I was screwed.

I realized I was still standing there, staring at the receptionist like I was mute. "Okay," I responded, trying to think of anything to say, "I'll just plan on seeing her, uh, next time we, um, cross paths." I turned quickly, to get out of there before I broke into incoherent mumbling. "Thanks so much."

Walking out, I turned left, headed to the Constitution Avenue side of the building and from there into Dirksen. I wasn't going anywhere, just walking, trying to decide on a next step. My amendment was in serious trouble, and I was completely blocked on doing anything about it.

As I reached the front of the building, I turned right, crossing another bridge over the lobby. A group of school-age girls, ten- to twelve-year-olds by the looks of them, all in school uniforms, were walking toward me in a semblance of order. They looked like Middle Eastern kids, maybe from some Arabic school, I thought, diplomats' children getting a tour of America's political system. As they passed I heard both Arabic and French, the clearer French of France itself rather than the more guttural French that their parents, most likely from North Africa, would speak at home.

North Africa.

Idiot, I thought.

I'd forgotten Mourad. I did have a Plan B, and I'd completely overlooked it. I left it aside because I didn't want to let Morocco in on the amendment. That was suddenly a very bad idea.

Now what was that woman's name, Mourad's secretary? The reception-ist, the gravel-voiced one he'd mentioned at the reception. God, what was her name? For all she drove me crazy with her questions about Michael, and my wife, and my job, for once I was going to enjoy calling her.

If I could remember her name.

Ayoubi.

Mrs. El Ayoubi.

I had a Plan B.

* * *

Two days later, shortly after 2:00 p.m., I approached Room 2255 in the Rayburn building from the long end of the hallway, avoiding the line stretching in the other direction. Sidling up to the guard, I said, "I'm switching with someone in the room," while the human rights putzes head-ing up the line snarled at me. I wondered for a moment if they recognized me, but thought, no, it's just human nature to snarl at line cutters.

Entering the mobbed room, I caught the eye of my human placeholder, sitting bleary-eyed in the back row next to Michelle, who in turn was scrib-bling furiously in her notebook. Jesus Christ, I thought, they're all the way across the room, and I'm going to have to schlep all over people to get in there. I leaned back as Larry approached so he could pass, accidentally pushing up against the woman behind me. In response to her low grunt of "hey, someone here," I apologized while others around me looked on in disapproval. I was making much more of a scene here than I wanted, but still, I thought, this is better than being in the hall before the hearing, where staffers could see me and harass me over our disaster of a client, Ernest Koliba.

This was another one of the innumerable "how-bad-does-Koliba-suck?" hearings that had been scheduled following Gangaran's death. It stood to be one of those where both sides on the political spectrum rolled out their best rhetoric detailing the many things the man had done wrong in the past year or so. Gangaran's murder was clearly a watershed event in that it brought out the full Africa Subcommittee, something rare in these late-session hearings, to rant and rail against the man and everything he stood for. It wasn't a pretty lineup: the Subcommittee included two members, Jack Tindal on the Democratic side and Republican Louis Hadle, both of whom had been at our February reception for Gangaran's visit. They both looked loaded for bear, and Tindal almost seemed to be looking at me, as if he recognized me. Oh, great, I thought, just what I need.

I leaned over to Michelle. "What did I miss?"

"Nothing."

"What are you writing so furiously?"

"Everything they say. Keeps my mind off the content."

I straightened, trying not to smile. It was true, if you focused on taking great notes at a hearing, you couldn't pay attention to the broader message, using half your brain to scribble down the last ten words you heard while using the other half to store up the next ten.

Opening my notebook to a new page, I took out a pen and leaned back, staring for a moment at the bald spot on the State Department witness's head. This was going to be a long hearing, with the head of State's Africa Bureau starting us out and a panel of three human rights groups following up. As usual, no one would testify from the other side, *our* side. Despite the popular perception that lobbyists testify all the time, that's only true when they represent voters, not foreign governments and especially not foreign dictators. No, Michelle and I would simply sit there and listen, take it all in, and report back to the client. What mattered, of course, was being there.

Normally, I'd duck an end-of-the-year hearing like this since it was unlikely to affect the actual legislation that would soon be passed. But this hearing was more like those meetings I had with my friends right after Gangaran died: they'd had to see me, to yell at me, to vent their frustrations. Same thing here: the Members, the staff, and even the human rights weenies all had to see that we were here, listening and taking notes. Even if they were all saying the same thing, over and over and over again.

Clearing my head, I began a run-through of where we were at this point. Our MNNA amendment was on track—sort of: I'd lost Will Richardson as my House-side help in Conference, but thanks to my first meeting with Alexis in her new job, we had a possible back-up in Toby Kelton. This was too soon to raise it with Alexis and Toby, because I needed to respect their tremendous annoyance over Koliba, but that should blow over by Conference, and besides, with the amendment already in the Senate bill, I might not even need them. So that was open.

Koliba's DOD funding was under threat, but even with all the screaming, it was still September and Congress always had an exceedingly short memory, so I was thinking he would probably come out okay. Our military aid for Africa amendment was totally up in the air, although my Plan B might work if I could get to Mourad in time and we could work it out.

And the Dungan, my client? Well, there was definitely more to do on that one, especially now that Sen. VanderMeer's efforts had been shot down. That's one of the real secrets of lobbying: you only have to win once to get something into a bill or report, and once it's there it's easier for you to keep it in than for your opponents to take it out. I had time to decide what it was I'd be doing.

A fist striking the dais rousted me from my daydreaming, and I processed the words "penny-ante dictator" as my eyes came into focus on Rep. Hamlin, the liberal Democrat from New York. Lots of New Yorkers on the International Relations Committee, I thought, their state home to a population that actually cares day-to-day what happens overseas, even when we're not at war. Hamlin was much like the rest of the New Yorkers, loud, boisterous, his face a searing red at the moment as he spluttered on and on about Koliba.

Glancing at Michelle, she seemed to be smiling a little. I suppose I must have started at the sound of the pounding fist, although anyone paying attention would have been prepared for it. Glancing at the panel, I could see that the members and their staffs, arrayed behind them in a cramped little row, were intent on the witness, still the poor State Department guy who seemed caught in the traditional witness's bind, trying to preserve his dignity while simultaneously preserving "the President's freedom of action in foreign affairs"—another misnomer that basically means, "hey, Congress, leave us alone, will ya?" Not an argument that ever worked on the Hill, but also not one any Administration ever let go of.

No wonder I never wanted to work for the government, I thought.

* * *

Two hours later, the meeting broke. Moving slowly along the wall as I headed for the door, the crush of people exiting holding us back, I noticed Rep. Tindal at the end of my row, waiting as people made their way out. I'd only met him once, at that Gangaran reception, and even then for just a few moments. He looked angry, very angry, just like he'd been throughout the hearing, lips pulled tight, face reddened, eyes like slits. God, I thought, he can't be looking at me. Michelle muttered something I couldn't catch from behind me, but I kept going, looking at the door and hoping I was imagining things. I wasn't.

"You work with Tom LeBont, don't you? At McPherson's shop?"

Several people turned to me, recognizing the name. Geez, thanks, bud, I'm likely to get stoned here.

"Yes, sir, I do."

"We met at your reception in February, didn't we?"

"Yes, sir, we did." When in doubt, go all polite and shit—that's my motto. Otherwise, you could have your head torn off.

"You tell Tom and Michael that the man has gone too far this time, and there are going to be repercussions."

We were in the middle of the crowd now, the people trapped behind us not even trying to get by and the ones with easy access to the door finding Tindal much more interesting. All of them were watching us.

"We'll tell him everything we heard today, Congressman."

He snorted. "You didn't even seem to be listening half the time."

Thank God in heaven, I thought, for Michelle's presence. I turned, pointed to her, and said, "She took our notes, Congressman." Looking back to Tindal, I continued, "Feverishly, in fact, from what I could tell. I'm sure she got most of it. And we will pass it all on. I promise."

He glared at me, his face still red, but maybe a touch of embarrassment in his eyes along with the anger. He paused, breathing slowly in, slowly out.

"You make sure you do." I could see he wasn't satisfied at that, but after a moment he turned to go. The crowd parted and then closed back in behind him, the wall of people reassembled, as if waiting for more.

To Michelle, I said, "Let's get out of here." As I turned back around, the wall parted again, opening to let us through, people grouped again in twos and threes, whispering among themselves as we left.

Chapter 17

Watching Senate Floor debate is kind of like watching grass grow, only less interesting.

In fact, calling what the Senate did with legislation a "debate" was a serious misnomer. It was more of a carefully choreographed dance where, except on the most contentious bills, the time and timing for debate were agreed to in advance and orchestrated through a maneuver called "unanimous consent," basically an agreement on what went next. When they didn't have such a deal ready, some Senator would point out there wasn't a quorum present—literally, as in, "Mr. President, I suggest the absence of a quorum," which was true about 99 percent of the time and a violation of Senate rules—and Floor debate would stop while the Clerk of the Senate called the roll to see who was there. The maneuver allowed them to turn the TV cameras off while they negotiated their next unanimous consent. As a result, you could go hours watching the television with only the occasional drone from the Clerk, calling out whatever Senator's name he'd gotten to and somehow never getting to the last name on the list.

Their other great trick, one they were planning to use later in the day, was "stacked votes," where they debated a series of amendments late into the night but didn't vote on them until the following morning, when they'd hold a series of five-minute votes. This way, most of the Senators got their beauty sleep, while the deadly dull debates were gotten out of the way. God forbid that they should actually have to listen to their colleagues debating legislation—there wouldn't be nearly enough time to make fundraising calls, or campaign for President, if they actually had to do *that*.

The Foreign Ops bill came to the Floor right around lunchtime, which is generally a bad idea but particularly problematic on days like this when the two parties were holding their policy luncheons, weekly strategy sessions on how to screw the other party's agenda. Americans like to think that Congress is there to do the nation's business, but in these days of deep partisan division, Floor debates are more like verbal dodgeball between twelve-year-old boys: "You suck!" "No, you suck!" It's generally well disguised behind positions that sound principled, but it's still just dodgeball.

Around 1:30 p.m., I was in the Senate gallery, looking down on the Senate Floor and hoping to somehow stay awake. I'd convinced Sen. VanderMeer to try once again to put something in the bill on freedom of religion in Kazakhstan, the amendment that Sen. Belkin had talked him out of during the Senate Committee debate. I wasn't entirely convinced it would fly, given Belkin's fight against the amendment in Committee, but it was worth a shot. And even if they talked him out of it, he'd be better positioned for the House-Senate Joint Conference where the bill would be finalized.

So far, discussion of the bill consisted of lame introductions by the Chairman and Ranking Minority Member of the Subcommittee, along with the obligatory compliments to each other and each other's staffs for their wisdom, willingness to collaborate, and all-around good-guyness. A couple of amendments that everyone had signed off on—mistakes, probably, in the printing of the bill, or items that fell to the floor on the way to the printer—were agreed to, but that had been about it. After all, those luncheons were still underway.

Sen. VanderMeer emerged through the Republican-side door as Sen. Belkin, running out of things to say, once again suggested the absence of a quorum, turning the television cameras off and suspending the "action" once more. I'd decided to turn up the heat a notch, sending VanderMeer to the Floor with a marginally improved amendment: I'd added a small proviso that would prohibit U.S. funds to any country undertaking a program of religious persecution against any group. After the way the two of them went nose to nose in the full Committee, I figured it had about zero chance of passing, but it might tell me something new.

The reason was simple. The Foreign Aid Appropriations Bill includes funding for the U.S. Export-Import Bank, the institution that provides financing and loan guaranties for America-led projects overseas. So when General Electric sold some country a batch of jet engines, or when Bechtel built a new power plant somewhere, Ex-Im would cover some part of the funding. That reduced the risk to the U.S. corporate seller, since no government would be stupid enough to default on a loan that the U.S. Government had financed or guaranteed. It was more grease on the wheels of international commerce.

The goal here wasn't to get the provision signed into law, but to try to find out who was behind Belkin's opposition to our earlier amendment. I figured that if it originated from Shaddock Mills, Belkin and Raymonda would make the argument based on U.S.-Kazakh relations and national security. If it originated with some oil company, or manufacturer, they'd go after him on the impact on U.S. commercial sales. The strategy depended on my hearing from VanderMeer what they'd said, but that would be easy: ever since Tom and I had gone in there, VanderMeer and his staff were my new best friends.

As VanderMeer approached Sen. Belkin, Raymonda converged on them from behind her desk, as if she didn't dare leave him alone. With the TV off, I was sure that virtually no one but me had seen them, but it was still more overt than I expected: Senators like people to think that they know what they're doing, and this came close to insubordination.

I smiled to myself, watching the three of them in a little triangle, VanderMeer appearing to describe his amendment to Belkin while Raymonda read through it. She was leaning in just a little, looking down at the paper but clearly listening while she read, splitting her attention between the story and the fact, VanderMeer's explanation and the amendment itself on the page before her.

She started, and I felt my heart skip a beat. I'd hit a serious nerve.

The rest of the conversation went by in slow motion, Raymonda ranting at VanderMeer in a quiet voice, waving the amendment and pointing at him, surprising Belkin as much as VanderMeer himself. The discussion went on for a minute or two as VanderMeer edged slowly away and finally caved. As he turned to leave the floor, with a glum nod to Belkin, I could see that Raymonda still had the amendment in her hand. That's probably not a good thing, I thought, rising out of my seat to head for VanderMeer's office.

* * *

"You look like hell."

"Yes, thank you very much," I replied, "and, well, you're a schmuck."

I wasn't in the best of moods, having come to Roger's office on my way to an early dinner with Charlotte, scheduled for five thirty. The Senate Floor debate was still going on and would continue go deep into the night, so for all I felt like crawling home to bed, I was stuck up on the Hill. The Senate leadership had insisted that the bill would pass sometime this evening, meaning that I could be there until 3:00 a.m. It wasn't something I was looking forward to.

I was troubled, mostly about Kazakhstan, and mostly because I was confused. I'd caught up with VanderMeer walking down the hall to his office and thanked him for taking the amendment to the Floor, telling him once again how we appreciated his willingness to stick with his principles. He thanked me, expressing regret that he hadn't succeeded and complaining about "that woman's" demeanor and words. I'd expected him to be angry with Ray, but he wasn't; he must have been getting used to her unique approach to the world around her.

My confusion came when he said that Raymonda had cited U.S. commercial interests *and* U.S.-Kazakh relations *and* Shaddock Mills *and* the Vice President's office, all in the space of what I remembered as being only about two minutes. That was a ridiculous amount to squeeze into that amount of time, but—well, but nothing, it just was. She almost can't be responding to all of them, I thought, and that only means that I don't know anything more than when I sent him to the Floor.

My frustration made me somewhat careless, and Roger's opening line was a sign that he was in one of his own special moods, the "you suck" one he cultivated most carefully. It didn't help that I'd interrupted a discussion he was having with some State Department morons, just walking in the door like I belonged there and, as I realized there was a meeting going on, stumbling back out like an idiot. Roger hated it when people just walked into his office, especially when doing so revealed, as I had done, the rare privilege of showing up pretty much whenever I wanted to. Now, having waited in the hall, trying to relax while he took his time finishing up, I'd been welcomed into his *sanctum sanctorum* despite my indiscretion.

"You here to insult me?"

"No, Roger, here to see if there's anything you need before I take a break to get some dinner."

"Yeah, right. Every time you try to do me a favor, it's because you've got something you need."

The man was right, of course, but I wasn't in a position to let that stop me.

Roger rose, lifting a stack of papers from his desk, and began to come around it to the right. That classic move, that first step in pushing me out the door.

"The coastal fisheries amendment," I said. Roger paused. "For Africa. The one you dropped out of the bill for me."

Three quick blinks. "I told you how to fix it." Shaking his head, he started forward again. I was running out of time.

"I've got a fix. Tonight. During Floor debate," I said. "And you've got to make sure that the managers take it."

Roger stopped. "Who?"

"Colbert. Who else?"

"I thought you said she couldn't get it done."

I handed him a manila folder, with three copies of the amendment and some talking points in case his boss needed them. "I talked Mourad into it, added in North Africa, and he convinced her to do it." I smiled at him.

He laughed, shaking his head again. "When does it come up?"

"Tonight." I looked him right in the eye, waiting to see his reaction. "Not sure when." That was true; in fact, I wasn't even sure of "if," but Mourad and I still had several hours to work on that. And it had to be tonight, since the Foreign Aid bill would only be on the Senate Floor this one night. It was now or never.

"Is that it?"

Is it ever? I thought. "You, uh, mind if I use your office as a base station? Michael's over at the Veep's lobby in the Capitol"—meaning, in these post-9/11 days, inside the Capitol Building security—"and I need somewhere to hang out while working with Colbert's folks"—meaning, inside the Senate office buildings' security perimeter. While the press always put lots of attention on lobbying restrictions, it was the heightened security due to terrorism that put the biggest crimp into our ability to walk the halls freely, and especially to go back and forth between the Capitol and the House and Senate office buildings.

"What about Harry's office?"

"Can't do it." With Harry being my link to Belkin on the MNNA amendment for the UAE and Belkin having rejected the Kazakhstan Floor amendment I just had VanderMeer offer, I felt I should distance myself just in case—but that wasn't something I could explain to Roger. "It would be too obvious."

He breathed in deeply and glanced at the papers in his hand before breathing out again. "What time?"

"Six o'clock, maybe six thirty. I've got dinner with Charlotte, and I'll come back here."

His eyes narrowed. "I'm not going to regret this, am I?"

Hey, don't ask me, I thought. "Nah."

✟ ✟ ✟

Charlotte was at Zaragoza, our favorite Spanish restaurant in D.C., when I arrived. No surprise there. I was on time, maybe a minute or two late, but she was forever early no matter where we went. Over the years I'd gotten used to being ready to leave ten minutes before we said we'd be going, because that was inevitably when she was ready to go. And no matter how hard I tried—and in Washington, with its ever-changing schedules and its tendency to always run late, I had to try really, really hard—I inevitably arrived after she did. It was maddening, more to her than to me, but every once in a while I found myself wishing I could get there before her. Like since Paris, my betrayal nipping at me. Like tonight.

"Hey, Sweetie," I leaned in to kiss her, and she turned up to me. From the little glimmer in her eyes, I figured that something was up.

"Hi, baby." She reached for her wine glass, a white, and took another drink. She was well into that glass, so she'd either arrived very early or was drinking really fast. From the size of the gulp she took, I was thinking the latter.

I flagged for a waiter and ordered a Merlot, the one glass I could afford to allow myself that night. While getting his attention, I wondered what Charlotte's drinking meant. She'd always been a pretty cheap drunk, not that she sought to get drunk the way kids do, but just that she had a low tolerance, especially when she wasn't eating. And like so many women, she wouldn't order something to nibble on with her drink to balance out the alcohol; that would mean too many calories. So she'd have a drink or two when she was in the mood without worrying about the effect. Sometimes it was okay, and sometimes she was sliding under the table before finishing her entrée. Tonight, we'd have to see.

"So how's your day been?" Another of my post-Paris guilt trip maneuvers, trying not to dominate our conversations, letting her go first.

"Oh, Heaney's such an asshole." She took another long swallow of the wine. So that was it—a bad day—which usually meant the whole sliding under the table thing if she was drinking this soon. Must have been an exceedingly bad day, I thought; Heaney was always as asshole.

"What now?"

"Oh, he reduced Karen to tears over some useless press release she wrote." Karen was the goat of the office; many Hill offices have them, especially the badly run ones, staffers who can't seem to do anything right. Like I mentioned earlier, elected Members of the House arrive in office with fewer skills in management, especially personnel, than anyone else in America, and they have total freedom on how to staff their offices. Job security—i.e., reelection—is completely divorced from how well the office runs: as long as they respond to constituent mail and have the necessary political skills, once they made it through the second election—i.e., getting *re*elected for the first time—they become a habit, and normally they're returned to office over and over. Such was the case with Heaney; no one back home knew what a gasbag he was, or just what an evil manager he was. He ran roughshod over the staff, and Charlotte had to try to pick up the pieces.

"She blew the story?"

"No, it was Heaney. He's been complaining about not being in the *Post-Courier* enough back home and that it's Karen's fault, so he insisted she do a release on him and this hearing he testified at." She shook her head and took another gulp. As the waiter approached with the Merlot, I ordered off the menu from memory, a *gambas al ajillo* appetizer to split, just to start getting some food in us; *zarzuela de mariscos* for me; and, with a glance and nod from her, the *pollo asada*, her favorite, for Charlotte. As he was starting to turn, she lifted her wine glass, waving it a little and pointing at it with her free hand. He nodded. "Karen had no way of knowing that Heaney's testimony, given to him by the guys from Tempest Water, would be completely contradicted by witnesses from four separate environmental organizations. The *Post-Courier* guy went after him like a buzz saw after the hearing, and Heaney went nuts."

"Gabe"—the office environmental policy guy—"should have caught that."

"Gabe wasn't in on it. Like I said, the Tempest guys gave Heaney the testimony, and he went with it without even checking with Gabe. Gabe was in the back of the hearing room in a flop sweat as he listened to Heaney—he'd already gotten the enviros' testimony earlier in the week." She laughed lightly and paused to take another drink. "He hid in the Committee room after the hearing, to avoid the explosion. I had to go find him, in a carrel in the back of the staff office, to figure what the hell had happened. From there it just got worse."

She looked right at me, her eyes still smiling, brown with flecks of green in this light as opposed to the green with flecks of brown that daylight would bring out in her. Her skin was slightly flushed, but from excitement, not the alcohol—she seemed to be burning through the alcohol, a sign that she was worked up.

After a pause, she said, "So my day was absolutely for shit. How about you?"

I looked up from the bread basket, where I was hunting for some distraction. She looked more relaxed; I figured that she'd needed to vent and had gotten it out. "So far? I've had one amendment killed on the Senate Floor, and I don't know why. Someone's fighting against what we're trying to do for the Dungan."

"The Dungan," she snorted, reaching for the second wine glass, which the waiter had just deposited. "Like the world needs a new amendment on the Dungan. What were you going for, $50 million in new equipment for that gas station?"

"Oh, God, don't start with me," I responded, laughing, as I turned to find the waiter again. "I get that all day from everyone on the Hill."

"I'm serious."

I turned, and whoa, she wasn't smiling anymore. That turn came quickly. "Honey…"

"No, I mean it," she said. "What are you doing for these people? Let alone Koliba. And why? Why do you keep doing it? Why do you want to stay?" She leaned back and turned, flushed again but this time darker, looking out onto Pennsylvania Avenue, out at the traffic, out at the people, looking anywhere but at me.

Oh, shit. I hadn't seen that coming at all. I turned then too and looked out with her, sinking as I did. I just hadn't seen this. "Jesus."

"Let's recap, Ed. Koliba's on the news every night, and all day long in the office, with new details all the time about how he's squashing democracy. You're out defending the man. The Dungan, your excuse for our still being in this city, no one even knows they *exist*." She stopped, staring, to let that one sink in. I waited her out. "Today completely sucked at work, and you know, it wasn't any worse than any other day this month, just a little louder than usual. And the career you're staying here for involves working for an absolute monster." Her voice was rising with every word, and her knuckles were white around her fork.

"Honey, the Koliba thing only went to shit a week ago, and we're coming up on the end of the year. Next year we probably won't even work for the guy." Or maybe he'd straighten up or get overthrown, so we'd be working for some other crazy African dictator. Jesus, I didn't know, and I didn't want to get into this now.

"I'm talking about now. How do you do this now?"

"Honey, there's nothing we can do. Sometimes we've gotta play the hand we're dealt."

"And how many years do we have to wait before you're the dealer? Before you start making your own choices?"

This was going downhill fast. And I had to get back to tracking the Senate Floor.

"Here we are, your *gambas al ajillo*." Our waiter was back. As he made room in the center of the table, I leaned back and exhaled slowly.

Charlotte watched me closely. "So you've got nothing to say?"

"No."

"Can I bring you anything else right now?" The waiter was still there, waiting for a pause in the discussion.

Charlotte pushed her chair back. "No," she said, "just the check. He'll take it."

Faster than I thought. Much faster.

"Sweetie..." I began to protest, knowing better but feeling like I had to try.

She stood, turning to take the coat off her chair while the waiter snatched at her wineglass to keep it from getting knocked over. "Don't start with me, you asshole. I'm going home. I'll see you whenever."

Watching her leave, swirling between the tables, the thing I noticed most was her ass, swaying as she negotiated the tight space and the over-high heels she'd worn that day. I loved her at that moment and hated where we were. The waiter, smaller almost than Charlotte, stood back now, and the customers around us were staring, but Charlotte seemed oblivious to all of it, and I was fixated on her weaving perilously between the cramped tables. She ducked a waitress as she slid past the cashier and made her way to the door and out. I looked at the waiter—this must have been when I saw everyone staring.

"Maybe if you could have the kitchen just pack up everything I ordered, I'll take it with me," I said, pushing the shrimp back toward him. "And I, uh, will take that check when you've got the chance."

* * *

Walking back from Zaragoza, I put in a call to Roger. "Just checking to make sure you're still there."

"Of course I'm still here, you idiot." Well, his mood hadn't lifted, so it looked like I was in for a fun hour or two before he stationed himself over at the Capitol for the last couple of hours of the debate.

"Need some dinner?"

"Can't leave."

"I'm bringing it in," I told him. I stopped walking for a moment and paused before continuing. "Charlotte and I had a fight, so you can choose between *pollo asada* and *zarzuela*. Just don't ask me what we fought about."

There was silence from his end of the line. As I started walking again, he said, "I can probably guess what you fought about."

"Yeah." I snorted, closing the phone as I was reminded just one more time what a lousy fucking fishbowl I lived in. It was bad enough that your entire social circle was predetermined by your job and your clients, without the fact that those parts of your life that should be private were spilled out all over the city because your best friend was the guy you lobbied three days a week, or your mother's sister was a Senator's wife, or whatever crazy fucking incestuous set of relationships drove your life.

I knocked on Roger's door this time before walking in. At least I've got something for him, I thought, turning the knob—might make the waiting less painful.

Roger watched me as I came in and put the bag on his desk. "What did you order?" he asked.

"The *zarzuela*."

"I'll take the chicken."

A peace offering. Not a common start from Roger, but I guessed that the idea of Charlotte and me fighting had calmed him down. He's a softie at heart, I thought, although I decided against voicing that feeling: he'd probably take it as a challenge and start chewing my ass off over something totally unimportant. I smiled to myself, for the first time in hours, and passed him the *pollo asada*. "There's an appetizer if you want it."

"No, thanks, I'm not that hungry."

We sat in silence for a few minutes, me just eating slowly while my mind raced in circles, Roger flipping through some notes that probably didn't need reviewing.

"I do need a favor, by the way," I said, taking another bite of mussel and speaking through it, "after the bill's off the Floor."

Roger looked askance at me. He was good at looking askance. "Hmmm?"

"Remember that girl I told you about a few months back, the one held prisoner in the UAE?" He nodded. "The client still hasn't released her yet, and I think we're going to get screwed in Conference if they don't. We snuck through Committee and Belkin can walk the amendment through tonight, but her parents' lawyers will catch it when the bill is reprinted."

"Of course they will," he said, glaring at me. "Tell the Embassy to straighten up and let her go."

"Tried that," I said. "I even tried a face-to-face with the Minister of Defense. It didn't work. They won't listen to us. I need you to tell them."

"Is that how it works?" He pushed at his chicken, looking carefully at a piece of breast meat before cutting into it. "We do your work for you?"

"Sometimes we have to save the client from their own stupidity." I said it as calmly as I could; it was a weapon I didn't like to use often.

His eyes narrowed.

"Get Fawzi in here," I said. Roger knew Fawzi from the many Embassy receptions he attended and from the annual single-malt scotch that Fawzi sent him at Christmas. For reasons I never understood, Arab Embassies always sent out the best Christmas presents. "Rip him a new one and tell them to let her go."

My Crackberry buzzed in my pocket. "CALL ME," all caps, rude according to geek etiquette but rather typical of Michael's messages. Ignoring it for the moment, I looked back at Roger. "It's the only way."

A long pause. With a grimace, he nodded.

The phone rang twice before Michael picked up. I heard nothing for a few seconds, but then I could hear him talking to someone in the background, "No, I know it's important. I'm sorry, but I have to take this." Into the phone, he said, "Yes, Mr. Ambassador?"

"Huh?"

After a pause, he went on. "No, Mr. Ambassador, I don't believe the Emirates will be discussed tonight." There was another pause, and I heard him say off-line, "Really, this is something I need to discuss outside. Sorry, Philip."

Galsworthy, I thought. He's trying to get away from Galsworthy.

"Would it help if I yelled into the phone at you?" I asked him, laughing.

"No, Mr. Ambassador, it's fine," he replied. "Let me just move over here where I can have some privacy."

"So this is just all about ditching Galsworthy?"

"Oh, shut up. He was trying to give me a ton of shit about Koliba." He must have been moving quickly, for his breathing was getting a little forced. "They don't pay me enough to listen to that asshole."

Michael, for all his strategizing and plotting on Koliba over the last five months, had been shielded from most of the Congressional rampages about him. The benefits of seniority – he could send us lackeys to sit through the shit and even duck it in the final stages.

"So what's up with Roger?"

"Enjoying some fine dining here at his desk."

"You didn't buy him dinner, did you?"

Like I needed this. Congress had just passed legislation prohibiting meals like this, but it wouldn't go into effect on the Senate side until January 1, and besides, I'd bought the dinner for Charlotte, not Roger. He was just eating it. "Is there something I can help you with, Michael? Or is this just a crank call?" I shook my head back and forth and waved my right arm in the air. Roger stared at me, looking confused.

"Fuck off. I need to talk to him."

"He's on the phone." Roger's eyebrows rose. "I'll have him call as soon as he's finished. Any sign of the bill?"

"That's what I need to ask him."

"Will do." I thumbed the 'off' button and lay the Blackberry on Roger's desk. "He's bored," I said. "It's six fifteen and the man's bored. You can call him when we're done."

"You've been working for him too long," Roger responded with a smile. "Tell me about it."

* * *

A knock on the door startled me, but it was only Mourad, who'd also positioned himself inside the Senate security perimeter for the night. His look was grave.

"She's gone."

"Shit, Mourad, she can't be gone," I replied, pointing to the TV. "They haven't done the amendment yet." Our coastal fisheries amendment, the main reason I was hanging around all night. Mourad had taken on the assignment of bird-dogging Erin Monaghan. His last report, an instant message at six thirty, had been that he'd talked to her, she knew the amendment needed to go that night, and she would do it. She couldn't be gone.

"The whole office is empty."

"Maybe she's at dinner." Even before glancing at my watch, I knew that was unlikely since it was well past 8:00 p.m.—shit, I thought, it's already eight thirty.

I looked over at him. "Do we have any options?"

"Not that I can see." He shook his head and looked over at the *gambas* still sitting by the television. I guessed that he hadn't eaten yet. "I gave Peter the folder with the amendment and talkers, and he was going to talk to Raymonda."

"What time was that?"

"Seven o'clock, seven fifteen, somewhere there."

"He's given it to her. I saw him talking with her a little after seven thirty, directly behind Belkin on the Floor." Senate committee staffers sat directly behind their Senators during Floor debates, keeping Senators on schedule with the things they needed to do, and serving as traffic cops working out deals with other Senators while their guy was talking. Some Senators needed their staffers more than others; like Raymonda had demonstrated earlier with Sen. VanderMeer, Belkin was definitely one of those. "And I gave mine to Roger, so we've got everything in place for when Colbert gets to the Floor to offer the amendment."

"Or she gets them to offer it on his behalf." Mourad walked over toward the television and reached for a shrimp. Just before taking it, he looked over at me.

I nodded. "Take the whole thing."

He popped the shrimp in his mouth and quickly grabbed another. He must have been starving. "But she's gone home," he mumbled in between chewing.

"I need to go check."

Mourad stopped. "She's gone. The entire fourth floor offices are dark. There's no one there."

"If this is going down the toilet, I need to be able to tell Michael I tried. Besides, I just need to take a walk." I pointed to the TV again, where Sen. Belkin was requesting unanimous consent to rescind the order for a roll call, that little nicety that would allow debate to proceed. "I've been staring at these assholes doing quorum calls for the last couple of hours, and I need to clear my head. Just keep an eye on them, and I'll be back."

Mourad grunted and let me pass by before heading for Roger's chair. Must be something about sitting in a staffer's chair, I thought; he's ignoring the other two chairs the same way I did.

As I reached for the doorknob, I turned back. "Don't touch anything, and I mean anything. Roger knows exactly where he left that pile of papers, to within a centimeter. He'll fry both of us if anything's changed when he comes back."

* * *

Ninety minutes later, Mourad and I were getting pretty punchy. I'd given up reclaiming Roger's chair behind the desk, as Mourad refused to get up to hand it back over. With my back to the door and my chair tilted dangerously back, I planted my feet on Roger's desk and, in between tossing an old tennis ball we'd found back and forth, was doing my Washington-renowned imitation of Sen. Frank Johnson, Roger's boss, barking out at Mourad for imagined transgressions: "What do you mean, you're not going to support the bill? What are you, French or something?" The trick was the odd, Clutch Cargo kind of way he held his mouth when he barked and the depth that came into his voice, as if he were reaching down into his belly to bring up a deeper, richer sound.

"So we're having a party?"

I completely missed the sound of the door opening. My arms flailed as the chair went over, and from the floor, I found myself staring up into Roger's smiling face.

Mourad roared with laughter, and from the corner of my eye, I saw the tennis ball moving in a high arc and then dropping down at me. Catching it with my right hand, I asked Roger, "How's the Floor debate going?"

He glanced over at his television. "What do you think?"

Roger carefully placed his folders on his desk, next to the others, and stood watching me as I scrambled to my feet and righted the chair. After a few moments, it became evident he was waiting for something else. Mourad started and then rose quickly from the chair, moving aside to let Roger by. A nasal sound, like an "mmm," emanated from somewhere inside him, which I took to be an expression of thanks. Sitting, he pulled the chair close to the desk and straightened himself out.

Mourad smiled at me as he came around to my side of the desk, the non-Roger side, where we belonged.

"So where is that idiot with the fisheries amendment?" Roger asked, reaching into the lower left-hand drawer of his desk. Bringing out first a white cloth and then a spray can, he sprayed several spots on his desk and began to wipe them in careful circular strokes.

My first thought was that he better not start going all OCD on me.

My second thought had me looking at Mourad, shaking my head no. No need to let Roger know yet that we had nothing. "Hasn't she been to the Floor yet? Last we heard she promised Mourad they'd do the amendment."

"Well," he said, "you're running out of time." He looked up at us, raising the cloth as he did, and blinked. "They're working on a unanimous consent to lock down the last five or ten amendments. Belkin's freaking out because they haven't done anything in the last two hours. Raymonda's cornering Senators, staff, anyone she can find to get the agreement finalized."

I noticed movement on the TV screen and nudged Mourad to turn up the volume.

"… that the order for a quorum call be rescinded, Mr. President." It was Belkin. It looked like they'd agreed on something.

"Mr. President, I send an amendment to the desk, which I am pleased to offer on behalf of the gentleman from New Jersey, Mr. Colbert." Mourad and I looked at each other. They couldn't be doing our amendment, so what the hell were they doing?

"Mr. President, this amendment will target funding from the military aid section of this bill specifically to protect the precious fisheries off the coast of Africa, including North Africa. These fisheries are threatened by overfishing by the fishing fleets of France, Spain, Korea, and other countries, and must be preserved."

It *was* our amendment. Those were the talking points I'd written, word for word, except that I'd used "precarious," not "precious." The fact that he'd mispronounced it, though, proved that he'd never seen them before, hadn't even read them before giving this speech—so it was a spur of the moment decision to offer the amendment. Because Erin had talked to Raymonda? Or because Raymonda was tired of Belkin complaining about having nothing to do?

"Roger, this is important." He was scrubbing again, in circles. He looked up. "Did you talk to Erin tonight?" He shook his head "no" and blinked. He could tell something was wrong. "Did you see her on the Floor?" "No" again, and much more blinking. Oblivious to the rag in his hand, he pushed his glasses up his nose.

I looked over at Mourad.

"She went home ages ago, Roger," he said. "We've been checking every hour or so, but there's no way she was here to give Colbert's clearance on the amendment."

On the television, Belkin held up the paper he'd been reading from, waving it for effect. "In fact, Mr. President, I would like to ask that I be added as an original cosponsor on this amendment. This is a fine amendment, and I am proud to cosponsor it."

"If the gentleman will yield," another voice cut in.

"I will be glad to yield to my colleague from Ohio."

The shot switched to the Democratic side of the aisle, where Subcommittee Chairman and Ohio Senator Robert Naylor was standing. "I would also ask that I be added as an original cosponsor to this amendment."

Roger started giggling, slowly at first, but as Naylor continued to expand on the amendment, longer and louder. His face contorted, he said, "You better make sure Colbert approved moving that amendment by the time we start the session tomorrow morning." Looking back at the desk, he sprayed another spot, as if he'd missed it earlier. "Or you are totally, and I do mean totally, screwed."

Within two minutes, the amendment had passed. Voice vote.

Mourad and I looked at each other. Roger, again, started giggling.

Chapter 18

Mourad and I were waiting outside Senator Colbert's office the following morning as Erin Monaghan approached; we'd been there since eight o'clock, to be sure we beat her to the office and could catch her on the way in. She saw us from a distance and, for an instant, seemed to think about turning around to walk away: she missed a step and almost tripped, as if she were pondering her options.

"Good morning, Erin," Mourad said as she approached. We'd decided he should take the lead.

She stopped and gave us a downtrodden look. "I'm really sorry, but ... well, we're not going to be able to help you with that amendment." She looked to the floor and sighed theatrically. "I'm so sorry. It is a really great idea. We just don't have the time to take it to the Floor."

There was a long pause. "Well, Erin," I said, "we actually have some *good* news, and maybe some bad news. But not that bad, I guess."

Mourad looked at me, uncertain.

"The Senate passed the amendment last night."

"Oh," she said, "that's great. Wow. That's terrific." She smiled at us.

"Yes, that's the good news," I continued. "The *maybe* bad news is, well, the Senate passed the amendment in Sen. Colbert's name."

Her mouth opened, slowly, as a look of shock spread across her face. I waited and, as Mourad started to say something, reached out to stop him.

We need her to react before we know what to do next, I thought, glaring at him in the hopes he'd pick up on that somehow. We waited.

After a seemingly interminable pause, she said, "I've never had an amendment pass on the Senate Floor before."

Well, technically you still haven't, I thought, but we'll let that go for now.

"It truly is a great amendment, and we feel proud being part of it," I said, giving her a determined look, one that said, "you're one of us." "The thing is, the Floor leaders on the bill had copies of the amendment, and we'd told them to wait until you spoke with them, but they moved the amendment on their own. At, like, nine thirty at night."

After a moment, I decided that a look of shock might help here, so glancing first at Mourad, I looked back to her, shocked.

Erin looked confused, while Mourad, clearly out of his league, looked serious but noncommittal.

"Here's what I suggest," I said, this time moving a little bit closer while going for conspiratorial. "You should take this to your staff director. The bill has already passed the Senate, but"—I paused, giving her a moment to panic combined with the small shred of hope she might hear in my "but"— "the Senate can still vitiate the vote"—wipe it off the books, pretend like it never happened, through one of their better and most arcane legislative moves—"so the Senator is totally protected." I paused again here and nodded meaningfully, letting it sink in. Erin looked at Mourad, and God bless him, he nodded too; he was getting into this. "But it would be too bad to lose such a great amendment."

She paused, as did I. It was up to her now, and all I needed was for her to figure that out. She looked at Mourad, and then back at me, and then at the floor. We waited.

"Okay," she said. "I'll be right back."

As the door closed behind her, Mourad smacked me on the left arm. "You sonofabitch, that was good."

"Yeah, well, you were great," I told him. "Completely useless. And ow, by the way." I rubbed my arm; this one would raise a bruise.

It was a good fifteen minutes before Erin came back through the door. But she came out smiling. "He says it's okay. We can leave it."

* * *

"So somebody's gotta have something good to report."

It was Michael, the following Monday, leading off our staff meeting in his typical jovial mood. At least, his typical mid-September-Congress-will-wrap-up-soon-and-you-haven't-done-everything-you-promised-yet jovial mood, meaning he wasn't very jovial at all.

Our victory with the coastal fisheries amendment was short-lived, as the continuing television coverage of the disaster in Golongo was giving us a major Koliba hangover. We were spending way too much time watching CNN reports from the capital; they'd finally snuck someone into Kinshasa, not the lovely Miss Amanpour, of course, but some unknown, unshaven rookie reporting from the tank-filled streets on the continuing rumors, innuendo, and general lawlessness. It was somewhat addicting, in that car-wreck kind of way.

Tom was back, glummer than ever since even he had been forced to start thinking ill of his client, and because he was feeling that the odds for accomplishing anything for Koliba were somewhere a few degrees south of zero. I was a little more sanguine than that, both because of America's general inability to pay attention to anything that happens in Africa for more than a week or two, and because Koliba's Congressional opponents, now numbering in the hundreds, weren't positioned to do much of anything bad this late in the year. The appropriations bill had already passed the House and Senate, and we had a month or two to go before Joint Conference. But I wasn't saying anything out loud, because the moment I did they'd hold me to it, turning the slightest comment that we might have a chance of getting out of this alive—no pun intended—into a firm commitment I'd have to meet. So I just sat quiet, hoping not to be noticed.

"Ed, what do we do?"

Well, there went that idea.

"Right now, nothing," I replied, staring back at Michael. "Our best plan is to sit silent and let the furor die down a little." To my left, Tom shifted uncomfortably in his seat. At least it seemed like he was uncomfortable, or at least wanted me to think so; he lifted up a little, shifted his shoulders and arms in one direction, his ass and hips in another, like he had a king-sized wedgie and was trying to shimmy his way out of it. Once he settled, as if for good measure, he coughed. I ignored his Mr. Subtle act. "It's still early in the month, and Koliba just isn't the kind of thing that stays on the front pages that long. We just have to lay low for now."

"They're not paying us to lay low, though, are they?" Michael was glaring at me, disgusted with my plan. Michael's biggest problem as a lobbyist was in being a man of action, a hoverer, someone who felt we always needed to be *doing* something. Like a chef who can't stop opening the oven over and over again to check on a soufflé, ruining it in the end. He never liked my theory that when you had a plan in place and knew it was working, you needed to let it play out. He was a three-yards-and-a-cloud-of-dust guy, while I was a Hail-Mary man all the way. This part of the year that always meant holding him back while watching that none of my carefully laid plans went to shit. Best way to hold him back?

"Michelle and I'll hit the House side again today," I said, "see what we can find." Three yards and a cloud of dust.

❧ ❧ ❧

"So what's the plan?" It was Michelle, on the she-slid-over side of the cab. She had an earnest look on her face, apparently not yet in on the joke that was this trip to the Hill.

Looking over, I wondered how long it had been since I'd shown that face, that open, friendly, I-believe-in-you face that she was wearing. Back somewhere before I stopped believing in the issues and started believing in the game, I supposed.

I leaned up toward the cabbie and spoke through the window in his plastic barrier. "Instead of Rayburn, just drop us at the corner of Second Street, just past the Madison Building of the Library of Congress." Looking into his eyes through the mirror, I saw that he knew which one I meant, the modern, anonymous block of stone and glass facing Independence Avenue, as opposed to the original, majestic Jefferson Building across the street.

"Why are we heading there?"

"Starbucks. We'll catch a coffee and lay out the plan," I responded. Turning to look out the window on my right, I continued, half to myself, "Or at least make one up."

Just about the worst thing you could do in this business was to argue in support of your client when the whole world was against you. That first day of meetings that we went to the Hill on Koliba, that was just to give people a chance to rant. With the end of the year still a couple of months away, with nothing on foreign aid moving, this was a good time to lay low, keep our heads down, and hope people would forget about us in light of the latest hurricane, or another Middle East hiccup, or coup rumors in East Kablooistan. Jeez, even the latest budget deficit numbers. Anything that would get their minds off Koliba for a while.

Besides which, sticking your face in just to talk to people was a horrible way to do lobbying. People in Washington never had time for meaningless meetings. They had time for a free lunch or dinner. They had time to get a cup of coffee if you bumped into them on the street. They even had time to catch a quick drink after work with you at the Pinnacle, or the Hawk and Dove if you were on the House side. But they never had time for you to stop by to blab.

Especially not when they were appropriators heading into the last couple months of the year.

"Goddammit, this is stupid."

"*What?*" Michelle seemed shocked. Jesus, I didn't mean to scare her, I thought.

"This." I waved my arms around the air, as if that meant something. "Running to the Hill. What's the fucking point?"

"I don't have any idea." She was staring now, her eyes a little wide, her mouth locked in an effort to say something more. Finally she spit out, "I, I, I, Jesus, you practically dragged me out to the cab with you. I assumed you knew what you were doing."

"Don't always assume that." The kid was starting to bug me, the way she always did. "You have to learn to have your own ideas. Koliba's not just my problem, for Christ's sake."

She stared at me for a moment, motionless. At least, as motionless as you can get in a D.C. cab rattling to a stop on a downtown D.C. street. "Well, shit, then," she finally said, "we'll just talk to people who don't even known Koliba exists."

Well, duh.

* * *

Six shots of watery Starbucks espresso later—three per espresso macchiato, the second more to kill time than because I needed it—Michelle and I set out on her simple yet elegant plan. If talking to our opponents about Koliba was just going to focus their attention on how to make him pay, and talking to our friends about him just going to get them to yell at us about what a lousy sonofabitch we were working for, we should just avoid the topic entirely. Doable. It would take a little luck, ducking anyone we didn't want to see while slipping in to see those we did, but that's a pretty routine operation in lobbying, knowing which halls were the least traveled, climbing an extra flight of stairs to get out off the high traffic floors, where the Committee rooms are, onto the quieter ones.

We entered Longworth on the south side, along C Street SE, the less-traveled side of the building. Turning right at the entrance, we headed to the stairs, toward our target, the third-floor office of Rep. Tommy Walston, Republican of Alabama, Chairman of the House Republican Conference, another darling of the right-to-life and religion crowd. He was from the same wing of the party as Henry Little, the loon whom Will Richardson had told me to ally myself with, but Walston was actually a reasonable human being despite the fire-and-brimstone attitude he adopted on the House Floor and in front of TV cameras. He served on the House Commerce and Small Business committees, a seemingly odd pairing for someone whose main face in politics was bringing religion and family values back in America. Truth be told, he was most successful at protecting jobs at the Boeing plant in his district and the Toyota plant next door, half of whose employees lived and voted in Walston's district.

One of the biggest lies in Washington was the one people told about knowing everything there is to know about everything. The dirty little secret was that most of them, even the best, only knew about their own sphere of influence: the foreign aid world, the defense spending world, the world of taxes and revenues, or of whatever their primary committee assignments might be, along with maybe, maybe some smaller subset reflecting a personal interest. Someone like Walston, good as he was, knew everything in the Commerce Department budget, how big it was, what it was for, and how he could squeeze a little "juice" out of it to the benefit of the folks back home. Other than that, he focused on the internal politics of Republicans in the House, whom he oversaw as head of the Conference.

Similarly, his staff was divided into a couple of people who focused on Commerce and Small Business, somebody doing defense and homeland security, some poor schlub who answered constituent mail, and a junior kid whose formal title should have been "Legislative Assistant, Kitchen Sink." This was the job in every office held by some pimply young kid, usually a Politics major from HomeState U, who didn't know his ass from a hole in the ground. In this office, it was Kenny Thurgood, tall, lanky, still just a tad pimply at twenty-four or twenty-five years old, with an odd habit of tilting his head to the left and down as he spoke to you, especially when he was tense. And he was tense pretty much all of the time.

That was the guy we were here to see.

"Kenny." Michelle put out her hand in greeting as Ken walked out from the back office, glasses slid far down his nose, shirt loose at the left of his waist, a grimace on his face. "How've you been?"

Michelle knew Kenny from grad school at Georgetown, where he was in the International Security Studies Program, a sort of elephants' graveyard where old national security practitioners went to die—I mean, teach. Old warhorses teaching young hopefuls—and hopelessly deludeds—in the intricacies of American foreign policy and national security in an age when none of us seemed to have a clue where the next threat was or would come from. It was a useful degree if you spent your two years in the program networking your way into the Washington establishment and laying the groundwork for a future career. Otherwise, like most master's programs in politics or policy, it was pretty much a waste.

Kenny came from among the hopelessly deludeds, the ones who think their degree will get them a job. Michelle had told me over coffee once that Kenny spent about eighteen months hunting around Washington in search of a national security position and took this sea slug of a job with Walston as an absolute last resort. Right after he got there, Walston had been voted in as Chair of the Conference, the policy organization for all House Republicans. It hadn't changed Kenny's job, and he spent about 10 percent of his time on foreign policy, but working for the Conference Chair was never a bad thing—and neither was knowing someone hidden away in that office. Kenny always welcomed Michelle when she visited, and I always encouraged her to visit.

This time was no exception. "You two free for coffee?"

Michelle snickered under her breath at the idea of me drinking more coffee, but I spoke first. "Sure, I haven't had a cup all day," I said, glancing at her in silent warning. This could easily kill another forty minutes if we were lucky.

As we headed out the door toward the elevator, I started in on Kenny with a discussion of the Dungan and their concerns about possible religious and cultural oppression by the Kazakh Government. Walking the halls, I blabbered through my stock speech while watching for anyone I might know, lest I have to duck behind a bush or plant to evade any Koliba discussions. The standard spiel rolled off my tongue without much effort, both because I didn't need Kenny to do anything and because I'd been doing it all year and knew it by heart. Kenny was fascinated, his questions pulling me into discussions of political differences among the Stans, and the relative levels of unpleasantness exercised by the Kazakh and Turkmen dictators. All in all, he had a good sense of the region, telling me he'd specialized in former Soviet states while at Georgetown, an interest he obviously kept up with since.

Standing in line in the Longworth cafeteria, I poured myself a massive cup of their watery coffee. Once again, when taste is missing, volume conquers all. While Michelle unobtrusively paid for the three coffees, undoubtedly violating some new ethics rule as she did so, I walked with Kenny to an empty table near the back, about equally far from the cash registers and the cafeteria doors. I'd learned long before that it was seldom a good idea to be surprised by someone walking in on you in the middle of a shtick.

As we sat, Kenny asked, "You guys work for Koliba, right? What's your take on the letter that's being circulated?"

I froze for a moment. Letter, letter, letter, nope, nothing buried in my head about any letter on Koliba. Must be new.

"This is the first I've heard of it," I replied.

"Of what?" Michelle asked, catching up with us.

"Oh, shit," Kenny said. "I probably shouldn't be telling you about it. It's pretty harsh."

I laughed at that. "Oh, that we'd expect. At this point, anything on Koliba's going to be pretty hard." I took a moment to slide into my seat, consciously relaxing my body. I needed him to see me as nonthreatening, to get that I was just another joe. "You know, half our business is telling the client what Congress thinks, not just asking for favors. We're two-way information sources, so the more we can tell them the better."

Michelle was looking at me as I spoke, her face showing much less than it would have just six months earlier. The intensity in her eyes gave her away, staring at me as they were with only the slightest crinkle at the corners, something only I'd notice. I smiled and looked back to Kenny. "I don't suppose you have a copy of the draft with you, do you?"

"I don't think I could do that," he said, looking over at Michelle. "I mean, we haven't even decided on whether we're going to sign it. Besides, I don't have it on me."

"No problem," I said. "We'll figure something out. Besides, we're here to talk about the Dungan anyway. Where were we, discussing the joys of yak milk, right?" I laughed again and slipped back into my spiel.

Twenty minutes later, watching Kenny trundle off down the hall, I turned to Michelle. "Follow after him and get that letter. I don't care how you do it, bat your eyes at him, give him the whole frigging Georgetown thing, tell him how Saxa the Hoyas are, how you Hoyas need to stick together, whatever, just get the letter."

"I thought you gave up on that a little easy." Michelle smiled grimly.

"I'd have had to drag it out of him," I said, "making him feel guilty about it. You can wheedle it out of him, and he'll give it up feeling like he's doing a buddy a favor. I do it—it's the last thing we get out of him. You do it—you've got a coconspirator for life."

Michelle stared at me for a moment before speaking. "Half the time when you talk strategy to me, I feel like I'm listening to Satan." Turning to follow Kenny, I could hear her continue under her breath, "What a crazy fucking job this is."

Well, that's one way to look at it, I thought.

* * *

Two days later, Michelle and I sat together in the third row of a House Foreign Affairs Committee hearing room, watching yet another assault on Koliba. I was pleased to see that the Committee was well into the Koliba debate by the time of my arrival, so I had the good fortune to miss much of it. Michelle looked miserable.

House Committee debates are always much more intense than Senate debates, more antagonistic, more spiteful across party divides, and just generally more unpleasant to sit through. I think that's why I liked this Committee so much more than its Senate counterpart; if you have to sit through four hours of deadly debate, there might as well be fireworks to keep you entertained. Michelle, however, didn't see it that way.

"How long's it been going?" I asked.

"Koliba? Ever since they began," she murmured, shaking her head.

"What's the issue?"

"Anderson," Congressman Ted Anderson, fourth ranking Republican on the panel and a raving madman of the party's lunatic fringe, "is trying to defend Koliba as an island of stability."

I started. Turning to scan the crowd, I asked, "Tom's not here, is he?"

"He came in about forty minutes ago," she said, looking surprised. "Walked in with Anderson. He's over by the other door, up against the wall. Why?"

There he was, ramrod straight, standing watch. Jesus Christ Almighty, I thought, he's decided to pick a fight. This one, I knew, he was going to lose: half the Republicans on this particular panel paid serious attention to human rights issues, and most of the rest of them were smart enough not to pick fights on the issue except when they had to. Which was more than often enough, given the White House's loathing of any Congressional meddling in such matters.

"Oh well, nothing I can do." I smiled at Michelle, who still looked confused. I straightened out in my seat and leaned over to her. "I'm glad you were here. If I'd seen Tom walk in like that, I'd have known he put Anderson up to it and would probably have strangled him." She looked over at Tom and back at Anderson, shaking her head.

Tuning in the debate, I decided that maybe this wouldn't be so bad after all. Anderson was being pretty nasty, and while he was clearly outnumbered, Koliba's opponents on the Committee were so consumed with responding to him, venting their spleen about our evil client, that he might be giving them the target they needed. With all this caterwauling, maybe they'd feel like they'd made their point on Koliba and stop worrying about him for the rest of the year. I could only hope.

My Crackberry buzzed in my pocket. I'd put it on silent, meaning that it had to be an IM from Charlotte. That was odd; she knew I was in one hearing or the other and wouldn't be taking calls.

I slid the device from my pocket and marveled at the stream of new messages. Charlotte's topped the list, but there were six others, all IMs, all about Richardson. "Ethics takes up Richardson" read the first, and the others mirrored that. Charlotte's said simply, "Call me now."

I shook my head. Larry Craig's two-step in a Minnesota airport restroom had pushed Will off the front pages for several weeks, but it looked like it was now his turn to be roasted over the slow flame that Washington and network reporters call "news."

Glancing out the window to my right, I paused. I hadn't seen Will since the news hit the *Post*, and hadn't tried to. I was still pissed at him, not so much for almost bringing me into his scandal, but for being so stupid as to do something like this in the first place. The city was teeming with—well, looking at it through Will's eyes—pussy, and he had to set up some completely crazy-ass scheme just to secure his supply? There was something entirely too sick about that, entirely too *Washington* about that, and I just didn't need it. I'd walked away from Will and didn't regret it.

I thumbed a note back to Charlotte. "Saw Richardson news." Send. "Will call when hfac done." Send.

I started to slip the Crackberry back in my pocket when it buzzed sharply in my hand. "Fuck," I muttered, almost dropping it. The vibrate on those things is pretty muffled when tucked in my jacket, but always freaks me out when it goes off in my hand.

"No. Call now." Another note from Charlotte.

That couldn't be good. She never, ever dragged me out of a hearing. Never.

I looked at Michelle and asked, "You okay here? You have it covered?"

"Yes," she said, looking around. "I think so. Why?"

"I have to go, and I don't know if I'll be able to get back in." I reached down under my seat for my notepad and copies of the bills. "You'll be fine. Just don't let Tom get too far off the reservation."

As I rose, she clutched my arm from behind and pulled. "What do I do?"

I sat back down and turned toward her. "Nothing. There's nothing you can do, so don't worry about it." I smiled to reassure her. "I was kidding. I do hope that Tom stops this soon, because Beach up there," I pointed toward the dais, where old-timer and longtime liberal Republican Tim Beach of Iowa was turning all sorts of shades of red, "looks like he's going to have a stroke listening to someone say good things about Koliba."

Seeing her relax a little, I continued. "Listen, kid. Most of the time we just play the cards we've been dealt. So don't worry so much about what's going to happen. What happens, happens. We're just along for the ride."

* * *

Heading out of the Committee room, I told the doorkeeper I was just running to the men's room and would be right back. That way, if it wasn't anything serious with Charlotte, there was a slim chance I might still be able to reclaim my seat.

Turning left, I walked quickly down the hall to the elevators and lucked out by finding the doors on an "up" elevator opening as I arrived. Two floors up, I turned left again and headed for the long corridor leading to Heaney's office.

Coming in the door, I said a quick hello to Joanna and, pointing to Charlotte's office, said simply, "She in?"

"Go ahead," she said. "I'm glad you're here."

As I entered the office, Charlotte was standing by the oversized window, her back to me, her arms crossed. From where I was standing, she seemed smaller than ever.

"Honey?"

She turned. She looked strained. "The FBI were here."

I walked quickly over to her and took her in my arms. God, she was small and felt smaller than ever as she put her arms around me. She was shaking. "What happened?"

"They came in and asked to talk to me." She pointed in the direction of her desk. "They closed the door, sat down, and started asking me questions."

"Jesus, what about?"

"Will."

Oh God, it was the Richardson investigation. But what? His house parties, the dinners? I'd never gone. Maybe my political contributions, the ones I'd been bundling over the years? But the law requiring bundlers to disclose their activities had just been passed and wouldn't even go into effect until January 1.

Jesus, I thought, I never believed we'd get dragged into this, and standing there, I felt a chill go through me. These fucking FBI investigations had gotten insane, beginning with the Duke Cunningham case, where his entire style of living turned out to be corrupt, and followed quickly by that idiot from Louisiana, William Jefferson, who hid cash in his freezer and incriminating documents in his Congressional office. These in turn pointed a beacon at the various investment property investigations involving Denny Hastert, Alan Mollohan, and the others who earmarked federally funded projects right next to properties they or their wives had invested in, driving up the value of their land to obscene heights. With all this floating around, the FBI had been rumored to be running a whole series of witch hunts into any Member of Congress whose conduct raised even the slightest suspicion. Most of the fuckers deserved it, but often it bled over to their staffs, who were mostly—and certainly in Charlotte's case—unaware of the goings-on.

"So why'd they want to talk to you?"

"They wanted to know what amendments Richardson might have slipped into the Chairman's bill." She looked up at me. "Can you believe it?"

I was confused. "What does that have to do with us?"

"With *me*, stupid, I review the Members' requests, remember?"

Oh Jesus, it wasn't me at all.

I was relieved, but the anger and fear in me spilled out. "Fucking A, Sweetie, *everyone* sticks shit into in the Veterans Affairs bill. It's a fucking Christmas tree." It is surely that, a bill for funding new VA clinics and hospitals and so Committee members could be looking over the Veterans Administration's shoulder. Mostly it's someplace to get on local TV talking about veterans, and how important they are, and how much a Member *cares*, truly cares about the plight of vets. I always found that the best way to tell when a Congressman was spinning a pile of bullshit was to count the number of times he used the word "care" as a verb; the more he said it, the more he was lying. Anytime someone said it more than ten times in a single speech, it was time to take him out back and vote the sumbitch out of office.

"Nothing personal, babe, but there's more shit shoveled into that bill than just about anything else up here," I laughed, trying desperately to lighten her up. I felt a small rumble in her, like something of a giggle.

"Hey," she said, pulling back to look up into my eyes. She was smiling a little. "That's my boss's Committee."

"Is he here?"

"No, he's already headed back to the district for the weekend."

"Yeah?" I said. "Well, then it's a bullshit assignment and you know it." She laughed and leaned back into me. I hugged her tighter and smiled slightly. She was calming down if she could laugh. There was more to learn here, but she was calming down.

But I needed room to breathe.

* * *

Leaving the office about twenty minutes later, I headed outside, into the stifling heat, just to get out of the building and away. I left Rayburn by the side entrance, the one facing Longworth, and turned right out the cavernous driveway toward C Street, and then left on C. I walked slowly; it was

September, but we were still in one of those horribly miserable D.C. sum-mer weeks, ninety-six degrees and the humidity at 143 percent. I didn't care, just needing to walk, away from that place where she'd been inter-viewed, away from the interview itself, and especially away from my own reactions to it.

I followed C Street past the rear side of the Longworth Building, the rear of Cannon, and finally, an eternity in this steaming heat, along the long back side of the Library of Congress's Madison Building. At the corner of 2nd Street, SE, I turned left and crossed the street at an angle, walking north again toward the Starbucks I'd been in with Michelle just two days earlier. It would have been somewhat shorter to come around the other way, turning left out of Rayburn and getting onto Independence there, but that was the main drag this time of day, Members, lobbyists, and staffers cross-ing between buildings and over to the Capitol, or up to where Independ-ence hit Pennsylvania if headed toward the restaurants and bars. The way I came, I had less chance of running into anyone I knew, and it worked.

I was sweating like a demon by the time I hit Starbucks, and looking at my reflection in a window along the way, I could see how wilted I was. At the bar, I ordered myself two bottles of water and my triple espresso. I carried the water to an open table near the side while waiting for my coffee, opened one of the bottles, and took a long slug.

"I hate this fucking town," I heard myself say aloud. "I really do."

Turning back toward the bar, I could see a startled customer looking over at me. I smiled, muttered "Bad day" to him, and headed for the bar to snag my espresso.

Stirring three sugars into the cup, I stared at the wall in front of me. There were so many things wrong with the conversation I'd just had with Charlotte. My reaction, thinking it was about me and not even considering it might be about Charlotte. The simple fact that it could have been about me, had I gone to that dinner Will invited me to, or had the FBI been smart enough to connect me to Charlotte. The fact that this was my life, hanging out with people like this who could flame out at almost any moment. What in God's name was I doing? And was there any way out?

Chapter 19

"Weenies," I said again. "Goobers. Doinks. Losers."

Alexis laughed, that light, airy, honest laugh that I was starting to think of as her signature. It wasn't a common laugh in Washington; most of us spent so many years laughing because we were supposed to, laughing at every lame-o attempt at humor by our targets of opportunity, that we'd forgotten what it was to laugh, to relax with people such that we'd hear what they were actually saying rather than filter it through the various things we hoped they would or wouldn't say while silently considering our options for how to react.

"They don't seem to be weenies to me," she said. "They seem to be entirely honest and focused. They have a goal, and they're pursuing it."

"But they're pursuing it like losers," I replied. "Look, I don't have anything against the human rights types, and I'm a big fan of democracy. But they're stupid the way they go about it."

"Why, because they don't take staffers and Members to fancy restaurants?" She was laughing at me again, this time a little more determinedly.

"No, it's not the money—it's what they ask people to do." I smiled at her, but I was serious. "Sure, nobody wants their wheatgrass sandwiches, but they can live with that because you've got us to feed you."

"Ouch." She laughed again. She'd insisted that she pay for this lunch, claiming it was more to thank me for helping her find the job than because of her ethics concerns, but I'd hit a nerve: maybe she'd had a few of those sandwiches I was talking about.

"Look," I laughed, "I'm not talking about their operating style. I'm talking about the substance of what they do. They do the job badly—they're all one-trick ponies."

"They're *committed*," Alexis responded. She leaned in, waving a forkful of chicken *cordon bleu* at me. She'd obviously been talked to a lot, which made sense—she was recognizable from her HFAC days, so most of them could act like they knew her; she was approachable, which many Foreign Ops staffers just plain aren't; and she wanted to learn the business. But she was also playing this pretty passionately, arguing their side with some vigor. It seemed to be a test, to see if I was just making fun of them for the hell of it, or if I was serious.

"Listen," I said, "it's comes down to something that's very simple: they live in a world of black and white, while the real world is almost all grays. They act as if human rights exist outside of balances of power, of power politics, of the uncertain political and geographic struggles in the world we all live in. Except for the Human Rights First, there's none of them that's worth a shit."

Human Rights First, née the Lawyers' Committee on Human Rights, traditionally focused first and foremost on the rule of law—freedom of the courts from government interference.

"What, you want them to lobby for police states every once in a while?"

"No, I'm not stupid either. But I want them to recognize reality." I glanced around us, but didn't see anyone I knew. I leaned in this time and, speaking more quietly, said, "Take Koliba."

She looked up from her lunch and responded before I could continue. "No, you take Koliba. I thought we weren't going to talk about him."

"We're not, but that's what I mean. All my Democratic Hill friends, or at least the liberal ones, want me to pretend I don't work for the guy, because it makes them feel better about being seen with me." I paused while I took a sip of wine and considered. I wasn't sure I wanted to go down this road, the fact that there were more and more people who insisted on ignoring the Koliba part of my life. As someone who'd always been the good guy, it just wasn't a role that I was comfortable with.

I took a breath before continuing. "Look, what's the sensible thing to do with Koliba? What *should* the U.S. Government do?"

"Cut him off. Prohibit all aid, and impose economic sanctions. The man is a killer."

"Thank you for your support," I said, laughing lightly. I raised my glass in a mock toast and smiled again. It was the answer I'd expected. "But what about the listening post?"

"What listening post?"

I glanced at my wine glass and then at the bottle, which was a little lower than I'd thought but not terribly so. How much wine had I had? "The U.S. has a secret listening post there, probably covers most of Central Africa. Why do you think we even argue about this guy? It's classified, but it's pretty widely known." Not that widely known, not *Washington Post* widely known at least. But several of the more senior Foreign Ops Subcommittee staffers that I'd talked to knew, which meant it was definitely out there. "That's why the U.S. cares, and why—at DOD's urging—Koliba got himself a lobbyist when he became President."

"Jesus, why the hell would they put a listening post there? The guy's a loon."

"Could you keep it down just a little?" I looked around again, reconfirming that there was no one nearby whom I knew or who appeared to be listening. My voice still low, I said, "I'm not supposed to know this, and neither are you. Like I said, it's classified."

She pursed her lips and looked into her wine glass. Watching her nervously, I took another gulp from mine. No wonder I'm so far ahead of her, I thought.

"It's a hazard of living and working in Washington," I continued. "Everybody knows a little something classified. Mostly it's the unimportant stuff, but even the unimportant stuff can upset State and DOD if they know you know it. So I try to balance between the 'need to know' and the need to be truthful."

"Why did you tell me?"

"Because I think you need to know," I said with a smile. "Look, I'm sorry. Maybe I shouldn't have told you, and yes, secret listening posts are a very big deal so you really don't ever want to talk about it. But you need to be able to trust me, and if you were to find this out two years from now, you'd be incredibly pissed. You'd feel used, even if I never asked you to do anything on Koliba."

She snorted lightly and, with a wry smile, reaching for her wine glass, asked me again. "No, seriously. Why?"

That hit me. I stopped, watching her, as she glanced at me out of the corner of her eye. Waiting, I tried to listen to myself for a second. If I was claiming to be telling her the truth, I felt like I should check to be sure it was what I actually believed. But my mind was a blank.

"I don't know. I... I'm not sure. Maybe I just need to talk to someone who's not going to stick a knife in my back. Maybe I need to think through why this is so hard." I looked down into my wine glass for a moment, but thought better of it. "I've never had a client go south on me like this. I've never found myself believing in someone at one moment, and then discover I was defending a monster." Elbows on the table, I drew the tips of my middle fingers along the edge of my brow. I could feel a major headache coming on.

"More importantly, though, I'm trying to make a point. One of the firmest rules in Washington is the simple fact that you can count on your enemies to be too stupid to do the obvious. Why is the post where it is? First, DOD thinks strategically, not politically, so I'm guessing that when they looked for a site, they based it entirely on geography—where will a listening post have the farther range? For all I know, they set it up twenty years ago under what's-his-name, the guy who ran the place before Koliba. The real question is why it's *still* there. That's the stupid part." I paused and took another drink. Even when I tell her, I reminded myself, she can't do anything with the information—her boss won't get involved in this one. "The human rights morons could get Congress to order it moved out of Golongo, and our support for Koliba would evaporate overnight. But they can't do that—human rights nerds oppose all things military on principle, and of course oppose NSA listening in to everything we do, so they can't even support the *idea* of a listening post. So they look the other way and end up fighting a losing battle every year because DOD's going to go ahead and pay Koliba's government the $20 million they promised them."

"Twenty million?"

"Twenty million." I was totally over the line now; Tom would kill me if he knew. "You didn't hear that either. All perfectly legal—there's a base agreement, funded out of the black part of the DOD budget. And that's my last Koliba secret, I swear."

"Shit," she said. She looked around, for the waiter perhaps, or maybe just to look away from me. "Maybe we should get out of here."

* * *

The following morning, I was back on the Hill, this time on the Senate side and this time actually having fun. My client had come to town, and I was shepherding them around the Senate. And enjoying myself thoroughly.

When I had proposed my fall visit to Chicago to meet with the Dungan-American Friendship Society, they'd countered with a request to bring their message to D.C. It was out of the ordinary and off schedule: usually this kind of meet-and-greet visit occurred in the early spring, when Congress was just getting going. We'd signed this client comparatively late in the year, though, and clients always wanted their time in the sun, meeting the Senators and Members of the House, rubbing shoulders with power. So here I was, toddling around the Hill with Bao, Charlie, and Hendrickson in tow. We'd already had a twenty-minute love fest with Sen. VanderMeer, our new best friend, and found ourselves—thanks to Roger's goodwill—in a face-to-face with his boss, Sen. Frank Johnson, Democrat of Michigan.

"Michael and Ed here have been very helpful in making sure that we're fully briefed on the importance of ensuring religious freedoms are respected in Kazakhstan." This was Roger, leaning in meekly to interrupt during a brief pause in the discussion, most of it between Hendrickson and the Senator, which had now been going on in a rather desultory manner for about fifteen minutes. We lost a good five minutes of that in nodding, bowing, and pointing one another to chairs, the way that so often happens with clients from Asian countries, and the rest of the time was a simple recitation of the reasons for our visit. After my brief intro and a wonderfully confusing series of statements from Bao about the Senator's lovely office surroundings and his graciousness in welcoming us, Hendrickson had taken over the discussion.

With Roger's help, we'd written the statement about "Michael and Ed" into the Senator's talking points for the meeting, but the Senator had either forgotten the point or, more likely, decided he wanted to keep all the glory to himself.

"Yes," admitted Johnson with an inscrutable glance at Roger. "Michael's been very helpful indeed. He speaks to me often about the mistreatment of the ethnic minorities in your country."

Jesus, I thought, I'm right in front of you. Would it kill you to notice my existence, just once maybe?

I was pretty sure that I kept my poker face on, but after the briefest pause, Bao leaned forward. "Yes," he said, "Ed is very knowledge." He looked over to me, smiled, and then nodded ever so slightly.

Sen. Johnson didn't blink, staring ahead at him for a moment before turning to Hendrickson. "Yet you know, John," he said, leaning forward. I struggled not to roll my eyes; he'd said it like a light bulb had gone off, when we all knew the bulb had burned out years before. "I really didn't understand the importance of keeping pressure on President Nazarbayev on these issues until you came here today and really laid it out for me. I want to thank you for that."

What a pile of shit. We'd written a one-page briefing for this meeting that told him more than he could have gotten from this conversation, and Roger had assured me that he'd walked the Senator through the memo the night before. So we all knew just how important pressure was and why.

"After you, my dear Alphonse," "no, you first, my dear Gaston," that's the standard ebb and flow of client meetings with a member of the House or Senate no matter how well you plan them out. The lobbyist is looking for a little credit, something to show the client that the member is aware of their existence and, even better, pretends like he works closely with them. The staffer's there to make sure that the member follows through on any necessary agenda items, doesn't forget who he's talking to or what the subject of the meeting is, and doesn't overcommit to some legislative proposal that's impossible—unless that's also part of the plan, commit to the impossible knowing he'll go down in a ball of glorious flames protecting a principle. Meaning the staffer's also there so he or she knows what mess they have to clean up when the meeting is done. And the members, well, they're actually there for the money, trying to show the client and the lobbyist how important they are to their successes, and hinting that without them—"if I lose the next election"—all those successes would go by the wayside. Even though the money doesn't actually change hands in this meeting, it's the giant invisible turd sitting in the middle of the room, to be paid out somewhere down the line again whenever the next fundraiser is scheduled.

From behind the Senator, Roger pointed to his watch so that both Hendrickson and I could see. "On behalf of Michael," I responded, "I want to thank you for the time, Senator. As I mentioned earlier, he's been unavoidably detained this morning, still in New York." It was sort of true, although the "unavoidable" was three shopping days with his wife Alice in Manhattan. "He wanted me to extend his best wishes to you and Gloria, and very much hopes to see you again soon."

Hendrickson looked confused for a moment, since Michael wasn't part of this conversation at all, but Michael was our main contact—and political contribution bundler—in the company's relationship with Johnson. I wasn't surprised by his confusion; my comment was aimed at the Senator, not Hendrickson.

"Oh, as do I," the Senator responded, undoubtedly counting in his head the several $1,000 checks Michael would bring to that next fundraiser, his, his wife's, his brother- and sister-in-law's, mine, whoever else's he could drum up. "Please be sure to tell him I'm looking forward to that."

Hendrickson's response was to step in front of me, as if I weren't there, and reach out a hand to shake the Senator's. Maybe he does recognize what I was doing, I thought, and wants the Senator to know it. "Thank you, sir," he said. "It has been an honor for me as always to speak with you. And please do remember the peoples of Kazakhstan." Holding tight to the hand, Johnson put his arm around Hendrickson's shoulder, leading him to the exit.

I rolled my eyes at Roger, mouthing "thanks" to him, and turned toward Bao and Charlie. Bao's eyes were gleaming, and he had a wide smile on his face. He probably wasn't sure what those exchanges had meant in detail, but he could surely tell that a short set piece had played out in front of him. He reached to take my arm, as he always did leaving our meetings, and turned to follow the Senator. "Surr-prises," he said quietly. "Always surrr-prises with you."

I laughed as we walked. Two meetings down, I thought, one more to go.

* * *

Late that afternoon, after I'd put them back in their cab for a ride to the airport, I headed over to Dirksen, to Roger's office, to follow up on the other issue I was working with him that day: our MNNA amendment for the UAE. Today was the day that Col. Fawzi had promised to report on the Government's decision on Karen Jameson; he'd scheduled a meeting with Roger for 2:00 p.m., and by now, three thirty, he'd be long gone and I could find out what had happened.

Except that he wasn't, as I discovered approaching Roger's door to find a large cloud of putrid cigarette smoke—not Roger's Marlboros, something infinitely worse—preceding Fawzi out the door. I would never figure out from Roger whether he'd been extremely late or whether the two of them had just spent an hour and a half bullshitting, but there was Fawzi, and there I was, caught checking up on him.

It's always difficult to convince people that you haven't set them up when they catch you in the act. In this case, though, Fawzi apparently figured it out beforehand.

"Ah, my friend," he coughed in that raspy voice, "there you are. I was sure that you would show up eventually." He laughed, harder than seemed wise given the precarious condition of his lungs, and put an arm on my shoulder affectionately. Or maybe so that I could keep him from falling over.

"Col. Fawzi," I said, glancing in at Roger before proceeding. He didn't give me any kind of sign, so I kept going in a noncommittal vein. "So good to see you, sir."

That only made Fawzi laugh harder.

"So can I guess you knew it was me?" I asked.

Coughing still, but at least able to stand up straight again and using his free hand to cover his mouth, Fawzi eyed me with a smile and nodded.

Roger called out then, seemingly tiring of the show going on in his doorway. "She's on an airplane right now—she was spirited out of prison this morning and released into U.S. custody. She'll be in New York sometime late tonight."

"She's free?"

Fawzi, after one final hack, shook his head. "She's been released into the custody of the United States Government. She is to be investigated as an international terrorist, and after that investigation the U.S. is free to decide her fate." He paused for a moment, sucking at his teeth before spitting a bit of tobacco to the floor. "Quietly, and without fanfare." He clapped his hand on my shoulder.

From the office, I head Roger's voice. "The family has agreed to this process. They'll see her at JFK, and it'll take a couple of months, but it will all be over."

"I did not *hear* that," Fawzi said, looking at me intently.

"Neither did I," I replied, smiling. I didn't need to; all I needed to know was the fact that the last obstacle to my MNNA amendment was out of the way. I turned back to my client. "Fawzi, my friend, you need to cut back on those cigarettes."

* * *

Ten days later, it was finally time for that dinner I'd promised Peter to talk about Koliba. I'd been able to dragoon Roger into joining us in the hopes of having some cover, but once we started getting into the topic at hand, I found that Roger was just as angry about Koliba as Peter was.

Dinners like this were pretty standard fare for me, in years when Congressional lobbying rules allowed me to pay for them. Like I mentioned earlier, the latest Ethics reform bill had passed, but the Senate-side restrictions wouldn't take effect until January, so I was still free to feed these two Senate staffers. The problem was, they knew me, all my tricks, and all my ways of talking around an issue without addressing the core complaint they were pursuing. I was defenseless, and they were out for bear.

"Look, I'm not trying to defend Koliba. And I know that the recent shit with Gangaran is probably less problematic than what he did with the courts earlier this year..."

Good God, I thought, listening to myself, I don't even believe what I'm saying.

Roger snorted. "How much have you been drinking? Turning Gangaran into chopped salad is 'less problematic'?" He looked at me as if I were strangling his firstborn. Perhaps I was; his Senator was a Democrat, after all, from a fairly liberal state.

"All right, all right, that didn't come out right." I was talking way too fast, struggling much too early in this dinner. We had just finished our salads and suffered our first visitation from Takis, the outgoing brother of the pair who ran the Pinnacle. Usually I could hold off the hard-core lobbying until the steaks arrived, but not tonight. Not with Koliba as my client.

Koliba was a particularly egregious example of the paradoxes of this business—a freshly minted, democratically elected President who promised change but turned to shit faster than any despot in history, even in Africa.

Africa's problem was the lack of viable governments or, as Weller always put it, "Africa doesn't have political systems—it has political leaders." From Mubarak in Egypt, down through Museveni in Uganda, Moi in Kenya and Mugabe in Zimbabwe, up through Mobutu in Zaire, Bongo in Gabon, the Eyadema family in Togo, up even to Ben Ali in Tunisia, Africa with rare exceptions was a series of "Big Man" countries where the President was the country, and the country served the President. The exceptions were glaring and most—like Nelson Mandela in South Africa—didn't last, falling back into the "Big Man" mode once their Mandela retired. Much of the blame lay with the colonial powers that left Africa in a shambles; someday, though, Africans will need to focus on the solutions, not on who was to blame for their political misery.

"I'm thinking the Committee report should state something like, 'The Committee sits in stunned disbelief,'" Roger continued, his left eye twitching at a rapid rate, "'at the shocking disregard of His Excellency President Ernest Koliba to pay the slightest attention to democratic norms.' How's that work for you?" Roger had the ability to be a complete dick when he wanted to be—"refreshingly direct," he called it—and tonight was one of those nights. "'The crushing of the judiciary demonstrates the government's complete indifference...'"

"Oh, fuck you."

"The Committee sits in sheer amazement," Peter chimed in, exchanging a hard, thin smile with Roger, "that you could think for a moment that the Committee would do anything other than *fuck* your client for his inexcusable..."

"No, really, fuck you—you know why I'm here." I was getting upset, mostly because I had to be there, but also that they were being so hard on me. I'd been hoping to walk away from this meal with some shred of dignity despite the fact that our client had been, well, pulling a Koliba. "Give me half a break here. Help me figure out what I have to do to survive."

"You don't get it, do you?" It was Roger again, ponging to Peter's ping, the two of them playing me the way they usually played the rookies. His entire face was ablaze with blinking and twitching. "Killing the Vice President was just the icing on the cake. It's the courts that matter in the long term, and they've completely trashed the judiciary. Political opponents come and go, get tossed in jail, and occasionally get assassinated like Gangaran. But without a free judiciary to challenge a head of state, you've got nothing. What about this don't you get?"

"So where are we?"

"You are screwed, my friend," Roger said evenly. "You are totally screwed."

And here, to my eternal gratitude, Takis returned, with our waiter and our steaks, smiling, breaking us up. "Here you go guys, here you go," he laughed, paying way too much attention to us. I looked around the room, thinking that some Senator must be complaining that we were too loud and too crude, ruining his efforts to get some poor bimbo staffer into the sack. Takis was the perfect owner for this restaurant, the Pinnacle, on this slice of turf—an old roughhouse a couple of blocks from the Senate office buildings on Massachusetts Avenue. Host to every member of the U.S. Senate and the wealthy lobbying class that wined and dined them, Takis never forgot a face and knew every name that mattered, although he never had any idea who I was until we started working for one of the fourteen or fifteen different Greek-American groups that lobby the Congress every year. After that, he at least recognized my face when I came through the door.

I took his arrival as a way out. "Takis, they're telling me how great Turkey is."

"Turkey, whaddaya mean Turkey?" He held back for a second, just a second, on Peter's steak. "Turkey's no good. You know that." Takis was Greek, not just Greek Greek but by-god-Goddammit-I'm-talking-out-of-his-mind Greek, the whole family was, totally wild about Greece and everything Greek and the whole cradle of civilization thing. It was a lot like my Dad with the Irish, you know, saving civilization and all that, if it hadn't been for the monks we wouldn't still have any copies of all those timeless Roman texts about all Gaul being divided into three parts. Having spent years working Dad into a lather, it was pretty easy to do the same with Takis. It was a little more dangerous to get Takis started, because he could go for hours if you let him, but I figured tonight he could see I was just using him to get out of a tight spot. And he saw right through me, as always.

"Those goddamned Turks, they're no good. I mean it." He gave us all a good, long meaningful stare. And then we laughed, and so did he, and he left us to our steaks mumbling to himself about them lousy Turks. And he had done it again, broken an ugly mood and let us get on with our night. We turned to other things, the overall budget situation, foreign aid getting cut once more, no funding for anything, and as we talked, my eyes wandered the room and my mind, half paying attention, wandered back in time as I asked myself, "How did I get here?"

The room was full of diners like me, supplicants appealing to a Senator, Congressman, or senior staffer for that little favor, or calling in that small chit, or just sucking up for the evening. Seeing myself repeated over and over around the room, I wondered when it had all gone wrong. The job meant something the first few years; at least, I thought it did. In those days,

I could actually believe that we were accomplishing something. What was different then? Was it what we were doing? The clients we had? Or was it me, not recognizing what a sleazy mess this whole industry—Washington—had become?

Peter asked me about Charlotte, and I laughed, pulling myself back to the conversation to tell them about her latest escapade, the House committee staff director who tried to pick her up at a crowded party—with me about ten feet away. Then Roger told Peter the story of Fawzi's near-death experience in the halls of Dirksen, laughing so hard at my transparent efforts that he'd almost left a lung where he stood.

It was so odd, but so very Washington, I thought, Roger, Peter, and I pretending that nothing had happened, moving on to other business, and laughing about our personal lives. We were pals again. Koliba was almost forgotten, and I told another story, and we laughed, and we commented on the steaks, and then the Redskins, and then they hosed me about my old girlfriend Raymonda for a while, giving me the same shit they always did about how it was my fault what an uptight bitch she was. At least I had dated a legend, I replied, and let it go at that.

So there we were, joking about old girlfriends, laughing, the unpleasantness behind us for now. Like everyone in Washington, best buds, at least until the next time we came nose to nose and screwed one another. Yes, indeedy, best of buds.

Chapter 20

"Jesus, Riley, what are you doing? Expecting to find something hidden inside?"

J. Riley MacGonagill turned his attention slowly toward me, away from the shrimp he'd been inspecting so closely. "Ah, it's the miscreant. How are you, Edward?"

I laughed, curious about the miscreant comment but even more so about the fact that Riley would be caught dead at one of Uncle Harry's fundraisers. Riley bore some time-honored grudge against Harry, the origins of which I'd never been able to draw out of him, but the two of them insisted on acting as if the other didn't exist. Yet here he was, having plunked down at least $1,000 to nosh with Harry and what appeared to be a much larger than usual crowd of lobbyists. In fact, the room was crammed with people, and after recognizing Riley's pure-white mane above the heads of the lobbyists around him, I'd been lucky to even get near him, given his prime location next to the shrimp bowl.

"So, do you think the shrimp is tainted? Or are you just calculating how much that one shrimp is costing you?"

"No, no, for heaven's sake," he replied, waving the shrimp in the air in front of him, "these things are just money down a black hole for me. I was more wondering how many I can consume before my gout starts acting up." With that, he popped it in his mouth, fantail and all, and grinned at me as he chewed.

"So what are you doing here?"

"Please, Edward, you must know," he responded with a shake of the head. "The whole damned firm is here." He waved airily at the crowd and dipped his hand back in for another shrimp. "They even flew in the entire Chicago office," using his latest catch to point toward the far corner.

Looking over, I saw a large group of suits gathered around Harry, all listening earnestly to him as he rambled, as usual, and raved. He seemed defensive, even from across the room, like he was trying to convince them that he was on their side. They were being very attentive and clustered around in a way one usually didn't see at a fundraiser, the things being primarily social occasions rather than serious opportunities to lobby a member.

"Hell of a crowd," I said. "Why are they all here?"

The group around Harry shifted and a small space opened, just as a thin man in a dark grey suit leaned forward gesturing to Harry, practically in his face.

Kincaid.

Riley and I spoke at the same moment. "Shit," I said. "You're kidding, right?" was his comment.

I turned to face him. "What do you mean?"

"It's you, Ed. Shaddock Mills is up to its ass in business with Kazakhstan, and your work for that sillyass crowd, the Dungeons, or Dangans, or whatever they are, has the government completely up in arms." He looked around for a moment and saw what he was looking for over by Harry. As my eyes followed his, I sensed the people around us glaring at me, or pointing as they told their neighbors who I was.

"I thought you said you weren't stupid enough to cause trouble for a firm so close to the Vice President."

"No, Riley, if I'm recalling right, *you* said that."

His eyes narrowed as he looked down at me. "Maybe I did. But whoever said it, you've certainly done the reverse. The Vice President is rumored to be livid, the entire D.C. office is here tonight in a command performance, and like I said, the whole Chicago office flew in." He waved again over toward the group by Harry.

"Harry's talking to my client," I said, almost to myself, turning away from Riley to stare over at Kincaid.

"Impossible, son," he replied, "he's talking to the man we use for political fundraising advisory services, Edward Kincaid. That's him in your uncle's face."

The room spun a little, losing all focus except for the bright circle that seemed to shine around Kincaid's face. My balance gone, I reached out to reach for Riley's arm, and at his sharp "ow!" turned toward him. There was a sudden sadness in his look, a recognition that something was going wrong. "Ah, Riley," I started, "he, um, he's..." I stopped.

The room was beginning to spin quite badly as I dropped my hand from Riley and headed through the door out into the hallway.

As I got to the top of the steps, I speeded up, jogging down the circular stair to the lobby, through the glass door, and out into the street. Stumbling to the sidewalk, I felt my stomach heave and moved quickly to the curb just as I retched once, hard, into the street. Well, mostly into the street, but partially onto the car just to my left. I closed my eyes and let my weight rest heavily on the car's hood as I struggled for control. For a moment, I felt the tightness easing, and I breathed in deeply. Then it was gone again, and I retched once, twice, fiercely, losing everything I'd eaten and then some.

"You know, it's actually quite tacky vomiting on a BMW when there's a perfectly good Buick right in front of you."

I laughed, coughing as I did, glancing left at the poor Beemer. I could see Riley out of the corner of my eye. He must have followed me out.

I looked down again, waiting in case there was more to come. Reaching into my back pocket, I pulled out my handkerchief and wiped my mouth. Riley waited patiently for me as I caught my breath, blew my nose, and dropped the handkerchief into the pile on the street. I can always get another handkerchief, I thought.

I turned to face him, about ten feet back from the curb, just far enough, I assumed, to avoid the stench. "How was the show?"

"No," he said, shaking his head, "no one would know anything other than the fact that you cleared out of there quickly." He turned back to look, as if to reassure himself that there was no one there. "As I left, I glanced over toward Harry. It looked like he might have seen you leaving. Kincaid was still talking, though, so he couldn't have seen anything."

I was staring down at his feet now, numb, still nauseous, and a little lost. Again, he waited.

"He's runs the board of the Dungan-American Friendship Society," I began. "Harry introduced us and insisted it be my client, not Michael's. And now he's all over Harry, and it must be about Kazakhstan, so it must be about me."

Something clicked in my head. "The address of the Chicago office, Riley. Shaddock's Chicago office. What's the address?"

He paused, looking surprised. "I'm not positive," he said, "but I think it's on East Wacker, right by the river. Somewhere in the 200s."

The elevator, the fucking down elevator that Kincaid gotten off of. They were in the same goddamned building as the Dungan-American Friendship Society, probably another twenty floors up in the frigging top floor offices. And I'd totally missed it.

I looked up at him, feeling the pain showing on my face, letting the budding knowledge that somehow this whole year had been a sham wash over me. "This is all so totally fucked."

"Yes, son, it is." He smiled ever so slightly. "Isn't it usually?"

My stomach lurched one last time, and I spun around. After a brief pause to regain my balance, I looked to the street. This time I targeted the Beemer.

* * *

My Crackberry buzzed again. Pulling it from the holder on my belt, I knew who it was even before looking at it: another call from Belinda. I ignored this one too.

I was in the Hart Senate Office Building, having come up the many stairs from the tunnels running under the Senate office buildings and over to the Capitol Building. I'd surfaced at the southeastern corner of Dirksen, the stairs nearest the Capitol, and turned right down the corridor to enter into Hart. I wasn't so much walking to anywhere as just walking, back and forth, down into the tunnels, across toward the Capitol, and back again into the Senate office buildings. Three calls so far from Belinda indicated that Harry wanted to see me, and soon, but I wasn't ready for that yet, not even ready to agree to the meeting.

If it had been another office, another situation, I'd have been forced to take the call: otherwise, they might have called Michael. Belinda, though, I knew I could trust, especially if she thought there was trouble for me. She'd show up at my apartment door at two o'clock in the morning if that was the only way to get my attention, but she'd never go past me to Michael like others would have. It gave me more time, time to think.

Not that there was all that much to think about. I could see that I was screwed.

As I approached the lower half of the massive Calder dominating the Hart lobby, I stopped. There it was, right in front of me, an unintentional *hommage* to the outrageous disconnect between substance and legislative action that lies at the heart of the American political system. Down here, on the lobby floor, the black pillars of steel representing mountains, the day-to-day legislative debate and occasional action that Americans see on their television sets. Up there, four stories over my head, the clouds, the hidden, nebulous behind-the-scenes insanity that was the reality of life and work in Washington, not just mine, but everyone's. For people like me, the rules were made up there, that place that no one outside Washington even knew existed, or if they did, saw like one sees massive cumulus clouds on the horizon.

And I'd broken the rules.

The imminent crashing down of my safety-net client, the Dungan, brought home the sheer absurdity of my work for Koliba. I'd listened to endless debates on Koliba's increasingly dictatorial hold on power, the undermining of the courts, the beatings of protestors and other opponents in the streets, and even the murder of his Vice President, but still found ways to prevent any serious damage. While Congress was focused on cutting nonexistent foreign aid funding to his government, I didn't have to worry since the real fight should have been on his listening post and the $20 million Pentagon payoff that came with it. The classified listening post, the one no one could actually talk about but that most of them seemed to know about. The one in the clouds.

Like I'd told Alexis, Washington had always been the world's largest sieve, with information leaking out all over the place so people could position themselves to win debates. Like Pakistan in the 1980s and early 1990s, before they exploded their first nuclear bomb. Everyone knew the Pakis were working on the bomb, everyone knew how far along they were in enriching the uranium they needed, and most everyone working on the issue knew that the critical breakpoint in the relationship came when then-Pakistani President Zia lied in a one-on-one meeting with then-Vice President George Bush, the old man, as to what degree Pakistan had already enriched its uranium. But most of the information was classified, as was the reason Bush knew the precise level of enrichment—spy satellites reading the heat signature of Pakistan's enrichment facilities—so no one could debate that part of the issue. The resulting debate was an unfocused "he said, he said" fight between those who thought Pakistani contributions to the war in Afghanistan were paramount and those who thought the main foreign policy goal of the U.S. needed to be nuclear nonproliferation.

Both sides lost, of course, when victory over the Soviets led inevitably to further civil war and from there to the rise of the Taliban. Pakistan not only succeeded in setting off its first nuclear device in May 1998, but also became the Taliban's main political and military supporter until sometime shortly after Sept. 11, 2001. That's when being friendly to our former Afghan ally Osama bin Laden became too hot even for them.

I turned, heading left down the central hall leading into Dirksen, not so much to go anywhere as to move. As I nodded to the bored, overweight cop patrolling the central hall, I wondered how many fruitless, mindless debates the Congress pursued in its desperate searches to "fix" the planet, country by country, by shaping each one into some version of our own increasingly corrupt and misguided political system, all the while that immovable forces like hunger, disease, population growth, and sheer human hatred of the "other" conspired against any effort to "fix" anything.

Coming to the end of that corridor, I approached the elevators to my left, ready, I thought, to go see Belinda. Senator Earl Ford of Tennessee, patrician elder of the Senate's minority, waited by the elevator with a nervous young staffer just behind his right shoulder. I chuckled to myself, reminded once again that Senators, unlike House members, seemed constitutionally incapable of going anywhere alone. As the elevator door opened, three young pages exited the elevator in a sloppy mess, one turning right toward Hart, the others to the left, deeper into Dirksen, and calling out to their compatriot, "this way!" None seemed to notice the Senator as they passed, and he certainly gave no indication of noticing them, in that *noblesse oblige* kind of way that Senators have.

Watching them, I tried to make my mind float back to my own first flush of innocence in the Washington scene, those first days of eagerness and excitement. Following the Senator into the elevator, I winced: it wasn't working.

What I couldn't get away from was the simple fact that I was helping Koliba. It didn't matter that the Congressional efforts to cut him off from any U.S. money were going to fail, or that my legislative legerdemain was making it a lot easier for everyone to skate through giving money to Koliba in a clandestine way, or even that despite Roger's screw-up on my coastal fisheries amendment I was still likely to win on that. What was starting to hit home was the simple fact that I was not only working for the leading candidate for this year's "Scum of the Earth" award, but I'd been winning *and* enjoying it.

Now that my cover had been blown, now that the Dungan had been revealed as a sham in someone else's political games, the truth was staring me in the face. And it was ugly.

* * *

I waited to return Belinda's call until I was right outside Harry's office. "Eddie?"

"Hi, Belinda. Is Harry in?"

"He's gone home," she responded. "An hour ago. I've been waiting here for you to call back. He needs to see you first thing tomorrow."

"I'm right outside. Wanna let me in?"

Belinda looked confused when she opened Harry's private door to the hall, his escape hatch for when constituents were camped out in his lobby. All members of Congress had them, although Senators' doors worked better because their offices were so much larger than the House ones—meaning their private doors were that much further down the hall from the ones mere constituents used.

"I've got a question for you," I said as I ducked past her into the office.

Belinda smiled. "I don't know what he wants. He just said he has to talk to you."

"It's not that. It's his contributions book. I need to see it."

The smile disappeared. Now she really looks like a librarian, I thought. But I resisted the temptation to continue.

"Eddie, I can't. I mean, I don't have ... a, um, book."

"August, just a few months ago. The morning of the Norman Hsu hearing." Hsu, the Hillary Clinton fundraiser who'd built political fundraising into his pyramid schemes, the better to convince his marks that he was legit. "I was talking to Harry about the new lobbying bill, and we got to talking about Hsu's contributions to Hillary and others." I paused, hoping she'd remember this. "He called you in and asked for the book." She looked down at the floor, remembering. I waited, but so did she. "He showed it to me. It lists every contribution he's ever gotten."

Belinda turned and walked back behind her desk. I could tell that she still wasn't convinced and was killing time while she thought about what to do.

"He's never raised money here," I continued, "so he hasn't violated FEC rules. He just keeps a book here so he can review the lists." I wasn't sure that was true; hell, I was pretty sure it wasn't, but it sounded good and even almost convincing. I needed to see that book.

She looked up at me one last time and then back down at her desk. She paused for a few moments. I waited. Looking up, she said, "You'll never tell anyone of this. Anyone."

She meant Harry. I nodded.

She turned back toward her credenza. From the left side, the bottom drawer, she pulled out a binder, comparatively small given all the money Harry had raised over the years, and turned in her chair. She held it to her chest. "Why?"

"I need to see how much trouble I'm in." I smiled at her. "And if there's any way out."

I could theoretically have done this from the FEC Web site, but that would just give me total dollar numbers and I'd have been forced to construct it from scratch. I didn't have time for that kind of search. The one thing I remembered from glancing at the book over Harry's shoulder was his color coding system, linking batched fundraising to the lead organizer of each event, and the affiliated numbering system identifying how many individuals had been pulled in and at how much each. It would give me a quick visual sense of just how bad my situation was.

"You can't take it."

"I need three minutes, just to glance through it." A look of pain crossed my face, inadvertently for once. "Please."

She handed it across to me.

Opening the book, I flipped randomly to the first of the blue divider tabs and found Kincaid at the top of the list. His number, 1-0001, identified him as the lead for all blue fundraisers; it took less than a minute to add up the first five tabs I flipped to and come up with $225,000.

I was fucked.

I'd been betrayed, used by Harry for some reason I couldn't figure out, but first and foremost, I was fucked.

"Thanks," I said, handing the book back to Belinda. "Will ten o'clock tomorrow morning work?"

* * *

I arrived home around a quarter past eleven, finding Charlotte on the living room couch, her back to me, wine glass in hand, reading. She glanced back at the sound of my arrival. "Hey, Sweetie," she called, a slight smile playing at the edge of her mouth.

I crossed the foyer, tossing my hat on the hall table and dropping my coat to the floor as I continued into the room.

Looking down for the briefest moment, I took her in. She was surprised, most likely at not getting the peck she'd been expecting, that lean-in and quick brush of a kiss that had become the norm. I moved a little further past her, around and then inside the arm with the wine glass, and got down on one knee. I took her face in my hands and kissed her, really kissed her, like I hadn't in so long. She giggled lightly and kissed back, a broad smile emerging on her face as she pulled back a little and squeaked, "my wine!" with more than a little urgency.

I reached to take it from her and placed it on the table. Turning back, I stopped, looking in her eyes, at her lips, at her chin and nose and cheeks and eyes again, all in a quick brush of a glance across her features, all exactly in place, exactly aligned the way I'd always known them to be. I breathed in sharply, needing air, and reached out to take her face in my hands again.

"Are you okay?" she asked.

I could feel the tension inside pulling at me then, a strain in my chest, a sob trying to get out. "I just, I just ... I need to be with you." God, please, I thought, let that be enough for now.

It was. I'll never know why, because I don't want to and I'd never ask. After taking a moment to put her book down, she reached out to me, her right hand against my face to bring me close, to bring me back to her. Pulling back, for air, to move, I bit her lower lip and pulled, tugged ever so gently, before moving to her neck. Her arms slid around my shoulders, holding me gently in place, giving me the freedom to move but pressing into me nonetheless, a pressing that gave in to my need as well as to her own. Sensing it, knowing, feeling it, I let go, stopped listening to the voices in my head, and lost myself in the moment, in what I'd risked, in what I'd spent so much time and energy undermining.

We made love there, on the couch, slowly, gently, frantically, passionately, back and forth, basking in the glow of the reading light as I took the care to reconnect with the parts and places of her. It was like making love to her for the first time all over again, full of surprises that carried only dim memories, of stretching, sliding my hands along the length of her, of feeling her hands and mouth more than ever.

And I felt the freedom, ever so much the freedom of being away, away in a place that was ours, just away. There was another place out there—I knew even as I made love to her—a place of clouds, and anger, and defeat, but here, here for these moments it was at bay and I could be at peace.

We moved to the bedroom and began again, more slowly, both of us sensing how different this was and needing to take our time, to enjoy one another in these new ways we'd forgotten. As our lovemaking headed to its crest this time, though, I could feel the clouds, the anger coming back, could feel them coming through. I drove her, drove her forward into orgasm once, twice, three times, to exhaust her, to push her limits, to push her closer toward sleep.

It worked. We lay in the aftermath, smiling against the weakness in us, against the labored breathing, and touched, lightly, carefully now, and I waited. I held her fingers in my mine, intertwined. We whispered little bits of thanks and love, listening to our breathing begin to slow, listening to each other slide away, she into sleep, me back into the mess I'd created of my life.

Turning on my side to face her, I watched Charlotte fading, the trademark twitching in her shoulder, the hand under her pillow telling me that she was edging deeper and deeper into her dreams. I watched her mouth slip open, watched her breathe, listened as the breaths became deeper and longer.

When I knew she was asleep, I rose and headed for the living room, to get the lights I'd say if she awoke, to get some water, to pee, whatever. I waited by the door, but she was sleeping soundly.

For a while, I just sat on the couch, staring out the window, drinking from a fresh bottle of red wine I'd opened. Round and round the day went, the ups and downs and more downs, the fundraiser, seeing Kincaid, walking the halls, seeing the book. How the *fuck* did I ever get to this point in my life? Somewhere along the line, I turned on the TV, for something meaningless to distract me. Around 3:30 a.m. I fell into a fitful sleep.

Chapter 21

I awoke to the sounds of Charlotte in the kitchen, small sounds, a spoon in the sink, the coffeepot being slid back into place.

I'd scarcely slept at all and never gotten back to bed. Once or twice during the night I'd gone back down the hall to our bedroom, finding her dead asleep. I'd pulled the blankets up around her, but she was too out of it to move, and I knew I was still way too wound up to join her.

Hearing her now, I lay still, listening. I needed to get up, to get to the Hill for my meeting with Uncle Harry. But I paused for a few more moments, listening to the quiet sounds of Charlotte's movements, the *snick* of the refrigerator opening, the clink of her coffee cup striking the counter, the whoosh of water running in the sink as she rinsed a plate. My eyes closed; I could see her precise, practiced movements.

Rising quietly, I padded into the hall and turned right into the kitchen. She turned to look at me. "You couldn't sleep?"

"Nah. It wasn't us, it was...I don't know." I reached around, pulling her close to me. "Good morning."

She leaned back into me, so light I could scarcely feel her, but somehow it seemed that if I stepped away she'd fall. "I'm worried about you."

I closed my eyes and breathed. And then again. "I know." I paused for a few moments, my mind racing but empty. "It's... it's just I don't know how to leave. This is what I do—this is who I am..."

"This is *not* who you are!" She leaned forward, pulling away, and turned her body to face me. "It's only what you *do*, and you can do other things."

Easy for you to say, I thought—you run offices. You can run any office anywhere, a law firm, local politician, you can run a store, manage a department, whatever. I beg for money from Congress or the administration—where else can you do that? I'm a shill, for Chrissakes. "I just thought I was coming into my own."

"You hate this town!" She wasn't angry, just earnest. But I wasn't ready yet, not for this, not now.

"No," I said, "not the town, only the fuckers who live here!" I laughed, almost a bray, hearing the thin edge I was on, so close to tears. "Sometimes I've hated what I *did*, not the town. Never the town..." Until now. I couldn't say it out loud, but suddenly, standing there, I knew it. I hated this place.

Charlotte was still, waiting for me, determined.

"Look," I said, "let's not start—I don't think I can do this right now." I let her go, stepping back, and turned toward the coffeepot. "I need some time."

She looked down and let her hands drop. I took my cup off the counter and, pouring, watched her from the corner of my eye. As she straightened the blouse that didn't need straightening, I knew she was finished and leaned back against the counter, facing her again. She started by me to the door, but stopped, leaning in to kiss me but pausing for a moment just before we touched. "You're not what you do." She kissed me, turned, and went out.

Well, I thought, now what?

* * *

From the frying pan...

"Son, I did you a favor."

You fat lousy miserable sonofabitch, I thought. "Harry, you gave me a sham client, lied to me from the get-go, and then sold me down the river," I responded, gripping the sides of my chair. "The whole fucking thing was bullshit, and now you're telling me I have to sell out the client. Fuck you!"

Harry leaned forward in his chair. "Don't forget who you're talking to here, son," he said, wagging a finger at me. "I'm still a United States Senator, and I'm still your uncle. So you just calm down here. No one fucked you. I did you the biggest goddamn favor I've ever done anyone. And now you're going to do what you have to."

God, I hated the man at that moment. "Harry. Just tell me what happened."

"What happened is that you've fucked up the easiest deal anyone ever had," he said, slamming his hand on the desk. His face was red, redder than usual. How much of this was a show just to scare me?

I'd gotten to Harry's office at 10:00 a.m., as promised the night before. He was waiting for me, pacing his office floor. He laid into me from the moment I walked in, but nothing he'd said so far was a surprise. There was still some game going on here, but he clearly didn't want to tell me what it was. I'd have to drag it out of him.

I wasn't sure it mattered, but I wanted to know. I *needed* to know. I'd spent a year chasing around the city because of him, and I needed to know what the hell was going on.

"The whole idea was to give these people a little representation, some coverage on what's happening in Washington, some information on the system."

"No, Harry," I replied. "That wasn't the gig." I stood up and stepped to his desk. "I was hired to ensure that the Kazakh government didn't oppress these people, the Dungan." I stopped, leaning on the desktop, getting as close as I could. "I wasn't told how. They left that to *me*. I did what they hired me to do."

"Well, none of us expected you to do so well, Goddammit!"

Ka-ching. "Us." I had him.

"Well, Uncle, what did *we* want me to do?"

"Goddamn you!" He rose from behind the desk, his gut first, his legs lurching under the weight. "It's not that simple."

"Harry." He stopped and turned, a little surprised. "It's that simple. You agreed to something with someone—presumably Shaddock Mills, or maybe just Kincaid." His eyes glimmered, and he looked away, toward the bookshelf behind him. "It involved me. I need to know what it was and what you expect now."

"There's nothing you can do." He looked a little sheepish now, guilty. "You have to stop trying to put more Kazakhstan language in the bill."

"Just tell me what the deal was."

"What does it matter, for Chrissakes?" He stared at me, but I stared right back and waited. He looked down at his desk, and after pushing some folder to the side, he said, "They have a client bidding on a pipeline deal. It's a multibillion-dollar project, but their French competition seems to be on the inside. They needed an edge."

The gears in my head processed that. "They were in on it from the start." That meant that everything I'd sent them, all my reporting, was going to my opponent, because my client was my opponent. "They needed a political problem in Washington that only they could solve."

"They needed something they could sell as a crisis, so they could save the day," he said. "You created the real thing. Now you have to pull it back."

I leaned forward in my chair and looked down at the floor. Oh God, I thought, I gave it to them step-by-step in the weekly reports we'd been sending, told them everything I was doing, not in detail but with enough information that they could counter me every inch of the way. No wonder I'd always felt like there was someone looking over my shoulder.

The pain in my stomach was back, not such that I'd be sick, just a dull lingering ache.

Problem was, there had to be more.

"Belkin," I said, first to myself and then to Harry. "Belkin. What did he get in Paris? What did you give him?"

He stopped. He hadn't been expecting that. "I... it wasn't... it wasn't anything at all..."

"Bullshit." I stood and approached his desk, leaning over it. "There's no way he gave you that and got nothing. What'd he get?"

Harry sat still, staring up at me.

"What'd he get?"

Nothing.

It hit me. "You gave him me. He's our UAE amendment, and he's with you on the Dungan. I cross you on this, and he screws us on the UAE. Right?"

Harry's head dropped for a moment, and when he looked back at me, there was something new in his eyes. It was almost respect.

As I watched him, it became a strange sort of sympathy, an almost fatherly sadness. I paused and felt a wave of defeat wash over me. "Fuck off, Harry." Turning from him, I exited through his private door.

* * *

The hammer fell three days later, when I met with Michael over drinks at the Hotel Mayflower.

"How did you miss it?"

Damn you, Michael. It was the right question to ask, and the one that had been bothering ever since I'd walked out of Harry's fundraiser.

"Jesus, Michael, I don't know," I said, "I Googled everything, and everywhere around this guy—he didn't show up anywhere tied to Shaddock Mills." I looked into my glass for a moment, before taking a long slug off of it. "Irony is, thanks to that bullshit lobbying reform act Bush just signed, next year I would have been able to find it. This year, well, it ain't like I didn't try."

We were in the Mayflower's lobby bar, a little ornate, a lot overdone, an open bar space in a bustling lobby full of tourists, dominated by a piano that no one ever seemed to play. It wasn't the Washington insider kind of place that one expected for this kind of meeting, but it would have to do. Besides, the Dom Perignon was real, and a nice touch.

"Such is life, right?" Michael raised his glass in toast to me, his friendly face on, but with an edge.

"That doesn't help me now, does it?" I emptied my glass, again. After a long pause, I said, "By the way, what are we celebrating?"

Michael, sliding the bottle from the ice bucket, said nothing at first. He slowly poured me another glass, and then topped his off. Returning the bottle to the bucket more carefully than necessary, he finally said, "Harry called me and said I needed to talk with you."

"We're celebrating that?"

He glared at me for a moment. I wasn't making this easy for him. Not that I had any intention of doing so.

"We never celebrated you getting the client," he responded, looking down into the glass. "We're celebrating that, and the fact that you've earned your 20 percent finder's fee."

I laughed, half in appreciation, half in amazement at his *chutzpah*. It couldn't be more of a payoff if he'd called it that.

"Harry calls you to shut me down, and you're trying to tell me it's a success? Jesus, Michael, I'm supposed to bend over for this?"

"Hey, chill out, for Chrissakes," he said, turning a little red. I'm finally getting to him a little, I thought, although we're still only down around level 2 out of 5, a medium rare. Still a long way to go on the Michael scale. "This isn't any easier for me than it is for you."

I took another long sip, and Michael grimaced at me. "What happened, anyway?"

"You tell me," he responded, relaxing a little. "All I know is that if we don't pull the plug on the Dungan, Harry's gonna create holy hell for our other clients. We've got no choice."

"Bullshit," I said. "We've got everything lined up for Conference."

Michael looked up from his glass with a smile. "You're kidding, right?"

I wasn't, but I might as well have been. Belkin could kill our MNNA amendment any time he wanted to. With the UAE a client that was virtually certain to renew and pony up the cash for next year's contract, Michael would have been crazy not to do what Harry wanted.

"It's always been a company client, Michael." I emptied another glass and leaned back, uncertain. And maybe a little bit woozy. "I guess it's not my call."

"No, my friend, it's not. And I am sorry about that." He leaned in and smiled and took the bottle in his hand. He raised it to me, and it was his real smile   he was "off," I marveled, the first time today—and I held my arm out as he filled my glass. "You might have avoided this if you'd played the client differently from the start. But you got the client and earned the deal: 20 percent."

"Blood money."

"Maybe." He emptied a third glass, keeping up with me but showing no sign of the alcohol's effect. Him and his hollow leg. "One last thing. Harry tells me I'm the one to tell the members and staff the amendment's dead. Personally." He tilted his head a little as he looked at me with a crooked smile.

Jesus, I thought. Harry doesn't trust me. That's a kick in the pants.

Shaking my head, I emptied my glass again and waved it at him again. Time for another bottle.

* * *

The next few weeks were like a demented dream, the disjointed kind where nothing made any sense but you kept walking from one scene to the next.

The normal train of events leading up to a Joint Conference had me working the halls, lining up the support I needed to get my amendments signed into law. That meant a lot of time walking from office to office, drop-by visits where I'd check in with people to make sure that my stuff was on track and that nothing new had popped up. But given my level of coverage on the Hill, it was hard to surprise me, so it was mostly a lot of time spent chatting people up with no heavy lifting.

There were two kinds of opportunities, the staged kind where I'd hang around in the halls outside someone's office around lunchtime to catch them on their way out, and the utterly random kind, trolling the waters to see what comes up on the line. During the year, I tried to do the latter at least twice a month, for three or four hours at a time; in the weeks before Conference, it was more like twice a week. Maybe it only worked because with three clients minimum at any time, I could always find a way to make lemonade out of any lemons I bumped into.

This year, though, this year was different. When the bill left the Senate floor in September, I still had one big issue to deal with—my Dungan client—and a couple of little bits to clean up if I felt like it. Once Harry and Michael lowered the boom on the Dungan, though, my year was basically over. I had to keep an eye on the UAE amendment and monitor to be certain Koliba got his money, but those were both fish in a barrel. I'd been going stir-crazy in the office and felt lost walking the halls of Congress. Still, with Michael back in the office, I decided "lost" would be a major improvement over "stir-crazy." So off to the Hill I went.

This day was luckier than most.

I'd gone back to see Kenny Thurgood, Michelle's friend from Georgetown, just on a lark, and had run into him heading out of the office with five of his friends. They were all wacko right-wingers, each and every one of them, but I was in a forgiving mood.

Just kidding.

This day I was the ultimate beggar, smart enough not to pretend I was a chooser, so when Kenny invited me to join them, I immediately said yes. It was always a good idea to cultivate new contacts, since you never knew when they might come in handy. Besides, like I said, I had nothing better to do.

Over coffee in the Rayburn cafeteria, we got into a long argument over freedom for missionaries to operate globally, a major foreign policy issue for the religious right. Most Christian religions, as well as the Mormons, put a high value on proselytizing. And what better place to go than the Moslem worlds, the ultimate infidels in Christian eyes. At least, that seemed to be a great idea until earlier in 2007, when a group of Korean missionaries got themselves kidnapped in Afghanistan. The end result was that their freedom had been purchased for $20 million. In cash. Turned over to the Taliban. So they could kill American troops.

A conundrum.

"Look, that's not the point," I said. "There are hundreds of millions of people around the world where you can go preach. Why go into a war zone?"

"The Word must be spread," one of them responded. It was Adam Childress, a tall, thin African-American who seemed the most avowedly Christian of the group and the one whose new job they were celebrating.

"Adam," Kenny replied, "please. There's holier-than-thou, and then there's just annoying." Several in the crowd laughed as, surprisingly to me, did Adam. I guessed that he was putting on a show for my benefit.

It was turning into an interesting discussion, in fact, as there was a dramatic range of differences within the group. Kenny seemed the most sensible, to me at least, maybe from the context he'd gotten going to graduate school. More likely, I thought, the prejudice that led him to value graduate school was probably more of a predictor than whatever he learned in the classroom.

"Look, I'm not disagreeing with you guys," I continued. "It's just that I think there's a time and place for everything, and it's not the time to be doing this in Afghanistan."

"True missionaries are prepared to die for their faith," Adam retorted, serious once again.

Jeez, I thought, he *is* annoying. "They do have that right, as long as they're the only ones to die," I said, leaning across the table to point at him. "I don't think they have the right to put U.S. troops in danger."

"My boss, for one," said Kenny, "thinks that there's a case to be made for that argument."

"So does mine." I looked up, surprised. It was Alexis—more good luck. I'd needed to find her, but wanted the informality of bumping into her. This was perfect.

I turned to Kenny. "I'm not sure we're going to make a whole lot more progress, here, do you?" He smiled and shook his head. I was starting to like this guy.

I stood and bowed to the table. "Thanks for the time, gang."

A chorus of voices responded. "No problem." "Thank *you* for the coffee." "Any time." Righties are so much more polite than the left, I thought, not for the first time.

Taking one last look at Adam, I asked, "By the way, what's the new job?"

"Foreign aid and defense approps for Senator VanderMeer."

Ka-CHING!

I must have stared; Adam smiled at me and said, "Probably not your favorite Senator."

I smiled back. "Actually, the Senator is a big supporter of one of my clients, the Dungan people of Kazakhstan." Adam's eyes widened, and his mouth dropped open a little. "He's concerned about protecting their freedoms."

"He talked about them during the interview," Adam said.

"We should meet up some time. I know that bill backwards and forwards and can tell you who's doing what to whom." I paused. "Just ask Kenny."

"He da man," Kenny said, smiling. "You should talk with him."

Adam looked up at me, still unsure, but—I could just about see the gears clicking—willing to take a shot. "Give me a call."

"Will do."

* * *

"Here you go." I presented Alexis with her tall cappuccino with an extra shot, and as always, she slid $3.40 across the table at me. I took it and smiled to her.

Sitting, I stirred raw sugar into my triple espresso while trying to decide the best approach. I'd talked her into a Starbucks run, on the basis that I'd already had two cups of the crap they served in House office buildings and couldn't take any more. We'd caught a cab as we walked out the Rayburn front door, and chitchatted during the brief ride up to Pennsylvania and 2nd. I'd caught her up on Charlotte, and she'd caught me up on her and Peter, something that still felt weird since I was so used to knowing Peter better than I knew her, and, well, our opinions of the dear boy differed. Let's leave it at that.

What I needed out of Alexis was news on our MNNA amendment and a status report on the Dungan. My dropping the first of those into my initial conversation with Alexis was turning out to be critical for us, now that Will Richardson had resigned, finally giving in to the reality of his disgrace. MNNA was still in play: staffers for the House side were playing it coy, not having decided to accept the amendment yet, so we definitely needed Kelton's help. If luck was what we made it—by always sticking our ideas out there, walking the halls and talking to anyone who would listen to us—this was one of those times when we needed the effort to pay off.

"So how do things look for Conference?"

I looked up. Alexis was looking relaxed, comfortable, like most of her issues were done. "Well, you tell me," I replied. "Has the Congressman talked to the House staffers about our MNNA amendment?"

"Oh, now it's *our* amendment?" She laughed, once again with that wonderful open laugh. Well, so far she's made it through the year without losing too much of herself, I thought; that's a good sign.

It had to be going well, or else she wouldn't be playing with me like that. "So he has talked to them?"

"Of course he has," she said. "You knew that, though."

No, I didn't. I hadn't been able to check in directly with the either subcommittee staffers, not since Michael went to see them about the Dungan. Partly because it was early enough that I didn't need to, but more importantly, I couldn't bring myself to. I just wasn't ready.

"How about your Dungan?" she continued.

"My" Dungan. My little beebles. I guessed I had come to think of them that way. My people from the Kazakh steppes, brave Chinese-origin peasants standing in the way of dictatorship. What an idiot I'd been.

"The references to Kazakhstan and the Dungan are being dropped from the bill," I responded.

"I know. Billy filled me in on what's going on." She took a sip from the cap, maybe playing for time, maybe not. "Why?"

She'd answered my question, which was how widely the story about the Dungan was known. The part I'd been worrying about had been how to get that out of her without telling her why. Otherwise, I figured I'd have to lie to her. So now what was I going to do?

I took a sip from the espresso, which for once had some value beyond the jolt it was going to give the rest of my afternoon. "It's a very long story."

"I have time," she responded with a smile.

I pondered, looking down at the table, then up to her, and then down again. "It's, uh, a problem with the client. Can I give you a rain check? Tell you some other time?"

The surprise showed in her face. I was expecting that kind of reaction; it wasn't an answer a lobbyist could get away with often. It was the first time I'd ever tried it on her.

"You need to?"

"Yeah, sorry, I do. That okay?" She nodded, with a quizzical look in her eye, something clicking. I took the coffee, swirled it to pick up the last bits of sugar, and finished it in one swallow. I reached for my coat.

"One last question."

Shit, I thought, I need her not to push me on the Dungan right now. "Hmm?"

"It's Koliba." This time *I* was surprised. Alexis never wanted to know about Koliba; she hated the guy on principle.

I left the coat where it was. "Ooo-kay."

"What do you need personally from this?"

"As we talked about, I think that dialogue between the U.S. and other countries is more important than how badly we slap their ..."

"No, not the company line. I mean you. Personally, you, what do you need? From the process? In the bill?"

I hadn't thought about it, since no one had ever asked. They generally either didn't want to talk about him or told me he was wonderful. And while I always knew what I needed for the client, it wasn't based on what I might *want*, but how much I could *get*. I closed my eyes for a second and cleared my head. Basically, I wanted the miserable bastard to die a horrible death, but that wouldn't happen this year, not in this bill.

I looked back at her, to be sure she was serious before I gave her an answer. I'd told her about the $20 million, so there was no point in lying. And I'd slipped out from under her first question, so this one I should answer. Okay, missy. "I want him to get his $20 million, and other than that I don't give a shit. If he's smashed around in the bill, fine, in the report, fine. Just let him get his money, and maybe he'll go away next year and I won't have to worry about him."

She smiled, thinly. I wondered what she'd been looking for and whether I'd given it to her. "That good enough?"

She leaned over and pulled her long coat off the chair next to her. "Yep."

* * *

"Charlie?"

"Yes. Who's speaking?"

"It's Ed, Charlie, Ed Matthews. Sorry to bother you, but I'm wondering if I could chat with you and your grandfather."

Another week had gone by, and it was the first time since the fundraiser that I'd been able to bring myself to call Bao. I knew that he couldn't have been in on the game that Kincaid had been playing, but I needed to hear it directly. I needed some kind of closure with them.

I'd steeled myself for the conversation. I was at home, on the fire escape, looking out over the many cars parked in the early snow, one of those mid-November snows that never lasted long in Washington. It was a quiet evening, about 9:00ish, so still around eight o'clock in Chicago. I'd played it close, in that Bao usually went to bed by eight fifteen or so, but I kept delaying the call, like I'd been delaying it all week.

"Ed, it's been a long time." Charlie paused, and I thought I could hear something in the background, perhaps him talking to Bao. "Grandfather and I were wondering where you disappeared to. Grandfather says to say he was worried."

"Thank him for me, Charlie." Sweet old guy. I took a sip out of the Merlot I'd brought out with me, hoping for a little warmth. "But there's a couple of things I need to know, if I can ask."

"Of course, please."

"Can you ask your grandfather why he set up the Dungan-American Friendship Society?"

"I can tell you that." Another pause, longer this time, for back and forth between Charlie and Bao. "It is as I remember. We had discussions with Mr. Kincaid and Mr. Hendrickson about our concerns for our people. Grandfather has been very worried in the months that he has been in the United States, and his conversations with Mr. Kincaid only made it more so."

I could feel a deadening creeping up on me. "How did you get to know Mr. Kincaid?"

"I attended an event at their firm about Kazakhstan, a discussion. It was close to my office. They befriended me and convinced me to bring my grandfather to America for a few months. They even helped with his visa."

Helped with his visa? An old Kazakh man, visiting his grandson for no apparent reason? That's an automatic "no" from Immigration and Customs

Enforcement, an absolute automatic no. Unless you have friends in high places.

"You asked them to set up the association?"

"No, this was their idea." Charlie laughed lightly. "They even insisted that we call it Dungan-American. We are the Hui people, and only outsiders call us Dungan."

I remembered reading that somewhere, some early research, but it hadn't meant anything. Now it did: the Hui are Chinese, and those Hui who emigrated to Kazakhstan or Kyrgyzstan were known as Dungan. The word didn't identify who they were—it identified where they lived.

"So when you came to Washington..."

"They asked Grandfather if he wanted to meet with a Senator, to tell the Senator about our people," Charlie replied.

"You were going to hire a lobbyist?"

"No." There was a pause and then an extended back-and-forth conversation in their native tongue. Another pause.

"Hello?" It was Bao.

"Hello, sir," I replied, slowing my speech down in the hopes he might understand me. "I apologize for interrupting. But I have something to tell you."

"More surrr-prise?"

I laughed lightly. "Yes, sir, but not a good surprise. I have failed in what I promised you. There will be no language supporting your people."

A slight pause. "But you try?"

"Well, yes, I did," I said, coughing. "But..."

"Not but," he interrupted me. "We ask you to try. You tried."

"Well, thank you..."

"A good luck day," he said. "With Senator. We meet you. Like I tell before, a very good luck day."

I paused slightly before answering. "Not so much for me, sir."

"Not your luck," Bao responded matter-of-factly. "My good luck day. I do not know your luck."

Chapter 22

It was scary walking into that last Congressional negotiating session, the Joint Conference, knowing that we owned the room, at least on our issues.

Michael, Wellington, Tom, and I all came in separately, me from standing with the *hoi polloi*, the great unwashed in the line snaking down along the corridor. I'd had Larry, my linestander, holding a place for me, but only got into the room thanks to him instead of my connections. Michael scurried in with a block of staffers, deep enough in a conversation with the Subcommittee Chief of Staff that he slid by the guard; Tom with Sen. VanderMeer; and Wellington, well, Wellington just walked right in the door, greeting the guard by name based on some unknown connection he'd made somewhere over the years. Weller knew the cops on the Hill the way that I knew the secretaries; he'd encountered them during his private after-hours briefings for senior members of the House and Senate, learned their names, tracked their careers. And those intel connections of his seemed truly priceless, presumably on people's natural assumption that, unless you were Valerie Plame, once you were in the spy business you were never *out* of the spy business.

I might have pulled the same trick, of course, if my good buddy Will Richardson hadn't gone and gotten himself forced out of the House for philandering. And I certainly recognized the symbolism of finding myself back in line—my Dungan work designated for the Conference trash heap, me dropped a couple of notches down on the Washington totem pole.

The room was small, like most rooms that Conference Committees were held in, and mercifully open to the public. Congress had long gone in spurts, alternatively keeping these kinds of meetings open when public outcry over earmarks forced them to, and keeping them closed once the outcry faded. This year, like most recent ones, the doors were flung so the public could see what Congress was doing. If anyone from the public—as opposed to us lobbyists—were actually to get into the room, they'd have no idea what was happening. But they would, nonetheless, be there.

From where I was sitting, in the back row, angled so that I could watch Toby Kelton and Alexis Chase, I didn't see anyone in the room I didn't recognize. There were only about thirty open seats, and most of them had been filled by people sneaking in the room the way Michael, Tom, and Weller had. Along with Mourad, the only foreign embassy official who'd made it, I was one of six people who'd gotten in the old-fashioned way, the others coming, from the looks of them, from various law and lobbying firms around town. No one I knew, and no one I recognized from Harry's fundraiser. Folks from Shaddock Mills had to be there somewhere, but I couldn't tell yet which ones they were.

Roger had called me at around 2:00 p.m. on the time and location of the meeting: 7:30 p.m. in a small House Appropriations Subcommittee room down in the basement of the Rayburn House Office Building. We'd been expecting the Conference to come this night, and I'd dispatched my line-stander—on call in the House-side Longworth Cafeteria since early morning—to get the line started. My guy got there fourth, good enough to get me in the room but disturbingly close to that locked-out seventh position in line. That meant that several calls had gone out before I heard about it, and ever since arriving at six thirty that evening—just in case things started early—I'd been memorizing the faces around me while chatting with Mourad. I didn't know any of them, and he didn't either, but then again it wasn't the lawyers who were making trouble for Morocco; it was the human rights weenies, the ones still trapped in the hall in that now unmoving line.

At 8:15 p.m., when they finally opened the doors after an unexplained delay, we pushed into the room, scattering to the seats in the back. The Members, staff, and hangers-on who'd squeezed in ahead of us were gathered around the Conference table talking quietly, deep in conversation as the lobbyists sought that last-minute, last-ditch maneuver that might squeeze another million out of the bill. Most of them are doomed to failure, I thought, waiting quietly in the back. Somewhere in that sea of people, though, there was undoubtedly a little piece of magic being worked on some issue that no one would ever hear of.

Looking to the crowd, I found Michael, on the other side of the room, working it hard. It was times like these that I remembered how good he was and why I'd been able to learn so much in so short a time. He was breezily chatting up just about everyone in the room, catching them all. It was the skill that separated him from the rest of us, and it was fun to watch.

Weller came over to greet me. He looked comfortable, relaxed. "Not a bad year, Ed. We're almost done."

"This isn't ending the way I wanted it to, Weller."

"Nothing ever does, Edward." He smiled down at me, caring in his eyes. "Listen, every year we think that we're out fighting for our clients, saving them from something bad, protecting them, protecting America. That's what it feels like from the inside. But over time, those years all slip by, pile up one after another, and the tide of history sweeps away whatever we've done or whatever we haven't.

"We're all just pieces of a puzzle that can never be completed, because the edges keep moving and reshaping and none of us ever fit together the same way twice. That's us as a company, it's you in the company, and it's your Dungan." He looked over at the Conference table, at the members, the staff, the suits, all clustered around it, maneuvering to get a last word in edgewise, a last bit of something. He continued, "Hell, it's all our clients."

Once again, Weller improved my mood, not for the reasons he thought, but it worked nonetheless. No matter what we did tonight, it wasn't the end of the world. Life would go on.

As Weller spoke, I'd been watching Tom, who was slowly working his way through the House Republicans gathering at the table. He was noticeably stiffer than Michael, but received by his targets with somewhat more appreciation: there aren't nearly as many Republican foreign aid groupies as there are Democrats, so they tend to be more warmly received when they make an appearance.

I waited until he closed in on Rep. Matthew Gunderson, Ranking Minority Member for the Subcommittee. I excused myself from Weller and joined him.

"Hello, Tom," I said as he noticed my approach. Sliding next to him, I extended my hand to the Congressman. "Rep. Gunderson, so good to see you again. Ed Matthews. I haven't seen you since your event last May." Fundraiser, that was, another in a long line, this one comparatively cheap at only $500.

He clearly had no idea who I was, but responded warmly anyway. Finally, I thought, a tiny touch of value out of a political contribution. "Of course, Ed, so good to see you again."

"I just wanted to say how impressed I am—we all are," I said, reaching out toward Tom to bring him in, "of the way you've stuck to Republican Party principles in this year's debates." Gunderson beamed and looked to Tom with a big smile. I continued, speaking slowly so he'd pick up on every word. "Your work in promoting American ideals, and especially promoting freedom of religion around the globe, are an example"—now he was looking back to me again, his face clouding just a little—"for all of us to follow. You should be proud for sticking by your principled approach."

Gunderson looked down to the floor, but Tom agreed with a grin. "Ed's right on point, Congressman. We are proud of the kind of work you've been doing."

Gunderson looked up over his glasses. "Thanks. Really." He looked directly at me and nodded, and then turned brusquely toward the table behind him. "I, uh, have to review my notes before we start."

Tom backed away with an "of course," but I remained where I was, just for those few extra seconds, without taking my eyes off him. Gunderson didn't look back, but I figured he could sense me there.

As I walked back toward my chair, Tom took hold of my arm. "Thanks. That was really nice of you."

"No problem, Tom," I said. I never would have gotten away with that with Weller or Michael, I thought. Tom's political blinders gave him a kind of childlike faith, especially in his colleagues. "Sometimes you just need to let people know you're paying attention."

* * *

"Mr. Chairman, I believe that the levels of funding being proposed for the African Development Bank are simply too low."

There were thirty ceiling tiles across, but I kept losing count of the tiles running down the length of the room. The more I tried to concentrate, the more my eyes would experience some kind of weird whiteout phenomenon where the lines ran together. Maybe it was the horrifically bad fluorescent lighting, and maybe it was just declining vision due to age, but I just couldn't seem to get the right number.

Rep. Jennings, a Congressional Black Caucus member, was speaking, droning on and on in a losing battle to increase the levels of funding for the ADB, the African Development Bank, one of a sea of such multilateral development institutions funded around the world. Their funding was off a little this year, I was assuming because of an increase in funding for the African Development Foundation—with which, of course, the ADB was not to be confused. Jennings must have had someone in his district, and maybe even someone in the room, someone who was big with the ADB, because he'd been chewing on this bone for about half an hour.

It was already 10:00 p.m., and we were still stuck in first of the many sections of the bill, on the multilaterals. This wasn't a good sign.

"Mr. Chairman, I'd like to suggest that we take a brief break. Perhaps we can work this out." It was Toby Kelton, in what was a peculiarly Congressional way of begging for mercy. A couple of them probably wanted to take Jennings out and beat some sense into him, but they'd satisfy themselves with cornering him in the Committee offices, just down the hall, and telling him that he'd fought long and hard and his constituent should be convinced that he was going down with the ship, fighting the good fight, but would he please shut the FUCK UP and let the Conference move on?

"The Committee is in recess for thirty minutes," the Chair replied.

Thank you, Jesus, I thought, most likely along with the rest of the crowd. I stood and stretched, stifling a yawn as my back and shoulders creaked. God, I was getting too old for this.

As I grappled with my advancing age, Kenny Thurgood walked over with his hand outstretched. "Hi, Ed," he said with a broad grin. "This is terrific. I'm so glad you suggested that I attend the Conference."

"Don't worry. It will get better," I said, turning toward him out of a twist. A little frown started to form as he reacted to my words. Ah, he's serious, I thought; he's been enjoying this. "I mean, the debates get even more interesting as the night goes on." In point of fact, that was only true if one took hard-core hallucinogenics, but I figured the kid probably never saw *Fantasia* and wouldn't get that joke.

He smiled again. "Great. I'm looking forward to it."

I'd convinced Kenny to attend the entire conference, telling him it was a chance to see how the worst of the process worked.

I glanced around us. There were a lot of people milling aimlessly, but no one near who mattered to our plans. Or to mine. Seeing Adam Childress standing over by his new boss, I waved and pointed him out to Kenny.

Kenny grinned at Adam, who smiled back. Well, I didn't get the smile, I thought, but that's okay—Kenny's my guy.

"Is your boss going to hang around all night?"

"He's in the office," Kenny responded. "Right about now he's taking a nap on the couch, but he's sticking around."

From out of the corner of my eye, I saw Michael by the door, signaling. It was time to catch up. "Thanks, Kenny." Pointing at Michael, I put a fatherly hand on Kenny's shoulder and said, "I have to run. The boss calls. You don't mind, do you?"

"Oh, no, don't let me get in your way," he said, moving back to let me pass. This guy is too nice, I thought with a smile as I moved by him.

In the hall, Michael, Tom, and Weller were gathered. Michelle was also there, looking mighty grumpy. She hadn't gotten into the room yet—the line was way too long, so she'd waited out in the halls until we could find a way to sneak her in. Even I had to admit there were few things more boring than waiting in the hall outside a Committee meeting.

"What do we have?" Michael asked.

"VanderMeer tells me that the MNNA amendment is agreed to," Tom replied. "One year, life of the bill."

"I've got the same from Alexis and Roger," I added. "Peter told me the same thing, but he may have gotten it from Alexis."

While the Conferees were technically still working on the first section of the bill, the action was in fact well beyond that. Most bills, and especially appropriations bills, were pre-negotiated by staffs before they even get to the open Conference Committee meeting. With appropriations, it was made easier by the fact that 95 percent of the bill is the same as the prior year's bill, just with different numbers. Then there was a bunch of miscellaneous provisions, like our UAE MNNA amendment; these got negotiated out like children divvying out Halloween candy: one for the

Senate, one for the House, one for the Senate, one for the… So this ten-hour Conference we were working our way through was something of a set piece, with maybe ten or twelve serious disagreements—with the big one this year being Iraqi reconstruction money—and the rest of the time spent speechifying a-la-Jennings and the ADB.

Weller looked to me with the thinnest smile on his lips. "You'll be here to confirm that in the morning?"

I nodded. Weller glanced at Michael, who also nodded. Turning to Michelle, Weller said, "Do you want to take my place?"

"No," she said, "I think I'll go too."

I shook my head, and must have snorted, because she turned to glare at me. As Weller walked away, Michelle paused, staring at me for another moment, and then trotted down the corridor after him.

Michael went on. "I've seen the Famagusta language they've agreed to—that's fine. So right now, we're batting 1.000."

"There is that little, um, Koliba kind of thing," I reminded him. Tom was looking particularly glum—we'd seen the language in two or three different versions, and they were all awful. But there was nothing there to prohibit his $20 million from going forward, which I assumed was what Michael meant. Tom, though, was still taking all the anti-Koliba vitriol personally.

"Koliba's getting his money," Michael said. Tom blanched and looked around: that was *secret* money, after all.

"So we're batting .800, I guess," I replied, with a thin smile. Waiting for a moment, I stuck in the dagger. "And then there's the Dungan."

Like a shot, Michael's face went red. "The Dungan language is out, and that's where it's staying."

"I know, Michael." I felt strangely calm, even for me. Partially it was the fact that I'd come to grips with the Dungan mess, and partially it was the way I more and more responded to Michael's anger, going deeper inside myself. "I know."

"Just don't fuck with me." He jammed his finger in my face. "Don't forget—I warned you that bastard Harry couldn't be trusted."

"Okay, okay, but I still read it that we're batting .600."

Still red—in fact, maybe even just a touch redder, if that was possible without a cardiac event—Michael turned and headed down the hall in the direction of the bathrooms. Or maybe just the long walk. Either way, I thought, maybe I should tone down the baiting just a little bit.

"Ed?"

I turned around. It was Michelle, halfway down the hall, standing alone. "Got a minute?"

"Sure." I walked over to her, curious. She waited for me to get close.

"I never wanted to be you."

"What?" She'd caught me; I wasn't expecting that. I'd had no idea *what* to expect, but whatever it was, it wasn't that.

"I wanted to work with you guys because you're the best in your business," she continued, earnest for once. There was something of a ferocity in her eyes, rather than the utter indifference I'd come to expect. "But that doesn't mean I want to *be* you. I just want to see how you operate. And staying here all night the way you will, I just don't need that."

I watched her carefully; she was so serious. "It's just not over until they all go home," I said, trying hard to sound less the grade-school teacher than I usually did when talking strategy with her. "Something could happen."

"I know that's why you need to be here," she replied. "But that's not me. A year from now, I'll be gone, doing the business from the 'access' side, not your process side. I'll never be the last one in the room." She looked down at the floor, kicking at a piece of something that wasn't there. After a pause, she looked back up at me. "I just had to say, I don't want to be you."

This time I paused, glancing back over my shoulder for a second and finding no one. I looked down. "I get it. You're right. You don't need it. Go." She waited. "Go. It's all right. And thanks for coming back."

She was smiling as she turned to walk away. I watched, impressed, and happy to know that at least someone knew where they were going.

"Hey," I said. She stopped. "I should have let you in on it more. Sorry." She turned and gave me a sad smile. After a few moments, she spun around, hurrying down the hall.

I turned back toward the conference, but as I approached the hallway, I found Peter blocking my way. "Got a sec?"

Great, I thought, what now?

"The DOD Appropriations conference just finished," he began.

"Okay."

"Koliba gets his $20 million this year."

"Oh." This was very strange: Peter never talked about classified programs, at least not to me. "Okay."

"We added something to the bill." He paused and, taking my elbow, pulled me back toward the hallway where I'd been talking with Michelle. It was empty, but Peter led me another dozen yards down the hall before continuing. Looking back over his shoulder and then down at the floor, he said, "The compromise was Alexis's idea."

The way he said that last bit, the tone he used, I wasn't sure if he was speaking to me or to himself, saying it out loud as if to validate it. I waited, still having no idea what he was getting at.

"The bill requires DIA to shut down the listening post in Golongo and open one up somewhere else. Hell, they could open two if they want—in working the deal, we gave them $60 million." He'd stopped, now that it was out.

She'd asked me what I needed, and I'd gotten it: the $20 million. *Then* she'd shut down the listening post. Jesus, the girl learned fast.

"Who knows?"

"The SecDef, the head of DIA, a couple of colonels who do the black budget." He paused. "Two or three members, and four or five staffers on Appropriations."

"Galsworthy?"

"Jesus, no, he'd tell the fucking *New York Times* and it'll be in tomorrow's newspaper," Peter snorted. "No one else finds out until it's shut down. It's the only way they'll get out safe."

"How long is that?"

"Three months, at the max. They need time to set up the exit." He looked at me. "You can wait that long?"

"No one's going to hear anything from me," I responded. There wasn't anything for me to tell anyone; we had a one-year contract, and thanks to this action we'd be fulfilling it. And there wasn't any point in telling anyone: there was nothing any of us could have done. "Thanks, Peter."

Walking back into the room a few minutes later, I looked around for Alexis and saw her in a far corner of the room, speaking with Kelton. She saw me first, and the two of them turned, facing me as they stopped talking. I pointed at her and smiled. She'd beaten me fair and square, the first staffer in ten years who'd taken a hypothetical like that and turned it into reality. I was impressed. You have learned much, Grasshopper, I thought. I smiled to myself and sat down for the next round.

* * *

By 4:30 a.m., the Conferees were getting to the end of the bill. Pretty much all that was left on their list of open issues was the fight over Iraqi reconstruction money. They'd actually spent forty-five minutes at one point berating Koliba for his evil ways, further evidence of the utter disconnect between Congressional debates and reality. Kelton was one of the people who piled on, maybe for my benefit, maybe just to gain more bona fides with the Congressional Black Caucus, who knows? In the end, they'd cut off any funds in the bill from going to Golongo without prior notification of the Committee, the standard aid cutoff.

At this point, there were only about fifteen of us outsiders left in the room, and at least ten of those were from various lobbying firms working for the Iraqi government and its many prime-ministers-in-waiting. In August, the lobbying firm founded by Mississippi Governor and former Republican National Committee Chairman Haley Barbour had taken a contract working for Iyad Allawi against Iraq's then-sitting Prime Minister. It shocked many of us to the core, mostly because almost no one seemed surprised: the U.S. was in the middle of a war under a Republican President, American troops dying to defend an incredibly inept Iraqi government, and a mainstream Republican lobbying firm had jumped into Iraq's political infighting. It was unconscionable and would have been seen as virtual treason in a simpler time, before money had completely taken over in Washington, but it slipped by as a one-day story in 2007. Once they got away with it, firms all over town were positioning themselves for this new shot at the Iraq gravy train, and any Congressional session debating the war and its aftermath was even busier than usual.

Across the room, one last soldier of the Shaddock Mills contingent remained. I'd tracked them down in the hallway conversations, listening in a little here or there during breaks until I could figure out who was who. A more senior colleague had made it up until the last break, but appeared to have given up shortly after they reconvened. The members had admitted before taking that last break that, while the Iraq reconstruction funding would take time, it was all that remained between us and freedom.

Kenny Thurgood, bless his heart, was still there. Michael and Tom had cleared out, the latter even paler than usual after these debates; he'd struggled to sit still during the Koliba conversation, and that was without knowing that he'd seen the last of his Koliba contracts. I'd committed to staying through to the end, as I did every year.

Adam Childress was still there too, with his boss, Sen. VanderMeer. That in itself was a bit of a mystery, since most years VanderMeer cleared out of meetings like this as soon as his issues were done. This year, though, he was hanging in.

"Mr. Chairman, perhaps we can break just one last time to consider positions on the Iraq reconstruction funding." This would be it, I knew. The members who remained had all made their speeches, designed to satisfy the various lobbyists present that they'd tried their best to win the day, but now it was time for the Subcommittee Chairman to get together with the State Department's lead rep, the Under Secretary for Politico-Military Affairs, to hash out some final compromise allowing the Iraq money—and the bill—to go through.

It was time.

While the members hemmed and hawed about their upcoming break, I slid across the row until I was behind Kenny. Leaning in close, I said quietly, "Kenny, if there's a time to deal with the religious rights issues your boss is worried about, I think this is it."

He turned and smiled. "I'll be right back."

* * *

"Mr. Chairman, I object. The provision is outside the scope of this conference."

"Outside the scope" was Congress-speak for arguing against a provision because it hadn't been included in the bill when the bill was debated in the House or the Senate. An extremely useful and powerful tool when it was true. Useless in this case, since both Committee reports had dealt with the specific issue under discussion, and both bills had a provision limiting aid to the country in question.

"Mr. Chairman, if I may." It was Sen. VanderMeer, with Adam crouched at his elbow. "I respectfully disagree with my colleague. Both bills contain a provision on this issue, in Title VI. This amendment is entirely within the scope of this conference." Glancing over at me from across the table, he smiled ever so slightly before turning back to stare at the Chairman.

I kept as straight a face as possible, the amendment in question being basically the same that VanderMeer had tried to offer on the Senate Floor at my request. Looking first at VanderMeer and then at Adam, I realized that my luck had decided to stick with me through the end of the year. Without Tom trying to get VanderMeer to push something positive on Koliba and without that chance coffee with Kenny and Adam, none of this would have been possible.

Rep. Gunderson, Tom's good friend the House Ranking Minority Member, sat uncomfortably in his seat, utterly unprepared for this amendment and seemingly unable to find a way out of it. Behind him, Kenny Thurgood and his boss, Rep. Tommy Walston, Chairman of the House Republican Conference, sat stone-faced. The House Republican Conference consists of every single Republican in the House and is a much more conservative group than the typical House Appropriations Committee member. Under a Republican President, with a very narrow Democratic majority in the House, it was impossible to get a foreign aid appropriations bill through the House without their support. Walston, with Kenny close behind him, had come into the room just as the Conferees were about to start up again with this one little thing they needed, a new, innocuous amendment they brought with them and handed to Rep. Gunderson so he could offer it on their behalf.

Walston was playing some serious hardball here.

The issue? A provision to prohibit Ex-Im Bank financing for projects in countries listed in Section 697 of the bill. As written, the amendment didn't name any countries, but Section 697 listed various limitations on aid to Central Asia—more colloquially, the Stans.

The amendment—very cleverly drafted, one would have to admit—inserted a new subsection (b) prohibiting any aid under any program to the country referred to in subsection (a) unless the President determined and reported to Congress that the country was not undertaking a program of religious persecution against any group.

The country mentioned in subsection (a) was Kazakhstan.

No Ex-Im financing meant no oil pipeline.

The President could waive the provision "in the interest of national security," a standard waiver. So you could argue that, if the White House really, really wanted the oil pipeline in Kazakhstan to go ahead, they could do it.

I glanced around the room. While the tension at the table had gone up about twenty notches, the few people in the audience barely seemed to notice.

The debate, if still quiet, had turned fierce. There was a level of resignation in the opposition and a sense that people just wanted to get out of the room. It wasn't all that much different from the last few hours, when people had been biting each other's heads off over Iraq.

I glanced over at my nameless Shaddock Mills counterpart. He'd been doodling. I'd been right: he didn't know the bill well enough to understand what was happening or why.

This was going to work.

* * *

After discussing the amendment for about fifteen minutes, the Members took an unplanned break. As those of us left in the room rose to stretch, Alexis rose from her seat and began to head in my direction.

I was expecting this, but didn't want to get caught in the room; my friend from Shaddock Mills might get suspicious. Heading for the door, I was almost out when Alexis caught up with me. "Can we talk, Ed?"

"Walk with me," I responded. Something a Member or staffer usually said to a lobbyist, not the other way around, but I was too close to let this slip through.

Heading into the hall, I turned left, toward the next corridor. There, at least, I thought we might have some privacy.

"What are you doing?"

I looked down at Alexis. She looked genuinely curious, not angry.

"Me?"

From behind us, a voice boomed, "What the FUCK are you up to?" It was Raymonda, barreling toward me, with Roger on his short legs trailing behind her.

So much for privacy. The Shaddock Mills guy was nowhere in sight, though, so I was still in the clear. "Ray, it's not me."

"Bullshit it's not you, you sonofabitch," she said, coming into my face. "You're pissed because you got screwed, and now you're trying to fuck with the bill."

"Ray, I've got no dog in this fight," I responded, surprising myself with how cool I felt. "You're stuck with what they're demanding, but it's not about my client. It's the loony-tunes right."

"Ed, be sensible." It was Roger. "Sen. Fuller insisted the Statement of Managers' language be pulled."

"Roger, I am serious." I looked him in the eye and held it for several seconds. "There's nothing on the Dungan here."

In a way, I was telling the truth. Most lobbyists in Washington pursue their clients' goals and don't care if anything gets in the way. Many of those are simply saying "no," the way the health care industry did when they decimated Hillary Clinton's dementedly confusing industry overhaul plan. Sometimes, though, what you do is a misdirection, a dodge, where you set loose the dogs of war on the powers-that-be and watch what happens. Like letting the religious right know that they had gotten absolutely zero out of this legislation, and telling them just the right moment to come into the room and drop a tactical nuclear device.

It's just that I wasn't doing it to help out a client. Not exactly.

"How do we fix this?" That was Raymonda. She must still have been thinking I cared.

"You can't," I responded. "There's no way out of the room but to take it."

"FUCK. YOU." Raymonda spat the words out, one at a time.

"You can't get the bill through the House unless the Republican Caucus supports it." All Appropriations Conference Reports had to pass each House of Congress one last time before going to the President, and getting Republican votes in the House for foreign aid bills had always been difficult. Even for Republican Presidents. "And even if we end the year with an omnibus CR"—an omnibus bill, the humongous kitchen-sink kind of bill that ends up funding the entire government at one shot—"your bill only gets in there if the House Minority Whip can say, 'the bill's got something in there for Jesus.'"

"They don't think that way, you asshole." Raymonda again.

"I know they don't," I replied, "and you know what I mean. Walston just made this their line in the sand, and they'll stick to it."

And don't think I was missing the irony here. This was the strategy I'd refused months before, right-wingers pulling Jesus out of their back pocket and waving him around like a prop. The whole idea of such a move had been one of the things I hated most about Washington, the way every belief could be twisted for political advantage, used as a fundraising tool or an attack ad or a speech to constituents to "rally the base."

But that was when I actually believed in the place. Not anymore. And more importantly, I figured out that no one else did either. We were all just playing an enormous board game, and winning and losing had nothing to do with the people or the country, it had to do with which party was ahead, what candidate was winning, who could suck more money out of the system than the other guy.

Alexis tried. "The bill has $200 million for Iraqi reconstruction."

"Right-wing Republicans in the House don't give a rat's ass about Iraqi reconstruction," I said. "They'll spend billions to blow shit up, but they think it's someone else's problem to rebuild. And besides," I continued, pointing back toward the Conference, "this is the religious right, and there's nothing in the bill for Jesus. Rebuilding Moslem houses doesn't change that."

"The White House will tell them to vote for the bill." Raymonda's turn. "They'll beat the crap out of them to get this through."

"Yeah, great," I replied, "but when the Omnibus CR is pulled together behind those closed doors, the leader of the House Republican Conference will say, 'my members need this provision.' It will go in, and it will stay in."

Roger stepped closer, nudging Raymonda back. She scowled, but ceded.

"Michael's going to kill you. He made a deal with Harry too, and you've shot it down." He put a hand on my shoulder, and his face screwed up in a single, massive twitch. "I'm serious about this. When that kid from Shaddock Mills reports back, Michael and your uncle Harry will both blow up."

This time I stepped in close to him, and they all backed up. "That kid doesn't even have a clue what you're fighting about, and if you tell him, you'll lose the bill *and* the Iraq reconstruction money." I looked at Raymonda. "Don't kid yourselves. This bill is going to squeak through in the best of circumstances, and now that they're focused on it, the only way that the Republicans in the House are going to let it pass is with this provision. Otherwise the whole compromise goes down. So don't say a fucking word, and take it as the best you're going to get."

They stared at me, that blank stare when wheels are spinning in people's heads. Waiting for a few moments, I saw that they couldn't find anything wrong with my logic. I turned back to Raymonda.

"The White House gets a national security waiver, so any Ex-Im deal they want will go through," I told her. "No harm, no foul."

"Fuck that," she spat out. "You sonofabitch, pass this amendment and the pipeline goes to the fucking French consortium."

Roger started. "Pipeline?"

Raymonda's eyes widened, and she turned a bright red.

At least now I know no one else was in on it, I thought. "Maybe next time your friends will try competing on price rather than by buying off a couple of Senators."

Raymonda glared at me, breathing heavily, her color still high. She started to speak, and stopped, started again. Moments later, she said, "You are dead in this town. Your career is over."

She turned, looking briefly askance at Roger, and stormed down the hall.

Roger was blinking furiously, a pleading look on his face. "Pipeline? Consortium?"

"Go ask her," I told him. "She has to tell you, and you'll be able to hold it over her for a very long time."

"And Michael?" he continued.

I smiled. "I'll worry about Michael. And I'll worry about Harry. You worry about the bill. Go ahead."

Roger stared at me for a few moments and headed after Raymonda. After several steps, he stopped, turning briefly to look back at me and wave, as if saying goodbye. Then he disappeared.

Alexis watched him until he turned the corner, and sighed. She crossed her arms in front of her, using her omnipresent folder as a shield again. Without looking toward me, she asked, "Do I want to know?"

"It's even more complicated than Koliba," I said. "Nice job on that, by the way."

She snorted and looked me in the eye. "What do you get out of this?"

I smiled. "Me? I get to sleep at night. I get to face myself in the mirror every morning."

Epilogue

Christmas week is the absolute worst time of the year to go to Paris. It's when everyone in France visits Paris, meaning that every major museum, church, and restaurant in the city is stuffed with people. And not just people: *French* people. The rudest people on earth.

Of course, Paris being Paris, it doesn't matter. It certainly didn't matter to Charlotte and me, back in our favorite hotel, the Hotel des Deux Îles on the Île-St.-Louis, dead in the center of Paris. For us, mobs or no, it was heaven.

Ignoring the crowds, we spent our time strolling the city streets, up the Champs Elysées for some serious window shopping, through the Marais for some serious shopping shopping, and into pretty much any restaurant we wanted for quiet dinners, an hour earlier than any decent Frenchman would have found himself eating but just the right time for us—it was one of those rare times when it paid to be the ugly American.

We'd left Washington right after the Conference and would be heading back only to pack. It was time to move on; Charlotte had been right all along. We didn't know where, and we didn't know what we'd end up doing. It was just time to move on.

* * *

It had taken another hour and a half for the Conference to wind up, as the members crossed all the *i*'s and dotted the *t*'s on their agreement. Glancing at my cell phone, I saw that we were approaching six fifteen, about the earliest I thought that I could call Charlotte.

Stretching as I stood, I looked around the room at the small number of us left. Committee members were heading for the exits, leaving the few remaining staffers behind to corral their files and folders. The Shaddock Mills kid was still there, observant to the end, unaware that he missed the amendment he'd been sent to watch for. There were no other lobbyists in the room that I could see, and only two or three Administration representatives left. Even most of the staffers were gone, especially those whose members had checked out early in the night. My new best friend on the Republican right, Kenny Thurgood, was still there, smiling broadly in the throes of his first big win; he and his boss looked as if they could barely restrain themselves from an enormous "high five."

It seemed almost peaceful after the craziness of the last few hours.

Walking over to Kenny, I shook his hand. At this point, I didn't care about being seen with him. "Don't forget—from here on out, you have to keep an eye on that amendment, and you have to keep an eye on my UAE MNNA amendment." That's what I had gotten from Walston in exchange for helping him to a "great victory" in Conference: he would make sure the UAE amendment was left alone as the bill moved forward.

Kenny nodded and shook my hand strongly. "Absolutely. That amendment is locked in."

I smiled. As he turned away, heading for the door, I flipped open my phone and speed-dialed Charlotte. The line rang three times.

"Hmm-ello?"

Good, I thought, I've woken her. "Hi, Sweetie. It's me. I'm not home."

"Hmm. No." There was a pause as she woke herself up. I could hear her take a deep breath. "Mmm. You're not home."

"Conference just ended, and I'm going to take some of the people out to breakfast. So I probably won't get home about ten o'clock."

"Okay." It was her little tiny voice, the squeaky one she had right after waking.

"Can you do me a favor?"

"Okay."

"Start packing."

"Huh?" That was a little more alert, a little more aware. Now she would wake up. I could almost see her, closing her eyes tight, forcing herself to focus. "What?"

"We're leaving. Don't know where we're going, don't know what we're going to do, we're just leaving." I paused, to let it sink in. "We've got the money, and we need to go. It's time."

"Are you okay?"

I laughed, to myself mostly.

"Better than I've been in a long, long time."

* * *

With all I'd been through, getting out of town was going to be the easy part. I'd gone to Michael late the afternoon following the Conference, after snagging a few hours' sleep at home. The Conference Report was well on its way to being incorporated into the massive eighty-kajillion dollar everything-but-the-kitchen-sink-end-of-the-year omnibus bill, and there was nothing anyone could do about it. That omnibus wouldn't actually be moving for days, and there would be moments for slipping this or that into or out of it; but that was the beauty of having the head of the House Republican Conference carry the amendment, because when he put something in a bill, it stayed.

I even got to break the news to Michael about what I'd done—no one else had the courage to call him up, and from the fact that Harry wasn't calling me up every two seconds, no one at Shaddock Mills found it yet either.

Michael took it relatively well, screaming at me for only about half an hour or so, maybe forty-five minutes, his face a bright, fire-engine kind of red that somehow didn't pop an aneurism or send his heart shooting out of his eyeballs. I took it about as well as I'd taken the UAE Ambassador's rant about our MNNA amendment, with the only difference being a serious twinge of sadness, knowing that this was the last time I'd ever get yelled at like this and thinking that, years from this moment, when I reminisced, this was one of the moments I would remember most clearly from my many wonderful years with him.

Looking back, though, I've realized that his heart wasn't in it. Maybe because of the time we'd spent together, maybe because he knew I'd protected him by having Kenny Thurgood and House Republican Conference Chair watching over our UAE amendment. Maybe he still liked me as much as Charlotte said he did. Whatever it was, while he needed to yell at me to make sure everyone else in the company knew never, *ever* to try a trick like that on him again, I know now he was playacting. Loudly, but playacting.

In the end, Michael and I made a simple deal: he gave me the $72,000 he'd promised me off the Dungan contract, and I disappeared from Washington, leaving him to tell the story however he wanted.

Charlotte quit her job the same day, giving her miserable boss the two-hour notice he deserved, once she was certain I'd signed the deal with Michael. We had nothing to go back to, other than packing up our house and shipping the stuff off somewhere.

Paris was our first stop, and it had been just a couple of days on the ground when we found ourselves at our favorite little café on the northwestern corner of the Île-St.-Louis, splitting a *Croque Monsieur* while admiring the flying buttresses of Nôtre-Dame. We still needed to decide how long to stay in Europe, how much of that $72K to piss away before deciding what to do next. I wasn't in any hurry, for I had a lot to catch up on, and a lot of Charlotte to reconnect with. We just needed some time, I'd told myself.

I knew that was a lie, the last one I was still allowing myself. It would take years to overcome everything I'd been and done. But at least I'd given myself the chance.

"So, my love," I said, reaching over the ubiquitous oil-and-vinegar tray to snag a few more *frites* off her plate, "you think there's any chance of finding a *Washington Post* somewhere in this godforsaken burg?"

Acknowledgments

This novel would not have been possible without the support and encouragement of the many mentors, colleagues, friends and associates I had over my years living and working in Washington, D.C. It arises, however, entirely from my own imagination, and represents a vision of Washington and the lobbying life that is entirely my own. Further, the opinions expressed by the protagonist are his own, and often significantly differ from mine, let alone anyone else's.

Thanks to Kim Stanley Robinson, for showing the way from a picaresque of random episodes to a plot. To Kate Wilhelm, vicariously, for her description of the writing process in *Storyteller*, which helped me to be more open to the recommendations of my readers. And to David Brin, for his encouragement and last-minute suggestions.

Thanks to Jim Langley, Joe Leventhal, Donald Wesling, and Dick McCall for taking the time to read the book in whole or in part and provide their thoughts.

Thanks to Kickstarter.com for helping finance the publication of this novel, CreateSpace.com for helping publish it, Zazzle.com for the giveaways on Kickstarter, and Gmail for serving as an unending storage of unending drafts. Thanks to Sam Fairchild, D'Anna Stanfield Tindal, Deb Bronston-Culp and Peggy Little for supporting the publication process.

Most importantly, my deepest thanks to my wife Elaine for her limitless patience, her great ideas, her careful editing, and her undying support for my writing. She lived it with me over our many years in Washington, stuck with me through the many lost weekends as I drafted, redrafted and redrafted some more, and encouraged me always to publish. Without her, I'd never have gotten this far.

6270471R0

Made in the USA
Charleston, SC
05 October 2010